WHAT THE SILENT SAY

EMERSON FORD

Storm
PUBLISHING

Ebook ISBN: 978-1-80508-908-7
Paperback ISBN: 978-1-80508-909-4

Cover design: Sarah Whittaker
Cover images: Arcangel, Shutterstock

Published by Storm Publishing.
For further information, visit:
www.stormpublishing.co

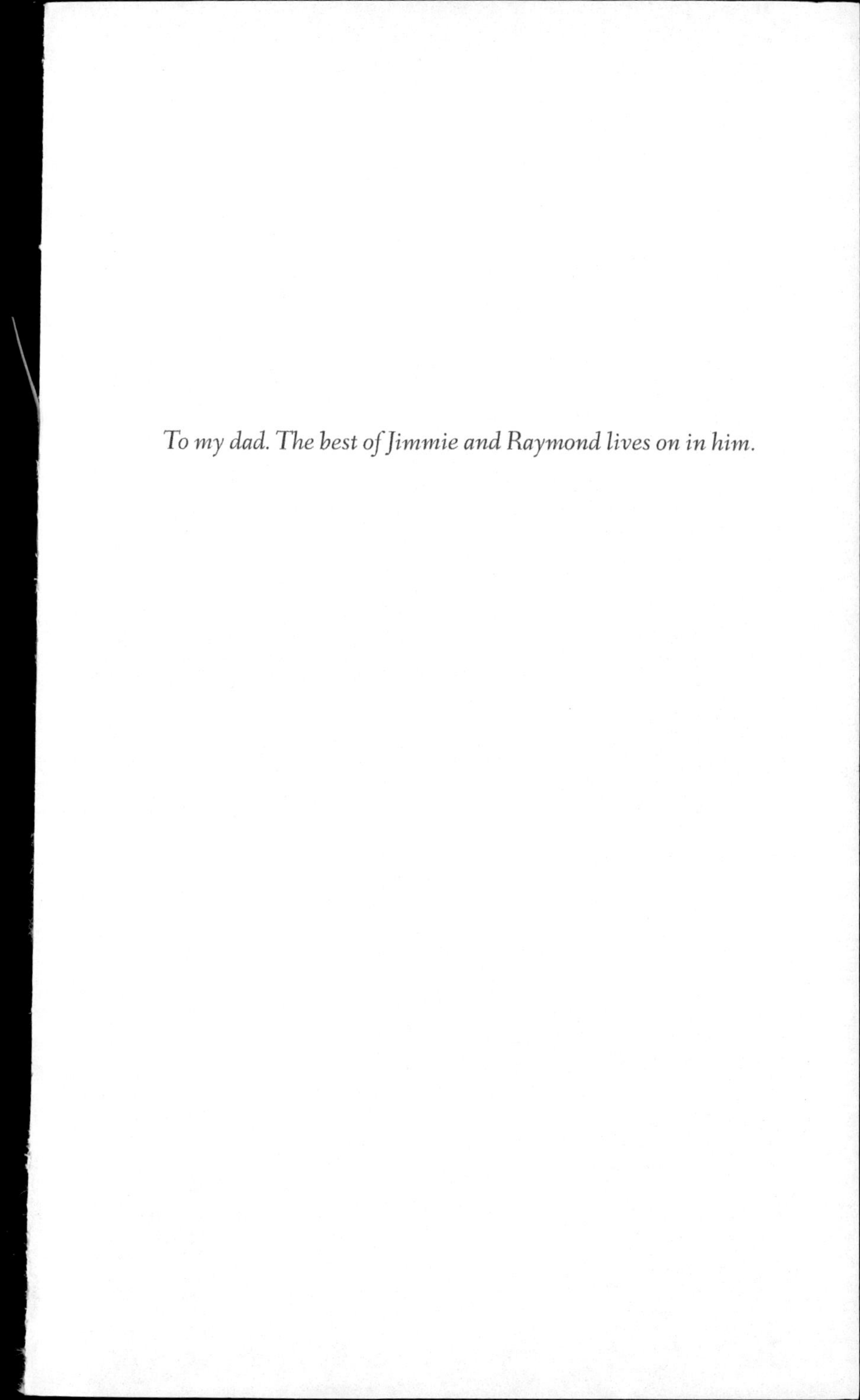

To my dad. The best of Jimmie and Raymond lives on in him.

ONE

A BIRTHDAY TOAST

April 1961
Florence, South Carolina

It was a comment in passing, the tail end of a birthday toast.

"Here's to you, my brother. Because of you, so many of us are home." He took a swig out of his fluted glass and plunked it on the table, sloshing liquid onto his white-knuckled fingers. A lock of blond hair fell across his forehead. "But you just couldn't leave things alone, could you?"

Mom's face turned ashen.

The room went quiet.

Dad pushed back his chair and stood next to him. Wrapping an arm around his shoulders, he leaned close, talking softly in his ear. "That's enough."

"Maybe it's time she knew." He tipped his glass to me and downed the rest in two swallows. "We were risking our lives in a war at her age."

My breath caught in my chest. This was about me?

"Mary, go and get the cake plates," Grandma Sarah said in a strained voice.

"But—"

"Go." Dad tilted his head toward the kitchen but softened his command with a wink.

A fight would get me nowhere, going by experience. I swallowed my sigh and made my way to the china hutch. Tucking plates into the crook of one arm, I kept one ear tuned to the dining room, catching only bits and scraps of their hushed voices.

"Why can't..."

"...give it time."

"...the letters in the desk..."

The plates pitched toward my chest in a clatter. The conversation halted.

For the rest of dinner, I kept a smile plastered on my face. I nodded in all the right places, responded to all their questions. When the dishes were cleared and the table wiped clean, I went straight to bed and crawled in with Mom's key ring tucked inside my fist.

At the end of the hallway, Mom pulled the chains on our cuckoo clock and nudged the pendulum into its rocking cadence, setting it for the next day. Shuffling down the hallway in her slippers, she paused at my room and peeked in, just as I'd known she would. I breathed a steady rhythm, taking care not to even twitch an eyelid.

She closed my door, disappearing in the darkness.

A minute passed, then two. The house settled into the cadence of the night—Dad's soft snore; the ticking pendulum; somewhere in the distance, the sad, low whistle of a train coming through Florence Station.

When I could wait no longer, I flipped back my blanket.

It hadn't been just tonight. My memories were dusted with knowing glances and hushed words, but I'd only lumped them in with all the other things I didn't understand.

Running my hand across the wall to guide me in the dark, I

slipped soundlessly down the smooth wooden hallway until my toes hit the white shag of our front room.

The grown-up room, I'd always called it. But now, the wall between childhood and adulthood seemed so thin it wouldn't take more than a pinprick to shatter it.

I sank my feet into the carpet.

The desk, with lamplight pooled in its glossy surface, drew me as if it were an Egyptian sarcophagus, and I, its robber.

I crept toward it under the glare of Uncle Festus, the name Mom had given to the severe man in the cracked oil portrait standing guard above the desk. Scurrying past him, I knocked the standing light off-kilter. I steadied it and lowered myself into the brass-studded leather chair. It took four tries before I found the right key and slid open the desk's drawer, a groan of wood too tight in its tracks announcing "*Intruuuder!*" I stopped and slid my eyes toward Festus.

Slowly, more carefully this time, I pulled the drawer so the squeaks came out in short, quieter bursts of mild alarm instead. There, pushed toward the back, lay a black portfolio of letters.

I flipped open the heavy cover. A letter toward the end slipped out and fell to the floor.

It was a landscape of wrinkles, stained in parts with watery brown as if it had fallen into the mud.

Dear Sweet,

Maybe one day I'll laugh, but I'm writing this inside a cave full of bones.

I'm tired of pretending things aren't as bad as they are. Okinawa is a burning, hellish place. Death has made a home here and welcomes us like we're straw for his fire. On the other islands, there were colorful birds and plants I'd never seen before, but here, it's just sulfur and rotting, sticking mud, dead men scattered as far as the eye can see.

I can't help but wonder how I got here. My whole life, I've tried to do everything right. And here I am, where nothing is right at all. I can only hope it comes right in the end, even with what I decided to do. Maybe then, you can forgive me.

Then, in a messier scrawl,

We're on the move. Don't know when I'll write next, but I'll send word as soon as I can. My heart's still beating, love. It's not over yet. Love you both more than I can say.

TWO

POCKETSFUL OF MONEY

May 1937
Florence, South Carolina

Fiddling with the keys in his pocket, Raymond leaned against the flagpole outside Jimmie's school, his gaze fixed on the faded-red doors at the top of the steps.

The bell rang, long and shrill.

Raymond pushed off the flagpole and puffed up every inch of his seventeen years.

The creaky doors opened. Students gushed forth like water from a busted dam, and there, at the tail end of the flood, bobbed Jimmie's towhead.

His brother stopped in his tracks the moment he saw Raymond. "What're you doin' here?"

Raymond took Jimmie's strap of books and slung it over his shoulder. "I'm not letting you walk home alone after what happened yesterday." His gaze flicked to Jimmie's fist-sized shiner, tight and round like an overripe plum. At five years younger, his brother needed Raymond, whether he liked it or not. "Ready to get back to fixin' the Ford?"

"As long as you don't make me go under it."

"Who'll reach the oil drum, then?"

"Try gettin' thrown from a car and tell me how you feel."

"Fair enough." Jimmie deserved a little leeway. The accident three years before had mangled Jimmie's back badly enough that it still pained him from time to time.

They hooked a left toward Guerry Street, where their modest two-bedroom home sat in a row with several other nondescript bungalows. "Those boys give you trouble today?"

"What do you think?"

Raymond clamped his mouth shut. He couldn't say what he thought. He'd tie those bullies to the tracks if it weren't against the law. Raymond cut through the front lawn and pulled a key from underneath a pot. "Wait here."

Jimmie plunked down on the steps.

Raymond grabbed two Coca-Colas from the icebox and sat beside Jimmie on their home's weather-beaten porch. Eyeing the dented and rusted-out 1925 Ford Model T parked in their driveway, he popped the tops off the bottles and handed one to Jimmie.

"They'll get bored and move on to someone else," Raymond said.

"They didn't start pickin' on me till Dad left." Jimmie downed half his drink in three gulps. "You think he's ever comin' back?"

The hope in his brother's voice made Raymond's heart sink. "He can't come home. He married her, didn't he?" Dad wasn't coming back. He'd met the wealthy Virginia three years ago on one of his sales trips to Charleston, and the temptation of a climb up her social ladder had been too strong to resist. Dad seemed satisfied with directing his sons' lives from a distance and seeing them for occasional visits.

Jimmie shoved his foot forward, leaving a scrape in the

gravel. "Being married didn't stop him from leaving us. He could leave her too." He took his bottle and blew across its top only to make a pathetic rasp of a whistle. He set it down on its side and kicked it away. "Dad left because I'm trash, just like those boys said."

Raymond set his bottle on the porch and lifted the car's hood. "Stop that. You're not trash, and you know it."

Jimmie followed him to the car and sat down against it, drawing his knees to his chest. "If only he would... if he would just..."

Love us? But Raymond couldn't remember one kind word coming from Dad, not even in his letters or during their short visits. "He just wants the best for us, is all. It's why he pushes us so hard." A lie, no doubt. Add it to the passel he'd told trying to make Jimmie feel better since Dad left.

"And what if after all that pushin', I can't be what he likes?"

Raymond turned his wrench around a bolt so hard his arm shook. It was the same question Raymond had asked himself, over and over, with no answer.

The muggy afternoon air settled around them, heavy and damp. Heavy, like the silence between them.

"You got something to say?" Jimmie asked.

"It's just... I want to fix everything, but I don't know how."

"Maybe there is no fixin' it." Jimmie lifted his head off his arm and studied his brother. "Maybe there are things even *you* can't fix. Don't make me go back to school, Ray. I can't stand being there."

A flash of heat ripped through Raymond, sparked by the quiver in Jimmie's voice. His brother was right. Raymond couldn't fix this. Nothing he tried worked—not waiting after school for Jimmie, not lying to him about Dad. Maybe it was time to tell Jimmie the truth. He pulled himself out of the engine and crouched at his brother's side. "Look at me."

"Leave me alone." Jimmie swiped his face with a rough, hurried hand.

"You know I love you, but you've got to quit this bellyaching."

Jimmie's mouth flopped open. "*Bellyachin'*?"

"You can't just give up. Sometimes you've got to do what you don't want to, like go to school even if you might get a beating. That's what makes a man a man—doing what needs doing even when it's tough."

"Easy for you to say."

"Dad ain't comin' back, Jimmie. He's not. And the sooner you realize that, the sooner you stop waitin' around for him to rescue you."

Jimmie's mouth trembled. "You don't know he's gone for good. Not for sure."

"Forget Dad. Stand up for yourself. Show those boys you're made of stronger stuff than they are." Raymond shoved a finger into Jimmie's chest. "Make them think twice before they mess with you again."

Jimmie stared at the ground and then at Raymond. A long moment passed, and then a spark lit his eyes, one that Raymond hadn't seen for a long, long time. "Just so we're straight, you're tellin' me I can sock 'em?"

"Only if they hit you first."

A smile cracked Jimmie's face. "Fine by me."

Raymond sat by his brother's side and bumped his shoulder. "I know you don't like me sticking my nose in your business, but you and me is all we got." Raymond pulled a cylinder head washer from his pocket and twiddled it between his fingers. "Promise me, right here and now. We'll always be there for each other, no matter what."

"I don't see as how you'll ever be in a pickle I can fix." He was quiet for a beat. "Did you figure out what to do about Dad wanting you to work for him?"

"Not yet." No matter how many different ways Raymond looked at it, he couldn't figure how to get out of Dad's plans. Everything hinged on keeping Dad happy—the house payment, their clothes, even the milk delivery for two growing boys. That support could be taken away in an instant if they didn't do what he wanted. The expectations were clear: once Raymond graduated high school in June, he would go to Clemson, the same military school Sellers men had attended for generations. Then he'd work at Dad's shrimping company down in Georgia, drumming up accounts as a salesman.

What boy in his right mind would turn down college and a ready-made job? But Raymond couldn't leave Florence. Mother and Jimmie needed him. And if he wanted a family of his own someday—and he did, more than anything—he couldn't be a traveling salesman like Dad and leave his wife and kids for weeks at a time, not if Raymond was going to be the kind of dad he needed to be. He wouldn't risk becoming like *him*.

"What if you told Dad you wanted to stay?"

"And be the first person to turn him down? No, thanks."

"How 'bout we make a deal? I stand up to the jerks, and you tell Dad you don't want to work for him when we visit in June." Jimmie held out his hand to Raymond. "Then you won't have to leave me."

A stone dropped into the pit of Raymond's stomach. How could he say no after all his yapping about being brave? If there ever was a pickle to be in, this was it. Dad was going to kill him. Raymond forced himself to grasp Jimmie's hand. "Okay. Deal." He pulled away, leaving behind the washer he'd been playing with. "Find where this goes, and I'll give you a nickel."

"How 'bout I split the nickel with you if you help me? Fifty-fifty."

"A nickel split fifty-fifty, huh? You playing hooky from math class again?"

"Why do I need math? I'll take my jitterbug on the road and make pocketsful of money."

"Is that right? And just how will you keep track of all that money without any math?"

"I can count to a million, and that's all I need to know."

"You got me beat there." Raymond chuckled and tossed the nickel to Jimmie. "Don't spend it all in one place, Jitterbug Jim."

THREE

BROTHERS AND SONS

June 1937
St. Simons Island, Georgia

Jimmie followed Raymond into the dining room and stopped short. It was just as fancy as he remembered, with a table decked in gleaming white and gold-rimmed china, but now an enormous bowl held up by fat porcelain cupids towered over the spectacle. No matter where he chose to sit, Jimmie would have to stare directly into the cherubs' rounded hind cheeks.

"You're late." Tall and sturdy with a hawk-like face, Arthur Raymond Sellers, Sr. sat at the head of the table, frowning at his watch.

Virginia laid her napkin in her lap with one hand and signaled for the food with the other. "Raymond. James. Take a seat. Your sister will be here any moment."

Jimmie pulled out his chair and leaned over to Raymond. "That hellcat ain't no sister of ours."

Raymond shoved an elbow into his brother's ribs. "Shh."

Their stepsister *was* a hellcat. She liked to think she was the favorite, and maybe she was. She lived with Dad all year round, while Jimmie hadn't seen him in months.

Susan walked in with a sickly-sweet smile tacked to her face and took a seat. "Hello, boys."

Dad peered around the cupids at Raymond. "Looking forward to Clemson?"

Raymond's face reddened. He glanced at Jimmie, a plea for rescue in his eyes.

Jimmie plowed into the silence. "I got to pitch at our last game. And I got a strikeout too."

"Oh?" Dad's head swiveled in Jimmie's direction. "And how's your math? Striking out there as well?"

"Matter of fact, I got an A on my last test." Jimmie had to have Susan beat there. She was long on looks but short in the brains department.

"So you've decided to finally apply yourself, have you?"

"Mrs. Thomas says I catch on quick. Said I might even pull off an A for the whole class."

Dad set down his fork, a spark of interest in his eyes at last. "Did she really?"

Warmth bloomed in Jimmie's chest. "Yes, sir. I'll find out as soon as—"

"Roger's agreed to escort me to the dance, Daddy." Susan's glance darted between the two.

Dad turned away from Jimmie and patted Susan's hand. "Now, didn't I tell you he would?"

Hiding behind the cupids, Susan shot Jimmie a look of triumph.

Uppity snot. Maggot eater. Phony, bug-eyed weasel. "You—"

"Have you taken the boat out yet, Dad?" Raymond asked, shaking his head a little at Jimmie.

"Oh boy, has he ever!" Susan exchanged smiles with their dad. "He took me to the bay just yesterday. It's our special place, isn't it, Daddy?"

Jimmie threw down his napkin and stood, scraping his chair against the floor. "You know what? I'm all wore out from our trip. May I go up?"

"Fine, fine." Dad waved him off and went back to sawing his pork chop.

Raymond caught up with Jimmie on the stairs going up to their room. "So, how about that cupid butt bowl?"

Despite himself, Jimmie chuckled. "I bet they paid good money for those cheri-bums."

"Whatever they paid, it was too much."

Jimmie stopped and faced Raymond. "Ray, I... I gotta tell you somethin', and I don't want you to be mad. Promise?"

"Of course."

"I lied, Ray. I told Dad I got an A, but I didn't. I got a C on that math test. Last time I got a C, Dad told me I had the brains of a catfish."

Raymond's mouth tightened. "I can't believe he said that."

Jimmie swallowed the ball in his throat. He was almost thirteen and too big for crying. "You still plan on tellin' Dad about staying in Florence?"

"I'll do it on Monday, right before we leave."

"Good. And there's one more thing you can do. Wanna help me leave a goodbye gift?"

Raymond narrowed his eyes at Jimmie. "What kind of trouble are you brewin'?"

Jimmie smirked. "You'll see."

With them leaving in an hour, Raymond couldn't put off talking with Dad any longer. He took a deep breath and raised his hand to the office door, rapping twice.

"Enter."

Raymond stepped onto the plush carpet of the inner sanctum.

Dad stood at a cart pouring amber liquid over ice. "Sit." He filled a glass with water and held it out to him.

Raymond took it and lowered himself into a stiff leather chair. Midday sun streamed in from the windows, setting the rich mahogany of the office aglow in the color of dried oak leaves. The air smelled of leather and cigar smoke, lemon polish and paper. Dust motes sparkled and tumbled in the soft rays of light, insensible to the coming storm between father and son.

Dad sat in his own chair. The air expelled from the seat cushion turned the motes into whirling dervishes. "How's your mother? She need anything?" He pulled a cigar from a box on his desk, snipped the cap, and set it between his teeth. The clock behind him ticked with each passing second.

A working car. A day off. You. "No, sir."

Dad brought a match to his cigar. Rotating it in the flame, he puffed, and a cloud of gray swirls dispersed into hazy union with the floating dust.

Tick. Tock. Tick.

Bead after bead of sweat joined together and ran down Raymond's spine. Dad did have a sixth sense about people. Did he guess what Raymond was about to do?

Dad set his cigar in an ashtray and rose from his chair. Standing before the window overlooking the garden, he clasped his hands behind his back and stared into the distance. "What's bothering you? I may have been gone from home awhile, but I still know my own son."

Raymond exhaled a deep breath. It was now or never. "The thing is, I... I don't want to go to Clemson. And I'm no salesman. Not like you." Dad would know that if he knew Raymond at all.

The next moment turned into two. "Oh?" Dad's voice was calm. Too calm.

"I'm thankful for the chance to go to college. I really am. It's just that I want something different. Besides, I can't leave Mother and Jimmie. They need me."

Dad turned around, his face a map of unknowns. "What could they possibly need that I don't provide?"

"Well, nothing, it's just—"

"If you get your degree and work for me, you'll have money enough to do whatever you like. Even take care of your mother and Jimmie, as you say."

"It's not about the money."

"It's always about the money." Dad dropped his smirk and put on a benign, kindly look. "Don't you want to get married someday? Have children of your own?"

"I could open my own mechanic's shop. I'm good at fixing cars. We wouldn't be rich, but we'd have enough." He pictured his children, happy. Free to be themselves. Confident enough to hug him and tell him what they're thinking. Trusting in him to give them only good for the rest of their lives. A person didn't need money for that. Give him a happy family—kids who wouldn't have to suffer for a lack of love—and he'd be set for life.

The mask fell from Dad's face. "Alright. Let's say you do that." He returned to his desk and sat in his chair. "You have a small mechanic's shop. You settle down and come home from a long, hard, thankless day to four squalling brats and a harpy for a wife. Beans for dinner, one pair of nice pants for Sundays. Hat in hand as you beg me for money to make rent." Red crept past his collar and spread into his jowls, the only hint of any emotion. "I won't do it. I won't give you one cent if you come begging."

"I won't." How could Dad even think it possible? Raymond would work four jobs before it ever came to that.

Dad tilted his head and studied Raymond with a sudden gleam in his eyes. "What are Jimmie's plans for after he graduates?"

Raymond blinked. Jimmie? What did Jimmie have to do with this? "I... I don't know."

"I need *somebody*, and if you won't do it, well, I could bring Jimmie on if I have to."

It was like a punch to the gut. Dad had set a trap, and Raymond had walked right into it. "He's just a kid, Dad."

"He's not as capable as you, but I suppose I could do the work to get him up to standard." His mouth tipped in a mocking smile. "Though it might be a fool's errand."

Raymond gripped his glass so tight he could've shattered it. Dad was no better than those bullies at Jimmie's school. "Jimmie's just as capable as I am. Maybe more."

"Oh? And your evidence of this is, what, an A on some math test? A fluke. You forget I raised that boy. He's too distractable."

Raymond studied his father, the stubborn set of his chin, his half-lidded eyes. Something wasn't right. If Dad cared this much about their futures, he would've never left them. "Why do you need us at all? Can't you use someone else?"

Dad blew smoke from his cigar stub, his iron gaze pinned on Raymond. "Because no one's going to say I didn't do right by my sons."

It was all to do with making himself feel better about leaving them? That figured. Raymond could barely keep his mouth from curling in disdain.

The future came to life as if it were a talkie flickering on a screen: Dad demanding excellence, Jimmie failing to provide it. Jimmie would be found lacking, day after day, minute by minute, and not just during a short visit. Raymond had seen Jimmie at the dinner table, savoring the crumbs of Dad's attention. His brother would do anything Dad asked of him if it gained him the approval he wanted. Underneath all Jimmie's bravado lay a tender heart. Given enough time and opportunity, Jimmie's wobbling confidence would be stomped into the ground.

"Send your brother in here."

Raymond's heart raced faster than a rat from a flooding hole. It wouldn't be fair to live his own life at the cost of Jimmie living his. What kind of brother would he be to sacrifice Jimmie's happiness for his own? "No." It had slipped out before he could think better of it.

"No?"

"I'll do it, alright? I'll leave Florence and go to Clemson." So he'd have to do what Dad wanted. It didn't mean he couldn't figure out a way to have what he wanted too.

Dad's eyes glittered. "And?"

"And I'll work for you after. But only if you let Jimmie do what he pleases."

"As long as what he does pleases me." Dad got up and clapped a hand on Raymond's shoulder, steering him toward the door. "Now, let's get you two to the station."

Jimmie's chin rested on the heel of his hand, his forehead pressed against the cool glass of the train car window. The scenery whizzed by in a blur of greens and browns, and his head hurt trying to pick out the details.

He dropped his hand and stared at his brother. Raymond had been awfully quiet since they'd left, and it had been several minutes since he'd turned a page in his comic book.

"D'you tell him?" Jimmie asked.

A space of a moment stretched between them. "Yep."

He dropped his hand and stared at Raymond. "And?"

"I'm going to Clemson."

Jimmie couldn't keep his face from twisting in shock. "But why?"

"He gave me a good reason to go."

"But what about staying and being with me? Ain't that reason enough?"

"Just drop it, will you? Trust me when I say it's better for the both of us."

Jimmie opened his mouth and then shut it again. Dad must've bawled him out, good and long.

"Was it that bad?"

"Yep."

Jimmie studied his brother's tense face. Raymond wouldn't have given up without a fight. He just wouldn't. Sometimes there was no talking Dad out of what he wanted, no matter how hard you worked at it. It would be plain selfish to let Raymond stay in the dumps about it. He shoved his brother in the side with an elbow. "Was it what we did with those cupids?"

Raymond smiled a little. "We're getting a whuppin' if they ever find out." He dug his fingers into Jimmie's ribs. "I never can tell you no."

"You're not feelin' guilty, are you?"

"Well..."

"Listen, no one—and I mean *no one*—leaves Dad's house without makin' fun of their butt bowl behind their backs. We did them a favor. 'Sides, Virginia can't know for sure it was us, not if she don't find those stupid cupids in the pond."

"Ha! She wouldn't be caught dead near that swamp."

Jimmie pictured Virginia in her pearls and stockings, heels stuck two inches deep in mud and swatting mosquitoes with her bony hand. Raymond was right—it'd never happen.

Raymond slapped his comic book into Jimmie's middle. "I'm gonna get some shut-eye."

But with Raymond's attention directed away from him, Jimmie's smile fell. He twisted the comic into a baton and leaned forward, elbows on his knees and head bowed.

Raymond was leaving.

Jimmie couldn't even imagine it. As far back as he could remember, Raymond had been there, watching over him. Telling him what to do.

His brother had to have had a good reason for backing down. He just *had* to. Raymond would still find a way to be there for him, no matter how far apart they were.

A little cheered, he turned his attention back to the scenery zipping by the window. How could Raymond sleep at a time like this? Every clack of the train's wheels sounded out *Home! Home!* to his ears, and he was near to bursting with it. The farther the train took them from St. Simons, the faster his heart beat. He stared out the window. The blurred landscape reassured him they were on their way back to South Carolina.

The second he got back, he'd strip off his Sunday suit and run naked as a baby into the water hole behind their house. He'd say *ain't* any chance he got and let his hair go any which way it pleased. He couldn't wait to once again be himself—just plain old Jimmie Sellers, back home where he belonged in nothing-ever-happens Florence, South Carolina.

FOUR

CLEMSON

November 1937
Clemson, South Carolina

Dressed in a cadet's uniform, Raymond strode across Clemson as if he'd been going there for years instead of just two months. He'd resigned himself to his fate and thrown himself into this new life, grieving the death of his plans. But as it turned out, the military school wasn't all that bad. It was nice doing something hard and not having a minute to think about Jimmie or home or what his life would be like if he weren't here.

"Hey, Ray! Wait up." Herbie Wade ran toward him.

"Hey there."

Herbie bent over his knees, huffing and puffing. "Shoo-ee. I've been following you since you left the barracks."

"Lost in thought, I guess."

They trod the pathway toward Tillman Hall where a bevy of girls from a local school waited to practice their dance steps with them.

"Excited?"

"No." Entertaining a bunch of tittering girls was a waste of time when he had a stack of assignments to complete.

"Aww, come on. There could be some lookers."

"Lookers?" Raymond gave him a disgusted look. "None you should be looking at. They're babies compared to us."

"Babies? They're not that young. My dad started going around with my mom when she was fourteen."

Fourteen? Raymond couldn't fathom it. That was just one year older than Jimmie, and his brother was still digging holes in their backyard to see if he could get to China. "They're just kids, Herbie." Raymond jogged up the last few steps and pulled open the door, waving Herbie in.

Reedy notes drifted from a gramophone in the corner. A buckshot of heavy floral scents pelted him. He resisted the urge to plug his nose. Someone needed to teach these girls that if they wanted to stalk prey, it was more successfully done if the boys didn't smell their predators from a mile away.

The girls in question stood in bunches around the punch-bowl and along the wall, gaping at him and Wade and the other cadets. Raymond pulled his collar.

The schoolgirls' matron stepped into the middle of the dance floor and clapped her hands. The gramophone's needle scratched against the record. "Thank you, gentlemen, for giving our girls an opportunity to dance with male partners. Your commander has promised me that you'll show these girls the respect and kindness suited to their age and innocence. Ladies, don't neglect to engage your partner in conversation even as you endeavor to follow his lead. Now, most importantly, make sure you enjoy yourselves." Her smile was more of a grimace. Maybe she didn't like being here anymore than Raymond did. She signaled to the cadet manning the player, and once again, music filled the room. The girls lining the walls stared at the room of cadets, anticipatory gleams in their eyes.

Raymond expelled a breath. "Into the fray, eh?"

Herbie didn't answer.

"Herbie?"

His friend had left Raymond's side, already making his way toward an especially breathless gaggle of teenage girls.

"That's a fine how-do-you-do," Raymond muttered. Abandoned by his friend and left to face all this alone.

Well, there was nothing for it but to get it over with.

A couple of unattached girls leaned against the wall. On his way to them, he passed an archway, and a slight movement inside caught his eye. He took two steps backward. From the shadows, a girl with apple cheeks peered at him through her spectacles then shrank back until she was completely shrouded in darkness.

Raymond tried not to laugh. He craned his neck into the alcove. "Hello there. Care to dance?" He reached a hand inside.

"No, thank you." Her quiet voice was firm.

He peered further into the darkness. She stood there, twining a curl around a finger, her eyes downcast. Poor girl. She was too young to be dancing with college boys.

Determined steps clacked behind him. "Look, you better get out of there." He jutted his thumb behind him at the approaching school mistress.

The girl looked past him. Her eyes widened. She leaped out of the dark with all the adolescent awkwardness of limbs she hadn't grown into just yet.

"Follow me." He grabbed her small hand and led her to the dance floor, where he guided them into a foxtrot.

She stumbled over his foot. "Sorry," she said, her head still bowed.

"It's alright. I won't bite." He glanced at the other dancers, who were chatting away merrily. "Say, you're pretty good at this. You must've been taking lessons for a while."

She shook her head, bouncing her curls.

A gangly cadet clomped past them with his partner. "I didn't know they let horses into Clemson," Raymond said.

She looked up, startled. And then she giggled.

Emboldened, he tried again. "I'm ever so glad I brought two lumps of sugar in my purse," he said in a breathy falsetto, imitating the horse-stepping cadet's partner.

She laughed again.

Victory. "How about them? What's he thinking?" With her hand still in his, he pointed to a couple by the punch bowl. The boy listened bug-eyed as the girl chattered away.

"I'm sure I wouldn't know."

"Oh, come on. Give it a try."

Just when Raymond thought he might've pushed her too far, she spoke, deepening her voice to match the cadet's. "I can't hear a word she's saying, but I'm not gonna tell her that and have her start all over."

Raymond laughed, perhaps for the first time since entering Clemson. "Thatta girl."

She smiled back, her baby cheeks not unlike Jimmie's. "My name's Evelyn."

"Thatta girl, *Evelyn*. How old are you, anyway?"

"Fourteen. *Almost* fifteen."

Raymond nodded. "My brother's thirteen. He dances much better than I do."

Her eyes fluttered up to his. "I think you're an awful good dancer."

"Don't let my brother hear you say that."

The music faded. Chatter filled the momentary silence. The music changed, and the gramophone pumped out an upbeat tune played by clarinets, brass, and piano, perfect for dancing the Carolina Shag. Raymond cringed inwardly. Jimmie had tried teaching him the steps a few years back but declared his big brother hopeless after an afternoon of tutelage.

Raymond stepped back. "Well, Evelyn, it's been a real treat. Don't partner up with any horses, alright?"

She looked down at her toes. "Mrs. Jones said we were allowed two dances with each boy. If you want to, that is." Peeping up at him, she caught a curl in her finger and twisted it like she had in the alcove.

He could barely hear her over the music and the crowd. He leaned forward. "What's that?"

"I said"—her voice strained—"we could dance another if you like." Her eyes skittered to the other boys waiting on the perimeter of the dance floor.

He must be the safest bet of the bunch. Better the devil you know and all that. "Well, I'm not any good at the shag," he spoke above the music, "but I'm up for it, if you are."

She smiled shyly and said something in reply.

A couple swooped by, their uproarious laughter obscuring her words.

"I can't hear in all this racket. What'd you say?" Raymond asked. He was almost yelling at this point.

"I said, I could be your bride."

Bride?

She gazed up at him with innocent eyes. He must've heard wrong. Or maybe she was pulling a joke like she had about the cadet at the punchbowl. "Bride? Why, I'm not looking just yet, but you can come back in a few years when you're old enough and ask again." He winked, letting her know he was in on the fun.

A fiery blush swept across her face. "*Guide.* I asked if you wanted a *guide.*"

Whoops. Raymond bit the inside of his cheek to keep from grinning. "Sorry. Couldn't hear you in all this racket. I would be glad to have your help. Will you?"

Cheeks still burning, she nodded. "Okay."

The dance went smoothly after that, with her giving him pointers and redirecting his steps.

Even Jimmie would've been proud of his attempt.

The song ended, and he dropped his hands from hers. "Thank you for the dance, Miss Evelyn."

She looked up at him, her eyes soft. "Thanks ever so much."

"Can I take you back to your hidey-hole?"

She nodded once like a queen granting favors from her throne. "Yes, please."

He led her back to the alcove and stayed with her until the next boy came along. His heart lightened when she smiled at the fellow and left with him. At least he hadn't scared her off from boys forever. She was a sweet kid. It had been nice playing the part of big brother again.

It struck him when he sauntered away that he'd forgotten to tell her his name. It was just as well he hadn't. She wouldn't remember him, anyway.

FIVE

A PEBBLE IN A SHOE

Evelyn's gaze followed his retreating back. Goodness, but he was handsome. And ever so nice. If only Mrs. Jones hadn't warned them not to monopolize any one boy's attention. She heaved a sigh.

"You alright, Miss...?"

"I'm fine," she answered glumly. Taking a turn with this boy was fine and all, but he wasn't the other fellow. The music faded. Relieved, she stepped back. "Thank you for the dance." She turned away before he could ask for another and returned to her alcove. She leaned her cheek against the cool plaster and closed her eyes. What was that first boy's name, anyway? She'd been too twitterpated to ask.

She peeked around the corner at the dance floor. The dancers parted, and for a moment *he* appeared, smiling down at another girl just like he had with her. Her smile fell. Just how many other girls would he dance with before the night was over?

Would he have stuck around longer, defying Mrs. Jones, if he'd seen her without her glasses? Boys went for Greta Garbos, not girls with Coca-Cola bottles wired to their faces. Evelyn took off her spectacles and tucked them in her pocket. Squinting at the twirling couples for his tall form among the other moving blobs, she stepped onto the dance floor.

"Pardon me!" a girl exclaimed, leaping out of her way.

Evelyn recoiled. "Sorry." She pulled the wired rims out of her pocket and put them back on. Dragging her feet to the coat check, she retrieved her cape and walked out the double doors of the auditorium. A light wind gusted, drifting through the thin fabric to her skin. She flattened one palm against her skirt, holding it down. With her other hand, she held the cape to her chest, where the breeze filled the bodice's pitiful emptiness. It was Mama's Sunday dress, but there hadn't been time to alter it. She flopped down on the concrete steps and set her elbows on her knees.

The wind scraped the dried leaves across the pavement and cooled her feverish cheeks. Propping her chin in her cupped hands, she kept an eye on the gate where her dad would appear at any moment. Would he be grouchy? Or would he be quiet, as usual? She twirled her purse on its chain around her finger. It wasn't his fault. It was because of the Great War. That's what Mama said, anyway. She also said he'd been quick to laugh and easy to love once, but Evelyn could no more imagine him laughing than she could imagine President Roosevelt asking her to tea.

Before long, a hulking shadow appeared in the distance. She sat up straight. "Daddy?"

The apparition grunted.

"Hi, Daddy."

"Honeybee," he said in a gravelly voice.

"I had a good time at the dance." She joined his side, and they veered onto the gravel path leading away from Clemson. "We danced the foxtrot and the Carolina Shag, and there was a waltz too, even though I don't think anyone does that one anymore. Mrs. Jones said it's important we know how to move in society, should our husbands come from the upper crust. Why do they call it that? Upper crust, I mean. Do rich people make their servants cut off their crusts?"

A breeze kicked up her hair and dress again.

He took off his scarf and tied it around her neck.

She snuggled into it and sighed, the tension from their one-sided conversation melting away in a bloom of joy.

Soon, they were home. Daddy climbed the porch steps and sat down, where he took out his whittling knife and a piece of wood.

"Well, good night, Daddy." She hesitated, but thinking of the scarf, she leaned down and gave him a quick peck on his pomaded hair.

He stared ahead, silent and grim.

She pulled open their front door and stepped into the warmth.

Her mother set her knitting aside. "You're early."

"It was the best night I've ever had." She twirled, her cape fluttering in a circle around her. "There was a boy, and he made me feel better about being there. You know how nervous I was."

"How was your walk home?"

"Oh, you know how Daddy is."

Mama's mouth pursed, just like Daddy's did when he was in one of his moods. Mama unclasped the cape. Pulling it off Evelyn's shoulders, she folded it neatly and set it over the arm of the seat behind her. "We have the last of the tomatoes to put up tomorrow. Best you get to bed."

"Good night, Mama." She kissed her mother's cheek and took the stairs two at a time to her bedroom.

Sitting at her dressing table, she took off her glasses and studied her profile in the mirror, lips puckered. Maybe she should try that new hairstyle her friend showed her. She'd be ready if that boy ever saw her again. *Bride?* She squealed. Oh, how she'd felt like fainting when he'd misunderstood her. After pinning her curls, she jumped on her bed and kicked her legs under her sheets. The quicker she fell asleep, the quicker she could dream about the nameless boy from the dance.

In the small hours of the morning, she awoke to angry voices filtering through the thin wall behind her headboard. She sat up, heart pounding. The voices stopped. It had to have been a dream. She'd never heard her dad say more than three words strung together. Unsettled, she laid her head back into the groove on her pillow and fell into a restless asleep.

She awoke the next morning disoriented and rushed to her door. Outside sat her shoes, polished to a shine. She breathed a sigh of relief. Everything was just as it should be. She slipped her hand into the right shoe and felt something lodged in the toe box. Smiling, she pulled out a smooth pebble, so round it could've been mistaken for a marble. It was the best part of every morning, seeing what surprise Daddy placed in her shoes.

Sometimes it was a peppermint, other times a beautiful leaf or flower. His cranky ways were just a cover for his kindness at night, a little game he played just with her. Every day she woke and looked inside her shoes for proof that he still loved her enough to play the game.

She'd even found a whole quarter once, wrapped in her worn socks and tucked inside. She'd hardly said a word about being ashamed of the holes in her socks, but still, he knew what would make her happiest. Sometimes she felt he was the only person who really did. He'd never said the words, but that quarter was a proclamation of love louder than any spoken declaration.

She got dressed and flew down the stairs. Wrapping her palm around the ball topping the end of the banister, she launched herself into the kitchen. Mama's back was to her at the stove.

"Good morning."

Mama didn't turn around to greet her. "Eggs are on the table."

Evelyn sat and tucked her napkin in her dress. Seeing a plate with toast, she smiled. Upper crust? She took her knife and severed the brown edges from the bread. There, now she was as good as anybody who had servants cut their crusts. She gulped down her food and drained her glass of milk, eager to get to school and talk about the dance with her friends.

She ran out the door and considered only in passing that Daddy wasn't sitting on their porch like he usually was.

When she came home later that day, she ran up the steps, stomach growling. What treat would Mama have waiting for her today? "I'm home!" She swung open the front door and let it slam into place. "Mama?" She sniffed. No tempting smells wafted from the kitchen.

Evelyn cracked open her parents' bedroom. Empty. Maybe Mama was in the garden. She dashed to the back door and looked outside. No signs of life, just like the kitchen.

A sniffling sound drifted from the cellar where they stored their garden's bounty in jars and baskets. "Mama?" Evelyn peered down into the musty darkness. The dim light filtering down from the kitchen fell upon her mother, who was leaning against the packed dirt wall. Her heart skipped a beat. "Why are you hidin'?"

Mama didn't answer.

Evelyn yanked the light cord, and the bulb buzzed to life. "What happened?" She remembered the empty porch. "Is Daddy—is he—is he... dead?"

"No, baby. He's not dead." Mama slid to the floor next to the jars of tomatoes. She held out her arms. Evelyn flew down the stairs and tucked herself into her mother's side. "He left us, Evie."

Evelyn pushed her away. It couldn't be. She ran up the

stairs and raced to Daddy's bedroom. The bed had been stripped of his potato-sack pillow and the closet emptied. She ran to her own bedroom and there, lying on her pillow, was a single daisy. She picked up the flower and crushed it under her shoe. Slamming her bedroom door behind her, she stalked back to the cellar.

Evelyn pointed up the stairs. "He should be the one cryin'. Not you." She fell into her mother's arms. Then Evelyn cried because Mama cried, but not for her own self. She was too mad at him for that.

"It's my fault," Mama said in a wobbly voice.

"You did nothing wrong." Evelyn reached up through the warm cocoon of her mother's arms and stroked her mother's cheek.

"I pushed him too hard last night. I wanted things to go back to the way they used to be. Before the war."

Evelyn laid her head on Mama's shoulder.

Mama's throat clicked on a swallow. "I wish you could've known what he was like before. How your father lit up a room just by pokin' his curly head inside of it. That man—the man I married—came back from France a stranger to me."

Unease crept inside Evelyn. What did it mean that she loved a man she didn't really know?

Mama wrapped a finger in one of Evelyn's curls. "I think it was easier for him to leave, knowing I keep waitin' for him to come back. He couldn't give me what I wanted, and I don't think he could stand it."

Poor Mama. Years of on-edge waiting, but he never really came back. And now, he was gone.

Mama pushed Evelyn away and peered into her eyes. "Don't you go thinking this has anything to do with you, okay? He loves you." She placed a hand on top of the pearlescent buttons leading a trail down the faded fabric of her work-worn house dress. "I know it in my heart."

Evelyn grabbed Mama's hands. "If I wrote him and told him we'd take him back just as he is, he'd come home, wouldn't he?"

Mama yanked her hands away. "I don't know, I don't know, I don't know! I don't even know where he's gone."

Panic fluttered inside Evelyn. She'd never seen Mama like this before. "Shhh, it's okay." She pulled her mother to her and hugged her tight. "It's alright. We'll be okay."

But would they? She'd never wake again to shoes outside her bedroom door, polished and ready for school. He wouldn't be there, making her feel safe at night, sitting on the porch and keeping strangers away. At least, that's what she'd always believed he was doing. Maybe Mama had been right, and he sat on the porch because he wanted to be alone.

Mama stood abruptly. "Evie, I... You're going to stay with Aunt Pat in North Carolina for a while."

Evelyn's mouth dropped open. Only a squeak came out in reply.

"Pack your bags. She'll be here tomorrow." Her mother went to the stairs.

"But I don't want to leave you. Mama, don't make me!" The last words came out on a sob.

Evelyn grabbed the hem of her mother's dress.

Mama yanked it out of Evelyn's hand. "It's for the best." She raced up the stairs. A door slammed. Quiet filled the cool damp of the cellar.

Evelyn wrapped her arms around her knees. Soundless tears leaked from her eyes. She pulled the pebble from her pocket and pitched it into a row of jars. It clanked and dropped with a soft thud on the hard-packed dirt. Evelyn pressed her hands against her ears, blocking the sound of Mama's weeping. She gritted her teeth against her own tears. There was no use in crying. Mama wouldn't comfort her. There was nobody left who would.

SIX

ON THE LAM

November 1937
Florence, South Carolina

Jimmie flung open the Ford's hood. Wires, cylinders, metal boxes, and bolts. The engine's smoke had to be caused by something, but what? He drew a fortifying breath. He'd watched Raymond work on this engine a thousand times. He'd just never paid attention since his brother would fix it without his help, anyway.

He glanced at the kitchen window. The gauzy hangings couldn't hide the outline of Mother's black dress and cloche hat with that floppy bow tacked on its side. She scurried behind the white curtains, but she wasn't quick enough for Jimmie not to see that wrinkle between her eyebrows carving a canyon, just like it always did when she was worried. He pinched his lips together. He either fixed the car in the next few minutes, or she'd be fired for being late to work.

"Think, dummy." What had Raymond said could be the problem if the engine smoked? Was the oil all used up? With a wrench tucked between his chin and his chest, he lay down on his back and scooted under the Ford. A flash of a memory, of metal and pain from the accident years ago, sent a shiver down his limbs. *You're okay. This car ain't moving. It can't hurt you.* He pulled himself toward the oil drum with two knobs on its side. Running his hand along the side of it, he twisted the bottom knob.

It didn't budge a bit. With all his strength, he pushed on the lever.

"Jimmie?"

He banged his forehead on the car and swore.

"Watch your mouth." Mother's sensible shoes peeped under the step plate.

Jimmie closed his eyes. "Yes, ma'am."

"I can't wait any longer."

"Just another minute." He grabbed the wrench. Ray should be the one fixing this. With a surge of frustration, he took his wrench and banged the knob.

Fluid shot from the drum onto his face and into his hair. His arms jerked upward to block the stream, a strangled cry escaping from his mouth.

His mother dropped to her knees. "Jimmie? What happened?"

He spit out the oil, angling away from the spray. "Stop looking at me."

She laid the side of her face on the gravel and peered under the car. "Oh, son. Here." She swung her arm under the car, waving a handkerchief.

His eyes stung from the dripping liquid. The fishy-smelling oil clung to his hair, his face, his clothes. "Go." He injected confidence into his voice. "I'll take care of this."

"Can you get to school on time?"

"It's just oil. It'll wash off."

She reached under the car and squeezed his leg. "If you're

sure. I have to start walking now if I want to make it in before lunch. Maybe Mr. Putman won't notice."

Mr. Putman not notice? That geezer paid more attention to the time clock than he did anything else, including his breath. Mother was as good as fired. Jimmie couldn't keep tears from welling in his eyes. "I tried my best. Honest."

"I know it's hard with Raymond gone. Thank you for trying."

Trying? Jimmie frowned. Failing was more like it. Now Mother would be fired, all because he couldn't do what Raymond always did so easily.

Mother's shoes clicked down the sidewalk. Sliding from under the car, he groped his way up the porch steps. He swung open the door, stumbled into the kitchen, and turned on the spigot at the sink. He placed his face under the tepid stream of water and scrubbed. "Stupid. Stupid!"

Raymond had told him to go to Mr. Hooper if there were any problems with the car, but Jimmie had wanted to show Mother he could take care of things himself. Ha! Load of good that did him.

If Raymond was here, he would've kept Jimmie from making things worse. Why exactly had he gone to Clemson, anyway? Jimmie had tried to accept Raymond's decision. He'd let it slide because he knew how hard it must've been to deal with Dad. Well, Jimmie was done with the not-knowing. He ripped the kitchen towel from its holder and rubbed his skin so hard his cheeks chafed.

He wouldn't get the answers by phone. The last time they'd talked, it'd been awkward. Raymond's friends had been in the background, laughing and having a good ol' time. Jimmie had to ask Raymond to repeat himself because of the noise. Before long, Jimmie stopped trying and hung up. He couldn't even remember Raymond saying goodbye. Jimmie gripped the sink's sides with his hands. There was nothing for it but to ask him why. In person.

He tossed his clothes in the washing basket and jumped in the tub. He rubbed his body with soap and sniffed his skin. The smell lingered, but at least he was passable for decent. He threw on some clean clothes and emptied his money jar. Ninety-eight cents. Not enough. He could ride his bicycle, but with it being four hours to Clemson by car, a bike ride would take too long. He'd have to thumb it to Clemson.

Don't be a dummy, Raymond's voice said in Jimmie's head.

"I'm doin' what I shoulda done a long time ago," Jimmie answered aloud.

He grabbed his pillowcase and strode to the kitchen. There wasn't much in the icebox besides an apple and a dish of left-overs. He stuffed the apple inside the bag and swiped a piece of bread and a handful of crackers from the pantry. Removing the bell from the crock, he cut a generous slab of butter and placed it on the bread, folding it in half. That ought to do—for a while, at least.

He stepped outside and slung the pillowcase over his shoulder. He'd have to walk the first part. No one would pick up a delinquent Jimmie Sellers in Florence on a school day. As soon as he reached the town's border, his stomach rumbled. Pulling out the butter sandwich, he sat on the side of the road and ate it in three bites. Just as he was wiping his hands on his shirt, a Cadillac trundled around the bend. He stood and stuck out his thumb.

The car slowed, and a pretty young woman with auburn pin curls peered through the passenger window. "Ditching school?"

Jimmie squinted at her. She looked nice and all, but so did skunks until they sprayed you. He shifted his bag to his other shoulder. "I like to keep my business to myself."

She smiled knowingly. "Get in. I can take you as far as Columbia."

Jimmie grinned. "Say, thanks, lady!"

Five rides and nine hours later, he arrived and, after getting directions, sat on the steps of his brother's barracks. And as if he'd conjured him with his thoughts, Raymond came around the corner minutes later with three other boys, slapping one of the cadets on the back and laughing at some joke. Jimmie clenched his teeth so tight his jaw ached. That was *his* brother. *His* best friend. He stood and stuffed his hands in his pants.

Eyes wide, Raymond faltered. "*Jimmie?* What're you doing here?"

"I could ask the same of you."

Raymond looked sideways at his friends. "See you later, fellas."

The boys nodded and eyed Jimmie as they walked away.

Raymond pressed Jimmie against the bricks. "What's so important you couldn't chase me down with a phone call?"

"Nothing's been right since you been gone."

"What happened?"

Jimmie hung his head. "I tried to fix the Ford, but I couldn't figure it out."

"Did you call Mr. Hooper?"

"*No,* I didn't call Mr. Hooper. I thought I could take care of it myself." Jimmie crossed his arms. "What did Dad tell you to make you leave?"

Raymond's gaze darted away. "You wouldn't understand."

"I have the right to know."

"Leave it alone."

"Just come home, will you? I don't want to do this on my own."

"I can't."

"Why not?"

"Because... I like it here."

Jimmie blinked back sudden tears. "More than being with me?"

Raymond grabbed Jimmie's shoulders. "Don't you ever think that. I'd never miss anybody more than I miss you right now."

"Doesn't seem like it from where I'm standing. You promised we'd always be there for each other."

"Can't we still?"

Jimmie bumped his head against the wall. "Why can't Dad just let us be?" Maybe it was because he was the youngest that he missed what everyone else understood.

"I've been asking myself the same question."

"So, what do we do now?"

"What we have been doing. I stay; you go home and take care of Mother."

"Because I did such a great job of that today."

"You tried, and that counts for something." Raymond hooked an arm around Jimmie's neck. "Look, I'm sorry. I'll try to come home more often for visits."

Jimmie side-eyed him. "Yeah? How often?"

"As often as I can. C'mon. I'm going to get you fed, and then we're going to go see a friend about borrowing a car." He froze. "Does Mother even know you're here?"

Jimmie gave Ray a sheepish grin.

Raymond flicked Jimmie's ear.

"Ow!" Jimmie rubbed at it. "What'd you do that for?"

"You know why. Call her first, then we'll work on getting you home."

SEVEN

COLLEGE CAFÉ

June 1941
Clemson, South Carolina

"Howdy, fellas." A young man with rust-red hair shellacked with pomade bounded up the steps and joined six other Army Reserve officers at the door of College Café.

Raymond stifled a groan. *Frankie.*

The newcomer slapped Lieutenant Harry Pulaski in the stomach. "Better lay off the donuts this time. Uniform's getting a little tight."

Harry took a menacing step forward, hand fisted at his side.

Captain Herbie Wade, the unquestioned leader of their group by virtue of both his rank and his commanding height, shouldered his way in front of Harry. "Leave it alone."

Harry was sensitive about his failed weigh-in the prior week. But more than likely, that's why Frankie had said it. Nothing ever stopped Frankie from doing what he liked. They'd done their best to tolerate him ever since they'd met at Clemson four years prior. It was either that or kill him. Frankie was like a bad cold—never welcome, hard to shake, and a guarantee of a bad time.

Raymond pulled open the door and stepped inside the diner. A waitress sitting behind the counter didn't take notice of them except to turn a page in the doorstop she was reading—judging by the thickness, a college textbook. Not a fashion magazine kind of girl, he guessed. Her lips read along to the sentences on the page, forming words he couldn't hear. But even if she had given them voice, he wouldn't have heard them, distracted as he was by the shape of her mouth.

A piece of honey-tinted hair escaped from the knot at the nape of her neck. Her hand moved to twine the silky strands slow and lazy around one of her fingers. The movement was familiar in some way. *She* was familiar. He cocked his head and studied her—her twining finger, the unusual color of her hair, her wired spectacles. Could it be the girl from that dance at Clemson? She'd been fourteen, then. A kid he'd felt sorry for. *Evelyn*, she'd answered when he'd asked her name. Just Evelyn.

The fan of her downcast lashes looked just as they had when she'd refused to look up at him at the dance, but this was a woman, not the child he remembered. The youthful bashfulness was now shuttered away behind a mysterious veil of feminine allure. Gone were the angles and lines of her adolescent limbs. Her arms were graceful curves framing a womanly figure, baby cheeks nowhere in sight.

He couldn't take his eyes off her. It was only after Frankie slammed the girl's book shut that Raymond noticed his friend had approached the counter.

Her head jerked up, her cheeks a mottled crimson.

"Frankie!" Raymond exclaimed.

Frankie leaned on the counter with one elbow and stared Evelyn down with a smirk. "Hey, Four Eyes. What's it take to get some service in this joint?"

Raymond stepped between them. "Hey, now. Just—"

"What's it take?" Evelyn put a fist on her hip. "Manners."

His heart went off like a Roman candle. No girl he knew could handle a guy like that.

Frankie bowed with arm extended. "Well then, Miss *Manners*, if you'd be so kind... Escort us to hither yon table and allow us to partake of the fare at this fine establishment. At your leisure, of course, my fair lady."

She raised an eyebrow. "Much better. Right this way, gentlemen." She called to the other waitress who'd just come out from a swinging door by the kitchen. "Rosie, I'm off my break now. Go ahead and put your feet up."

"What were you thinking?" Raymond hissed to Frankie.

Frankie shrugged. "What? She was loafing on the job."

"Didn't you hear her? She was on her break."

Evelyn approached with their menus. "Follow me, gentlemen."

Errant wisps of dark golden hair brushed the nape of her neck, tempting Raymond's attention downward, but determined to be a gentleman, he dragged his gaze to the top of her head. He couldn't block his peripheral vision, though, and even that told him she was a knockout. He'd thought her lips distracting, but oh no—Miss Manners was a distraction in all kinds of ways. He trailed behind her like a barge pulled by a tugboat, helpless to do anything other than follow in her wake.

Raymond sat at the table and reached for the menu Evelyn held out to him. He willed her to look at him, wondering if she'd recognize him, but she moved to the next man without a return glance. Maybe it wasn't the girl from the dance.

He sighed and closed the menu. He could recite it backward from memory, anyway. Any Clemson student short on cash and far from Mom's kitchen could. Advertisements promising tasty home-cooked meals in Clemson's newspaper drew young, hungry men like lions to the kill.

Evelyn left for the pot of coffee.

Frankie turned and watched her walk away. On the back of his head, two tufts of hair sprang from his heavily pomaded waves, looking a little like sprouted horns. Raymond smirked. Never had the fellow looked more like the devil he was.

Frankie turned around, grinning. "Bet she won't loaf on the job after this," he sing-songed behind his menu.

"Knock it off, Frankie," Wade warned.

"She's a peach, huh? A real peach." Frankie waved his hands in the shape of an hourglass and winked. "I'm gonna tell her I'm free on Friday night 'cause I know she's dying to ask."

"A lot of good it'll do you after what you did. Leave her alone," Raymond said.

"Yeah, or what? Some girls like a man who knows what's what."

Raymond slapped Frankie's head with a menu.

"Ow!" Frankie laughed and flicked his own menu with his forefinger and thumb. "Alright, alright. Who said I wanted to date Polly Perfect, anyway? I know plenty of girls who don't insist on manners, if you know what I mean."

Wade put his hands behind Frankie's neck and pretended to strangle him. Too bad Wade wasn't doing it for real. Maybe it was time for a distraction. "Congrats again on the promotion, Herbie. I'm surprised they still let you hang out with us lowly LTs."

"We'll always be friends."

"Friends who salute each other." Raymond spread his hands in front of him as if he were showcasing Wade's name in lights. "Captain Herbie Wade."

"Alright, enough of that. You gonna get some donuts?"

"You bet I will." Raymond would never turn down one of College Café's cinnamon-dusted donuts. They were so good even a pinup prepping for a photoshoot would go back for seconds.

Evelyn took their orders and brought their food, seemingly

unfazed by their attention. If only he could see inside her head. It was like when he itched to get below a car's hood and figure out what made it run. He choked on his coffee. He shouldn't be thinking about getting under anyone's hood. He knew a lot less about females than he did mechanics.

Raymond hung back after the others paid their tab and left the diner. He ran his fingers through his hair and approached the counter, where she was cleaning seats. "Excuse me, miss?"

She glanced up but didn't stop wiping. "Did you want a donut for the walk home?"

"Uh, sure. Thanks."

She lifted a glass dome and tucked a donut in a folded piece of wax paper. "Anything else?"

"I'd like to apologize for what happened with my friend. I didn't know I'd have to muzzle him so you wouldn't get harassed."

She looked at him over the rim of her glasses. "Do you often mop up your buddies' messes?"

"He's not my buddy. And yeah, I do. Especially when the messes involve girls studying... history?" He looked pointedly at her book on the counter.

The side of her mouth tipped. "Differential equations."

Fascinating. He'd expected a lot of things, but not... that. "Beauty *and* brains. I'd hate to ask what you read for fun."

A smile cracked her porcelain cool. "Comic books."

"You just keep getting more and more interesting." He stuck out his hand. "Raymond. Raymond Sellers. I've never seen you in here before."

She wiped her hand on her apron and put her hand in his. "Evelyn Noble. I just returned from North Carolina to be with my mother. It's my first week on the job. Look, I'm the one who's sorry. I was so wrapped up in—"

"Differwhatsit angulations."

She laughed. "*Differential equations*. I—"

"You've nothing to worry about, Miss Noble. Don't let Frankie make you feel bad for his lack of social graces. So math, huh? It's nice when people don't let their minds go to waste."

"Is that so?"

"Next time I come in, I'll pour my own coffee, and you can keep reading. Consider it my contribution to society, letting your brain do what it does."

"Hmm. No one's ever buttered me up by complimenting my brain before."

"I'm just curious. Why study that"—he gestured to the book —"and not something else? Like, something easier to pronounce."

"Something tells me you know exactly how to pronounce it."

He laughed and lifted his hands. "Guilty as charged."

"I guess... I guess I love numbers and how they make sense. There's no wondering at the outcome when you put them together. There's comfort in knowing there's an answer, even if you haven't arrived at it yet. Nothing else in life is like that."

"I get it. When I fix an engine, I know it'll start if I can put everything in its proper place. It's like a puzzle."

"Exactly. It's the same way with math. For me, at least." She leaned close as if she were about to share a secret. "It also helps you pass the National Teacher Exam."

"So, a teacher, huh?"

"After I finish two more years of college and ace the test, yes."

"You know what I always say—why shouldn't a girl use her brains if she's got 'em?"

"You always say that, huh?" Evelyn shook her finger at him. "You, charmer, are welcome back any time, but don't bring your friend along." She grabbed Raymond's empty coffee cup and put it in a tub of dirty dishes behind her.

He leaned an elbow on the counter. "You don't remember me, do you?"

She picked up the tub and handed it through the window to the fry cook. "Should I?"

"Dancing lessons? At Clemson?"

"Dancing less—" She turned around, eyes wide. "Dancing lessons? That was *you*?"

Raymond couldn't keep himself from grinning. "That was me."

Her gaze skimmed over his frame. Her face flamed. "You look... different."

That was true enough. He'd only been seventeen then. Toothpick skinny with the shaved hair of a new cadet. A late bloomer, so his mother said. If the mirror didn't lie, four years made the difference between a boy and a man, his shoulders now broad and jawline sharp. "I could say the same about you." He didn't inspect her for changes like she did him, seeing as he'd decided to be a gentleman. Besides, he'd seen enough to know already.

"A lot can change in four years."

"So where have you been all this time?"

"In North Carolina with my aunt."

"But you're back. For good?"

"For now." She leaned forward on the counter, propping herself with flattened palms. "I have one question for you."

The serious tone in her voice made his heart jump. "Yeah?"

"Was that horsey hoofer from the dance one of the boys you brought with you tonight?"

Raymond barked out a laugh. "No. He's back at the stables, eating his oats and hay."

She groaned. "That was *terrible*."

"I know, but you didn't give me much time to prepare."

Her grin softened. "You were really nice to me that night,

Raymond. Life got hard for me after that, but thinking back to our dance always made me smile."

"So you thought of me, huh?"

She turned around and started a pot of coffee. Angling her head back, she smiled. "I did."

He'd expected her to quail at his boldness. "I don't know anybody quite like you. But I have a feeling you're worth the knowing." He tapped the counter and stood. "I'll see you again soon, Miss Evelyn Noble."

"Until then, Raymond," she murmured.

He lifted his hand. His back bumped into the door. He grinned at her and turned round. Pulling the door, he stepped into the muggy night air. Slipping around the building's corner, away from the glass-walled front and Evelyn's line of sight, he thrust a fist in the air and gave a voiceless shout. He strolled down the path to the boarding house, his steps so light that the only thing keeping him from Fred Astaire-ing home was that he didn't know the first thing about tap dancing. So his heart did the tap dancing for him and carried them both in song the whole way back.

EIGHT

SUNLIGHT AND SUN TEA

August 1941
Clemson, South Carolina

The basket sat on the grass beside their quilt, sandwiches and drinks still packed inside. Raymond lay on his back with one arm folded across his chest, the other at his side, his face dappled by shadows and sun. Evelyn lay beside him, not so close that their shoulders touched, but close enough that she could feel his heat.

"You awake?" he asked.

She let her head fall to the side and met his gaze. "Yes."

"C'mere." He pulled her closer to him.

Her insides erupted in wildfire. They'd never been so near before, his sturdy, masculine body contrasting with her softness.

She dared to lay her head on Raymond's chest, and he wound his arm under her neck and around her shoulder.

A light breeze wafted over them. She closed her eyes, listening to his slow and steady heartbeat, and breathed in the sweet scent of grass and sun-warmed pine needles. They'd dated for the six weeks he'd trained at Clemson, and after he'd moved down to St. Simons to work for his dad, he'd returned for several weekend visits. In between, they sent each other letters —sappy, heartsick ones Evelyn had read dozens of times. Rosie, her friend and fellow waitress, squealed each time Evelyn arrived at the diner and pulled a new one out of her sweater pocket.

He shifted to his side, gently moving Evelyn's head to the quilt instead of his chest so he could look into her eyes. He plucked a blade of grass and ran it over her cheek. "Are you happy?"

"Of course I am."

"Even with how little we see each other?"

She forced a smile. "I'd be happy with just one day if that's all I get."

Raymond laughed a little.

"What?" Evelyn pushed his shoulder back gently.

"Darlin', it wasn't too long ago you were trying to get rid of me."

"Which I'm lousy at, apparently."

He snapped his fingers. "I almost forgot to tell you. I ran into Frankie yesterday."

"*Your* Frankie? From College Café?"

"He's not *my* Frankie. But I got to thinking..." A devilish look danced in his eyes.

"Oh no. What did you do?"

"I didn't think there was any harm in inviting him to meet us for dinner tonight. To catch up on old times. Wouldn't you like to see him again?"

Evelyn poked him in the chest. "No. I'm not sharing our time with anybody else." She poked him harder. "You're a real troublemaker, you know that?"

He laughed. "I love it when you get mad."

"Oh, you do, do you?" She tickled him under his arms.

He pushed her hands gently to the quilt. "I do." He smiled softly at her, his eyes crinkling at the edges.

"Good thing because you'll probably be seeing a lot of it." She curled a finger in the hair at his temple.

"Maybe I just wanted you to feel better about my next question. What if we saw my family instead?"

"Oh." Her stomach tightened. They hadn't met each other's families yet. It would be one step further into making this real. "When?"

"How about now? We could drive up, stay the night, and I could have you back tomorrow in time for your lunch shift. Jimmie and I'll sleep outside on the porch while you take our room. What do you say?"

"*Now*?" Her hand went to her hair.

He grabbed her hand and pulled it to his lips, kissing her palm. "You look lovely."

* * *

Florence, South Carolina

The house was immaculate. A little nicked and frayed, like most households still bearing the scars of the Depression, but it was well-ordered, unlike the home she lived in with her mother.

Sarah, Raymond's mother, bustled them into their kitchen and sat them down at a small table, where four place settings were laid. She set a dish of cookies on the table. "I like to have the sweets first, don't you?"

Evelyn settled in, nodding her thanks. "I can't say I mind it myself."

A soft breeze drifted through the open window above the sink. The white cotton curtain swelled, sending sunlight dancing across the mint-green hexagon counter tiles and the worn linoleum floor. Her bracing muscles relaxed.

"I was glad to get Raymond's call." Sarah used her apron to pull a tray of golden-topped yeast rolls out of the oven. "We've been so anxious to meet you. Jimmie should be here any minute."

Evelyn shot a worried glance toward Raymond, who only smiled and took a sip from his glass of sun tea. Having never had siblings, she wasn't sure what to expect. Would Jimmie be resentful of her barging in on his time with Raymond? From what Raymond had told her, they were awfully close.

"What's Jimmie been up to?" Raymond asked.

Sarah placed the rolls in a basket and covered them with a heavy blue-and-white checkered cloth, tucking them in like they were those Fabergé eggs Evelyn had read about in her preparations for the history portion of the teacher's test. Going by Raymond's raptures about his mother's cooking, the comparison wasn't far off. "I hardly know, he's so busy with his friends."

Loud stomps sounded on the porch steps. The screen door screeched open and then slammed shut.

"Speak of the devil," Raymond muttered.

There were two loud thumps—what Evelyn could only guess were shoes being taken off and dropped to the floor. A teenage boy with sun-bronzed skin and hair so blond it was almost white bounded into the kitchen. He stopped short at the sight of Evelyn and gave an appreciative whistle. "Who's this?"

"Watch it." Raymond stood, scraping his chair against the floor. "That's my girl you're whistling at."

"You can't bring a looker like that into our house and expect me not to—"

Raymond slapped a hand over his brother's mouth and gave Evelyn an exaggerated polite smile. "Excuse me. I'll be just a minute." He swung Jimmie out of the room.

The raucous sounds of what could only be wrestling followed, punctuated by the boys' laughter.

Evelyn sneaked a glance at Sarah. "Should I be concerned?"

"Oh, I just let them get it out of their system." Sarah took a small nibble of her cookie and put it back on her plate. "It's been a while since they've seen each other."

Evelyn eyed Sarah for any hints of resentment. Raymond had most likely replaced some of his visits home to see her. The last thing she wanted was for Raymond's mother to nurse a grudge against her. "Mrs. Sellers—"

"Sarah." She smiled, the crinkles at the side of her eyes deep, like Raymond's.

"I know time is precious, especially with him living away from home."

"Oh heavens, don't you give up a moment with him. I'd be worried if he didn't want to spend all his time with you, a nice girl like you. We still get our visits in. But now that we're alone..." Sarah passed the plate of cookies. "Tell me about yourself."

"There's not much to tell. It's just me and my mother. I work at a diner and plan on being a teacher. Once I finish my degree and pass the exam, that is."

The brothers popped into the doorway, breathing heavily, their arms draped over each other's shoulders.

"I keep telling her she's ready," Raymond said. "She could probably pass with her eyes closed, she's that smart."

Evelyn tore off a piece of her cookie and crumbled it between two fingers. It had been a small point of contention between them, her not taking the test yet. She had to know child development, contemporary affairs, history, science, and literature. Math, fine arts, reasoning, and teaching methods, even though she'd never stepped foot inside a classroom. And that was only a partial list. Raymond believed her capable, but it would take years for her to feel ready.

She stood and held out her hand to Jimmie. "Hello. I'm Evelyn."

He returned her smile with a friendly one of his own. "You already know I'm Jimmie."

While they'd been talking, Sarah had set the table with a roast chicken, black-eyed peas, and the rolls. "Dinner's ready."

Sarah served Evelyn first, then her boys, and herself last.

While the others talked, Evelyn buttered her roll and studied them. They were relaxed and happy in each other's company. Raymond fit in the domestic scene. She pictured her and Raymond eating at their own cozy kitchen table covered by a cloth embroidered with yellow jessamine and their intertwining initials. She looked up and caught Raymond staring at her, his mouth tipped at the side. Her cheeks burned, though he couldn't have known what she'd been thinking about.

Sarah peeked at Raymond over a forkful of black-eyed peas. "What do you make of Germany invading Russia?"

Raymond's face grew troubled. "It's not good, not for anyone."

Sarah set down her fork as if she couldn't stomach another bite. "First Poland, then Denmark and Norway. The Netherlands. France. When will they stop?"

"Britain held them off. Hitler's not invincible," Raymond said.

"America can't stay isolated from these troubles forever. Soon enough, we'll find them at our door."

Evelyn's heart took off at a clip. No one she knew wanted or expected America to get involved, especially after the disaster of the Great War. Hundreds of thousands, dead; her father, a ghost. For what purpose? "Raymond? Do you think America will enter the war?" He'd be the first to go, him being a soldier in the reserves.

His hand covered hers. "No one's going anywhere." He winked at Jimmie. "Though I wouldn't mind giving Hitler's army a run for their money."

"Me neither," Jimmie said around a mouthful of chicken. "I'll show those—"

Sarah gave him a playful tap on the back of his head. "Don't talk with food in your mouth."

Jimmie gave Evelyn a sheepish grin. "'Scuse me for bein' rude, Miss Evelyn."

It would've been much more fun growing up if she'd had a brother like Jimmie. She smiled. "It's alright."

"Enough of this war talk." Jimmie took a big gulp from his glass and set it down with a *thunk*, sloshing water onto the table. "When are you two gettin' hitched?"

NINE

SAFE AND ALONE

December 10, 1941

Dear Evie,

Thank you for your last letter. I'd much rather hear about your day in person, but your words have kept me going between visits. The past five months have been the happiest of my life. I still can't believe the prettiest and sweetest girl alive likes me back. I know things are different now after the bombing at Pearl Harbor and with America joining the war, but they don't have to be different for us. Until they give me marching orders, I plan to go on with life as normal, and that includes visiting you every chance I get.

I'd made up my mind long ago to be content working for my dad, and I am. I've worked hard at making the best of it. There's been no reason to think things won't turn out okay, even if my life looks different than I thought it would. But all that feels upside down now with this war. I worry about Jimmie doing something stupid with me gone. I worry about Mother too. She has Jimmie for now, but I can't see him not joining up as soon as he turns eighteen when I'm out there having an adventure without him. Then there's you, but my reasons are purely selfish there, as I don't want to be without you. Seeing as I'm in the reserves and will be called up whether I like it or not, the best I can figure is if I give this soldier business all I have, the quicker I'll be able to come home. I'm determined that everything comes out right in the end for all of us, war or no war.

I'd like to settle things between us before we find out what my orders might be. As to what I want to settle, I think you might guess. If all goes according to plan (and if Dad is amenable), I'll come up for the church's annual Christmas dinner. I'll stay a couple of nights at the boarding house, and we can enjoy a few days together before I go home to Florence.

Counting down the days,
Raymond

* * *

December 1941
Clemson, South Carolina

Evelyn stood outside the car, holding open the passenger door. "Bye, Mama."

Hands still on the steering wheel, her mother leaned over and peered at her. "You walkin' home? It's cold out."

"Rosie said she'll give me a ride."

"Alright, then."

An uneasy silence stretched between them. Mama tucked one of the pieces of her chopped-off hair behind an ear. She used to take such pride in her long, auburn waves. It had been a shock seeing it gone when Evelyn returned.

Four years apart had been enough to do its damage, it seemed, even though Evelyn had been back for months. The distance between them had grown only wider when Evelyn started dating Raymond. Mama had made it quite clear she didn't want her to date a man in the Army, and Evelyn, caught up in the rush of new love, hadn't listened. "Well... see you tonight."

Evelyn closed the door, and Mama drove away without another word.

A shiver ran through her, but it had nothing to do with the weather.

Raymond had written that he wanted to settle things. But instead of providing reassurance, his words had done the opposite—they'd pushed her into a corner.

She advanced toward the two-story brick building where the church's Christmas party was being held. She opened the door, and blessed warmth wafted over her, thawing her nose and cheeks. The tinkling notes of a holiday song swirled in the hum and chatter of the crowd. Gold- and red-striped ribbons hung from every doorway and fixture, while tinsel shimmered on the boughs of a spindly pine. If not for the sea of drawn and pinched faces, the idyllic scene could have come straight from a recruitment poster—a call to protect exercises of freedom like these from the darkness encroaching their shores.

Evelyn scanned the partygoers. Raymond wasn't among them yet. Rosie, waiting beside a table laden with turkey and trimmings, waved her over. Evelyn stepped into the somber crowd and began to make her way toward her friend.

"I heard the Japanese are on their way to Alaska as we speak," the matronly town librarian said, her penciled eyebrows pinched together.

"They wouldn't dare!" The woman's worried expression mirrored the librarian's.

"Of course they would. Look what they did at Pearl Harbor.

My John went straight to the recruiters when he heard Roosevelt's speech on the radio."

Evelyn stood on her tippy-toes and craned her neck above the women.

"Did they take John?"

"No. His bum eyes and all. But mark my words... every man'll be gone before we know it."

Evelyn's heart dropped. "Excuse me." She pushed past them and arrived at the table where Rosie waited.

"Hello, dear." Rosie's shiny red lips pecked Evelyn's cheek.

"Hello. Hungry?" Evelyn asked.

"Starved! You'll have to roll me out of here."

Dear Rosie. Not even a war could dim her sparkle.

They went to opposite sides of the table and began to pile food on their plates.

"How's it going with Raymond?"

Evelyn avoided Rosie's eyes. "Fine."

"Oh, *Evie*. You're not getting cold feet because of the war, are you?" Rosie leaned forward, her eyes wide like a puppy's when he begged for a bone. "Nobody's a guarantee. Why, you might leave here tonight and get hit by a bus."

"Rosie!"

"But that uniform of his!" She fanned herself with a napkin. "Ev, he's just the dreamiest."

"It's hard enough as it is without you pressuring me."

"But there'll hardly be anybody left if you won't date any boys in the service. Are you just going to date... *nobody*?" She whispered the last as if it were a treasonable offense.

"I'm perfectly happy with my—"

"Books?" Rosie's pert little nose wrinkled.

"No. *Life*." Evelyn slapped a spoonful of mashed potatoes onto her plate.

"What if he asks you to marry him? You wouldn't say no, would you?"

Evelyn shrugged. She loved him more with each day that passed. What would it be like a week from now? A month? If it was unbearable to say goodbye now, it would be unthinkable to fall for him any deeper.

"A man needs someone to fight for. Just think of the morale boost you would be." Rosie clasped her hands to her chest along with the knife she'd used to cut a slice of pie. "Why, he'd win the whole war if only to come home to you!"

Evelyn gently took the knife from Rosie's grasp. "You're a hopeless romantic, Rosie." She set it on the table and smiled at her friend. "I'm not marrying anybody just because there's a war on."

"Evelyn Noble, that is the most unpatriotic thing I've heard anybody say. Think of it as doing your part for the war effort."

"And which boy are you going to marry to do your part?" Evelyn shot back.

Rosie's eyes darted about the hall as if cataloging her prospects. "I'd marry more than one if I could," she said. "I might have to, since there's an extra boy without a girl because of *you*."

Evelyn bit back a laugh. "Oh, dear. Willing to commit bigamy for the cause. You *are* serious, aren't you?"

Tears collected in Rosie's baby blue eyes. "I just can't stand the thought of them shivering in their foxholes, thinking the world's gone on without them. If they had a girl, one of their very own, maybe it wouldn't feel so cold and lonely over there." She blinked away unshed tears. "I'd give Raymond a go, except he only has eyes for *you*."

Evelyn had a feeling the next time she saw Rosie, her friend would be flitting out of a church with some Joe on her arm and a newly placed ring on her finger, doing her part for the "war effort." Marriage to a military man marching off to war wouldn't be easy, but Rosie couldn't see for the stars in her eyes. What if Rosie's husband didn't come back from the fight as he used to be? What if he didn't come back at all? What would happen to those stars then? She'd seen it before—the glimmer in Mama's eyes, gone. Their home a dark, quiet mausoleum holding the memory of a man who'd never died.

The specter of her father rose before her again, as it had been doing more of late.

He'd been the first to abandon her. Then, it was her mother, who pushed her away when Evelyn needed her most. And the time at her aunt's house was lonelier yet. She was ready for something sure, something steady. For someone who wouldn't leave, no matter how hard things got. It wasn't exactly the same as Raymond being sent away, but that didn't change the way it felt.

War had left its mark on the Noble household. It left its mark on her still. It wasn't Raymond's fault, but what she needed was a sure bet.

"Hello, ladies. May I join you?"

Evelyn's stomach dropped. He'd come. The rest of the room faded away. He gazed into her eyes with a heat so strong her resolve weakened. All she could think about was reaching for him and never letting go.

Rosie peeked at Raymond, her eyes sparkling and cherry red lips parted in a glossy O. "Why, Raymond! It's been too long. I was just telling Evie that I wanted to get some of that wassail over there. Wasn't I, dear?"

"Rosie!" The rat wouldn't even look her in the eyes. "I don't think you—"

"Have fun, you two." Rosie winked and turned on her heel.

"So." Raymond looked at her expectantly.

The bends in Evelyn's elbows and knees began to sweat. "So."

As if her body had a mind of its own, she leaned into him and placed her head on his shoulder.

He wrapped his arm around her and spoke softly into her ear. "Hello, Miss Manners."

She closed her eyes. It had been a dream, meeting him. A silly dream she'd gotten swept up in, and she hadn't stopped to think. *Let me have just one more minute like this. Just one. Then I'll give him up.*

He pulled back and tucked a strand of hair behind her ear. "I missed you."

The tenderness in his eyes condemned her as a traitor. How could she sit like this with him with what she was about to do? "I... I missed you too."

"How's your studying on preferential undulations going?"

A laugh escaped before she could stop it. She playfully swatted him. "*Differential equations*."

"That's what I said."

"You'd think you'd have figured out by now how to pronounce it."

"Then I wouldn't get to see you laugh." He grabbed her hand. "Evie, I..."

She pulled away. "Can we go outside? It's stuffy in here."

"What about your food?"

She placed it on the table. "I'd rather talk."

"Alright. I could do with a little privacy."

She held on tight to his hand through the crowd and outside the building until they stopped at a bench sitting underneath the canopy of an oak.

"Here." He unwound his scarf from his neck and smoothed it on the bench. "The seat is cold." He stood before her, his eyes easy but his body tightly wound as if he restrained himself from something. But from what? She could hardly remember the young Clemson cadet she'd met at the dance. In his place was this self-assured Army lieutenant in the olive drab wool and khaki uniform of a soldier.

She sat, crossing her feet at the ankles. "Thank you."

He joined her on the bench and wrapped an arm around her. "I don't know why you don't like the cold. It's a relief after summer."

Heat from his body seeped through her coat down to her very skin. "Mmhmm."

His eyebrows knitted together. "You okay, Evie?"

She pulled a string at the end of his scarf, untwisting its threads. "I'm just wondering... what will you be doing, do you think? In the war, I mean." If he pushed paper or fueled the planes—anything at all out of harm's way, maybe she could allow herself to be with him.

He placed his hands on hers, stopping them from shredding his scarf. "Nervous about me being a part of it?"

"Y-yes."

"With the way things are going, we won't be over there for long. Everybody I know is joining up. Why, there'll be two of us for every one of them."

"You didn't answer my question."

He gave her a quizzical look. "The infantry. I thought you knew that."

The feeble light of hope inside flickered and died. She couldn't live every day fearing he wouldn't come home. She just couldn't, not after what she'd been through already. There was nothing else to do but end it now, before it got harder. "I wish you luck, Raymond. I really do. But..."

He stared at her. "But what? What's wrong?"

"What's wrong?" She laughed without humor. "You're going to war. That's what's wrong."

"I know it won't be fun or easy, but it doesn't mean we can't be together. That's what I came to say. I can take care of you. You won't have to work at the diner anymore. You can teach. Evie, I want us to get—"

She put her fingers on his lips. If he said another word, she wouldn't be able to go through with it. "I'm sorry, Raymond, but I don't want this."

His head reared back as if she'd struck him. "You don't want this?" he repeated slowly, as if she'd spoken a foreign language.

"It'll just be too hard."

He hauled himself to his feet. "What are you talking about? Of course it'll be hard, but we can get through it. Together." He dropped once again to the bench and gathered her hands in his. "What is it, really? I can fix it if you just tell me. Is it your mother? Does she not want us together? Because I can talk to her. I can assure her that I'll be good to you. I can change her mind."

With tears welling in her eyes, she stood and kissed his cheek. "I'll pray for you every day." She wouldn't ask him to look her up if he made it home safely. She couldn't have her cake and eat it too, especially after a betrayal like this.

"That's it? You're just leaving?"

She nodded, throat too tight to speak.

"I don't understand. I thought you... we..." His jaw worked. For a moment he was all too still. Then he locked his gaze with hers, his eyes glinting in the moonlight. "I'm not wrong about us." He cupped his hand around her jaw and ran his thumb over her cheek. "And I know you feel the same."

Evelyn closed her eyes and swallowed.

"Why won't you just try, Evie?" he whispered.

"Stop making this harder."

After a long moment, he slipped his hand away from her jaw. "Alright. If this is what you want, I won't force you." He grabbed his scarf off the bench and stood, holding it out to her crushed in his hand. "You're cold. You can throw it away later for all I care."

She couldn't bring herself to reach out and take it.

He groaned. "C'mere." He looped the scarf around her

neck and tied it in a swift knot. All in the work of a moment, he stepped back, his face drawn. "Goodbye, Evelyn."

She turned her back to him and walked away even as her heart chided her for it.

It was for the best. He would leave, and she would continue to work at the diner, go to college, and study for the teachers' exam.

Alone, alone, her heart pounded the words to the beat of her steps.

Just as I want it, she argued. *Safe.*

But alone.

TEN

ARRIVAL OF THE YANKS

March 1942
Fort Jackson, South Carolina

> *"Nothing has made me feel more certain of our victory than the efficiency which your division displayed at the end of only eight weeks training. If the United States can go on turning out divisions like that, victory will be ours much sooner than I had thought possible."*
>
> *—Lord Mountbatten, after his review of the 77th Division*

Ignoring the chatter of his fellow officers standing near him, Raymond stared across the grassy expanse of the parade field. Thoughts of Evelyn haunted him, just as they always did in moments like these. Shortly after leaving her at Christmas, he'd been called up by the Army and sent to Fort Jackson to help lead a new division. He hadn't been able to stick around Clemson and try to shake some sense into her. Not that it would have done any good.

The idea of working for Dad had become bearable once he thought Evelyn might marry him. Raymond would have worked happily for him if it meant he could come home to her. She'd have been the bright spot in all this miserable mess. His gaze came to rest on a pile of grass clippings lying by the side of Fort Jackson's parade field. The steam rising from the mound reminded him of the mug of coffee he'd have every time he visited Evelyn at the café. He scrubbed his face with his hands. This was pathetic. *He* was pathetic, comparing steaming mulch to coffee. He shouldn't be thinking of her, anyway. She wasn't thinking about him. She'd made that clear enough when he'd seen her last at Christmas.

Besides, he had a job to do, and he'd better turn his attention to it. He studied the gate at Fort Jackson's entrance, where buses bearing the 77th Division's first round of draftees would arrive at any moment.

These men, plucked from their civilian lives in the North, were New York City toughs and shopkeepers, muscled laborers, coal miners, and farmhands from the surrounding states. They wouldn't look like soldiers, take orders like soldiers, or fight like them, either. How would Raymond, a guy whose biggest scars came from roughhousing, get the rumored hard-as-nails Northerners to listen?

"Yoohoo! You listening?" Harry Pulaski waved a hand in front of Raymond's face.

"Guess I wasn't paying attention."

"I asked Wade if he knows where we're going." He turned again to Wade. "Who's it gonna be? Hitler or Hirohito?"

Wade squinted in the sun, staring past Harry, Raymond, and Frankie to the gate. "That's above my pay grade, Harry."

Rumors fed the engine of every conversation, and Wade, being closer to the top than any of their company, fielded questions day and night about where they'd end up. Come noon time, he'd have an entire roster of enlisted men asking him too.

Harry's mouth turned down at the sides. "Mama says she'll

write the colonel if I don't let her know soon. Like I'm keeping it from her on purpose."

"Tell her Uncle Sam's your mother now," Wade said.

"Not if you want me to live."

"A snowball's chance in hell of that, Harry. Your mama'd never off her baby."

"Shut up, all of you." Frankie brought a finger to his collar and pulled, revealing a red and blotchy neck. "I'm sick of your yapping."

"You're just cranky 'cause it's hot," Wade said.

"I don't care as long as they gimme a gun and ship me wherever it is," Harry said. "I'll send 'em to hell quicker than green grass through a goose."

"Don't tell your mama. She'll write the chaplain too," Raymond said.

Chaplain Taylor leaned over. "Felt my ears itch. Up to no good?"

Raymond greeted the man with a grin. Even though the minister-turned-soldier was the oldest man in the battalion, he had enough energy to outpace the lot of them, which he did every morning when they went for their runs. It motivated everybody to run a little faster, seeing that short-cropped, graying head leading the pack.

Frankie jerked a nod toward Harry. "This guy said he's going to send the Japs straight to—"

Harry slapped a hand over Frankie's mouth.

The chaplain's mouth twitched. "You boys in need of one of my sermons?"

"We're still recovering from your last spanking," Raymond said.

A faint rumble sounded just beyond Fort Jackson's gates.

"Here they come!" Frankie whooped.

The men quieted and got into position.

A logistics major stepped beside the 306th Battalion's

commander, Colonel Smith, and waited in front of the other officers.

A bus stopped, dumped its load of men, and went on its way. Bus after bus, the Yanks tumbled out, joking and roughing each other up, just like Raymond and his friends, but only... rougher. Most were grizzled and scarred with wild looks in their eyes. Some had shoulders as wide as doorways, the kind only hard labor could've produced. Did they let former rock-breakers into the military? Maybe, with a war on.

The major shouted above the din. "Pipe down for your instructions!"

A voice carried over the commotion, loud enough for all to hear. "Yeah? Says who?"

A deathly quiet fell over the crowd. The major stepped forward, murder in his eyes. Colonel Smith slapped his folder into his adjutant's chest, stopping the man's advance.

Raymond looked over the newcomers. Who was brave enough to talk back to a major?

All draftees but one stared at their shoes as the square-shouldered big-shot colonel scanned them like a bear searching for fresh meat.

That recruit stared at the colonel and yawned—yawned!—as if he were at Sunday luncheon with his best girl's family. Pomaded ebony waves added three inches to his average stature. A swollen, bent nose, a scar-puckered cheek, caterpillar eyebrows, and battered hands the size of skillets made it clear the man had never let his size get in the way of winning any fights.

Colonel Smith stalked toward him.

The men parted like the waters of the Red Sea.

The colonel stopped in front of the private, who folded his arms and stared back with a smirk.

Raymond exchanged glances with Harry. Leading a platoon

with this draftee in it would be a nightmare. He could endanger the whole operation.

"What's your name, soldier?" the colonel asked, voice cold with rage.

"Solomon. Mitt Solomon. But that's Mr. Solomon to you." He side-eyed his pals, no doubt hoping for a reaction. But they only shrank into their shoes, most likely bracing for an explosion from the man shooting fire at Mitt with his eyeballs.

Still as a statue and every line and curve of his face as hard as stone, Colonel Smith was silent. His eyebrows lowered into a line of resolve above his glittering eyes.

The only sign that Solomon noticed was a tinge of red rising above his collar.

Raymond's stomach knotted. As much as the draftee might deserve this, no one wanted to be on the receiving end of the colonel's ire.

"Alright, *Private* Mitt Solomon, lug everyone's gear to the barracks." The draftees' eyes swiveled to the mountain of bags lying just beyond the buses. "After that, you'll scrub pots in the mess hall with your toothbrush. Congratulations. You're the 77th's newest potato peeler. Hope Army life's everything you dreamed it would be." Colonel Smith turned to the rest of the men. "The rest of you, follow Lieutenant Pulaski to chow. *In an orderly, quiet fashion.* Dismissed."

The men formed lines behind Harry, sneaking looks at Mitt as they passed him. The mess hall was the last place anyone wanted to be unless they were eating chow, and even then, not so much. Kitchen patrol was the bottom of the barrel, the lowest rung on the ladder—monotonous labor with no thanks in return for whipping up dinner for thousands of men at a time. It couldn't be easy to make food taste good when recipes measured ingredients by the gallon, but at least the mess hall would keep Mitt far away from Raymond's platoon.

"The Army must be trolling prisons for draftees," the colonel said to his nearby officers. "Keep an eye on that one."

A few days passed. The men settled into their new routines and were filtered into various units. Raymond had just received his own platoon's roster the day before. He stood in front of them now, gathered at the rifle range. The motley crew was a sea of freckled baby cheeks, graying hairs, and paunches over cinched belts. Their hooded eyes stared back, sizing him up.

Did they see someone they'd obey without hesitation, or some buttoned-up twenty-two-year-old kid with spit-shined boots?

He brought a stealthy hand to his tidy hair and mussed it a little.

One of the men noticed and smirked.

What am I doing? Raymond brought his arm down.

He was no shavetail lieutenant fresh from Officer Candidate School—if he counted his time at Clemson, he'd been at this for years. He'd model discipline. Duty. Loyalty. Courage. He'd do everything he could to turn his soldiers into a powerful, fighting whole, and himself, among them. They didn't know it yet, but he planned on being their best bet of coming home to their sweethearts.

He set his shoulders back and lifted his chin. "Today begins your training on the M1 rifle. Don't mind the grease. It's been dipped in Cosmoline to protect it from rust and the elements. Your job is to take the rifle apart and clean every nook and cranny until it's fit to be fired."

Raymond nodded to SSG Kalberer and SGT Oliver, who went down the line issuing rifles. He squinted at their backs, trying to decipher who was Kalberer and who was Oliver. Even after being at Fort Jackson with them for over a month, he had a hard time telling them apart. Wide-shouldered and square-jawed with large pearly whites and curly blond hair, he might've pegged them as twin Hollywood stars in their regular lives if he didn't already know Kalberer was a teacher and Oliver, a construction worker.

"Separate into squads, and we'll run you through disassembly of your weapons, one piece at a time. Clean each part with solvent and rags, then reassemble. No one leaves until your weapon passes inspection." A few grumbles rippled through the men, but Raymond didn't let his gaze waver. "Follow my instructions to the letter. Be thorough and attentive to detail. You might want to speed through it, but trust me, it'll add more time than it saves. Even if it takes all day, your rifle better be so clean your mother would stir her stew with it."

The men spread into three circles. With Kalberer and Oliver directing the other squads, Raymond stood in front of the third with his already-cleaned rifle laid out on a makeshift table. He showed them the different parts of the weapon and then put it back together while they watched. Releasing them to their own weapons, he meandered among the squads and oversaw the disassembly of weapons.

After some time passed, Private Jasper Hall's furtive tones drifted over to Raymond from several yards away. "Takes too long to clean each piece by hand. We dump the parts in the gas, pull them out, and abracadabra! Clean as a whistle and ready to put back together."

Private John Mahony scratched his head. "I don't know, Jasper. The LT seemed to want us to follow his instructions exactly."

"Who cares? He won't neither, seeing as we'll have our rifles put together lickety-split."

Raymond kept his back to them so they wouldn't suspect he was listening. First day and Raymond already had a mutiny on his hands. The regular punishments for insubordination wouldn't work on a population used to much worse. If it was this hard to get his men to follow a simple set of instructions, how difficult would it be when he commanded them under fire?

He took one step in their direction but halted. As hard as it was to sit back and let them make a mistake, he hadn't earned their respect yet. They might grudgingly obey, but if he let them fail, maybe they'd learn they should've listened to him in the first place.

"You got a better idea?" Private Matthew Peach held up his hands. "I'm with Jasper. My skin's burnt clean off."

Private George Benjamin shook his head. "You're supposed to dunk the *rag* in the gas, you idiot. Not your hands." The black-haired private sat cross-legged on the ground finishing up his rifle, seemingly undisturbed by Jasper's idiocy.

"You won't be saying that when you're eating chow before the other squads," Private Hank Allen said.

Jasper jutted his thumb toward Allen. "Now someone's talking sense. Listen, you can either use your brains or waste your time. You with me, Benjamin?"

"No, thanks."

"Okay, Grandpa. Guess some people ain't bright enough to reckanize genius when they see it. Allen! Mahony! You in? Walter, you too?"

"I'm game," Private Bobby Walter said. He cupped a handful of parts and brought them over to the tub of solvent. Looking straight at Benjamin, he dumped them in.

It took every bit of Raymond's willpower to hold himself back from grabbing the private by the collar and dragging him away from the tub.

One by one, the others joined in, and everyone's rifle parts lay co-mingled in the gasoline. All but Benjamin's.

"Don't say I didn't warn you," Benjamin said.

"Why don't you shut up?" Peach, splayed out on the grass with his hands behind his head, kicked Benjamin's foot with his own. "Goody two shoes."

Benjamin's mouth clamped shut, looking for all the world as if he were about to explode.

Jasper cackled. "Just our luck, getting this dried turd in our squad."

That did it. Raymond couldn't sit back and let Benjamin take grief at the service of some lesson. He stepped into their circle. The men shot to their feet and stood at attention. "I don't see any rifles ready for inspection. Except for Benjamin's, that is. Private? Your rifle."

Benjamin shot the others a *Ha! I told you so* look and handed Raymond the weapon.

"Well done. You want to tell me why yours is the only one ready?"

The private lifted his chin, staring at the others. "I think that's a better question for Jasper, sir."

Jasper's mouth dropped open. "*Traitor.*" He took a menacing step toward Benjamin, fists clenched.

"Hey, hey, hey!" Raymond pushed his fingers in Jasper's chest. "Cool it, Private. Benjamin, you're dismissed to chow."

"Yes, sir." Benjamin gave the others a mocking glance and strode away with Jasper's glare pinned on his back.

Raymond turned his attention back to Jasper. "Want to tell me what happened?"

"Well, sir, I—I had an idea to save time."

"And?" Raymond asked.

"I thought if we put all the parts together in the gasoline, it would make it easier to..." His voice trailed off as he looked at Raymond's face.

"Was that part of my instructions?"

"Well, no, sir, but—"

"You know, I heard they're having apple cobbler for supper. *With* ice cream," Raymond announced. "And you know how fast it melts out in this heat."

Mahony crossed his arms. "We'll be there, sir."

"Will the ice cream, though?"

Mahony gave no answer.

"I'd start pulling those pieces out if I were you."

Raymond walked away, palms sweaty and heart thudding in his chest.

Time would tell if he'd taken the right tactic on the rifle range. He'd give them an hour to cool off and come to their senses. In the meantime, it wouldn't be a bad idea to find whatever ally he could in the platoon. Raymond slipped through the flaps of the chow tent.

On a bench farthest from the grub line sat Benjamin. Instead of tucking into his food, Benjamin was flipping pages in a small book, staring at its contents.

Raymond grabbed an apple and tossed it in the air, catching it in his hand. He arrived at the table and gave a pointed look at the man sitting beside Benjamin. "Scoot."

"Who are you to—" His eyes caught sight of Raymond's lieutenant bars. He shut his mouth and scooted down the bench.

Raymond sat in the vacated spot. "Private Benjamin."

Benjamin looked at him, surprise in his eyes. "Lieutenant?"

"You a reader?" Raymond pointed to Benjamin's book.

Benjamin was quiet for a moment, as if considering whether to open up to his commander. "My boys and I like to go on walks, collect leaves. Put 'em in a scrapbook. Thought I'd add to their collection while I'm here." He took out a leaf from between two pages and held it up, inspecting it in the shaft of light coming through the cracks in the tent walls.

"That so?" Benjamin was a dad. The only one in the platoon, maybe. "I didn't know you had kids."

"Wanna see a picture?"

Raymond smiled. "Of course."

Benjamin pulled out a sepia-toned photograph with scalloped edges from his shirt pocket and handed it to Raymond.

The two boys were young in the picture. The oldest had his arms wrapped around Benjamin's leg like a vise. He didn't look at the camera but stared into the distance with wide, serious eyes. The baby on Benjamin's shoulders gripped handfuls of his father's hair and was caught in the middle of a belly laugh. That's when Raymond saw it—Benjamin's fingers, frozen in time tickling the baby's foot. Benjamin's wife must've been behind the camera, because the look in the man's eyes could only be reserved for a lover.

Raymond cleared his throat. "Nice family." He handed the photo back. While Benjamin tucked it back in his pocket, Raymond studied him. The private seemed different to him now. A little less rough around the edges, maybe.

Benjamin took a bite of his cobbler.

"How's dessert?"

Benjamin stopped mid-chew and swallowed. "Pretty good."

"Glad you didn't listen to those knuckleheads back there?"

"Guess so."

Raymond leaned forward with his forearms on the table. "First time you held a rifle?"

"I'm an accountant in my other life, LT. The closest thing to a weapon I've carried is a pencil."

"Don't see as how a pencil'll do much good out here. Have you given any thought to what you want to be trained on?"

"I was thinking the radio, sir."

Raymond nodded once. "Alright. I'll tell you what. We'll get you trained on the radio after basic. What do you say to that?"

Benjamin sat back with the first smile Raymond had seen on his face since he'd arrived at the post. "Well, that'd be nice, sir."

"Don't worry about the others. They'll come around. They're just not used to following orders."

Avoiding Raymond's eyes, Benjamin put the leaf back in the book carefully and tucked it in his pocket. "It don't matter to me either way, sir. As long as I get home, they can say what they like."

Raymond headed back to the practice field in the dusky glow of sunset. He broke through the trees and entered the open expanse of the rifle range. There his men sat in a huddle, sweating over the guts of their rifles spread out on canvas.

"I don't get it. Why won't this piece fit?"

"It's the right piece. Just won't screw all the way."

Mahony's arm shook with the effort. "C'mon! Go in, you lousy screw!"

"Lemme try," Peach said. He ripped the rifle from Jasper and twisted his tool with a grunt.

"Get a hammer!"

A hammer? With a rifle? If there were ever men in need of direction, it would be these soldiers of his. "That's enough."

The men jumped and covered the mess behind them by standing in front of it.

"Give me the rifle." Raymond took it from Peach and studied the buttplate screw. "Looks like the screw won't work with this hole." He looked up at their defeated faces. "Don't feel bad. The manufacturing process isn't perfect. Everyone take your rifle and remove this screw right here. Go through each rifle and try every screw until you find the one that fits. If the screw's too loose, move on to the next one."

They did as he said, and Raymond stood back with his arms crossed and tried not to laugh. They looked like a bunch of chickens studying a card trick.

After some time, Peach raised a perfectly put-together rifle in the air and whooped. "I got it!" He faced the others. "Told you my idea would work."

Walter rolled his eyes.

"Well, it did!"

"Peach, go get yourself some chow." The private grinned broadly. "The rest of you, finish your rifles. You're almost there," Raymond said. He couldn't help but add, "Though I hate to inform you the ice cream's gone."

A strangled cry escaped Mahony. "But what about the cobbler?"

"I told Private Solomon to hold some back. Just a warning, though... he was hungry when I left 'im."

Mahony cursed. The men whipped around and got back to work on their rifles.

Raymond stayed close and gave direction when needed. The platoon had made it to the end of the day without combusting but not without its feuding, insubordination, and grudges. At least that Mitt Solomon hadn't been a part of things. The platoon might not be left standing if he had.

ELEVEN

BETTER THE ARMY THAN THE CLINK

The next week, Raymond took his platoon to the rifle range and lined them up to fire their weapons.

Some distance away, Mitt sat on an overturned bucket next to the mess tent, dicing his onions on a slab of wood and watching the proceedings.

Raymond came beside Angelo Martinelli. "Alright, just like I showed you."

The soldier brought the rifle up to his shoulder and angled his elbow by his ear.

Just as Raymond adjusted the private's positioning, a shout came the direction of the tent. "Bring your elbow down, Marti! You ain't dancing with ya sister."

Martinelli dropped his elbow to his waist.

"Just ignore him," Raymond said quietly, lifting Martinelli's elbow a fraction. "Now, nice and easy."

Martinelli shot into the air high above the targets.

Mitt howled with laughter. "You'd win us the war if there were Japs in those clouds. Point the gun at the target this time, ya dope."

"Stay out of this, Private, or you'll be cleaning latrines,"

Raymond called across the field, barely containing his frustration.

Next to Martinelli, Allen prepared to shoot, with the butt of the rifle cradled between his cheek and his shoulder.

"If ya shoot it like that, you'll be at the Pearly Gates in time to beat the lunch rush," Mitt yelled.

Raymond swiveled in Mitt's direction. "Private Solomon!" His hoarse voice boomed across the meadow. "Get your can up here. Now!"

Mitt tossed his knife to the side and ripped off his apron. By the time he made it to the firing line, Raymond had steam coming out of his collar.

Without a word, Raymond held out a rifle.

Mitt looked from the gun to Raymond.

"What's the matter, Wyatt Earp? Don't you want to show 'em how it's done?"

"No problem, boss." Mitt pulled the gun to his shoulder, lined his sights, and pulled the trigger.

Crack.

Bullseye.

One of his men let out a long whistle.

Raymond's gaze whipped from the target to Mitt then back to the target again. He'd never seen someone shoot like that. Not even Kalberer.

Raymond took the rifle from Mitt and handed it to the man on his right. "As you were, Private," Raymond said, jerking his head in the direction of the mess tent.

Mitt strutted like a rooster back to his bucket, undoubtedly crowing over how he'd bested the lieutenant.

Raymond's mouth curved in a sly smile. Who cared if his attempt at a lesson had fallen flat? It looked like the 77th had a secret weapon.

. . .

Raymond rapped his knuckle on the colonel's door. "Sir?"

Smith motioned him in. "Lieutenant. Make it quick."

Raymond approached his commander's desk and stood at attention. "It's about Private Milton Solomon."

"At ease." Colonel Smith took a protracted sip from his mug of coffee. "Ahh, yes. I heard about his little stunt on the firing line."

"It wasn't a stunt, sir. He didn't even wait to settle his sights. Just pointed and shot. Perfect bullseye."

"So? He has an attitude I'm not sure the Army can tame. Who's to say he won't turn around and use his skills against us?"

Before he could think better of it, Raymond blurted out the impulse that had been nagging him ever since the firing line. "Sir, I want him in my unit."

Smith's mouth flattened. "I don't like it."

"I'll take full responsibility for him. Any mishaps will be on my head." He nodded once to press home his confidence, but inside, his stomach quivered. What was he thinking, risking his standing in the unit for an untried man who would most likely be unimpressed with Raymond's guardianship? Raymond could barely handle the men that he had. But there was something in Mitt that begged to be discovered.

Smith sighed and rubbed the bridge of his nose under his glasses. "I've been of half a mind to declare him unfit and throw him back to the streets where he came from," he muttered. He studied Raymond for a long moment. "Maybe all he needs is a little personalized persuasion. And someone willing to give it." He tore off his glasses and threw them to the desk. "Sounds like that person is you."

"Yes, sir."

"Alright. Persuade this Solomon it's in his best interests to shape up. Order him to the rifle range tomorrow at 0530 to help set up, and then get him qualified on the rifle. If he doesn't show, kick him to the curb. I may feel like taking a gamble with him, but I'm not stupid."

"Kick him back to the KP curb or to the out-of-the-Army curb, sir?"

"I had a shaved-off fingernail in my potatoes yesterday. Get him out of here and away from our mess as soon as you can trust he'll be an asset to the platoon." The colonel put his spectacles back on. "Dismissed."

Before Raymond could take two steps, the colonel called out, "Wait."

Raymond turned around.

Smith stood and flattened his hands on his desk. "Maybe I am a little stupid. He's too good a shot to give him a choice. Drag him from his cot by the ear if you have to. I want that boy in line regardless of his inclinations. He'd better cry red, white, and blue tears of gratitude that he's one of us by the time you're through with him. Make it happen, Lieutenant."

Later that morning, Raymond sent his platoon on a run with loaded rucksacks on their backs. On his order, they'd filled them to the brim with heavy objects—rocks, ration cans, and filled canteens. Raymond led from the front with his own pack, weighted down with books.

It was a moment of reprieve, time with his men behind his back and not at his front, challenging him with their hooded gazes.

By the time they were halfway through the run, there was so much collective caterwauling behind him it was like he escorted a herd of cats. He ordered the offenders to the side of the road to do push-ups, and when it was all over, he'd commended Benjamin emphatically in front of the others for completing the run without complaint. That was his first mistake.

For the rest of the day, Benjamin had a target on his back. When Raymond sent the worst of the perpetrators to run the route again with Sergeant Kalberer taking lead, more bullies popped up to take their place. Raymond gave his men the harshest lecture he knew to give, and, irritated by the lack of contrition on their faces, he ended it by spontaneously announcing that Benjamin was going to be an assistant squad leader. That was his second mistake.

His men had been technically obedient after that, but with Benjamin looking downright miserable and the rest of the men's attitudes barely in check, Raymond was ready to call it a day. And he wanted to add Mitt to the mix?

Home had never felt farther away, even at Dad's. The letters had helped, filled with Mother's recounting of Jimmie's escapades and Jimmie bemoaning Mother's undivided attention. But mail call never brought the only letter he really wanted. Evelyn's.

"Enough," he groused. It was done between him and her. Over. He had to move on and quit moping. He had Mitt to get to, anyway. Raymond strode to the mess hall, head bowed.

"Hello there, Lieutenant Sellers."

Raymond held back a groan. All he wanted to do was get this talk with Mitt over with and wash off the grime from the day.

In the dusk, the 306th's chaplain walked briskly to him, a hand lifted in greeting.

"Hello, Chaplain."

"How's it going out here?"

Raymond shrugged. "Doing my best."

"And your men? Getting along?"

"If you could call it that."

"Tough day, I gather."

Taylor was looking at him with such genuine care,

Raymond didn't have the heart to rebuff him. He sighed. "Trouble's brewing among the men."

"It's a big task, turning these men into soldiers."

Raymond took off his hat and slapped it against his leg. "Especially when their lieutenant doesn't know what the heck he's doing."

"If it's any comfort, the other units aren't faring much better. These Yanks sure are giving us a run for our money." His eyes twinkled. "Maybe that's the kind of spirit we need. We'll just have to figure out how to harness it."

Raymond stared at Mitt, wiping down the mess tables in the distance. "It's just that I have to do this right." How could he explain the suffocating feeling he had every time he stood in front of his men? "The better I train them, the better chance we have of coming home, but I can't seem to get that idea through their thick skulls."

"You can't control what happens, Raymond. All you can do is your best and leave the rest to God's keeping."

Easy for him to say when the Army was depending on Raymond to do exactly that—control his platoon to the best of his ability so they could adapt to the unpredictable.

Mitt dumped a bucket of dirty water onto the grass outside the tent. The private looked like he was almost done with cleaning. "Excuse me, Chaplain. I have one more thing on the agenda for today. And, uh, thanks for the talk."

"Well, alright. Anytime."

"Sure thing, Chappy."

Setting aside the chaplain's words, Raymond jogged over to the tent and pushed aside the flaps.

A kerosene lantern hung from a support pole, the light softening Mitt's face and making him look more like a little boy than a man from the streets. Raymond bit back a laugh. A tuft of hair stuck up on the back of Mitt's head, making him look exactly like Jimmie did when he woke up in the morning. "Hello, Private Solomon."

He didn't look up from his work. "Yeah?"

Raymond would set aside salutes and *sirs* for the moment. A bigger battle lay ahead of him, and he wasn't going to get shot down on the march to the battlefield. His platoon might be a mess, but the colonel trusted him to take on the biggest loudmouth the battalion had. Raymond straddled a chair and rested his arms on its back. "I think we need to get a few things straight here."

"Which are...?"

"Stop your work and listen."

Mitt threw his rag back into the bucket, sloshing water onto the table. "Okay, fine."

"Like it or not, this is the Army. That means you have rules to follow. *I* have rules to follow. You need to get your act in line or you're not going to survive your stint with the 77th."

Raymond's words were met with stony silence.

"What do you think all this is for?" Raymond jerked a thumb behind him to the rifle range. "You think we're just playing pretend? There's an enemy out there that's a whole lot more prepared to kill you than you are them. You wanna let us do our job and keep you from getting killed, or do you wanna go your own way and take your buddies down with you as you go?"

Mitt shrugged.

"We don't make these rules to annoy you. Any second you take to question an order is the second you and your fellow soldiers get killed. Rules make you listen. Rules keep you safe. That's all it is, Solomon. It's not personal."

Mitt scooped the rag from the bucket and twisted it, squeezing the water onto the plank floor. "I'll keep that in mind."

Raymond narrowed his eyes. Two could play at this game. "You know what? Forget I said anything." He play-acted a yawn and raised his arms to stretch. "Not everyone can hack it. Why don't we just forget the whole thing? Send you home, no hard feelings."

Mitt swung around. "Now wait just a minute, Sarg—"

"Lieutenant."

"So I gave you a promotion. Who cares? Listen, I never said I couldn't hack it."

"Demoting me to sergeant isn't a promotion." Raymond rose from the chair and grabbed it by its top rail. He swung it around and placed it back under the table. "We can have you on the first train out of here tomorrow morning." Raymond patted Mitt on the shoulder. "Not everyone's cut out for the Army."

Mitt shrugged off Raymond's hand. "And who said I ain't?"

"The colonel."

"Oh, he did, did he?" Steam would have shot out of Mitt's ears if he had the mechanics for it.

"You think he's wrong? From what the mess sergeant said, you don't listen, you're disruptive, you don't care to learn, and you don't even want to be here. Why should I keep you around and put the lives of my men at risk while I'm at it?"

"I never said I don't wanna be here. I'll be the next Alvin York if you want, just..." Mitt clamped his mouth shut and fixed his eyes on Raymond. "Don't do it. Don't send me back."

What waited for Mitt back in New York that made going to war preferable? "Why do you want to stay?"

Mitt looked away and shrugged. "Better the Army than the clink."

The hair on Raymond's arms stood on end. Mitt wasn't a felon, was he? Last he heard, the Army didn't take too kindly to convicts joining their ranks. But maybe the guy was ready for a fresh start. "Alright. Be the best private the 77th has on its rosters, and I'll consider it. Don't even think of mucking up training, and I mean it. Make your mother proud."

He took a menacing step toward Raymond. "And what makes you think she ain't?"

Raymond stood his ground. "Well, is she? She teach you to act like a two-year-old?"

"My mother's a good woman."

"Then she wouldn't be too happy with what you're doing out here, would she?"

"You know what I do to wise guys who assume too much?" Mitt's hand clenched at his side.

"What you used to do, you mean? If you're going to try and stick it out, you can't do what you did before the Army." Raymond looked pointedly at Mitt's fist.

Mitt opened his mouth and then shut it again. He crossed his arms and stuffed his still-fisted hand under his armpit.

"Hey." Raymond reached out and jiggled Mitt's shoulder. "Lighten up. With what I saw you do on that field the other day..." Raymond whistled. "We could use a guy like you on our side. How'd you learn to shoot like that, anyway?"

Mitt dropped to the bench across from the lieutenant and slouched over, hairy forearms resting on his thighs. "You wouldn't believe me if I told you."

"Try me."

"You really wanna know?"

"Alright, alright. I don't have all night—"

"My old man was a cop."

A laugh sputtered out of Raymond. "Of all the ideas I cooked up in my head... are you kidding me?"

"Nope. Now, I never actually got to shoot his gun, but he let me hold it sometimes. I was as surprised as you when I hit the target."

Raymond's bark of laughter turned into a hacking cough.

Mitt slapped Raymond on the back a few times. "You okay there, bud?"

Raymond waved him off and stood up to go. "Fine. Fine."

He pointed at Mitt. "I've got other fish to fry. I want you with the boys on the firing line tomorrow. Be there at 0530 on the dot to help me set up. You stick to my side like glue, you hear me? Maybe, if you're a good boy and eat all your peas for the next few months, you'll be released from the mess hall for good. You'll join us every morning for training after you're done with preparing breakfast. No more putting slop in the trough if you play things right. You alright with that?"

"Yeah. I'm alright with that, boss." Mitt's grin left no doubt that he was, in fact, okay with that.

"Oh, and Private? It's lieutenant—not *boss*."

"You got it." Mitt saluted with two fingers and the wrong hand, but Raymond let it slide. He hurried away without looking back before Mitt changed his mind about trying.

Raymond trudged through the tall grass, the *slip slap, slip slap* of his dew-dampened trousers the only sound in the silence of a slumbering camp. Stars twinkled above him in the dissolving inky light. Peace covered Raymond like one of their Army-issued, thick woolen blankets. Warmth spread from his heart to his limbs with the joy of the morning, in the beauty, in the quiet. Everything seemed right and good, and as natural as breathing, a quiet prayer of thanks sprang to his lips.

He'd entered the mess tent last night half hoping Mitt would throw in the towel and refuse to show. If Mitt gave up, Raymond wouldn't need to worry about him coming in and blowing up his already problematic platoon. But he'd left feeling... different. He wasn't sure why, exactly. Maybe it was because Mitt had become a challenge Raymond didn't want to lose.

Almost to the rifle range, he drew to an abrupt halt. Mitt leaned against a tree with one shoulder, eyes zeroed in on

Raymond's approach. "You scared the pee outta me, Solomon. 0530 not early enough for you?"

Mitt shrugged and pushed off the tree. "I had to wake early to milk the cows."

No cows at Fort Jackson. No chickens to feed, either. No reason for Mitt to be there an hour earlier than required. Maybe Raymond had gotten through to Mitt after all.

In the distance, lights bounced across the field in cadence with the bumps in the road as a jeep laden with target rifles approached the range.

"You want me to unload those rifles... sir?" At that word, Mitt pursed his lips as if he'd taken a swig of curdled milk by accident.

Raymond bit back a grin. *Don't hurt yourself there, bud.* He motioned to the jeep with his head.

"Hey there, Mitt." The jeep's driver, Martinelli, greeted Mitt with a grin.

"How'd you get roped into this?" Mitt raised his fist and lunged as if to punch Martinelli but stopped just before his fist made contact.

Martinelli laughed. "Volunteered. It got me out of guard duty."

"Yeah, yeah. Let's get this over with." Mitt moseyed to the back of the vehicle, moving as slow as molasses from an overturned jug, and lifted a case of weapons out of the back of the truck.

Raymond went to work setting up targets, and just when he'd adjusted the last one, a loud curse rent the air.

Mitt was shaking out one of his hands. He grabbed a wooden box of rifles and dumped it on the ground without ceremony. He kicked the crate, and in an explosion of fury and color, let loose with a crescendo of curses.

Raymond blinked. *He's creative. I'll give him that.* He strode toward the private. "Lemme look at it."

"I'm fine. It'll take a lot more than that to take me out," Mitt said but stuck his hand out for inspection anyway.

One of Mitt's fingers, red and a little swollen, had a jagged, bleeding fingernail.

"Can you move it?"

Mitt yanked his hand from Raymond's grasp. "Yeah, I can move it." He wiggled it in front of Raymond's face.

Raymond batted Mitt's hand away. "Have the medics assess it when you're done here. It's not bad enough for you to get out of finishing this."

Another expletive slipped from Mitt's mouth.

"Watch it, Private. Cursing won't help you unload weapons any faster." Raymond went to the back of the truck and heaved out a box of rifles. "Another set of hands will, though. Since you're missing one of your own."

"Har, har, har. What's your next stop? The USO?"

Raymond ignored him and crouched to inspect the crate of rifles Mitt had dropped.

The salty private walked away from him and grabbed another load. He set the box on the ground in front of Martinelli and leaned on the truck's open window. "So, what's with Mr. Squeaky Clean back there? What'd they call him back in school—Holy Rabbi?"

Mitt clearly believed he was out of earshot. Raymond took a fortifying breath. Mitt might be older, harder, and hairier than Jimmie would ever be, but if Mitt needed a big brother to keep him out of trouble, Raymond was plenty experienced with that. "Actually, they called me *Parson*," he called over to them.

Mitt slowly turned around, his face schooled into a look of nonchalance. "Yeah, well, it fits."

"Forgot I was here? You better get used to me babysitting you." Raymond grabbed the last box and shoved it in Mitt's chest. "Someone a mile away would've heard you."

Mitt hefted the container and propped it on his shoulder.

"Babysitter my... backside. I'm ancient enough to have sandwiches in my icebox older than you."

"Then act like it."

Side by side they carried the rifles closer to the shooting line. "Did they really call you Parson?"

"They did."

"Popular guy, huh?"

"Listen, there's cursing, and then there's *cursing*." Raymond bit back a laugh at Mitt's unimpressed face. "You can't talk like that in the Army, Solomon. Officially, you understand. We have rules about that. No one cares what happens when the bullets fly, but for now, clean it up."

"You hear confessions too, Parson? Jews don't normally go for that sort of thing, but I've got some stuff I gotta unload off my chest, LT. We're talkin' a lot of *juicy* stuff."

"I'm not that kind of parson." Or any at all, for that matter.

"What kind are you, then? Besides the word-cop kind, I mean."

"The kind that's telling you to get your finger checked out. Get to the medic. You need to be ready to ruck it with us tomorrow. You're done here."

"It's not even bleeding! Look..." Mitt waggled his finger. "It ain't broken. I don't need a doctor to tell me that."

"That's an order, Private. Go."

Mitt sighed. "Okay, okay, I give. See you around, Parson."

"Lieutenant."

"Fine. Lieutenant." Mitt set off and within a few yards, stubbed his foot on a rock. Another expletive shot out of him. Mitt's head whipped around to see if Raymond noticed.

Yeah, he'd noticed.

TWELVE

A LITTLE SOMETHING MORE

April 1942
Clemson, South Carolina

A man approached the counter and plunked his money down. "Thanks for supper. It was just as good as it always is."

Evelyn grinned at the balding school superintendent. He came in every day for tomato soup and a grilled cheese sandwich and refused to be served by anyone but her. "See you tomorrow?"

He set a toothpick between his teeth and studied her.

Evelyn brushed discarded cinnamon and sugar into her palm and clapped her hands over the wastebasket. "You alright, Mr. Cabot?"

He took his toothpick out of his mouth and pointed it at her. "You still want to be a teacher?"

At the appraising look in his eyes, a tiny spark of hope lit in her heart. "I do."

"I got a passel of teachers who joined up and left me in a bind. I don't see as how we can replace half of 'em, so many are gone. You interested?"

Evelyn cocked her head to the side. He had to know she was still a long way off from meeting the requirements. "But I'm not done with college yet, and I—"

"With the bind I'm in? You can take as long as you want to finish."

She could barely keep herself from rounding the counter and giving that man the biggest hug of his life. For the first time in months, she buzzed with optimism. "I would love to! Oh, Mr. Cabot. Thank you for taking a chance on me. I won't let you down."

A grin spread across his face. "Thank *you.* As long as you pass the National Teacher Exam in June, the job is yours."

Her hopes plummeted to her toes. "But... I'm not at all ready." If she took the test and failed, there wouldn't be a chance to retake it with the school year starting shortly later. It would be mortifying to leave Mr. Cabot in another lurch.

"If it were up to me, I'd hire you on the spot, but the board is all caught up in this new test like it's the answer to all our problems. You're a bright one. You'll do just fine."

How could he possibly know that? "Can I have a little time to think about it?"

The smile on his face drooped. "I suppose you can have until Monday. I know I'm springing this on you at the last minute, but I sure could use the help."

"I appreciate the extra time, Mr. Cabot. I'll let you know as soon as I decide."

He tapped the counter once. "Alright, then. Bye for now."

As soon as he left, Rosie sidled up to her and bumped her with her hip. "What was that all about?"

"Mr. Cabot asked me to consider teaching."

"Why, Evelyn, that's great news!" Rosie wrapped her up in a big hug. Then she pulled back, an exaggerated frown on her face. "Though I'm sad you'll be leaving me."

"Don't get too sad just yet. I don't think I can take it."

"But Evie, this is your chance to do what you've always wanted."

"I'm just not ready."

"You've been studying since the day we met."

"I don't want to fail."

Rosie threw up her hands. "What have you got to lose by trying?"

Her friend was no better than a bulldog with a meat bone between his teeth. "I'll take it when I'm ready."

Rosie looked down her pert little nose. "We'll see."

Evelyn didn't like the look in Rosie's eyes. It always meant trouble was just around the corner.

The next day at work passed without another comment from Rosie, which made Evelyn even more suspicious. But her shift came to an end, and Evelyn began to think Rosie might've forgotten. "I'll see you tomorrow."

Rosie's head popped up from beneath the counter where she'd been digging around for more wax paper. "Wait!"

Evelyn narrowed her eyes. "I'm tired, Rosie. I want to go home."

Her eyes flitted to the door and back again. "I was thinking you might want to take the leftover lemon pie to your mother."

"What are you talking about? The diner hasn't had lemon pie for weeks."

A cat-like smile crossed Rosie's face, and she pushed past Evelyn, her eyes focused on something by the door. "Never mind the pie."

The bell rang, and in walked Samuel Lewis, an old acquaintance from their childhood. Evelyn started. "Samuel! Why, I haven't seen you for ages." If it weren't for his pinned jacket sleeve where his right arm would've been, she'd hardly have recognized him. He was tall and well-built, a man in every respect, though he still had those angelic blue eyes and his golden-blond hair. "Hello, Rosie." He nodded at her friend, a sparkle in his eyes. "Evelyn."

"Can I get you a donut? Some coffee?" Evelyn asked.

He exchanged glances with Rosie. "That sounds nice."

Rosie nudged Evelyn toward Samuel. "You just got off, Evie. Why don't you join him, and I'll bring a plate of donuts." It was less a question and more a command, the way she'd said it. In a lower voice, she said, "He teaches at the school and knows all about the test."

She had to hand it to Rosie—this was one strategy Evelyn hadn't seen coming.

"On the off chance he might be able to help, I'll humor you."

"That's all I ask."

Evelyn walked Samuel to a table. He held out her chair for her, and she settled into it.

Samuel glanced down at her, a kind smile on his face. "I take it she didn't tell you I was coming."

"What exactly did she tell you?"

"Can we ease into it after I get my coffee?"

Heat sprang to her cheeks, despite the glint of humor in his eyes. "How terribly rude of me. Samuel, please, tell me what you've been up to since we last saw each other."

He took the seat across from her. "I'm teaching."

"What do you teach?"

"Mathematics at the high school. It's a harder position to fill apparently, so my missing arm didn't present a difficulty in getting hired." He dropped a lump of sugar into his coffee, crushing it with his spoon. "Good thing I love numbers. They present a guaranteed outcome when nothing else in life is like that."

She glanced at him in surprise. "I've thought the very same."

He smiled at her and took a slow sip of his coffee. "Speaking of teaching..."

Evelyn laughed. "That was very smoothly done."

"When Rosie mentioned your name, all our happy times in Mrs. Simmons' class came back like it was yesterday. Remember when Rob lost his pet rabbits in the school—"

"—and Mrs. Simmons was finding baby rabbits for months?" Evelyn shook her head. "I still don't know how they survived that long to have litter after litter."

"I do." He sat back with a self-satisfied smile.

"But how? No one knew. Unless you..."

He fluttered his angelic eyes at her.

"You *fed* them?"

"It was the most fun I'd had in ages."

Evelyn shook her head. "I have to say, you've surprised me, Samuel Lewis."

He slid his cup out of the way and leaned forward. "The test is hard. There's no getting around it. But I can give you some pointers and help you along as best I can. It'd be nice to have you around the school, just like when we were younger."

She glanced away from the bold appreciation in his eyes. "Thank you, Samuel. That's very kind, but I'm not sure it's worth the effort."

"If you're willing to give the exam a shot, I'm free tomorrow after school for a study session."

"I-I'll think about it."

He stood and laid down a dollar. "See you tomorrow, hopefully."

"Alright, Samuel."

As soon as he walked out the door, Rosie slid into Samuel's vacant seat. "So?"

"I have to say, I'm not even mad. It was very thoughtful of you."

"He's stuck here for the duration of the war, you know. He

can't join up because of his arm. He tried, but they turned him down. He's about the only handsome boy who hasn't left yet."

A wave of sadness washed over her, remembering the conversation at Christmas when Rosie had tried to convince her to stay with Raymond. "Samuel just wants to help me with the test. Nothing else."

"Even so, I don't think he'd mind it being a little something more."

THIRTEEN

THE TEST

April 15, 1942

Dear Jimmie—

So, I hear you've enlisted. The recruiter took your word for being eighteen and made you a cook after you divulged your old back injury. What's done is done, but no son of mine is going into this war as a slop slinger. I've put in a call to an associate of mine, a Mr. Gerald Sloane, who has made room for you to take the next Army General Classification Test at the reception center (details enclosed). I have served him in a prior circumstance and have not had cause to call in a favor until now. If you do well, he has promised to get you into the first phase of pilot training. Come to St. Simons as soon as you graduate and study for the exam under my supervision. Do not waste this opportunity.

—Dad

* * *

St. Simons, Georgia

Life with Dad was already complicated. Life with Dad as teacher was downright unpleasant. He was like a pit bull with a rabbit between his jaws. From the time breakfast finished until long after supper's dishes were cleared away, Dad loomed over him, goading him until his answers were perfect. Each time they made progress on one concept, they simply moved on to the next, Jimmie forever chasing that elusive pat on the back.

It would all be worth it if he passed the test and got out of being a cook. What was the point of enlisting if he couldn't join Raymond on the front lines?

But by the second week, Jimmie no longer cared if he made Dad mad. He had to get out.

He stuffed pillows under his blanket and joined his friends for a night on the town—friends he hadn't seen once since coming to the island. He drank, he smoked, he laughed until his gut hurt, reveling in the glorious act of frittering away the minutes as if they were nothing.

Hours later, belly still aching from laughter and booze, he stepped up to the entrance of Dad's house and quietly turned the knob, opening the door. He peeked inside. All was dark and quiet, so he tiptoed in.

Not a second later, a lamp switched on. Jimmie jumped against the doorframe. Slowly, his eyes adjusted to the light.

There Dad sat in an upholstered chair under the glow of the green-fringed lamp hovering above his head like a Venus flytrap.

How had he known? Then again, Dad had written the book on sneaking around.

Dad hooked a finger under his necktie and loosened it. Slow and deliberate, he pulled on one end until it slipped from his collar and pooled in his lap. He fingered the brushed wool lining. "Where have you been?" His voice was as smooth as a snake's belly.

Jimmie squared his shoulders and kept his head high even as his stomach threatened to empty the contents of the night's fun. "I went out for some fresh air."

"You don't sound sure about that." Dad rose from his chair and stalked toward Jimmie. He leaned forward, sniffing his son's collar. "I didn't know fresh air smelled like cigarettes and beer." He inhaled deeply once more. "And five-cent perfume."

Jimmie smoothed his hair into place with a shaky hand. "You know I haven't had any fun since I came down here."

"Empty your pockets."

"But Dad!"

"No buts. I want all your spending money. Every cent of it."

Jimmie stuffed a hand into his pocket and pulled out a fistful of coins. Walking over to the desk, he dumped his money on the glass top. The coins clattered as they landed, a nickel rolling off the table, over the woolen carpet and planks of nut-brown wood until it came to a stop at Dad's shoe.

"What if I'm out and get hungry? I don't wanna bum money off the boys again."

"You needn't worry about the boys' goodwill because you're not going anywhere for the rest of your time here." Dad grabbed Jimmie's shoulder in a vise grip and marched him over to the desk, shoving him into the chair with a jostle. "You'll sit your rear end in this chair and get to work. Time to grow up, son."

Jimmie ripped his arm away, chest heaving. He was a grown man at seventeen, and here he was, being pushed around by his own dad.

"I'm starting to have serious doubts you have what it takes to do this."

Jimmie stared at the top of the desk, his face burning.

"Well? Do you have what it takes? Don't let anyone cast doubt on your character if it isn't true."

"I've done my best. Honest, I have."

"Prove it." Dad pulled out a stack of writing paper from his drawer and slapped it on the desktop. He shifted a manual from the corner of the desk until it lay beside the blank sheets. "Copy this guide, word for word. I want to see your completed work first thing in the morning."

"But that'll take hours!"

"You should've thought of that before you went out on the town. Too much coddling ruins a man. We've your mother to thank for that."

"You leave her out of—"

"Oh, you can be sure I'll leave her out of this. What was I thinking, putting you boys in her charge? You think just because I left, I can't have a say in how your life turns out, but I'm still your father."

"I wish you weren't." The words flew out before Jimmie could stop them.

Dad's lips parted. Pain etched itself across his face.

Jimmie had never talked like that to Dad, not ever. "I didn't mean—"

"Get to writing," Dad said in a more subdued voice. "Time for us to see what you're really made of."

Heart knocking against his ribs, Jimmie entered the bright, high-ceilinged classroom. Sunlight streamed in from the east-facing windows and ricocheted off the polished wooden floor. He shielded his eyes. Small tables with metal chairs dotted the room, most of them occupied by the other test-takers. Jimmie inched his way to a desk at the back out of reach from the slanted rays and sat down.

A line of uniformed men sat in a row of chairs at the front observing the applicants taking their seats. Jimmie glanced at the others ready to take the test. They didn't have the square-jawed and broad-shouldered confidence he expected of soon-to-be pilots. Maybe they were just here because their dads had connections too.

Jimmie relaxed into the hard wooden seat.

A balding man with a rack of ribbons on his uniform stood at the front as his assistants delivered exams to each desk.

Jimmie's hands itched to leaf through the stack of papers in front of him. Imagining his dad's reaction if he were sent home for disobeying directions, he locked his fingers together in his lap. Dad expected him to pass this test, so that's what he would do.

The man with the ribbons cleared his throat. "When I give the signal, turn the page and start the test." He glanced at his watch and waited a few seconds. "You may begin."

Jimmie flipped the cover page. The proctors wandered the room, passing through the rows and occasionally looking down at the exams. One came close and angled his head, glancing at the sheet half hidden by Jimmie's arm. The man frowned.

Were his answers so wrong the man knew it at a glance?

Jimmie hunched over the exam, casting a shadow over the rest of the page.

The proctor took the hint and moved on.

Jimmie flipped through the pages, trying to find a question he could easily answer. There. The first question on page three seemed easy enough.

Private Billings bought some books for $9. He sold them to his bunkmates for $10, making $0.25 on each book. How many books were there?

The moment he set his pencil to paper, the lead broke. Swearing under his breath, he grabbed another pencil, but by the time he'd returned to the test, the answer had already flitted out of his head.

Concentrate, you dummy! He shook out his writing hand and circled an answer.

Finally, progress. He moved on to the next question.

A HALCYON atmosphere pervaded the camp.

Halcyon? What the heck is a halcyon? And what did that have to do with flying a plane? What did any of it have to do with anything? He glanced up at the clock. Fifteen minutes had passed already? Time to knuckle down and stop panicking. He went through the questions, one by one, circling letters even if he didn't know the answer and ignoring the images crowding in his head—his scowling dad, Raymond surrounded by the cackling enemy, and a plane going down in flames, the plane he wouldn't be piloting because he couldn't pass this test.

"One more minute," the bald man announced.

Jimmie looked up, startled. One minute? He still had half the test to go. In a panic, Jimmie spent the rest of the time circling a random letter beneath every unanswered question.

"Stop."

Sighing, Jimmie loosened his iron grip on his pencil and set it down.

"Close your booklets. Remain in your seats while we collect your tests." The head proctor signaled his assistants to move toward the desks.

Jimmie sat back and peeked at the other applicants. Their faces were pinched and drawn, appearing as shellshocked as he felt.

Maybe he had a chance after all.

He draped his jacket over his arm and walked past the proctors. It was only after he exited the building and turned the corner that he collapsed against the brick building and loosened his tie. There was nothing to do now but go back to Dad's and wait.

Jimmie put on his hat and reached for the doorknob.

"Where you goin'?"

He scowled and whipped around to face the stairs. "Stay out of my business."

Clomping down each step on shiny red pumps, Susan trailed her hand down the banister rail, eyeing Jimmie like he was the mouse, and she was the cat. "Didn't Daddy say you had to stay close in case a certain letter came?"

In a flash, he imagined grabbing her by the neck of that ridiculous floofy dress and tossing her over the side of the staircase. "I'm just goin' out for fresh air."

"I'll tell."

How old was she? Twelve? Jimmie crossed his arms and stared her down. "Go ahead."

Instead of yelling for Dad like he expected, she smirked a little and lowered her voice as if she shared a secret. "The letter came."

The breakfast in Jimmie's stomach churned. Two weeks had passed in strained interaction with Dad, waiting for the test results. Jimmie's heart jumped with every knock at the door, every ring of the phone, every creak of the mail slot. How long did it take to grade a handful of tests, anyway?

Dad hollered from his office. "Jimmie!"

This was it. The letter had come.

He hurried past Susan and entered Dad's office.

Dad was smiling—smiling!—and holding out a letter. "It's here. Open it."

Jimmie hesitated.

"Go on." Dad tossed it at him, and Jimmie caught it against his chest.

Dad returned to his seat behind the desk. He placed his elbows on the arms of his chair and steepled his fingers, an anticipatory gleam in his eyes.

Jimmie glanced from the letter to his dad. He'd spent collective hours imagining this moment. If he passed, he'd get one of Dad's rare nods of approval. He might even introduce Jimmie to his friends. *This is my son. A pilot,* he'd say with a lift of his chin. He'd wear that smug smile of his when he was proud of something he'd accomplished. Except this time, it would be Jimmie who had accomplished it.

And if he failed the test?

Well, he'd melt into his shoes and die of shame.

He slid his thumb under the sealed flap and ripped it open.

There it was, in the open space between two paragraphs.

Second quartile.

Dad leaned forward. "Well? What does it say?"

"I... I don't know. What does second quartile mean?"

Dad's smile fell. "Let me see that." He got up from his desk and ripped the letter from Jimmie's hands. "The results have been tabulated and..." Dad's eyes darted over the letter.

Jimmie's heart beat so hard it drowned out the rest of his dad's words. "Did I make it?"

"*No*, you didn't *make it*." Dad slapped the letter on his desk. "Looks like you have some more work to do."

"What do you mean?"

"I'll call Mr. Sloane and see when he can fit you into the next test." He was already reaching for the phone on his desk.

His father's clipped tone was already relaying a request for another favor to Mr. Sloane as Jimmie slunk out of the office. He trudged up the stairs to his room, kicked off his shoes, and crawled under the covers, wishing his bed would swallow him alive. At this moment, Dad was probably apologizing to Mr. Sloane for his screw-up son.

He looked to the empty twin bed across from his. If only Ray was with him now. He'd wrestle Jimmie out of his misery.

Was it really worth another try at the test?

Maybe he didn't have what it took, and maybe his father could never be pleased.

If that was the case, why not chart his own course? He did have a backup, after all. Jimmie flung off the blankets. He shoved his feet into his shoes and jerked his shoelaces tight. He loped downstairs and opened the door to his dad's office.

"A few days ago, I went to the recruitment office."

A stunned look crossed Dad's face. "Don't tell me you took that cook job after the strings I pulled."

"I talked to someone from the Navy. Just in case the test didn't pan out. This time I didn't mention my back, and he said they could take me on as a machinist's mate on a bomber crew."

"A gunner? On a Navy plane?" Dad's bewildered voice matched his face. "Why would you do that when you could be a pilot in the Army Air Corps?"

"Why do pilots get all the buzz anyway? I'll be the one doing the actual shooting."

His dad's mouth flopped open. "Do you want to get yourself killed?"

From where Jimmie was standing, he'd rather risk that than coming up short one more time. "It's a war, Dad."

"I'll report you as underage."

"No, you won't. You don't want to be seen as unpatriotic, do you?"

"It's illegal."

"Any seventeen-year-old boy can enlist if their parents sign off on it."

Dad ground his lips together.

"Thanks for trying, but I think we both knew the pilot thing wasn't going to work out."

He walked past his dad to the stairs. He'd gather his things, sleep at the station, and take the first train back to South Carolina. He didn't need to be a pilot to show Dad what he was worth. He'd still become a war hero, and he'd do it without Dad's help. As for danger? A gunner in the air had to have about the same odds as an infantryman on the ground, so if Raymond could hack it, so could he.

FOURTEEN

OF WHIMS AND WAR

April 1942
Fort Jackson, South Carolina

Raymond turned on his side and punched his pillow. He'd been awakened by a dream of Evelyn—again. It had been over four months since he'd last seen her. He'd left the Christmas dance assuming he'd never see her again, and he hadn't. He'd moved on from Clemson to Fort Jackson, focused on the mission before him. Intent on forgetting what lay behind him. Telling himself she couldn't have been clearer in her disinterest. But he still thought about her, especially at night when he lay in his cot without Army business to distract him. Thoughts turned into restless dreams, dreams into discontented mornings. Time hadn't lessened the tenderness he felt toward her or the ache in his chest when he told himself to forget her.

If only there hadn't been tears in her eyes when she'd said goodbye.

He sat up and ran his fingers through his hair.

His weekend pass sang a siren song of possibility—that he'd read her wrong and that she'd been waiting for him to come back to her all this time. That if there was even the smallest chance, he should take it, especially since the time he had left in South Carolina dwindled fast. Rumors were that they'd be moving on to another camp soon.

He dropped his feet to the floor and pulled on his trousers. His mind went to work, knocking out the supports of his good intentions one by one, giving himself justifications to do what he'd already decided to do. It couldn't only be the war that was bothering her, could it? He knew plenty of couples who were chugging along despite it. What if he'd offended her? He couldn't go overseas with that on his conscience. How could he be a soldier if he didn't even have the guts to fight for the woman he loved? He slipped on his shirt and swiped the weekend pass off his bedside table, stuffing it inside his pocket. The only thing to do was to drive to Clemson and find out once and for all where he stood.

He borrowed Wade's car and drove the two hours, tapping out his apprehension on the wheel. Once he'd settled the question as to whether he had a chance or not, he'd be able to go back to the business of preparing for war without this distraction.

He drove into the old familiar parking lot of the diner and straightened his tie. Setting his hat on his head, he exited the car, bounded up the diner's steps, and pulled open the door.

Evelyn sat on a stool reading a book, her face propped by her hand and the glow of a hanging lamp wrapping her in its soft light.

Seeing her again after so long nearly knocked the wind out of him. The curve of her fingers. The slope of her neck. A delicate chain with a single pearl nestled in the dip at the base of her throat. She was even more beautiful than he remembered, if such a thing were possible.

She called out without looking up from her book. "Kitchen's closed. We open again at six." Besides the fry cook spraying down the grill behind the order window and one elderly couple finishing their pie, she was alone.

Retrieving a mug, he brushed her arm in the process.

"Raymond!" She jerked to her feet.

"No, no. Don't get up." He poured coffee into his cup and put the carafe back on the burner. "Remember the deal we made? I serve myself while you continue your date with the numbers."

"If my boss finds out—"

"I'll tell him the only reason I buy his coffee is to see you." Raymond sat down on the high stool at the counter. "If he's got a head for business, he won't make a fuss." He crossed his forearms on the counter and leaned forward. He could feel the warmth of the hanging light enveloping him in the same golden glow surrounding Evelyn. "Go on. Don't mind me."

He whipped an Army manual out of his back pocket, pretending to study it.

She set her jaw, and turning her back to him, she began filling saltshakers with a little more vigor than necessary.

Twist. Pour. Twist. *Thunk.*

Twist. Pour. Twist. *Thunk.*

"Do you have any donuts left?" Raymond asked, as innocent as a lamb.

A saltshaker went down with the loudest *thunk* yet. She turned around and stared at him. After a long moment, she retrieved the sugared treat from under a glass dome and plunked it on a plate. She set it in front of him with a flourish and leaned on the counter with her hands. "Once you get an idea in your head..."

"I can't let it go," he finished for her.

"Bye, Joe!" she called out to the man cleaning up in the kitchen. "Thanks for offering to close up. This gentleman just needs his check."

Joe lifted his hand. "Got it."

She disappeared behind the counter and then straightened, her handbag hooked around her forearm.

And his scarf wrapped around her neck.

He stared at it. He might not be the biggest lady-killer, but even he knew that a girl didn't wear the scarf of a boy she hated.

"What?" Her hand dropped to the scarf.

"My scarf. You kept it."

Her face drained of color. She slowly unwound it and handed it to him. "Here."

"I told you to keep it." Raymond surveyed the parking lot. No car picking her up, no new football-sized boyfriend waiting, either. "Can I walk you home tonight?"

"What for?"

"So we can talk."

"It's over between you and me."

Oh, but it wasn't. Not if she still wore his scarf.

"I'm seeing someone else, Raymond."

Out of all the things he'd prepared himself for, this hadn't been one of them. "So who is this other guy?"

"He's kind and... kind. He's helping me with my teacher's exam."

"Huh."

"What?"

"You just don't sound too excited about him, is all."

Her shoulders sagged. "Well, truth be told, I think he's more interested in my friend Rosie."

"And... are you okay with that?"

She scooped her book into the crook of one arm. "Why are you here?"

"One walk is all I ask. If I can't convince you on the way to your house to give me a chance, you can give me the boot. I promise."

A war played out on her face. The side in his favor better have bigger guns. "*And* if you want me to leave right now and never talk to you again, I will," he amended. "Even if it means never eating a warm, delicious cinnamon sugar donut from College Café ever again. Promise."

She sighed. "Okay."

"Okay you want me to leave, or okay I can walk you home?"

Evelyn's head tilted, and she narrowed her eyes. "Okay you can walk me home."

"Okay, then."

Her mouth twitched. "Well, c'mon, then. You've got one hour. Give it your best shot."

He plunked two quarters on the counter and took a big bite out of his donut before he threw it back on the plate.

He held open the glass door for Evelyn, and she stepped past him into the scent of sweet yellow jessamine hanging heavy in the night air, the flowering vines twisting over the walkways and trees surrounding the diner. Under the light of the rising moon, Raymond and Evelyn ambled in silence to the end of the parking lot, gravel crunching underneath their shoes.

"When's the exam?"

She was quiet for a moment. "It was today."

"Today? But you're here."

"I'll take the next one."

Still a sore subject, apparently. Raymond held his hands behind his back and twisted to face her. "Do you know I don't even like coffee?"

She stared at him. "You can't be serious. You drank it every time you came into the diner."

"It was an excuse to have you come back to the table."

"You're crazy."

"Not usually." He peeked at her. "What I can't figure out is if I was going crazy when we saw each other at Christmas."

Evelyn refused to meet his eyes.

"Do you remember our first dance?"

She looked up at him in surprise. "Of course I do."

"May I?" He reached toward her, and she hesitated for a moment before putting her hand in his. Electricity shot through him. He wasn't prepared for what it would be like to touch her again. With a gentle tug, he pulled her to him, and she naturally fell into the rhythm of his dance.

"It feels like so long ago," she said in a small voice.

They swayed a little. He held her in a proper dancing position, never pulling her closer than one of those chaperones would have allowed with her ruler. "You were a scared bunny hiding in that alcove, and I wanted to rescue you."

"I was a silly thing, wasn't I?"

"No, not silly. You reminded me of my brother."

"Why?"

He nodded. "You were just a kid. Fourteen years old and never been danced with. Am I right?"

"You were the first." She sighed and let him pull her a little closer. He rested his chin on her forehead. "I don't know why you remembered me. I hardly said anything worth saying."

"Oh, but you did. If I recall, you proposed to me."

Evelyn sucked in a sharp breath and pulled away. "I did not!"

"Oh, but my sweet, you did. You offered to be my bride."

Evelyn let out a cry of protest.

"And do you remember what I said in return?" Raymond asked. "I told you I wasn't looking just yet but to come find me in a few years and ask again."

"Now, you know that's not what I said. I asked if you wanted me to be your *guide*."

"The music was awful loud." He eyed her with mock suspicion. "*Guide*'s different enough from *bride* that I think I would've heard that."

"Really!" Even in the pale light of the moon, the apples of her cheeks deepened in color.

He laughed and twirled her around with his arm stretched

upward. "Alright, I'm obviously in no danger of another proposal tonight." He dropped her hand and stepped back. "Thank you for the dance, Miss Noble."

She put her hands on her hips. "I'm sure you've been laughing about me ever since that dance."

"Never! Honestly, I found it awfully..." he trailed off for a moment, gazing into her eyes, "...adorable." He leaned his shoulder against a tree and crossed his arms, grinning at her.

"You make me sound like a puppy."

"A really *adorable* puppy, though."

She laughed. "I give up! You make it very hard to be mad at you, you know that?"

"Why on earth would you want to be mad at me? I just called you adorable."

"Weren't you supposed to be convincing me to give you another chance?"

"I'll be on my best behavior from now on. Promise."

"Just how good is your best, anyway?"

He stared at her for a moment then pushed off the tree. "Good enough." He came closer. "Evie..."

She took a step back.

He stopped. "Why'd you end it with me? I thought you liked me."

This time, it was Evelyn who took a step forward, face earnest. "Oh, but I did!"

"Did?"

She hugged her arms to her waist and stood there, quiet and grave. "Did you know my dad fought in the Great War? He was in the infantry. Like you." She gave him a pointed look. "He dragged whatever happened over there like a sack of rocks tied to his shoes. It must've been terrible, but he never spoke about it. He didn't speak about anything at all, really. One day, he just..." Evelyn waved her hand as if searching the air for a way to explain a betrayal that must've cut too deeply for words. "He left. Without a word. Like our home was just a stopping place to somewhere else."

Raymond's stomach knotted. The undercurrents from Christmas now took shape into capsizing swells.

"I haven't heard from him since. Not one letter, not one phone call. Last I heard, he's in California near his brother. We get updates sometimes, but not from my dad."

Raymond could relate more than she knew, but even his father's monthly one-sheet letters were better than nothing at all. "He loved you, Evelyn. There's no way he didn't."

"Sometimes I wonder what we did, what *I* did to make him leave. But the truth is, it wasn't my fault. It wasn't his. If it wasn't for..." She squared her shoulders. "Soldiers aren't for me, Raymond. Not with another war on."

They stared at each other. A tingle of challenge tempted him to tatter her words as if they were dried leaves he could burn to ash. There had to be an answer to this predicament that brought them together. To refuse happiness on the chance it could be lost? She was wrong. They could rebuild what their fathers tried to destroy. They could do it together. And if he had to work for his dad, let it at least be with her beside him. With her, he could bear anything. But how could he convince her of that? "C'mon. Let's get you home."

He held out the crook of his arm. She hesitated before tucking her arm in his.

They moved once again down the path, and Raymond reached for the canopy of flowering dogwood blossoms above them. He trailed his fingers over the flowers, stirring their fragrance, and a petal fluttered to Evelyn's hair. He stopped. Holding her gaze, he reached toward her hair. She held her breath as he slowly extracted the petal from one of her loose curls.

He lowered his hand with the petal in his fingers and moved tentatively toward her cheek. He allowed himself the briefest of touches, a gentle brush with his bent fingers as if she were a doe poised for flight. She turned her head into his palm and closed her eyes.

He dropped his hand and waited for her eyes to meet his. The only thing he could do was speak from the heart. He'd tell her the truth and hope she'd hear that and not his words if they came too rushed or too strong. He couldn't change her father's leaving, but there was one thing he could say with any kind of certainty. "My father also left. Almost ten years ago."

Evelyn put a hand to her throat.

"But you see, my father's a hard man. He doesn't have an excuse like your dad has. I can't even say for sure he loves us. Maybe he loves himself more than he does anyone else." He shook his head. "I made a promise to myself long ago that I'd never do to my wife and children what my father did to his. The thought of doing that makes me sick. I'd rather die." He gently grasped her shoulders. "I don't leave the ones I love, no matter what. I'm not my father or yours."

"But the war—"

"Pretend there isn't a war. Pretend we could be together every day from here on out. Would you do it?"

Tears filled her eyes.

He'd promised he'd give her up, and he would, if that's what she wanted. He'd leave and she'd remain a dream to him, a beautiful dream he'd think about whenever life got ugly or hard. As bad as her rejection would hurt, it would be worse to wonder what might have been if he hadn't given it another try. He waited a beat, and when she didn't respond, he dropped his hands from her shoulders. He'd wanted an explanation, and he'd gotten one. He wouldn't force her.

He placed the petal in his shirt pocket and took a step back. At least he could leave knowing that he'd given it all he had.

They stopped at the gate in front of her house, and she faced him, her eyes full of some simmering emotion Raymond couldn't decipher. "Thank you for walking me home, Raymond."

He nodded and shoved his hands in his pockets, clenching them so he wouldn't weave his fingers through her hair and pull her toward him for a kiss.

She took a few hesitant steps toward him until she stood mere inches away. "Since you love coffee so much, I'll be sure to have a fresh pot ready the next time you come in," she said, her voice trembling.

He couldn't breathe. The next time?

Lifting her lips, she placed the briefest of kisses on his cheek and just as quickly pulled back, her face lit in a fiery hue.

"Evie, what—"

"I'm saying okay. Let's pretend." She turned away, and without glancing back, she opened the white picket gate and hurried up the path to her front door, disappearing into the house.

Raymond stood frozen outside the gate. He didn't know exactly what had changed her mind, but somewhere along the way between Holly Street and 5th, she'd decided he merited another try. In return, he'd never give her cause to regret the decision she'd made; he would show the both of them that some men stuck around and stuck it out, regardless of whims or war.

FIFTEEN

IN FOR A DIME, IN FOR A DOLLAR

June 1942
Clemson, South Carolina

Two months later, Evelyn sat on a painted bench, her head resting against the brick wall outside the diner. A cool spring breeze ruffled her work dress, tickling her skin. It wafted over every curve and valley of her, and she closed her eyes, reveling in the delicious freedom from the heat.

Footsteps crunched through the gravel. She couldn't stop the smile that slowly spread across her face.

"Ready?"

She opened her eyes and squinted up at him. "You're late."

Raymond glanced at his watch. "Am I?"

"You missed the donuts, I'm afraid."

His face lightened. "Who cares about donuts? You're the one I came to see."

He grabbed her hand and pulled her to her feet. She retrieved her books from the bench, but he didn't let go. She tilted her head away from him, hiding her blush.

"I hope your mother didn't go to any special trouble. She knows I'll eat anything, right?"

"I told her, but you know how it is. Just make sure you compliment her hot milk cake. She makes it special for company." The fact that Mama had made anything at all was a victory, but Raymond didn't need to know that. It had taken her awhile to come around when Evelyn had told her that things were back on with Raymond. She didn't speak to Evelyn for a week but finally moved on as if nothing had happened. What she actually thought, Evelyn couldn't know.

"By the way... thanks."

"For what?"

"For inviting me over. For introducing me to your mom."

She could hardly avoid it much longer. The opportunities to do so dwindled with the division leaving for Virginia within the week. She tugged his hand. "We're going to be late."

"We have plenty of time." He smiled down at her. "Let's enjoy the walk."

They strolled along the gravel path, hand-in-hand, following the road to her house.

"How's it going with your platoon?"

"A little better. That Mitt Solomon's been a surprise. If you'd told me he'd turn out like this the day he arrived, I'd have said you were lying."

The humor in his voice made her smile. "What do you mean?"

"He's the same fellow, in some ways. Still has a hard time with regulations and such, but he's trying. It's the others I'm worried about."

"Why?"

"Ever since that fuss with the rifles, they've been giving Benjamin a hard time. Mitt's the only one who lets him be. Oh, the men behave themselves ever since my last set down, but they aren't friendly, if you catch my drift."

"Poor Benjamin."

"I can't force them to be friends, but I need them to at least get along before we—"

"We weren't going to talk about that, remember?" How could they pretend there wasn't an impending goodbye if he kept mentioning it? She'd only just agreed to exchange letters while he was overseas. Thinking of him leaving dredged up old feelings—feelings that had almost kept her from being with him.

He sighed. "Sorry. How's studying going?"

When she'd ended her study sessions with Samuel, he'd been disappointed but understanding. Well, not too disappointed. He'd gone out for a date with Rosie that very night. Now, they were engaged. Samuel had encouraged Evelyn to not give up on the test, but Raymond's return was enough of the excuse she needed to put it off for longer. "I'm still not ready."

"I don't see how you'll ever get more ready than you are now."

"Yes, but what if I fail?"

"Oh ye of little faith." He lifted her hand clasped in his and kissed her knuckles. "*I* would hire you if I were in charge of a school."

Evelyn backhanded him playfully in the stomach with her hand still held in his.

They stopped in front of her house, the gate swinging by one hinge. He'd never seen their home in the daylight. Evelyn's eyes roved over the slanted picket fence and the sagging front stoop, trying to imagine how it looked from his point of view, with the rotting roof and the rain gutter torn away and lying against the red brick. The house showed the neglect of a man's hands. But the flower beds were tidy and the porch swept. Evelyn had made sure of that. She caught Raymond's gaze scanning the yard as well. He squeezed her hand.

The front door squealed open, scraping against the porch's

warped wood floor. Evelyn dropped Raymond's hand. "Don't forget about the cake," she whispered.

Her mother poked her head out, holding the door open with an arm swung to the side. "Come on in."

Raymond climbed the steps and took over holding the door. "Hello, Mrs. Noble. I'm happy to finally meet you."

A ghost of a smile cranked the side of Cora's mouth upward before it dropped again. "Welcome, Raymond."

They walked into the front living room. Muted light filtered through the drawn curtains, blanketing the atmosphere in a lethargic haze. Stacks of newspapers and correspondence lay on the side tables. Pieces of wallpaper peeled away from the walls in the South Carolinian humidity. The gray atmosphere rubbed against Evelyn like sandpaper. She glanced at Raymond, but he only followed Mama to the small kitchen table, set with their unchipped china and the Dutch boy and girl salt and pepper shakers her dad had brought home from the war. Evelyn had never seen the shakers outside of the cabinet before. At least Mama was trying.

They sat at the table, and her mother placed a square of cornbread on Raymond's plate. She ladled beans over the cornbread and handed him the saltshaker. "I know a man likes to salt his own food."

"That's mighty thoughtful of you, Mrs. Noble." He shook the shaker once over his beans.

Mama prepared two more plates and put her hands in her lap. "Evie says you're the praying sort."

Raymond nodded and said a quick grace. Evelyn's mother dug into her food as soon as the "Amen" was uttered. Raymond picked up his spoon. "So, Mrs. Noble... I heard you're a teacher."

"I am." She stuffed another spoonful of beans into her mouth. All Evelyn could hear was the sound of her mother chewing.

"And do you enjoy it?"

"It's work."

Raymond glanced at Evelyn and back at Mama. "It must be nice, being around kids all day."

"I suppose."

The table dissolved into quiet.

"Mother made her hot milk cake, just for you," Evelyn said.

"You don't say," Raymond said, with a glint of humor in his eyes. "That just happens to be my favorite, Mrs. Noble. How'd you guess?"

She shrugged. "There's no one who doesn't like cake."

"Well now, that's true enough." Raymond paused for a moment. His eyes pensive, he brought a spoonful of food to his mouth.

The rest of the meal passed in stuttering silence, interrupted only by Raymond's awkward attempts at conversation and Evelyn's efforts to lower Mama's hackles.

When their plates were nearly empty, a look of determination passed over Raymond's face.

He was going to try again, despite all evidence to the contrary that Mama would want to hear what he had to say. Evelyn put her hand on his knee and squeezed, but he ignored the warning.

"I was wondering if you and Evelyn would like to—"

Mama clanged her fork down on her plate. "You want to explain why you're seeing my daughter when you're going off to fight a war?"

"Mama!" Evelyn wanted to fold in on herself and disappear. No, she wanted Raymond to disappear. Not for good, but from her house.

Raymond laid his hand on hers. "No, it's okay." Raymond wiped the side of his mouth with his napkin. "Mrs. Noble, I—"

Her eyes narrowed into a slit. "Don't *Mrs. Noble* me." A

flush swept from her throat to her face as if she were a lobster thrown into a boiling pot. "There's nothing you could say that would change my mind about you. Why don't you just save her the heartache and leave now?"

Evelyn stood, scraping her chair against the floor. She couldn't bear seeing him stumble through trying to find an answer for what she herself little understood. "Mama, why don't you go rest on the couch while Raymond and I do the dishes?"

"Oh, so you do dishes, do you?" Mama looked Raymond up and down. "Alright, then." She walked out of the room, taking some of the gray with her.

Evelyn breathed a little easier, except for the food sitting in her stomach, a burning, heavy lump. She filled the sink with hot water, sensing the heat of Raymond's eyes on her back. He brought the plates over and dunked them in the basin.

They stood side by side, her washing dishes and him drying them with a dishtowel.

Evelyn whispered furtively to Raymond, her eyes on the dish she was scrubbing. "I'm sorry. I thought it would be different. I don't know why." She passed the rinsed plate to him.

He set it in the rack without drying it and grabbed her hand. "Look at me."

She raised her gaze to his.

"I don't mind. Honest, I don't."

He was just telling her that to make her feel better. Raymond was her first bit of real happiness since Daddy left, and Mama had to go and ruin it.

He took her hand and brought it to his chest still cradled in his hand, water dripping down their forearms. With his other hand, he cupped her face and brushed his thumb across her cheek. His face lowered, inches away from hers.

She didn't know if he'd closed the distance between them,

or if he'd waited for her to move first. All she knew was that kissing him was the sunshine she'd heard about but never felt on her skin. Not like this, and never in her home. She closed her eyes and gave herself over to the warmth uncurling in her body. How quickly things had changed. Only six months ago she'd been pushing him away. Now, it was more important than anything that he not give up on her.

He broke away, and her eyes flew open. He glanced through the doorway to the living room. "We'd better get back to your mom."

Evelyn reluctantly returned to washing the dishes, handing them to Raymond to dry. She avoided his gaze, knowing he was gauging her reaction to what had just happened. Before long, the plates and serving dishes were stacked in the cabinet and the utensils placed back in the drawer. Raymond and Evelyn came out to the living room and found her mother sitting on the couch, staring out the window.

"We're finished, Mama."

"Sit, then." She handed them each a slice of cake and a fork once they were settled on the settee.

What was Mama playing at? Why was she serving him cake when earlier she'd almost thrown him out of the house?

Raymond cleared his throat. "I noticed your gutter came off, Mrs. Noble. I'd like to come by and fix it tomorrow since I'm here for the weekend."

Her mother stopped mid-chew. "I guess I can't say no to that."

Evelyn looked back at Raymond, an apology in her eyes. "That'd be nice, Raymond. Thank you."

After a few quiet minutes of eating cake, Raymond stood. "Well, ladies, thank you for the wonderful food. I enjoyed meeting you, Mrs. Noble. I'll be by tomorrow with my tools."

Her mother stuffed another bite in her mouth. "We'll see," she said, so only Evelyn could hear.

Evelyn stood, following him to the door with a sinking heart. Kiss or no kiss, he'd never come back to do the gutter. How could he, with how Mama had treated him? No girl could be worth this trouble.

After he left, she closed the door and leaned on it. "What on earth is wrong with you, Mama? I'm ashamed of how you treated him. He was nothing but nice to you."

"Nice? Lot of good that did me." Mama gathered the plates and stood. "I tried, Evie. I tried to reconcile myself to the idea of you being with him, but I just can't do it. He'll break your heart, Evie. Mark my words. He'll break your heart."

"Mama, please. Be nice to him. For my sake."

"I did you a favor. He won't be back tomorrow."

Evelyn swatted down her own doubts. "He isn't like that, Mama. You'll see."

The next day, Evelyn strolled home after working the morning shift, taking deep breaths of the fresh air mingled with sweet jessamine. As much as she was thankful for her job, she could do without the smell of grease and coffee chasing her home on her clothes. All she could think about during work was whether Raymond would be there when she arrived home. She knew he wasn't the type to go back on his word, but even so, nearing her driveway, she stopped short. There, perched on a ladder against her roof, was Raymond, chiseling away at the rotting wood. Relief flooded through her. "Raymond."

He twisted around. "Hey there, doll." He climbed down, grabbed a drinking glass from the porch, and met her at the fence. He drained half the lemonade and lowered the glass to his side.

She eyed the drink. "Where did that come from?"

"Your mom." His eyes twinkled.

Mama did that? "Really?"

"Mmhmm. She even brought me a sandwich." He brandished a plate from the porch.

"A—a sandwich? But what changed?"

He shrugged. "I came back." He paused. "But it mighta had something to do with that little set-down you gave her after I left."

"She told you about that?"

"Well, no. But you just confirmed it. It must've gotten to her because there's ham *and* cheese in here." He grinned and took a big bite of his sandwich.

"You came back, after everything?"

He swallowed his mouthful. "What kind of guy do you take me for? I'm not going to kiss a girl and leave her."

"Shh!" She cast a furtive glance toward their open windows. Just as she feared, her mother was there, watching. She dragged him to the opposite side of the hedge, away from her mother's view.

The playful glint in Raymond's eyes faded. "What's the problem?"

"Do you know why my mom is like this?"

"Your father left."

"Yes, he left. Because of what the war did to him."

Raymond's mouth ground into a straight line. "So we're back at this again? I already told you, I'm not your father."

"But how can you know it won't happen to you?"

"Because... because... I just know!"

"But I don't. That's the problem."

"Do you even hear yourself?" He ran his hands through his hair. "I love you, Evie, but you're a chicken."

She gasped. She didn't know what shocked her more—Raymond telling her he loved her or him calling her a chicken. "A *chicken*?"

He narrowed his eyes at her. "You sure had me fooled.

Where's the Evie who put Frankie in his place? She seemed like the kind of girl who wouldn't back down from a fight." He stepped closer to her. "And why won't you take the teacher's exam? You were ready before you even started studying, and you know it. And what about me? You gotta take a chance sometime."

"I *am* taking a chance. We'll write, and then we'll see, when you get back..."

"No, none of this halfway stuff. I'm talking a real chance."

"Easy for you to say."

"You know what? It's not. You think it's easy for me, going off and leaving you?"

"I didn't say that."

"You weren't really going to give me a chance, were you? You were going to play it safe until you knew what would happen. This is a game, and I'm just your pawn. Well, make your move, Evie. What's it gonna be so I can know where I stand before I have to go?"

A cry escaped her open mouth, and tears tumbled down her cheeks.

"Oh, Evie." He grabbed her, hugging her tight. "I'm sorry. I shouldn't have said all that."

"No, I'm sorry. You're right. You're right about all of it." Her head lay against his chest, his steady heartbeat settling her tempest.

"What are you thinking?" His voice rumbled against her ear.

She tilted her face to his. "You really love me?"

He stilled. "Yes." One word, spoken without hesitation. With the same surety he was asking of her.

His accusations had been hard, but true. Somewhere along the way, she'd lost her nerve. "I... love you too."

"Will you take a chance and marry me, Evie?" He brushed a

strand of hair off her forehead. "I might not know the future, but I can promise I'll love you and protect you as long as I live."

She closed her eyes. It was enough, for now. She nodded and laid her head back on his chest. She'd known there'd be no going back after saying she loved him—and that's exactly why she'd said it.

SIXTEEN

THE ARMY GOES ROLLING ALONG

June 1942
Fort Jackson, South Carolina

Mitt yawned and wiped the tears at his eyelids with his thumbs. How much longer could he keep up with juggling both jobs? He'd had to get up before the crack of dawn to dice potatoes in the mess hall before joining Company A on the grassy field. Something had to give.

It hadn't been easy adjusting to the life of a blisterfoot. Sometimes his mouth cranked off before he could stop it. Sometimes his gear didn't pass inspection. But he had to hand it to the LT—the guy had stuck to his word and was turning him into a soldier.

It had been days since the last time he'd messed up. When would he be released from kitchen patrol? It was the whole reason he busted his backside, day after day, working two jobs like a putz.

The man in front of him leaned to the side, and the sunlight shot straight into Mitt's eyeballs. He winced and squeezed his eyes tight. The sparkling red orbs behind his eyelids danced and swirled. The platoon's jabbering faded into black static.

Someone smacked the side of his head. Mitt startled awake and swung to face his attacker.

"Whatsa matter, Mitt? You tired or somethin'?"

Mitt grabbed the front of Martinelli's shirt. "Be glad we got too many witnesses."

"Ooh. Big talker."

"Wanna see?"

"What I can't see is why they drafted in a guy like you in."

If Martinelli only knew.

Mitt rubbed at his scar, a jagged ridge down the side of his face. The day he'd gotten it had been the blackest day of his life. Even worse was what had happened afterward when he was kicked to the streets. Everyone back home expected him to fail. Seemed like everyone here expected it too. Well, he wasn't going to give them the satisfaction. They'd have to tie him up and ride him out on a rail before he went back home. "I wasn't drafted."

Martinelli gave an incredulous laugh. "You signed up for this?"

"The morning after they bombed the harbor." At least he had one thing over the others. He wasn't forced into service. He'd marched up to the Army office and signed up, all on his own. What would the colonel say to that if he knew? Looking back, Mitt couldn't say why he'd joined up. Maybe he was bored. Maybe he was tired of being the bad guy and wanted to be the good guy for once.

"Well, ain't you special? Just because you—"

"Shut up. Here comes the LT."

Sure enough, Raymond walked their way. Mitt let go of Martinelli's shirt and fell into position beside Benjamin, Walter, Jasper, and Mahony.

Raymond stopped in front of them. "Any questions before you run the course?"

Mitt had one. Walls, ropes, poles, pits, and wire—if this was what war was like, why all the fuss? He yawned. "Just like the playgrounds we had in the Bronx. Trash piles and construction zones, sir."

"Then you should have no problems with this. Remember you're racing against the clock, not each other. Help each other out just like you would in battle, alright?"

Just then, another platoon trickled back from the course, mud splatters painting the men's legs and forearms.

"Things might be a little slippery after the rain last night," Raymond said. "Make sure you keep a good grip."

The rain had only left puddles. As long as he didn't have to swim through them, he'd be okay. There'd never been much opportunity for swimming on the streets of New York City. "Piece of cake, sir," Mitt said.

"We'll see about that."

Mitt tamped down the fire that had flared at the LT's words. When would Mitt stop having to prove himself—when the war was over? Maybe if he was first through the obstacle course, the LT would finally get it.

"Now line up at the start in order of squads."

The men crouched at the starting line, with Mitt, Benjamin, Walter, Jasper, and Mahony in the front.

"Ten minutes. Ready?" Raymond clicked the button on his stopwatch. "Go!"

Mitt hurled himself forward and grasped the metal bars of the horizontal ladder. *One-two. One-two. One-two.* He swung his hands from bar to bar. At the end of the ladder, he released his grip and fell to the ground with a thud.

He ran and threw himself down before a spread of barbed wire hovering above a patch of dirt. Keeping his head dipped, he bear-crawled forward.

Jasper huffed and puffed beside him, dragging his stocky frame under the wire. Benjamin and Walter were only a few feet ahead.

Jasper grabbed Benjamin's boot.

"Get off me!" Benjamin shook his leg and flung Jasper's hand away from him.

Mitt propelled himself out of the pit and sprinted toward the wooden wall with Jasper, Benjamin, and Walter neck and neck behind him.

They crashed into the wall.

Jasper scrambled up Benjamin like a ladder, jamming a boot into his neck.

"Watch it!" Benjamin yelled, gripping Jasper's legs to keep him from toppling.

Jasper hoisted himself over the top and made an obscene gesture at Benjamin. "Try to keep up, Grandpa." He disappeared over the side.

Mitt slammed the wall with a flat palm. "Jasper, help him up!"

The LT shouted from the other side of the wall.

In the next moment, Jasper appeared at the top of the wall again, shooting fireballs at Mitt and Benjamin with his eyes. He shoved his hand toward them. "C'mon! I don't got all day!"

Mahony pushed Benjamin out of the way and reached for Jasper's hand.

"Oh no, you don't!" Mitt grabbed Mahony with one of his frying-pan hands and yanked him to the ground.

"Oof!" Mahony lay there like a cockroach giving up the ghost, his legs and arms flailing in the air.

Mitt motioned Benjamin over and crouched with his back to the wall. "C'mon, Benge."

He eyed Mitt, hesitant.

Mitt's first-place finish was fading with every second. Well, so what? He couldn't let them dogpile the guy like this. "Go!"

Benjamin stepped on Mitt's thigh and then his back. Groaning, Mitt straightened his legs, lifting the private.

Benjamin levered himself onto the ridge of the wall with Jasper's begrudging help. Benjamin reached a hand toward Mitt.

They clasped hands, and Benjamin pulled. They tumbled to the ground on the other side, Mitt landing face-first in the mud.

Mahony must've gotten help from someone else because he landed beside them.

Benjamin pulled Mitt to his feet. "You okay?"

Mitt swiped a hand over his face. "Let's go."

They ran toward a cargo net stretched from the ground to a platform above it, passing Jasper doing pushups on the side of the course with the LT standing over him with hands on his hips. Mitt grinned. Good. Jasper could use a good spanking.

Benjamin sprang to the net like a spider on its prey, with Mitt next, only a few feet below him.

Before Mitt could climb a rung, Benjamin's boots crashed into him.

What the...? Mitt looked up. Benjamin hung by his hands, swinging by one hand on a swoop of rope. Walter was grinding his boot into Benjamin's shoulder.

These clowns were a part of the platoon and Mitt still had to prove himself? He may have missed a lot being in the kitchens, but he'd never seen Benjamin do anything to earn this amount of grief. "Knock it off, Walt!"

Walter finally lifted his boot off Benjamin and crawled off the web. Benjamin righted himself and, with Mitt beside him, climbed to the top and descended the ladder from the platform.

They slithered through concrete tunnels, scaled a twenty-foot pole, and sped across a shaky rope bridge spread over rushing water without further incident. A short sprint to the finish, and they collapsed onto the gravel at the end of the course.

Wheezing, Mitt flopped his arms to his sides. He turned his head to Benjamin. "Where's Jasper? I'm gonna kill him."

Benjamin lifted his head and peered in the distance. "There. By the latrines with a bucket. And Walt."

Heh. Mitt closed his eyes and settled his breathing. Served them right, cleaning toilets. "Don't let 'em get to you, Benge."

"It's fine."

"Keep your head down. They'll move on to someone else."

"I said, I'm fine."

"Just giving some friendly advice. Take it or leave it." Mitt's breathing slowed. The sun was sizzling his skin, but he was too tired to move. The gravel may as well have been a down-filled mattress. His mind grew fuzzy. He closed his eyes, and the black static returned.

A cool shadow blocked the red glow of the sun through his eyelids. He opened his eyes.

The LT hovered over him. "I'd like a word, Solomon."

The down-filled mattress became a bed of gravel again, every piece jutting into Mitt like tacks. What had he done wrong now? "Yes, sir." With a grunt, Mitt got up and followed Raymond. They stopped several yards away under an oak tree.

"I saw what you did at the wall."

The wall? Did the LT think he was in on Benge's bullying? "I swear, it wasn't me."

Raymond grabbed his shoulder. "Calm down. You're not in trouble."

"I'm not?"

"Why would you get in trouble for sticking up for one of your fellow soldiers? Thanks for helping Benjamin."

Mitt picked a piece of imaginary lint off his shirt. "It's just an obstacle course."

"Not to me."

"So why's Benge getting ganged up on?"

"It's a long, stupid story about rifles going back to our first days here. Now look, the colonel and I had a little talk about you yesterday."

Ah, here it was. The real reason the LT wanted to chat. "Checking up on me, huh?"

"Actually, he was checking up on me. Wanted to see if I was doing my job. I told him I thought you were going to be a real asset to the team. Thanks for proving me right today." He smiled at Mitt, then. A real, genuine smile, as if Mitt had done something really impressive instead of something any decent guy would do. "You're done with kitchen patrol. For good. Report to the company at 0500 tomorrow morning."

His heart skipped a beat. "You serious?"

"As a heart attack."

It's what Mitt wanted, wasn't it? But now that it was about to happen, his stomach didn't feel right. Peeling potatoes and cutting onions was safe. No one died if he messed up. "You sure 'bout this?"

"You're ready to be a part of this platoon. In every way. See you bright and early tomorrow."

Warmth pooled in his chest. The LT believed in him. "I'll be there." His mouth went dry as soon as he spoke the words. There'd be no going back now.

"Oh, and Mitt?"

"Sir?"

"Why don't you go wash up?" The LT pressed his lips together.

Mitt lowered his nose to his underarm and sniffed. He exhaled a hearty sigh. Nothing but the manliest of men could smell that ripe. "Wash up?"

"It's your face."

Was the LT making a joke about the scar on his face? Mitt

didn't take him for being that kind of guy. Mitt narrowed his eyes. "What's wrong with my face?"

"It's..."

"Yeah?"

"Dirty."

Dirty? Mitt looked at the other soldiers. "So's everybody else's."

"Just trust me on this, alright?"

Mitt rubbed his face and felt crackles of dried mud flake off. He shrugged. "Okay, sir."

"Dismissed."

Mitt strode to the shaving station near the showers. Gripping the wood shelf, he peered into the mirror. Oh. Tracks of dried sweat cut through the mud layering his face, one thick line coming from each corner of his eyelids. Mitt grinned. He turned down his mouth and exaggerated a fake cry into the mirror. He looked like one of those crying clowns from the circus.

The door to the latrine swung open. Jasper, holding a bucket in each hand, jerked to a stop, water splashing over his boots. He gaped at Mitt.

"What you lookin' at?" Mitt put up a fist. "Scram."

"You need the chaplain, or..."

"What do you take me for? A sissy? Get outta here."

Jasper backed out the door, still eyeing Mitt until the door swung closed between them.

Mitt turned back to the mirror and made the face again. He froze in the middle of an especially ridiculous contortion. *What am I doing?*

He'd just wanted to see what it looked like to cry. He'd never cried, not even when his pop had kicked him to the streets. And if he could handle that without crying, he could handle leaving the kitchen and joining the war effort for real.

He turned the spigot and splashed water onto his skin. After he'd scrubbed every inch of his face, he glanced in the mirror again. *Now that's a face worth lookin' at.* He waggled his eyebrows.

He dipped his fingers in the water and flicked droplets onto his image in the mirror.

No more kitchen patrol, no more goofing off. It was time to get serious about this war business.

SEVENTEEN

A LEAP OF FAITH

June 1942
Clemson, South Carolina

Raymond stood beside Jimmie at the church's beribboned altar railing, trying to pay attention to his brother going on and on about leaving for his military training in the next few weeks. He glanced again toward the double wooden doors at the end of the aisle. At any moment, they should swing open and reveal Evelyn, bouquet in hand. At least, he hoped they would. Would she come? He'd worked awfully hard to get her to this point. The memory of her walking away from him at Christmas haunted him still.

Had she truly been able to let go of her fears? She'd only wanted to marry him after he'd come back and fought for her. He pushed down a twinge of guilt.

A few friends and relatives were scattered in the pews. Their two mothers were in the front row—his, with a smile as wide as her face, and Evelyn's, well, her mother had come, and that was as much as could be hoped for. His father, on the other hand, couldn't be bothered to do even that. It had been a whirlwind, pulling off a proper wedding with the 77th's move to Camp Pickett, Virginia, in two days' time, but he was certain there'd been enough notice for his dad to take the train from St. Simons. No matter how awkward the occasion would be for him, a father didn't miss his son's wedding.

Evelyn's father hadn't shown up either, not that they'd expected him. A pit formed in his stomach. Maybe Raymond would go off to war and leave her for good, just like she feared. Maybe like her father, Raymond would come home a wreck, unable to speak or love her like she deserved. She'd be miserable, and all because he'd taken her first *no* as a suggestion. She'd even put a pin in her plans to be a teacher until he went overseas.

"*Hello*?" Jimmie waved his hand in front of Raymond's face.

Raymond dragged his gaze back to his little brother. "Sorry. What was that?"

Eyes snapping with emotion, Jimmie gave a pointed look at the doors and then back to his brother. "Stop looking at those doors, Ray. Everyone's here who's going to be here."

Raymond's breath hitched. "You saw her?"

"I'm talking about Dad, dummy. 'Course Evelyn's here. Why wouldn't she be?"

If only Jimmie knew. "I'm not waiting on Dad."

Jimmie shook his head. "Still can't believe he didn't come."

"He sent a telegram with his best wishes this morning."

"How nice," Jimmie said in a flat voice.

"He hasn't seen Mom since the divorce, Jimmie. It would be hard for them."

"Mom would've put up with it for your sake."

Raymond grabbed Jimmie's shoulder. "Hey, thanks for being here. It means the world to me that you're walking Evelyn down the aisle."

"Speaking of..." Jimmie nodded toward the back of the church.

It was then that he saw it—the movement of a small bouquet of flowers through the cracked doors. Raymond's heart thumped. She'd come.

"Time to get you hitched." Jimmie padded away from Raymond over the plush red carpet to the back of the church.

A chair scraped against the wooden floor. The pastor's wife sat down at the piano to his right. The tinny strains of the wedding march filled the mostly empty room, and the doors at the back swung open.

Sunlight cut a path down the aisle. At the end of the beam stood Evelyn, her golden hair wreathed in a warm glow. Clutching a bouquet of white daisies, she gazed at him with a soft smile and stepped forward on Jimmie's arm.

It had seemed a dream before now, marrying her—a dream where he'd wake up without her arriving at the church as he waited. She had good cause not to show up, but still, she came. She made her way down the aisle, holding his gaze. The joy in her eyes eased his fear a little.

They arrived at last, and Jimmie let go of her. "Welcome to the family, sis."

She kissed his cheek. "Thank you, brother."

Jimmie's cheeks flamed. "Alright, get on with it." He left them and sat in the front pew beside their mother.

Evelyn slipped her small hand into Raymond's.

He wanted to tell her she was beautiful. That he loved her and would do everything he could to make her happy. But he'd say the only thing that really mattered to him in that moment. "You're here," he whispered.

"I'm here," she answered, squeezing his hand.

He scarcely heard the prayer before the minister turned to him. Raymond's heart beat fast and hard. Could he let her go through with it? Everything he'd ever wanted—a wife, a family of his own—was on the verge of coming true. He had everything to gain in marrying her, but if things went wrong, she'd bear the worst of it. How could he do this to her, knowing what she risked?

"Raymond, will you have this woman to be your wedded wife, to live together after God's ordinance in the holy estate of matrimony? Will you love her, comfort her, honor and keep her in sickness and in health, and forsaking all others, keep yourself only unto her, so long as you both shall live?"

A rebellion leaped up in him, swift and fierce. "I will."

A few more words, and she gave her own assent. There was no turning back now.

After the ceremony, their mothers were invited by the pastor to give the happy couple their first congratulations. Mrs. Noble hung back, deferring to Mother, who kissed Raymond's and Evelyn's cheeks with effusive exclamations of joy.

Evelyn turned to Mrs. Noble and wrapped an arm around her neck, giving her a quick peck on the cheek. Her mother only pulled away and nodded at Raymond, her eyes brimming with unshed tears. "Take care of her," she said in a tight voice.

"I will, Mrs. Noble. I promise." As solemn as an undertaker, he nodded once, underscoring his pledge.

Raymond left Evelyn's side and engulfed his brother in a hug. "You're still my favorite brother."

"Your only brother," Jimmie said.

"Can you believe I just got married today?" He pointed Jimmie in Evelyn's direction. "Now that right there is a beautiful woman."

"Alright, alright. Enough of that lovey-dovey stuff. Don't forget you promised to come back to visit Mother first chance you get, okay? I worry about her, with me leaving for training."

"Camp Pickett's only a four-hour drive from here. She'll get sick of us."

Evelyn approached them.

"Well, good luck with this one, Evelyn." Jimmie jerked a thumb toward Raymond. "You're gonna need it."

Evelyn slipped an arm around Raymond's waist and rested her head on his shoulder. "Now you tell me."

"You can't back out now," Raymond said, smiling and looking down at her.

Jimmie rolled his eyes. "Don't you two have somewhere to be?"

Yes, they did. "Ready?"

She nodded. "Ready as I'll ever be."

* * *

Camp Pickett, Virginia

Raymond carried Evelyn over the threshold and kicked the door closed with his foot. "Home, sweet home." He set her down on her feet gently.

"You sure you can't stay the night?" Without Raymond holding her, the darkness pressed in, cold and quiet.

He flipped the light switch. The room was empty, save for a bed stripped of linens and a washstand with a pitcher. "Hate leaving you here." His gaze traveled the empty room. "If I didn't have orders to report back tonight, I'd stay." He kissed her forehead. "I'll be back before you know it. Promise."

He could smuggle her into Camp Pickett in his duffel bag, but a honeymoon spent sleeping in the officers' barracks would be even worse than Evelyn staying by herself in this boarding house miles away from the 77th's new training ground. With time dwindling before the division left, Evelyn would follow Raymond as other Army wives followed theirs, staying in hotels and boarding houses and seeing their husbands every chance they got. At least they'd had one night together before coming to Virginia. Heat rushed to her face, remembering. "I'll be okay." She suffused her voice with a confidence she didn't feel.

She pulled him by the collar and pressed her lips to his, driving away any thoughts not having to do with how much she wanted to kiss him.

He enclosed her in his arms and kissed her hard. "What a honeymoon, huh?"

"I told you. I don't need one. I'm just happy we don't have to be separated just yet."

"I'll be right back." He left the room and came back carrying a trunk. Giving the room another once-over, he rubbed the back of his neck. "Sure you'll be alright? I didn't think to ask about blankets."

"Go. I'll figure it all out tomorrow."

He pulled her close. "Don't forget to lock up." He kissed her again and left, closing the door behind him.

She fell back onto the bare mattress, dress and all.

How had she gotten here? One day, she was dating Samuel —if you could even call it that—and the next, it seemed she was married. She'd set aside her test preparations in the whirl of events and informed Mr. Cabot she wasn't going to take him up on his offer after all. Raymond made her promise to come back to it, but for now, Evelyn had a reprieve.

She must've fallen asleep within seconds, because the next time she opened her eyes, midday sun streamed through the bare window. The room looked emptier than it had the night before, every nook and cranny exposed to light. She stretched her hand across the mattress, the space beside her blank and cold.

A knock sounded at her door. She glanced at her wrist-watch. *Noon already.* Who could possibly be visiting her when she knew nobody in the area?

The knock came again, this time multiplied into several brisk raps.

Evelyn dropped her feet to the floor and ran her fingers through her hair. "Just a moment."

She turned the key, cracking the door open a few inches. Two ladies, each with her own version of welcome on her face, stared back. A thin, raven-haired woman grinned widely and budged her way in. "I'm Thelma. We saw you walk in last night, but..." She halted. "Why, you poor dear! Where are your things?"

Evelyn's eyes darted from Thelma to the other woman. "My things?"

Thelma's friend smiled shyly at her. "I'm Dorothy," she said. Her blonde eyelashes and eyebrows disappeared against her pale skin. "Our husbands are with yours at the 77th."

Evelyn relaxed a little. "Oh. Well, hello. I'm Evelyn Nob—Sellers." She blushed at her stumble. "Our trunk is over there." She pointed to a wooden trunk beneath the window.

Thelma made a beeline toward it. "Where are your curtains?" she asked from the recesses of the trunk.

Evelyn blushed even harder. "I didn't think to bring any."

Thelma shushed her. "Don't you worry. You're in good hands now. Why, Dorothy is the best seamstress this side of the Ohio. Do you have any bedding?"

"We married in a rush with only a few days to prepare. I assumed the boarding house would have linens..." Should she have known to bring bedding? The two ladies stared at her, most likely appraising her capabilities as a wife. Only two days in and already failing.

Dorothy marched over to the window and measured it with her apron strings. "Isn't that just like a man, not to think of telling his wife these things?"

Thelma clucked. "I'll be right back. I have some extra bedding you can borrow until you get your own."

Evelyn exhaled the tension that had been building since Raymond left. The ladies' display of solidarity meant more to her in that moment than any borrowed blankets or sewn curtains would have.

Dorothy grabbed a broom and went to work sweeping the dust out of every corner. She chattered away as she worked, spilling her stories as if she'd known Evelyn for years. She and Thelma followed their husbands from camp to camp, renting rooms nearby at each training post and waiting for visits when training allowed, just as Evelyn planned to do.

"The ones with children stay back, of course. Thelma will have to return home soon," Dorothy said.

"But doesn't she want to stay?" Evelyn asked.

Thelma entered the room with her arms full of linens. She laughed a little. "Of course. I just want to be near my mother when the baby comes." She deposited her load on the bed and pulled out a pillowcase from the pile.

"Oh." Evelyn glanced down at Thelma's waist. "I didn't know."

"It takes a while for the first ones to show. Thelma here's still flat as a flapjack, lucky girl," Dorothy said.

Evelyn looked down at her own waist. She'd be happy if she didn't have to go back home anytime soon. She had little enough time as it was with Raymond. She went to one side of the bed and Thelma to the other. Together, they pulled the sheets smooth and stretched the coverlet.

The door creaked open again.

"Hello there, ladies. Can I steal my wife?" Raymond poked his head inside, a small bunch of freshly picked wildflowers in his hand.

Cheeks afire, Evelyn straightened. "I didn't think I'd see you this soon."

Dorothy leaned her broom against the wall and joined Thelma, who was already making her way to the door.

"We'll come by tomorrow and see how you're getting along." Thelma squeezed Evelyn's forearm. "Each of us has a room here, so holler if you need anything. One of us will come a-runnin'."

"Thank you, Thelma. Dorothy," Evelyn said.

The two women passed Raymond, smiling knowingly at him. Evelyn's blush deepened.

"Thanks for taking care of my wife." He turned and looked straight at Evelyn, emphasizing the word *wife*.

Her stomach fluttered.

"Mind if I stick around for the rest of the day?" he asked after the ladies disappeared into the hallway.

Evelyn laughed softly. "Oh, I suppose not." She leaned on the opposite side of the doorjamb.

He pulled her to him and kissed her.

"I missed you," she said, sighing against his mouth. "But why are you here?"

"Wade was tired of my mooning about and told me to take the afternoon off."

She took the flowers from his hand and carried them to the washstand. "I thought you said soldiers don't do things like take afternoons off," she said, arranging the flowers in the pitcher.

"We don't, but not everyone's arrived at Pickett yet. I don't expect I'll get any more breaks for a while."

"What did you have in mind?"

"Oh, lots of things."

She didn't miss the teasing note in his voice and pulled him into the room. "Well, let's not waste a minute."

EIGHTEEN

INTO THE SHADOWS

February 1944
Fort Pierce, Florida

They settled into a routine, and before long, the golden days of summer shifted to fall then faded into the gloomy gray of winter. Before Evelyn knew it, they were well into their second year of marriage. Raymond spent most Saturday nights with her, and on especially happy weekends, he'd get Fridays too. Then the division moved from camp to camp, and Evelyn followed, exchanging forest picnics for swimming in the ocean. The longer they went without news of him leaving, the more she had allowed herself to dream that enough time would pass that the Army wouldn't need the division at all. But with the buildup of Allies in England and the heavy losses in Tawara in the Pacific, it was getting harder to hold onto that hope.

One Saturday, Evelyn stood at the window staring unseeingly at the children playing a game of kickball in the street. Her fingers followed the line of wood separating the panes of glass, scraping the dried paint with her nails.

Raymond's boots clomped up the narrow wooden stairs.

She dropped her hand from the window and took a fortifying breath. She couldn't put it off any longer. He needed to know before one more week passed.

His footsteps stopped outside their door. The handle turned and creaked, but instead of the door swinging open and him rushing in with his usual fervor, the handle stopped. Why did he hesitate? She shifted her head to the side, listening. After another beat or two, the handle turned again, and she returned her gaze to the window. He entered the room, his steps approaching slowly, quietly. He snuck up behind her and placed his hands on her waist. He bent his head to nuzzle her neck. "Hello, sweet."

"Hi." She turned and wrapped her arms around him, and they stood there, holding onto each other. She concentrated on the steady thumping of his heart and the rise and fall of his chest. If only they could stay like this forever.

"How was your day?" Raymond asked against her hair.

"Hmm?"

"Your day. How was it?"

She opened her eyes and pulled back from him, sliding her hands to his waist and hooking her fingers through his belt loops. "Interesting."

"Mine too."

The look in his eyes made her heart skip a beat.

He pulled at her hand and dragged her to their makeshift table—his Army trunk with two pillows on the floor. On top of the trunk, Evelyn had placed a jar with stalks of dried lupine to brighten their temporary dwelling. The flowers sat on Thelma's embroidered potato sack beside other artifacts from their first months of marriage—sand dollars from the beaches around Fort Pierce, a smooth river rock from Virginia, and sparkling sand from Camp Hyder, Arizona, poured into a small bowl with a candle she lit whenever Raymond joined her for dinner.

"Is yours a good interesting or a bad interesting?" Raymond

sat down and leaned across the trunk, intertwining his hand with Evelyn's.

"A complicated interesting."

"Sounds like your interesting's a little more interesting than my interesting."

Evelyn smiled a little. "So, are you going to tell me or not?"

"You're not going to like it."

Her heart leaped into a frantic rhythm, his words like a starting pistol. Evelyn pulled her hand from Raymond's and sat back. "Then don't." It was too soon. Much too soon, especially now.

She scrambled to her feet and went back to the window.

He didn't come closer as she expected. She turned around and glanced at him. He stood behind her with his hands in his pockets, face half hidden in shadows. "We knew this was coming."

"I know." She went to him and folded herself in the safety of his chest once again. "Tell me."

"The division's moving to Hawaii. Soon."

"Will I be able to come?"

Raymond shook his head. "After jungle training, we're shipping off to—"

She put her fingers to his lips. "Don't say it."

He kissed her fingers. "Alright. I won't, but—"

"We're having a baby."

Raymond paled. He glanced at her waist with wide eyes. "We're... you're... but how do you know? How long until... you know..." He made a ridiculous downward motion with his hands, which she supposed indicated her giving birth.

Evelyn bit her bottom lip to keep from laughing. She'd never seen him so flustered. "Four months, maybe. I—I didn't know, not until Thelma put it together for me. I feel stupid, but Mama never talked with me about it."

He stood quiet for a moment, and she knew he was running

calculations in his head. It wouldn't take him long to arrive at the same conclusion she had. "I'll be gone."

Reaching for his hand, she placed it on her abdomen. "Meet your son."

"Or daughter."

"Or daughter." She moved her hand over his, and they stood there, connecting with the life growing within her.

"I know the timing's hard, but it'll all work out."

She bit back a retort. How could he be so confident? *He* wasn't the one who'd be left on his own. He wasn't the one who had no idea how to do this. "How do you know?"

"Because it has to. I'll make sure of it. It's not ideal, but we're having a baby." He picked her up in a bear hug, and her feet left the ground, eliciting a breathless laugh from her. He set her down.

"How do you feel?"

"Hungry."

"I'm serious. I don't want you going through this alone." He took her hands and pulled her down to sit on their mattress. "I've been thinking a lot about this, ever since I found out two minutes ago..."

She shook her head and laughed.

"What if you moved in with my mother?"

Evelyn sobered. For all the practicalities of this conversation, it made an unclear future all the more real. "I suppose it's worth considering."

"Not just considering. I know how hard it is with your own mom. It'll be even harder for you if you have to tiptoe around her at the same time you're dealing with me being gone. Besides, with Jimmie gone for training, Mother will be lonely. It could be good for the both of you." He rubbed the back of his neck. "I admit, it would take a load of worry off my back. But if you want to live with your own mother, just say the word."

Evelyn turned the idea over in her mind, imagining what it

would be like to live in such a warm and cheery home with her mother-in-law. The tension in her stomach loosened a little. "Do you think she'll have me?"

"Nothing would make her happier." Raymond tucked a strand of hair behind her ear. "I don't want you worrying. Everything's going to work out just fine. We're going to have ourselves a little baby, and when I come home, we'll be the happiest three peas in a pod."

She moved into his embrace, but with her face hidden in the cradle of his shoulder, her smile dropped. She'd known this day would come. She'd known from the moment he showed up at the diner, smiling and perfect, ready to fight for another chance.

It had been wonderful, just as he'd promised. They'd loved each other with all the fervency and elation that came from the wonder of being together. But the longer they went without hearing any concrete plans from the Army, the more she'd begun to hope. It had seemed daring to make plans at first—wrong, even—but somewhere along the way, dreaming turned into believing, and she'd been laughingly unprepared when the time finally came. Unprepared and pregnant.

"How long do we have?" Evelyn tucked her hands between the wall of his chest and hers.

"A few weeks. Days, maybe."

She pushed away from him and pasted on her bravest smile. "The sun should be setting over the bay. Why don't we go and watch it?" She held out her hand to him. She'd known she'd taken a chance when she'd said yes. The time had come to see where her leap of faith would land them.

NINETEEN

ALL THEY HAVE IN THE BRONX ARE FIRE HYDRANTS

July 1944
Guam

The sun shimmered off the water in waves of distorted light, hypnotizing the men staring toward Guam, an American territory captured by the Japanese. The 77th would be joining Marines and soldiers already knocking down Japan's ring of outer defense, island by bloody island, life after precious life—men once bearers of light now ash scattered across foreign sands. After two years of training, the 77th was finally at war.

Raymond stood at the rails without touching the painted gray metal brought to smelting point by the fury of the sun. It had taken two weeks to travel from Hawaii on the transport ship, every day hotter than the last. The first night at sea, Raymond had learned better than to sleep below deck. He'd have baked in his bedroll if he hadn't gone topside to escape the trapped heat below. Now they waited in the waters of Agat Bay, melting in a floating oven.

He'd last seen Evelyn over four months ago, the roundness in her belly barely showing. A hint of new life. Of hope. And now he was here, staring at the billows of smoke rising from within the island's jungle. She was due any day now. Maybe had given birth to their baby already. Was Evelyn okay? It should be illegal, carrying a double portion of fear into battle.

"What I wouldn't give for a cold glass of pineapple juice at the Royal Hawaiian," Walter said, scratching the prickly heat rash traveling up his neck.

"Juice?" Mitt snapped. "What are you? Seven?"

Raymond closed his eyes, imagining the cold, tangy juice pouring down his throat.

"Who says a grown man can't like juice?" Walter asked.

"And who signed off on us leaving Hawaii just to sit here and fry? Some pudgy full bird in his office is my guess," Mitt said. "You got any scoop on when we're getting off this thing, LT?"

Raymond's daydream of swimming in waterfalls of ice-cold pineapple juice evaporated at the sound of his name. "Your guess is as good as mine."

"Can't wait to get off this tin can." Walter blinked through the sweat dripping into his eyes.

Mitt jutted his chin toward Guam. "I'd rather be here sweating like a sinner in a church pew than over there in that mess."

Raymond couldn't disagree with that. They'd all heard the tales from Japanese prisoner of war camps—stories of unspeakable acts done to those they captured. Europe seemed a safer bet from where Raymond stood, but maybe that was just because it would get him out of the Pacific and away from an enemy he couldn't understand.

Colonel Smith strode to the front of the battalion. The murmur of voices quieted, leaving only the sound of flags snapping in the wind and the ship's engines groaning beneath them.

The colonel's gaze traveled across the men, who were shoulder to shoulder, packed like sardines. He mopped the back of his neck with a handkerchief and folded it in a neat square, slowly creasing each edge before placing it back in his pocket.

The nervous gesture unsettled Raymond.

"Let's get to it. Recon elements report harassing activity—rifle pits, trenches, and barbed wire enforce enemy beach defense, with their mobile artillery and tanks in support. Mop up once ashore and push east toward Mount Alifan. Repulse enemy patrols and clean out caves as you go. Our ships and planes have worked round the clock to soften things up, but we won't know how successful it's been till we're on the ground. No one wants another Saipan."

No, indeed. The *banzai* charge in Saipan killing the last of thirty thousand Japanese soldiers had clarified what the enemy would resort to, even in the face of sure defeat: the fight would continue until every last Japanese man, woman, and child died in the effort, along with countless Americans in collateral damage.

"I must inform you that there's been one small change to our plans." The colonel paused for a moment. "We won't have the amphibious vehicles promised to us. You'll be taking Higgins boats to shore instead."

Raymond exchanged glances with Mitt. Higgins boats wouldn't be able to navigate the perimeter of coral surrounding the island, as far as he could guess.

"Best case and in the highest of tides, the boats will have a clearance of just two feet to get us within wading distance. Worst case, and likely, in my opinion, is if we have a delay. The boats won't get over the coral and you'll have to swim to shore with the weight of your gear on your back."

Raymond closed his eyes for a moment. Even the best-case scenario held the potential for disaster.

Mitt cursed under his breath.

"What a crock," Walter said. "Worst case is a Jap slug between your eyes."

Raymond elbowed him in the ribs. "Stow it, Private."

"You think we'll have to swim like he said?" Mitt asked.

"If we do, we'll be okay. We all got our swim training, remember?"

Mitt didn't answer.

The colonel glanced from face to face. "I've been with you from the beginning. I've watched you transform into a superior fighting force with every possible advantage of training. Tomorrow, you'll show the world the Army fights just as hard as those leathernecks do."

"Yes, sir!"

Raymond's throat clogged with the weight of what was to begin tomorrow. What had started at Fort Jackson would find fruition at daybreak.

"I'm proud to send every last one of you into battle. Be ready to disembark at 0400, sharp. Oh, and don't forget to keep your *sirs* and salutes in your pockets while on the island—you don't want to put a target on your leaders. Fill your canteens, take your Atabrine, and give 'em hell, boys. That is all. Chaplain?"

Chaplain Taylor stepped to the front, and everyone bowed their heads. "Yea though we walk through the valley of the shadow of death, we will fear no evil..."

The next morning, the men climbed over the side of their transport ship down nets to the waiting Higgins below. One by one, boats packed with platoons roared through Agat Bay en route to Guam's shore.

"A three-hour late start." Raymond's mouth settled into a grim line. True to Colonel Smith's prediction, the go-command had been delayed for several hours, and the low tide would prevent the boats from getting over the coral. They'd have to wade or even swim to shore over coral and shell craters while keeping their weapons above water as best they could.

"Looks like we ain't getting door-to-shore service," Kalberer said.

Thirty men from Raymond's platoon crammed the interior of their boat. Each carried their rifle, a machete, two bandoleers of ammunition, grenades, a belt of ammo, an entrenchment tool, two canteens of water, a full battle pack with rations, and a gas mask. Some also carried tools of their specialty: radios and phone line reels, mortars, and machine guns. The weight of it all was enough to pull a man underwater.

Past Guam's placid beach line, shells exploded on the slopes of Mount Alifan and columns of smoke rose deep within the jungle surrounding its base. Thoughts assailed Raymond of Evelyn and their coming baby, of his promises and assurances of his return. *Please let this go off without a hitch. Please help me lead my men and get us out of here alive.* He mouthed the petitions over and over as the island pressed closer into view.

They peered over the side of the Higgins as soldiers closer to shore disembarked from their boats and struggled through the treacherous, coral-choked waters. In the distance, a soldier was sucked under the water by the weight of his gear. Too far to help, Raymond and his men could do nothing but watch, knowing their turn in the surf would come within moments.

Raymond glanced at Mitt, whose face was ashen and still as stone. "You okay?"

"Fine," Mitt said in a gruff voice.

"You're green."

"I—I..." He paused. "I can't swim, LT."

What a time for jokes. "C'mon. What's wrong?"

"I—can't—swim."

"What do you mean, you can't *swim*?" Raymond's last word dropped like a thunderclap. "You were trained in Hawaii just like the rest of us."

"If you hadn't noticed..." Mitt gestured wildly to the burning island in the background and the men churning in the water in front of them. "This ain't Hawaii, LT!"

Raymond shot him a look of fire. "You wanna try that again?"

"Maybe I forgot."

Raymond took in Mitt's sickly face. Mitt didn't forget. He was afraid. Raymond gentled his voice. "You can wade, can't you?"

Mitt studied the sea again. Raymond willed his gaze not to follow Mitt's to the place where the soldier had just slipped beneath the surface moments before.

Before Mitt could answer, the boat slammed into something hard, jerking the men forward. Raymond grasped Mitt's arm. Then came the ear-shriveling screech of metal being scraped. The boat listed to one side.

Raymond yelled, "Everyone off! Now!"

The engine cut. The chaos in the water spilled into the boat, with soldiers securing their gear before climbing out like rats fleeing a sinking ship.

Mitt turned panic-stricken eyes to Raymond. "We're too far out!"

"Get in the water!"

Mitt's arms shook trying to secure his chin strap.

Raymond swatted Mitt's hands aside and tightened the strap for him. He shoved Mitt toward the side of the boat where others scrambled over the edge. "Don't forget to hold the gunwale before you drop."

Raymond checked the progress of the rest, and when he turned back around, Mitt was nowhere to be seen. Raymond bent over the side and peered into the water. There, several feet below, Mitt flailed about, choking on mouthfuls of water, trying to stay afloat. Raymond cupped his mouth. "Take off your pack!"

Mitt's head bobbed under the surface.

Fear gripped Raymond's heart and jerked it into his throat. He disentangled himself from his gear and dropped it to the floor of the Higgins. Vaulting over the side, he plunged into the water. He gasped. The water shocked every nerve and muscle to attention. *Move!* he commanded his limbs. He swam over and released the private from the weight of his gear. Hooking an arm around him, he pulled Mitt's head above water. He couldn't let a man go down like this on their first day of action. "Hold on! I'll tow you in!" Raymond shouted over the din.

With an out-of-his-mind soldier clamped onto him like a barnacle, Raymond struggled to stay afloat.

"I can't do it, Parson!" Mitt slipped under.

Raymond yanked him up once again. "Your mama gonna like getting a letter from me?" Better to make him mad than let him carry on like this and kill the both of them. "Dear Mrs. Solomon, I regret to inform you..." Mitt clambered higher up Raymond's back, pulling them both beneath the surface. Raymond strained upward, grunting with the effort. He broke the surface and spit out water. "That your idiot son... drowned... before he ever fired a shot." A wave crashed over Raymond, slapping him in the face and knocking them forward.

"I'm gonna die!"

Raymond's arms cramped. His legs were turning to jelly. He didn't know how much longer he could stay afloat with Mitt attached to his back. "Kick your legs, for the love of Pete."

Mitt finally let go and paddled like a fish wriggling to get off the hook.

Raymond swam to him. "Stay with me. I'll pull you up if I see you go under." Mitt jerked his head up and down, his eyes still wide with fright. Together, they moved toward the shore. "If I recall, I'd signed off on your swimming."

"I faked it," Mitt said, a growl in his voice.

The private was mad. Good. Maybe now Mitt would forget

that he had forgotten how to swim. "You can't fake swimming. You either can"—a wave crashed into his mouth, and Raymond spit out the salty water—"or you can't."

Solid ground bumped against his boots. With one great, final push, he strained out of the water. It was like trying to pull a suction cup off the ground straight up, and Raymond and Mitt plopped onto the beach with synchronous groans.

Heavy padding of boots sounded behind them. "Off the beach, boys." Oliver ran up to them, half-crouched, and jerked both Raymond and Mitt to their feet. "Move to the tree line!"

They stumbled through bullet-pockmarked sand into the safety of the trees. Mitt and Raymond collapsed to the ground, sucking air from the effort and surrounded by the rest of the men in their platoon.

"Well, that went about as well as expected," Oliver said between heavy pants. He bent over, hands on his knees and his head lifted to face the soldiers littered about him on the jungle floor.

"Well, Parson, now's your chance," Mitt said.

"What're you talking about?"

"You said it yourself—no one cares about swearing when things get hot."

Raymond rolled his eyes.

"You're not tempted? Not even a little bit?"

"Shut up, Solomon."

"Alrighty then. I'll say enough for the both of us." Mitt let loose with a stream of curses under his breath so foul Raymond blinked. "Lighten up, LT. That steam'll burn ya if you don't let it out every once in a while."

Kalberer pulled Raymond to his feet. "Glad you made it."

"Everyone accounted for?" Raymond's eyes roamed over the soggy crew.

"They're all here."

"Injuries?"

"You and Mitt got the worst of it."

Raymond reached a hand to Mitt, still sprawled out on the ground below him. "You okay?"

"Am I okay?" Mitt ignored Raymond's hand and jumped to a crouch in one fluid movement. He stood, wiping the sand from his pants. "Never better." That old cocksure grin was back on his face.

"Solomon..."

Mitt shrugged. "Hey, all they got in the Bronx are fire hydrants. Can't expect me to be aces in water deeper than my boot tops. I owe ya one, Parson."

"You bet you do, and I'm gonna save it for something real good."

"I'll see if I can scrounge any spare gear for the two of us since ours is swimming with the fishies." Mitt thumped Raymond on the back and strolled toward a huddle of men.

The dirty dog. Raymond didn't know whether to laugh or put Mitt to work digging latrines. Not that they had time for that. "Hope you haven't forgotten how to shoot too, Solomon!"

TWENTY
JIMMIE GOES TO WAR

July 1, 1944

Dear Jimmie,

Hope this letter finds you safe. All is well here. Susan is married now. Home is lonesome without her, but she and her new husband spend every Friday night with us playing bridge. He just completed his training as a pilot with the Army Air Corps and will head to the Pacific soon. He's a smart and accomplished young man, and as a brother-in-law of sorts, he could be an ally if needed. Write him and welcome him to the family.

I've enclosed five dollars for incidentals and stamps. I assume you don't have enough money to post your letters to me as I haven't received one from you yet. I'd pass on the updates your brother sends, but he reports that the two of you exchange letters regularly.

Best wishes,
Dad

* * *

Tinian Island

Jimmie slung his bag onto the top bunk. The moment his arm arced over his head, pain shot down his spine. As quickly as it came, the pain passed. He exhaled and stretched his torso by twisting from side to side. He'd have to remember to take it easy. The days of travel from their training grounds in Honolulu to Tinian Island had done a number on his back. Although he'd scammed the Navy into letting him become a gunner despite his previous back injury, Jimmie didn't have to be stupid about it. His back rarely bothered him anymore. A twinge here and there, but he was fine enough to man a machine gun in a plane.

He stepped back from the bunk. Hands on hips, he surveyed his new kingdom: wet socks slung over the rungs of bunk bed ladders, mosquito netting drooping into frothy puddles on the floor, and boots lying beside each bed with scrape marks in the caked-on mud showing each man's half-hearted attempt at cleaning them. The floor was made of broken-up ammo boxes laid down on crushed coral, an uneven foundation for the oversized tent meant to house Jimmie's crew.

He stretched with one foot on the bottom rail to lay out his bedroll on the top bunk's plank board. Grinning, he climbed the bamboo ladder and spread out on his very own seven-by-three-foot rectangular oasis in the middle of the topsy-turvy Pacific. At least it was bigger than his vacation home—the waist turret of a PB4Y-1, the Navy's version of the B-24 Liberator.

Good thing being a cook hadn't worked out. This was the most fun he'd had in ages.

The path to victory depended on those disaster-prone planes. Luckily for the Allies, there never seemed to be a shortage of men foolhardy enough to crew them. Not even the bomber's nickname of "The Flying Coffin" gave Jimmie pause. The more time he spent training in the gunner's seat, the more concerned he should've been by the number of mishaps the plane had, but he wasn't.

When he'd arrived at the training grounds, he'd studied the plane from nose to tail, listening carefully to his instructors and making notes he'd review in his head when he lay on his cot back in the barracks. For the first time in his life, Jimmie worked toward something all on his own, without Raymond waiting in the wings to get him out of any scrapes or his dad breathing down his neck. No one in the Navy questioned whether he had what it took—they just expected him to do it.

He pulled out a thick packet of letters from his bag. Mother wrote like clockwork, and so did the girl he had on hold back home. She'd let him kiss her in the back row of the picture house every Friday night. Even his dad had written, but that was just because he had to. Dad's letters, mostly unopened, went under his pillow with the rest of them.

On the nearest pole holding up the roof of canvas, he pinned a picture of his mother and one of him and Raymond lounging on the steps of their home. Raymond's arm draped lazily across Jimmie's shoulders. He'd smiled for the camera, while Jimmie looked up at his older brother.

Jimmie pulled out a wrinkled and worn copy of *The Fighting Yank* comic book. Across the front was his brother's compact script: *Be like Yank. Show 'em how it's done. Love, Raymond.* The cover showed Yank, the hero, lounging on Hirohito's throne with debilitated Japanese soldiers littered about him in distress. Yank had singlehandedly brought WWII to a close with one wild battle. Jimmie ran his finger over the sunken ridges of his brother's signature and placed the comic book in his back pocket.

Tonight, they went on their first mission. He wasn't stupid enough to think Yank would swoop in and save the day now that they were in the war for real. Jimmie would have to do that all on his own. And he would. He'd shoot down every red-sunned flyer in his sights and come home in one piece. So would Raymond, if Jimmie had any part in it.

He glanced at his watch and leaped down from the bunk. Time to head to the runway and meet up with the crew. They flew in less than an hour.

At the runway, the painted girl on the side of their plane greeted him with her perpetual wink. Ensign Schnepp, their bombardier, was peering into *Dirty Gerty*'s bomb doors.

Jimmie sidled next to him. "What's it going to be? Search and rescue? Recon? Bombing run?"

"Just your regular old night patrol."

"Fine by me." From what they'd been told, night patrol was a wild card. There'd be no telling what would happen.

Captain Jensen and his co-pilot, Paskett, radio operator, Bobby Chatham, ball turret gunner, Charles "Jack" Jacquette, and Norman, the gunner opposite of Jimmie in the waist of the plane, trickled onto the runway, joining Jimmie and Schnepp.

"Enjoy her shine while it lasts. It won't be pretty for long." Jensen slapped a hand on the plane's fuselage. "Just a quick pre-flight briefing and then up we go, alright?"

That was one good thing about Jensen—he wasn't a nag. As he'd told them before, if his crew members didn't know their jobs after a year of training, nothing could fix that level of stupid.

The rest of the crew of twelve arrived. After the briefing, Jimmie climbed inside the plane and headed to his starboard station. Satisfied that all was as it should be, he went to his seat behind and below the cockpit for takeoff and buckled in. His stomach fizzed, just like it did on Christmas mornings.

The plane's engines roared to life.

Jimmie grasped the cylinder head washer he'd put on his dog tag chain. The washer's once-sharp edges were worn down from seven years of wearing it. He'd carried it with him ever since the day Raymond dropped it in his hand, the circle of metal linking him to the best friend he'd ever had. If anything might bring him luck, it would be this.

The plane rumbled and creaked down the runway.

It hefted into the air. Jimmie dug his boots into the floor, pushing against the pressure sucking him into the seat. A concerning *ping* ricocheted throughout the cabin.

The bone-jarring rattle settled at last, and he relaxed his feet on the floor. Nothing seemed amiss after the earlier *ping*—no missing panels or a dangling catwalk. He dropped the washer back to his chest and, after unbuckling his seatbelt, headed to his station. Just as he'd been taught for months, he put his hands on the Browning's handles and swiveled the gun perpendicular to the plane, training his eyes upon the sea.

The wind whistled through the fuselage, tangling his hair, the vibration of the plane lulling him into a trance. "Where are you in all of this, Ray?" he whispered, scanning the murky depths. Last he heard, the 77th had landed in Guam. The thought of Raymond being that close to danger made him want to vomit.

The only downside to night patrol was how much time he had to think.

His thoughts meandered to Dad's letters, safe under his pillow back on Tinian. Odd that Dad kept writing, with no responses from Jimmie. He pushed down the niggle of guilt he'd been fighting since he'd seen the letters earlier that day. He'd write Dad back when he had something to say. It wouldn't matter that Jimmie hadn't become a pilot if he became a bona fide war hero instead.

TWENTY-ONE

BAPTISM IN GUAM

July 1944
Guam

Raymond sat on the jungle floor with his boots beside him, twisting his socks and wringing out every drop of water that he could. "Alright, Kalberer. Tell me what we're dealing with."

"The only real problem is lack of ammo and a few water-logged weapons. We can make do with the rest that we're missing."

"Like?"

"Canteens, rations, e-tools, a few helmets..." Kalberer shrugged. "Full battle packs went down, sir."

"HQ's working on resupply. Put men without helmets at the back of any movements." It wasn't even 1400, and he was ready to call it a night. Almost everything they needed to fight lay at the bottom of Agat Bay, stripped by greedy waves and jagged coral fingers. They didn't even have a radio, and without one, they'd be as good as a plane with blackout curtains hanging in the windows. "Benjamin? See if the cap has an extra radio."

"You got it, LT." Benjamin disappeared through the thick vegetation.

Out of the dense jungle rose Mount Alifan and the rolling land of its foothills. Up there, the 305th fought with the Marines to capture the mount, while the 306th—Raymond's battalion—had orders to relieve the Marines across the beachhead. If all went according to plan, they'd spread out in linked formations and push the Japanese off the island, each company in its own sector.

Benjamin returned with a SCR-536 handie-talkie radio. Mitt followed close behind, a hefty portable flamethrower strapped to his back, a couple of helmets dangling from each hand, and bandoleers of ammo draped around his neck.

Raymond finished tying his bootlaces and stood. "You two are a sight for sore eyes."

Mitt set the bulky flamethrower on the ground. "Couldn't get them to cough up more than this."

Raymond lifted the ammunition from Mitt's neck. "We'll get by. What's the situation at company, Benjamin?"

"About the same across the board. Everyone's scrambling for gear."

"Take the flamethrower, Oliver." If anyone could handle the hefty contraption, it was Oliver. The sergeant had tree trunks for legs and sledgehammers for arms.

"Yes, sir."

Raymond spoke louder for the rest of his men to hear. "We'll push to Alifan, mopping up as we go." He just had to get to the end of the day with all his men alive. *All you can do is your best and leave the rest to God's keeping,* Chaplain Taylor had said. Well, it was time to find out if his best was good enough. "Be on the lookout for enemy patrols. Scouts out."

"You heard 'im. Move out, Walter, Jasper," Kalberer said. "The rest of you, wedge formation."

The men straggled farther and farther apart in the virgin

jungle, tripping over the forked goat's foot vine looping in and out of the ground. Red blooms from wild hibiscus trees known as *pågu* peeked through the dense foliage, surprising splashes of color in an otherwise unvarying blanket of green. They hacked at vines as thick as forearms with their machetes while muffled explosions and pops from nearby firefights drifted through the impenetrable tangle of *åkgak* trees and their sword-shaped fronds. Sunlight disappeared in the tangle. Hemmed in by the suffocating profusion, they could only follow the upward slope of jungle floor leading to the mountain and hope they wouldn't get lost.

All at once, light broke through the canopy in stabbing streams of brilliance. The murky jungle gave way to a field of rolling grassland punctuated by trees and shrubs, with a coconut grove just beyond it.

At Raymond's nod, Jasper moved into the field, keeping cover in the scrub. With weapon at the ready, Walter stayed at the edge and scanned the landscape for enemy movement. In cautious, quiet steps, Jasper continued across, and Walter followed at a distance. Jasper reached the coconut grove and gave a forward signal to Walter, who in turn motioned to Raymond.

One by one, the soldiers crept into the field.

A low groan emerged from the sound of distant firefights. A tank? Raymond signaled his men to a halt. He lowered his hand, and they crouched in the tall grass.

A full minute passed in quiet.

Raymond took a cautious step forward. The rest of his men followed suit, inching their way closer to the grove.

A plane roared overhead with a hail of bullets. The platoon dove to the ground.

"It's one of ours!" Mahony yelled.

"What?" Raymond glanced at the sky. The plane was

turning around for another run at them. Oliver was right. One of their own planes was strafing them.

Oliver grabbed the signal panels and ran into the open field, waving at the plane as if he could take flight himself.

The pilots must've received the message because the firing stopped. The plane flew past them and over the trees.

Raymond grabbed the sergeant by the collar, dragging him down to the ground. "You almost got yourself killed. But thanks. You saved our bacon."

"Enough to earn your Lucky Strikes?"

One of the perks of being an officer: better cigarettes in your rations. "You bet."

Walter gave the *all-clear*, and Raymond stood. "Anybody need a medic?"

"We're okay, LT," Kalberer said.

"Move out, then."

Hours passed without sight of the Japanese. By the time the waning sun dipped closer to the horizon, Raymond was almost ready to throw flares and draw the enemy out of its hiding place.

He spotted a cave ahead—a half-hidden crag in a cliff they'd have missed if they stepped any farther. It might've been an ambush if they had.

On Raymond's command, Oliver led the way up the hill to the rocky slit, while Peach and Martinelli trained their rifles on the opening.

Allen pulled the pin from a grenade and lobbed it into the hole. He scrambled back just before the grenade exploded, and Peach and Martinelli fired their weapons into the cave.

The enemy fired back from the bowels of the cavern.

"Return fire!" Oliver pointed his flamethrower and filled the hollow with a fiery stream.

Three blazing Japanese soldiers leaped outside.

Raymond startled. He didn't know what he'd expected, but

it wasn't the enemy screaming in agony. In training, they'd acted out the fight, but this was real. He was at war. He was leading men in battle and those men Oliver routed from the cave—the enemy—were dying. Shots rang out from his soldiers' weapons. He flinched. *Dead*, he amended.

On his command, men were dead. He bit the inside of his cheek until he tasted metal. The Japanese were the ones who'd started this when they'd bombed Pearl Harbor. No, it started earlier, with their torment of the Chinese and any peoples they deemed the weaker. And only when enough of the Japanese were killed could everyone go back to how their lives used to be. It was just the way it had to be. It didn't mean it changed who he was. He would go home, enjoy being a husband and a dad, and forget all this ever happened.

He motioned his men forward. It was almost dark, and night was when the Japanese did their dirtiest work. They moved on, and just as the light was fading, they arrived in a pocket of trees big enough for them to bed down for the night.

Raymond signaled them close. "Solomon? Work on defensive measures. Make do with what you have. You'll make your own trench right there, at the opening of the trees. The rest, two to a trench, one on watch while the other sleeps. Stay in those holes till sunup."

Two by two, his men branched out and laid down their gear. Without Mitt, Benjamin was left without his usual partner. Raymond turned to Benjamin. "It's you and me tonight. Get to digging."

Raymond stuck his shovel into the earth, and it scraped against something hard. He stooped and clawed at the dirt with his fingers. Five inches under the mud, he found a layer of coral and limestone. Just great. How would they get the trenches deep enough for protection? Raymond hit the coral with the side of his shovel and made a crack big enough to work at with his entrenchment tool. In time, he and Benjamin had a hole big enough to cover them to their shoulders. It would work if they crouched.

They climbed in just as deepest dark descended in the jungle. Raymond pulled a leaf from his pocket and leaned forward. "Here," he whispered.

Benjamin took Raymond's offering, a question in his eyes.

Raymond mimed opening a book and putting the leaf inside. "For your book."

Thanks, Benjamin mouthed. He pulled the book from his trouser pocket and carefully placed the leaf between its pages.

The moon was a narrow sliver, bright enough so the trench mates could see each other but not much more than that.

A trailing eerie green glow lit his men's faces from flashes of light blooming and arcing in the distance. The Japanese were out there, using flares to find Americans lying low under the cover of night.

A strange bird warbled somewhere beyond them. Another soon joined it. The first bird answered. They weren't like any birds Raymond had heard before, but then again, everything was different out here. The birds sounded almost... human. The hairs on Raymond's neck stood on end.

"Got to pee," Mahony whispered across the dark.

"Stay down," Raymond whispered.

It was too late. Mahony had already crawled out of his trench.

"Get back!" Beads of sweat dripped down Raymond's spine.

Something rustled in the grass just outside the perimeter.

Mahony dove back into his hole.

A glimmer undulated in the pitch black.

"Hey. You boys." A heavily accented voice spoke from the darkness.

Raymond's hand tightened on his weapon.

The undulation became a shadow, creeping toward them. "I American. No shoot. A-okay. Coca-Cola. Wash-ing-ton."

The clearing erupted in fire, and the shadow dropped.

"Ceasefire!" Raymond yelled.

The platoon's firing stuttered and slowed, halting within seconds.

An enemy grenade exploded ten yards away. Raymond gripped his weapon so tightly his fingers locked into position. A drop of sweat hung from the end of his nose. Every impulse screamed at him to wipe it, but he forced himself to leave it alone.

A shadow materialized from the trees, then another. One by one, Japanese soldiers crossed the platoon's perimeter. Five, maybe six soldiers. They were so close and the night so dark, Raymond could only pray the rest of his platoon's training kicked in when they saw what he did.

Three sounds rang out, so muddled together Raymond couldn't determine what happened first: the sound of surprise, the thump, or the grunt.

Yelling Japanese soldiers rushed the trenches.

"Jap in the hole!" Mitt shouted. There was a sickening crack of a rifle butt hitting flesh.

"D'you get him?" Raymond shouted over the noise.

"He's down," Mitt said. "No, wait." A shot rang out. "Now I got 'im."

Walter lobbed a grenade over Raymond's head. Distinctly American curses punctuated the explosion.

"Hold grenades!" Raymond yelled. It was too dark to be throwing them without having a good idea of where they'd land.

Enemy movements ceased. Were they all dead or had they vanished into the trees? No one in the platoon made a sound. No one moved a muscle, not even as the night gave way to deep orchid and the lavender-tinged bronze of early morning.

TWENTY-TWO

THE LITTLE HOUSE ON GUERRY STREET

March 1944
Florence, South Carolina

Evelyn stayed on the wharf and waved Raymond off until his ship faded into the hazy line between sky and sea. She then cried on the train all the way from California to South Carolina and collapsed, weeping, into Sarah's arms at the depot.

Sarah slid anxious glances toward her throughout their drive to her home on Guerry Street. She wouldn't let Evelyn carry her suitcase and commanded her to leave the trunk until tomorrow, when a friend would come and help them move it into the house. Evelyn settled into the boys' room, taking Raymond's bed, of course, and lay there, numb and buzzing, her face swollen and eyes red. When Sarah came in to check on her, she pulled off Evelyn's shoes, put a pillow under her legs, and turned out the light without a word.

The next morning, Evelyn skulked to the kitchen.

"Good morning."

Evelyn jumped.

There, at the kitchen table, the older woman sat, rag curls wrapped in a scarf and her hands encircling a mug with steam rising from it. "How'd you sleep?"

Evelyn rubbed her hands over her slightly rounded abdomen. "Well enough for a pregnant lady." But it hadn't been just that. She could hardly sleep being in Raymond's old room, thinking of him writing his high school essays at that desk in the corner, starting his habit of sliding his shoes under the bed, leaning out the window beside Jimmie to have those spitting contests Raymond had told her about. This house was so full of him, Evelyn couldn't tell if it comforted her or made their separation that much more painful.

"Have you and Raymond decided on any names?"

"Arthur Raymond, if it's a boy, and Mary, for a girl."

"Those are fine names." Sarah took a sip of her coffee and eyed Evelyn above the rim of her cup. "Do you want to call your mother?"

Evelyn shook her head. "We haven't talked in ages." But neither had Evelyn called her. A twinge of guilt silenced her from saying more.

"I'm sure she'd want to hear from you. Why, she's close enough, she could drive up for a visit."

"I don't think so."

"Raymond didn't tell me what happened between you two. Only that it was hard. I didn't ask any questions, either, but you might be surprised how a baby can be a bridge between people." Sarah's gentle expression soothed any offense Evelyn might have taken to the correction.

Evelyn ran her hand up and down her robe belt. Maybe she should give Mama a call. "Alright, I'll give it a try."

Sarah directed her to the hallway. The telephone sat in a rounded nook in the wall with a wooden ledge, and just below it was a chair and a side table with a pencil and a notepad.

She dialed the number and lowered herself into the chair. It rang and rang. Evelyn picked up the pencil and drew a flowering vine around the paper's edge. By the time Evelyn drew a swing extending from the vine, Mama picked up.

"Noble residence."

"Mama, it's me. Evie." Silence met her on the other end. "Are you there?"

"Where are you callin' from?"

"I'm in Florence. With Sarah. Raymond's left."

There was another long pause. "Are you comin' home then?"

"I'm having a baby."

"Oh, Evie." The chastisement in her voice was unmistakable.

"I just think it'd be easier to—"

"—there's no room—"

"I wasn't asking." Evelyn blinked back tears. "Do you think we might see you?"

"Sounds like you don't need anybody else."

Evelyn wound the telephone cord around her finger so tight the tip of her finger pounded.

"Raymond was worried about his mother being alone with Jimmie gone. I'm helping her just as much as—" She closed her mouth. Why was she explaining herself? Mama had just told her there was no room for her and the baby. "Well, you know where to find me if you want to see us."

The line went dead.

Evelyn held out the receiver again and stared at it.

The child in her womb kicked and dragged its heel under Evelyn's ribcage. She dropped the handset back into its cradle and laid her hand on her stomach. The baby kicked again, and for a moment, Evelyn connected with the life growing within her, hand to heel separated by just dress and skin.

Like a slap of an ocean wave, it hit her. She was going to be a mother.

Her breath hitched. Cold swept over her. The room swirled and righted again.

What did she know of being a mother?

Mama had been loving until tragedy hit. Though she'd always been strict, she hadn't been stingy with her affection and had always listened to Evelyn's rambling without too much impatience. She'd even sewn Evelyn a new apron every year, the progression of styles and fabric matching Evelyn's changing interests. The day Daddy left was the last time Evelyn could remember being held by her. When Evelyn returned from her aunt's four years later, Mama was someone else altogether. Did it all hang on such an unsteady balance?

If Raymond didn't return, if he came home broken, this little one inside her might one day field excruciating phone calls like the one Evelyn just endured.

Come home, she willed into the void across the ocean, to wherever Raymond was. *Please, come home to us.* If he were here, he would keep her from being a mess of a mother.

* * *

July 1944

Sarah dropped the curtain back into place and shook her head. "It doesn't look good." The rain had been falling for days. With the relatively flat landscape of Florence, there was always a risk of flooding in the summer when they caught the remnants of Caribbean squalls that had moved up the coast. The road in front of their house had become a rushing river. "And with your time so near."

Evelyn gripped the bookcase. *Nearer than she thinks.*

It had been four months since she'd moved in with Sarah, and almost a full day since the pains had started. She'd convinced herself they were the practice ones Sarah had warned her about, but as the hours ticked on, it became more difficult to ignore that these pains were steady, relentless, and building in their intensity.

So she tried harder to pretend they weren't happening. Evelyn canned tomatoes and scrubbed the grout in between the counter tiles with lemon peels and salt. She dusted their books and wiped floor corners and the staircase railing with a damp rag. Sarah came home from her work at the piano store and joined the cleaning, making jokes about Evelyn feathering her nest but none the wiser as to her daughter-in-law's condition.

Then the storm knocked out their power, casting the house in late evening darkness. Evelyn went upstairs and lay on her bed, wide awake, counting the seconds between lightning and thunder. But the lightning illuminated Raymond's desk, the pile of his letters at her bedside, their wedding day picture. With nowhere else to lie down, she shut her eyes tight and stayed in her room with its constant reminders of the person she wanted most to get her through this. All night, thunder crashed and shook the house, one wave riding the other, just like her contractions.

She'd come downstairs that morning, stopping halfway down to get through another crushing spasm. If she could be with Sarah, in her calming presence, she might be able to face what she could no longer ignore was coming.

Evelyn gripped the bookshelf and doubled over in a cry of pain, clutching her belly with the other hand.

Sarah rushed to her side and helped her to the sofa.

"Oh, honey. How quick are they coming?"

She couldn't meet Sarah's gaze. "Every two minutes."

"When did it start?"

"Last night."

Sarah's face crumpled in lines of worry. "My sweet girl. Why didn't you tell me it had started?"

Evelyn couldn't speak through the pain and waited for it to retract its claws from her abdomen. "I was afraid."

Sarah brushed a strand of hair from Evelyn's forehead. "It's too late to go anywhere. Especially now that the rain's blocked the road. You're having your baby right here. And soon."

A protest sprang to her lips but was just as quickly cut off by a groan that had burgeoned from deep within her. Evelyn swung her head from side to side through it, hoping that communicated her feelings clearly enough.

Sarah leaped to her feet. "I'll go find help." She put on her galoshes and ran out, slamming the door behind her.

The minutes were interminable, the house quiet except for the rain slashing against the window and the rolling thunder. The urge came to bear down, and her body could deny it no longer. She gave in and did what her body commanded. Her cry pierced the darkness. The sound terrified her more than the quiet had.

Evelyn closed her eyes and dropped her head on the back of the sofa. Alone, alone. Raymond wasn't here. Mama wasn't here. Even Sarah had gone.

Voices broke through the haze. Cold drips of water fell on her skin. Evelyn opened her eyes. Two sopping wet people bent over her, the drips coming from their bedraggled hair.

Sarah lowered herself to her knees and grabbed Evelyn's hand. "Honey, we're back. I brought Opal."

The nurse kneeled beside Evelyn. "Don't you worry. We'll take good care of you."

Opal took charge, assessing Evelyn and barking orders to Sarah to prepare for what was imminently coming.

Another cry welled up in the deepest part of Evelyn. Something shifted. "I can't do this!"

"Yes, you can, honey," Sarah soothed.

Evelyn tried to clench her knees shut. Everything was

changing. Her body, her life was being pulled, faster and faster, toward a murky end, and she couldn't stop it.

Opal propped up her back. "Evelyn, let go. Push as hard as you can."

She did as commanded, again and again. "I can't," she said, tossing her head back and forth.

"Yes, you can." Sarah ran a soothing hand across Evelyn's forehead. "You're so close. Just once more."

With a sob, Evelyn gathered every last bit of her strength and pushed. Agony gripped her flesh, tearing, devouring her down to her bones.

A squalling cry filled the room.

"A girl, Evelyn! You have a beautiful baby girl," Sarah said. "Your Mary is here."

Evelyn fell back against the sofa's arm. Incandescent shimmers dotted her vision. "Is she okay?"

Sarah choked out a laugh through her tears. "Take a look."

Evelyn turned her head and caught sight of a mewling, pitiful soul being wrapped in a blanket Sarah had crocheted.

Oh. Oh. She was small, so much smaller than expected, with flailing, wrinkled limbs fighting Opal's gentle ministrations.

Mary's cries grew more strident. "Are you sure she's okay?"

"Your daughter is as healthy as they come." Opal handed Mary to her.

Evelyn's arms dipped with the weight.

Dark golden wisps of downy hair peeped from beneath a cotton cap. Evelyn couldn't resist running a thumb lightly over the silky strands and the delicate curve of lashes lining Mary's swollen eyelids.

All this, because of the love between her and Raymond. It was a staggering return for such a timid leap of faith. His love had been reward enough, but oh, she would have said yes much sooner had she known it would lead to this.

Raymond would be overjoyed if he were here to see this.

An unbidden image flashed across her mind of a tired, desperate Raymond hurtling into battle.

Evelyn trembled, whether from the thought or from giving birth, she didn't know. She closed her eyes and hugged Mary close.

She's here, Evelyn willed him to hear across the distance. *Your daughter is here. You fought for us. Now fight for her.*

TWENTY-THREE

THE FIRST HIT

July 1944
Guam

"What a day, LT. What a *day*!" Mitt yawned. "Our own plane shooting at us, then those Japs—"

"Move out, Mitt. No time for chit-chat."

Raymond signaled to Kalberer. "Tonight, no one leaves their hole. If they have the urge to relieve themselves, they go where they are or wait till morning. *And* they hold fire until there's a definite target." If they weren't careful, the platoon's mistakes would pile up faster than Raymond could fix them.

"Could've used more warning last night. We need trip wires, LT. Noise-makers. Tin can rattles."

"Use the men's ration cans. For now, we go fast and link up with those Marines. Let's move."

The men gathered their packs and started the journey north to Yigo. They scaled slopes and slid down narrow gorges, sometimes passing other patrolling platoons, the clay mud turning their uniforms a rusty red hue and the coral shredding their boots. They pushed on, passing thatched Chamorro huts and red-tinged broken dirt farm fields, marching through the driving storms and steamy heat and soaked to the skin in sweat and rain.

Toward the end of the first day, they veered onto a road safely behind enemy lines, irrigation ditches lining the muddy route.

Martinelli swore and stumbled into Raymond.

Raymond moved to steady him but grasped air. The private was bent by the ditch, retching.

In a heap at the bottom of the ditch lay Guamanian Chamorro women and children, mangled and unmoving. Innocents. He recoiled, blinking back hot tears. The men who did this, these were the men they were up against? He yanked Martinelli's arm. "Keep moving."

"I'm gonna murder them," Martinelli whispered hotly.

It wouldn't be murder if it was justice. "Save it for our next run-in."

"Can't we bury them?" Peach asked quietly.

"We have to keep moving."

Peach let out a sound of disgust. "They ain't right in the head."

Maybe Peach was right. How could thinking, feeling human beings do such a thing? He'd heard how the Japanese treated the Chinese. They'd done this and much worse, just because they considered the Chinese inferior. Half of him hadn't believed it. But seeing it? If he ever had a moment when he wondered why he was here, he now had his answer. It was right to put a stop to the Japanese advance, even to the death. What kind of man could leave behind what Raymond saw in the ditch? Didn't the Japanese have families? Kids? A flash of Evelyn, their unborn baby, in the enemy's hands, and something new coiled in his stomach. Something hard and hot.

The men trudged past Raymond, some eyeing the ditch as they passed.

"Don't look."

For a long time, no one spoke. They only hacked their way forward with their machetes, keeping one eye on the path and one on their surroundings for any sign of the enemy.

Mango trees, their limbs bent with their burden of ripe fruit, lined the trail, a good sign that the Japanese hadn't been through yet. The supply-starved enemy wouldn't have resisted so easy a solution to their hunger. The fruit dangled so low, Shirley Temple could have picked them.

A flicker caught Raymond's eye.

His machete froze.

He signaled to the others, and they dropped into the vines.

He steadied his breathing. A patrol of Japanese soldiers a hundred yards away was advancing toward the overgrown mango grove.

Raymond motioned for quiet. The enemy was now trudging through the jungle's unkempt foliage toward the platoon's hiding place.

Soon, boots marched past his line of vision. Raymond didn't dare lift his head to appease his curiosity about the men passing by.

One of the men stopped within feet of where Raymond lay.

The man took a bite out of a juicy mango. He devoured the fruit, slurping down the fleshy bits. An agony of seconds later, the man tossed the mango pit into the tangle, right at Raymond's face, and stepped forward. The soldier joined the rest of his group. The Japanese were now surrounded on all sides by Raymond's platoon.

There wouldn't be a better opportunity to attack than this.

Raymond gave the signal.

The jungle erupted in rifle shots.

The enemy grabbed their weapons and returned fire.

Raymond set his eyes on the closest of the enemy, who was aiming his weapon at Allen. Raymond pulled his trigger. The man dropped into the foliage. Heart thumping, Raymond swiveled to find another target.

At the edge of the tree line fifty yards to their left, a mortar round landed.

Palm tree shards and red clay earth showered over them.

"Where'd that come from?" Mitt yelled.

"There!" Kalberer pointed to the mango grove.

Another round hit the ground, several yards closer than the last one.

Mitt found his targets and fired. The mortars went silent.

A Japanese soldier rose from his hiding place and shot at Peach. The private fired back several rounds without a hit and reloaded his rifle, his fingers fumbling.

Raymond targeted the man attacking Peach. The bullet struck, and the force propelled the enemy backward into the vines, the last of the enemy to fall.

But it hadn't been soon enough.

Peach crumpled to the ground.

"Peach!" Raymond hurried to the private's side and pressed the heels of his hands into the rust-red seeping right below Peach's ribcage.

The private groaned.

"Radio!"

Benjamin ran it to him and cast a worried glance at Peach.

Raymond held the receiver to his ear. "Man down in 3rd Platoon!"

A staticky voice came through the other side. "Sit tight and wait. We've got others in the same boat."

Peach didn't have time to wait. "Solomon. Go get help!"

Staring at Peach, Mitt didn't move.

"*Go!*"

Mitt jerked to action. He gave Peach's shoulder a quick pat, then hurried away.

Raymond removed his hands and lifted the shirt above the

wound, exposing the full reality of Peach's condition. His stomach dropped. No way could a man survive with a wound like that. "Well, looks like you got yourself a ticket to some babying from a pretty nurse."

Peach grinned then grimaced. "Worth it," he ground out.

Within a minute, Marine medics broke into the jungle, Mitt running behind them.

The medic who inspected Peach shook his head at Raymond, confirming his worst fear.

"He'll need to be evacuated," the medic said aloud. They moved Peach to a stretcher and lifted him up.

Raymond jiggled Peach's boot. "You did real good today, Peach. We sure showed those Japs what's what, didn't we?"

Peach's gray and sweaty face flopped to the side toward Raymond. He tried to speak through clenched teeth.

"Don't say anything. Just get better. We'll be here when you get back."

The stretcher carried the soldier out of sight. Raymond turned to find his men staring at him. He wouldn't be able to sugarcoat it. They'd have known the moment they laid eyes on Peach that he probably wasn't coming back.

"They'll patch him up and send him back, good as new."

It was a lie, of course, but he couldn't bring himself to reveal the truth. "Let's head out." They had to keep moving. The longer they stayed still, the more of a chance another one of them went down, just like Peach.

TWENTY-FOUR

GUNNER DOWN

Tinian

Jimmie stood at the edge of the airfield and took in the sight of *Dirty Gerty*, sitting pretty and ready to go. The plane must've required fewer fixes than usual to be available so soon after getting docked in repairs. It was a good sign for the night ahead. He never did feel comfortable getting on a plane that sat with the mechanics for too long.

Looking at her, his chest swelled.

When she'd arrived in Hawaii, she'd just rolled off the factory line—all tight lines and smooth, unbroken color. Now, patch jobs marred the pristine surface, her replacement parts painted in mismatched blue and gray. Subsequent missions and haphazard landings had pockmarked and scraped the paint, leaving scratched aluminum peeking through the motley blue. Inside, her seats were cracked and worn, her handles and knobs dull from the time they spent in the grip and twist of sweaty hands, the floor no longer shiny and smooth but dingy from boot-tracked grime.

The blemishes told the story of the crew and its plane better than any words ever could.

Dirty Gerty was a banged-up victory machine, and he'd helped turn her into one.

Planes, ships, trains, radar stations, buildings, little tin cans floating on the ocean—anything belonging to the Japs, he smoked. And he was good at it too.

Back home he'd been Jitterbug Jim, the boy who gave himself too often to fun. The cut-up, the clown. To his father, the ne'er-do-well. Jimmie *had* been a mess-up, and maybe he still was, but out here, he was Jimmie, the sharpshooter. Jimmie, the brave. Up there, he was allowed to be someone else. He pulled his weight, and no one had any reason to suspect he'd do anything different.

One of his fellow gunners, Norman, stared up at the plane, paintbrush clenched between his teeth.

"Hey, Norm. How's she looking?"

The man took the brush from his mouth. "'Bout as good as you'd be if you rolled off the runway into a pineapple grove."

Jimmie shook his head. It was one thing after another with her. She'd dropped a wheel they'd scavenged off a burned-out PB4Y after *Gert*'s last landing gear incident. Jimmie patted her side affectionately. Good ol' girl. He hadn't been killed yet, not for lack of her trying.

"D'you hear about *Pop's Cannonball*?"

Jimmie's stomach dropped. Not Mac. "What happened?"

"Mac and his crew went down over Palawan. *Blunderbuss* is doing the recovery."

Jimmie grimaced. Retrieving dead crewmen's bodies was his least favorite mission. "Shame." Commander Harold McGaughey had been the most aggressive, reckless pilot in the entire squadron. A man didn't necessarily want to fly with him, but he couldn't help but admire the stunts he'd pulled.

"Coulda been us, you know."

"Not yet anyway."

"Not yet." Norman brandished another paintbrush out of his back pocket and handed it to Jimmie. "Help me with *Gerty*. I wanna get her just right."

Jimmie laughed. The bikini-topped girl got more upkeep than any other part of their plane. Maybe they wouldn't have so many mechanical problems if they paid more attention to the rest of it. He took the brush and climbed the ladder to the nose. After he finished, she was as perky and pretty as she ever was.

The rest of the crew arrived and boarded. Jimmie slipped into the belly of the plane after them. He entered the fuselage and went over to his starboard station.

"Ready?" Norman asked, standing on the port side and checking his stores of ammo hooked on the wall.

"You betcha." Jimmie lifted the canisters away from the wall and let them fall back, the heft telling him they were full. He ran his hand over his gun, feeling for any cracks or bends. "Okay, Betsy," he whispered to his gun. "You gonna take good care of me?" Releasing the cover latch, he peered inside, clicking it closed once again and jiggling it, making sure it was secure. A few more checks, and he stepped away, nodding once. "Let's strap in."

They headed to their seats near the front of the plane and buckled in for the ride. The plane rattled faster and faster down the runway, metal parts rubbing and squeaking, the floor vibrating under Jimmie's feet. After dozens of missions, Jimmie's stomach still clenched on takeoffs. Raymond would've suggested praying, but Jimmie and the Big Guy were on the outs, especially after this past weekend. What else could a fellow do on an island but drink contraband booze and gamble away his paycheck?

He'd do it again if temptation came knocking. More than likely, God didn't hear prayers from people who weren't really sorry. Jimmie would have to try for luck instead. He clutched the cylinder head washer in his fist.

The plane hefted into the air and settled into cruising altitude. Jimmie unbuckled and walked to his station. They had enough fuel for a thousand miles out, a thousand miles back, and twenty to spare if they needed to fudge it a little, which they often did, gliding in on a cupful of gas. It was his favorite part, the coming back. Nothing would ever beat the feeling of touching down facing the tangerine-tinted horizon after a riotous night in the sky.

He pulled his goggles over his eyes. Kissing his fingers, he touched the pinup he'd taped to the curved metal encasing his swivel-mounted Browning machine gun and tucked his comic book between the wall and his seat. He donned his gloves and gave Yank a two-fingered salute. "You know the best thing 'bout going up, Norm?"

"What's that?"

"No mosquitos."

Norman laughed. "Except for the ones that hooked onto us before we climbed aboard."

Jimmie gave himself a quick rubdown over his flight suit to kill any stowaways. *Stupid buggers.* He stretched his neck to one side and then the other. "You think Tokyo Rose'll mention us again? The *Blue Raiders*." Jimmie looked sideways at Norm. "It has a nice ring to it, don't it?"

Good ol' Tokyo Rose, the catch-all name troops gave to the English-speaking Japanese women whispering demoralizing propaganda across Pacific airwaves. She'd not only mentioned them in her last broadcast, she'd given them a nickname—the *Blue Raiders, Blue* for their planes' painted underbellies, *Raiders* for their exploits.

"Must be hitting some Jap nerves."

"Good." Tokyo Rose didn't scare him any. If anything, the squadron's confidence grew a little too robust after hearing their names over the radio. Making the broadcast was just as good as making one of Ernie Pyle's newspaper columns.

Captain Jensen's voice came through the intercom. "*Pop quiz. What do you boys in the back have to do when we ditch* Dirty Gerty?"

"*Did he just say when? I think I heard him say* when, *boys,*" Norm said.

"*You're just askin' for trouble, sir,*" Chatham said.

"*Okay, you knuckleheads*—if. *What first?*"

Schnepp's voice piped through the system. "*Get behind the bomb bay, put on our Mae Wests, lock arms, and lay back with our feet up against the bulkhead.*"

"*Ding, ding, ding. Good job, Schnepp. You get a cookie. What do we do once we hit water?*"

"Once *we hit water?*" another gunner asked.

They'd better not have to ditch. He'd seen the afterward often enough. He'd gone on mission after mission trying to find crews that had disappeared without a trace—no wreckage, no oil slick, no radio contact beforehand. Nothing. Just... gone.

If a man bailed out, he had a chance if he didn't die on impact. A chance, but slim. Whenever *Dirty Gerty* found a ditched plane, sometimes the crew had been in the water for days, half hanging on to life as they rode above the water on wreckage or in rafts.

Jimmie searched the sea out of the side of his eye for a flash, a change in colors, a movement of any kind. The moon, hanging high above them, illuminated their watery path in ripples of white on the black of the deep.

He followed the ripples to the horizon.

The ocean was so vast, and they were alone. The hair on the nape of his neck stood on end. No escort over vast, open water, blanketed by inky darkness on a ramshackle plane known for its mechanical failures. If they had to ditch her in the ocean, no one would even know, not unless they had time to radio someone before they went down. Finding a downed crew was like trying to find one uncooked grain in a sea of cooked rice.

Jimmie rubbed the survival map of the Pacific tucked in his flight jacket, printed on silk so it would float.

"What's the first meal you're gonna eat when you get back?" Norman asked.

"Easy. Mother'll be waiting for me at the port, a big basket filled with her biscuits. Cut in half with cold butter and honey in between. I'll eat three in one go." His mouth watered. He remembered how his teeth used to bite through the thin, crunchy outer layer, then the soft, pillowy inside. "That's all I want. Just some of Mother's biscuits. How 'bout you?"

"Meatloaf," he said without hesitation. "Meatloaf and Mom's famous mashed potatoes. She puts in chives from her garden and cream on top. They're nice and fluffy-like. She whips 'em good with an egg yolk. That's the secret. Don't tell nobody, okay?"

Jimmie grinned. "I guess I can do that, Norm."

They continued to skirt the coastline in search of ships camouflaged with island foliage. One hour. Two. The vibrating aircraft lulled Jimmie into the third hour.

He was jolted awake with Jacquette's voice coming over the intercom. "*We got a couple of Sugar Charlies. A sea truck too. Dead ahead.*"

Jimmie squinted. Sure enough, straight ahead were three supply transport vessels nestled into a small cove.

The plane rose from fifty feet to one hundred, positioning to drop a load on the ship.

"*Handing off to bombardier,*" Jensen said.

Jimmie waited for the whine of bombs dropping through the air but heard nothing.

"*Hung up in the racks,*" the bombardier announced.

"*Go again.*"

"*Aye aye, sir.*"

Nothing, again.

"*Want me to knock 'em loose?*" Jimmie asked. He'd have to scamper down the catwalk over the bomb bay open to the whipping waters below. The explosives would have to be jettisoned at some point before they landed, anyway. If he timed it right, they'd fall right on their targets.

"*Forget the bombs. Strafe 'em, boys.*"

The plane swooped back down to fifty feet, the gunners holding fire on the way in so they didn't trigger an explosion in the front of the plane.

Once they got close enough, the gunners opened fire, and a trail of bullets shredded the palm fronds and brush the Japanese had used to disguise the ships. Miniature geysers marked the trail of their bullets in the water. Jimmie followed the ships through his sights and fired. Hot shells landing on Jimmie's boots made the cabin smell like burning rubber.

One of the Sugar Charlies burst into flame.

Just as they flew over the second ship, it exploded into a fireball, thrusting *Dirty Gerty* into the air.

Jimmie's stomach flipped. Aloft, he held on to his gun. It swung to the left, and he slammed into a hanging ammo box. Searing pain shot down his spine and radiated to his chest. He dropped to the ground, hands slipping from Betsy to the metal floor. The noise faded to a dull roar. Jimmie's vision flickered to black.

Norm shook him awake. "Jimmie. *Jimmie.* Get up."

Jimmie grasped Norm's arms and pulled himself to a standing position. A wave of agony surged through him, and he doubled over with a strangled groan.

He steadied his breathing and clutched the handles of his gun. With every ounce of strength he had left, he straightened his body. Black dotted his vision again.

Breathe. That's it. Look at the clouds. Look at the water. It was then he noticed telltale puffs of smoke rising from a pile of debris on the coastline close to the ships. Volleys of red anti-aircraft fire tracers arced through the air in the plane's direction.

"*Incoming!*"

The plane heaved upward. Jimmie slapped his hand on the wall for support.

"C'mon!" Norm hit the side of the plane.

Jimmie gave up fighting the downward pressure and slid to the floor.

Within seconds, the plane settled into a gentle cruise over the open ocean, out of range of enemy fire.

Norm hurried to Jimmie and knelt beside him. "You okay?"

Jimmie tried to turn and look at his injury, but it caused another paroxysm of pain. "Can you look and tell me what you see?"

Norm lifted Jimmie's shirt and whistled. "You're gonna be black and blue for weeks. Think anything's broken?"

"Feels like it. Keep quiet about it, will you?"

Norm shook his head. "Negative, flyboy."

Jimmie's breath hitched. "Jensen'll put me on ice. You know he will."

"Yeah? And he'll skin me alive if he finds out I didn't tell him."

Jensen had made it crystal clear that anyone who endangered the mission in any way would be thrown into the brig, but Jimmie couldn't be taken off the crew. It would kill him to stay down while the others went up. "How'll he find out if you don't tell him?"

Norman plugged his headphones into the intercom box, looking at Jimmie the whole time, one eyebrow raised. "*Jimmie's hurt.*"

TWENTY-FIVE

A RAIN-FILLED TRENCH

July 31, 1944

Dear Sweet—

I just received word about our little Mary's arrival over the radio. I'm so excited I can hardly see straight! Tell me everything about her, even if it seems boring to you. I'm glad she's a girl and not the boy you wanted, for she won't be in any army when she gets older. Could you send something of hers I can carry with me? I want to hold her close to my heart, just as she surely is.

How are you feeling? I wish I could've been there with you through it, but at least you had Mother. As for me, I'm plugging along just fine. It's really the pits out here with nothing to do but dream of being back home with you. I'll write more once we settle in the next place. I don't mind the moving, as long as it brings me home to you.

All my love,
R.

* * *

July 1944
Guam

Arriving at a break in the thick vegetation behind enemy lines, Raymond signaled his men close. "Command Post reports enemy lines have moved on to Yigo. You can relax for the night, but keep your eyes and ears open. Dig your holes, and then eat. Benjamin, defenses."

"Roger that." Benjamin walked toward the perimeter of their camp, a bundle of wire and two cans under his arms. He passed by Jasper and Mahony. "Hey," he said, nodding once.

They ignored him and kept digging their holes.

Raymond's mouth tightened. In the States, the situation with Benjamin and the others had seemed to work itself out. After the obstacle course, there'd been no more incidents that required his intervention. Mitt was friendly to the private, and Raymond had no reason to think all was not well. But there was something about being here, in the jungle and at war—it was like he saw and felt everything twice as clearly. Maybe in training he'd been so focused on their survival that he'd missed the one thing that could pull them down.

Raymond approached Jasper, Allen, Mahony, and Walter, who were busy setting down their gear and pulling out their entrenchment tools.

"Listen, we need to talk about Benjamin."

The men glanced at each other.

"You going to rail on us about being Benge's friend like Mitt does?" Mahony swatted at the flies circling his fruit bar.

"I'm not asking you to be friends. I'm asking you to be friendly. Catch the difference?"

"I'm suspicious of a guy who keeps to himself, LT."

"Maybe he keeps to himself because of how you treat him."

"All due respect, but where I come from, a guy's only quiet for two reasons. They're either planning the best place to stick you with their knife, or they want nothing to do with you."

A flash of irritation gobbled Raymond's cool. "You make nice, or I'll bump you down to buck private. All of you—bring him into the fold." He looked from man to man. They murmured their agreement, all except one. Stony silent, Jasper stood, arms crossed.

"Mahony, get over there and help him. *Nicely*," Raymond said.

Mahony lifted his hands in surrender. "Okay, LT." He stuffed the rest of the bar into his mouth and slung the strap of his rifle over his shoulder.

"And you." Raymond pointed at Jasper. "You're gonna share Benjamin's hole tonight." A little forced proximity under his watchful eye might do the pair good.

"Fine."

Raymond stopped him with a hand on his arm. "I'm serious. Make a real effort, will you?"

Jasper dropped his smirk. "Okay."

The LT was out of his mind if he thought putting him with Benjamin would fix anything. Benjamin was a stick in the mud. A good-time killer. A snitch. All Jasper needed to know about him he'd learned the day Benjamin offered up the plan with the rifles to the LT. But he'd humor his commander and try to get through the night without *accidentally* discharging his weapon into Benjamin's foot.

He rolled his eyes at himself. "Accidental" discharges? Maybe there was something to what the LT said.

He approached Benjamin, and without a word to each other, they flipped coral and clay in an orchestration of movements fast becoming second nature. Fat raindrops began to fall from the sky, and in minutes, they were bailing water and jungle debris out of their hole with their helmets. Once it became clear they weren't budging water levels, they threw their shovels aside and hopped into their shallow dug-out trench.

The damp cold crept into his boots and up his legs, into his fingers and on to the tips of his nose and ears. The coated nylon of his poncho may as well have been newspaper. Water dripped into Jasper's eyes, and rivulets of rain carried muddy debris down his neck and into his boots. He tried to ignore the creeping, crawling creatures the water washed into their trench and settled into the cradle of mud and water, packed in so close his boots knocked against Benjamin's hips.

Jasper scanned the dense jungle for movement in the fading light. In the quiet, the LT's plea echoed in his head. He sighed. "You think Peach made it?"

"Hope so."

"Me too." When Benjamin didn't say anything else, Jasper tried again. "Where's home?"

"New Jersey."

"Got family?"

"A wife. Two boys."

Benge had kids? The thought gave him pause. "You miss 'em?"

"What kind of question is that? 'Course I miss them."

"Tell me about them."

Benjamin's head sank even lower into his poncho as if he were a turtle retreating into his shell.

"C'mon. What else we got to do?"

Benjamin wiped the drizzle from his face. "Fine." He was quiet for a beat. "Nate is my littlest. Loves to talk your ear off. Sometimes, he chatters at us through his door. Thinks we can hear him." Benjamin shrugged. "It's pretty cute."

Jasper smiled despite himself. "Your other?"

"Michael." Benjamin gave a long, hard sigh. "Look, I don't really want to talk about this."

"I just didn't realize any of us were dads."

"Michael's... well, he's... he's smart. Smarter than anybody I know. Adds up numbers a mile long, all in his head. He doesn't talk much, but he could do my job better than me."

"What'd you do before you got called up?"

"I was an accountant."

"An *accountant*?"

"So?"

"So things make a lot more sense now. You're a 'go by the book' kind of guy, aren't ya? A real rules-follower."

"You still raw about your dumb idea to dump all those parts in the gasoline?"

"It was called being creative."

"Whatever helps you sleep at night."

"I sleep just fine." Jasper stuffed his hands under his armpits. He was done talking. He'd done his duty by the LT.

After a long moment, Benjamin spoke. "It's just... I can't afford to mess up out here. My boys need me."

Boys did need their dads, it was true. Jasper had never had one—or a mom, for that matter. He didn't have anyone, really. He'd been raised by a sister, and she was too busy with the rest of her brats to pay him much mind. When he was little, he'd have given anything for what Benjamin's boys had. "It ain't right, them putting dads out here. They should be working supply or pushing paper." Jasper shook out the puddle of water collecting in his poncho with a crisp *snap*. "Tell you what. I'm gonna keep an eye on you and help you get home. It don't matter what happens to me like it matters for you."

"Worry about your own self." Benjamin yanked his slipping poncho higher over his neck. "I don't need you getting killed for my sake."

"Your boys waiting back home are all the permission I need."

"Look, can we stop talking about them? Please? It's hard being away as it is."

Jasper never had been moved much by talk of defending family and freedom. Freedom for him meant going back to the streets and scraping a living together under the nose of those rich snoots back in the city. But he'd fight for making sure those boys got their dad back. "I wouldn't have been so mean to you if I'd known you were a dad."

Benjamin was quiet. "You got a girl back home?"

"Nah. Unless Mahony's counts."

"Yeah, right. He wouldn't know what to do with a girl if he got one."

"Well, you did, if your boys are proof of that."

Benjamin rolled his eyes. "As if you know."

Jasper grinned. The wind picked up and blew more rain into their trench. "Reminds me of the monsoons back at Camp Hyder. Remember those?"

"Yeah."

"D'you get a pass and visit the Grand Canyon while we were there?"

"Nope. Saw pictures, though."

"Pictures are peanuts compared to the real thing, Benge. Feels bigger than the Pacific when you're out there." The little black-and-white drawing of the canyon in Jasper's schoolbook resembled lines left behind by a rake in the dirt compared to how it looked in real life.

"Nothing's bigger than the Pacific."

How could Jasper explain it to somebody who'd never seen it? Opening the door of the dusty car and stepping out into the wide-open space—there were layers of rock and infinite sky, cracks in the earth as long as they were deep, as if God had stuck his fingers in the ground and tried to pry the world apart with his own two hands.

He'd glanced at the canyon floor. Everything swayed. His foot slipped a little, and in a flash, he saw his body at the bottom. He'd never felt more scared in his whole life—not until two nights ago, when those Japs came through their camp. Over here, he was back walking the edge of that canyon line with the rolling fear of plummeting.

"You awake, Benge?"

No answer came. Benjamin's chin was tucked against his chest, a light snore coming from his open lips.

At least one of them was getting rest in all this muck. An involuntary shiver ran through his body. Rain dripped from Jasper's eyelashes to his cheeks, down his neck, down, down between sucking cloth and clammy skin and into the pool of gritty water. He closed his eyes and let the water claim every crevice of him, even as his body clamored for escape.

TWENTY-SIX

WALTER

July 1944
Guam

"I wish you'd shut your trap. I told you. I'm not interested," Mitt whispered hoarsely. Even though the Japanese had been pushed out of the area, he wouldn't be surprised if there was trouble hiding around the corner.

"What, is it 'cause she's not Jewish?" Martinelli asked.

"No, it's 'cause she's your sister."

"*Non fare lo scemo.*" Martinelli pressed his thumb and fingers together and shook them in Mitt's face. "I'm not asking you to marry her."

"Put your claw away." Mitt batted Martinelli's hand.

"She's a nice girl. A teacher."

"And what am I gonna say to a teacher?" Mitt pointed a stubby finger to the puckered scar running from his forehead to his cheek. "You don't get this by being the teacher's pet."

Behind them, Mahony leaned forward. "Where'd you get that scar, anyway?"

Mitt shot him a murderous look. "I walked into a door."

Martinelli shouldered Mahony back. "C'mon. My pop never lets her out to have a little fun. She'll never leave home at this rate."

"Why d'you wanna get rid of her so bad? She got moles or somethin'?"

Martinelli whipped out a small photograph. "Take a look at this."

Mitt took a quick peek. And then another. He wasn't partial to brunettes, but he could make an exception for Marti's sister. "I'll think on it."

Martinelli grinned. "Told ya."

Raymond whipped his head around. "Keep it down."

Mitt shut his mouth tight.

Though nothing had been said since the almost drowning, Mitt suspected he was skating on thin ice. He had to get things back on track—show the LT he still meant business.

Raymond put his pack on the ground. "We stop here."

Mitt took off his gear and sat back against a vine-covered tree. Raymond stood with Kalberer and Oliver, huddled over a map the LT had sketched during one of his radio communications with Captain Wade.

Raymond signaled Mitt over. "Listen up. Company A will cut a swath across the base of the mountain to the east of where we stand." Raymond pointed to the map. "Here, and there, with our platoon on the far right. Reports of harassing fire indicate they've dug in close to this ditch. We have to clear it before the company can move forward. Oliver, you'll take point and patrol with your squad. Mitt, your squad will provide cover fire, with the other squad in support in case I need to pull it into action."

Oliver crossed his arms. "Enemy strength?"

"Estimated to be less than twenty. But there'll be more in the surrounding areas. It'll likely be a recon by fire exercise until they show themselves. Watch for buried explosives during maneuvers." The LT folded the map and tucked it into a plastic wrapper. "Japs are on their last leg out here. Let's finish this up."

Oliver nodded once. "Let's go, Solomon."

After a final weapons check, the unit moved out in a column with one squad to the side and one to the rear. After some time on the path, Jasper lifted his rifle over his head from a crouch, signaling the enemy in sight.

Mitt's and Oliver's squads inched forward.

The ditch was quiet. A good sign. Coming against them with the element of surprise raised the chance of victory, especially against an entrenched enemy.

On command, the squads opened fire.

The enemy sprang to action, returning a deafening salvo.

"Left flanking!" Oliver yelled. Under the cover of heavy fire, the team ran to the side of men carrying automatic rifles.

They alternated, flanking and firing, moving closer and closer to the ditch.

Almost as soon as it started, the enemy's fire ceased. With shaking hands, Mitt kept his gun raised. It was easy. Too easy. He craned his neck and peered toward the trees past the ditch and the hilly slopes beyond, sensing eyes watching the back of his head. He shook off his shivers and crept forward with his rifle.

Walter threw a grenade into the dense thicket lining the ditch. In the next moment, the explosive was tossed back out toward the platoon.

Walter scrambled out of range of the explosion. "Get out and surrender!" He took a slow step forward, rifle trained on the cowering Japanese soldier obscured by the brush.

Mitt kept his weapon trained on the enemy. "Back off!" What was Walter thinking? He wouldn't be able to see what he was dealing with until it was too late.

Walter ignored him. "Good food, clean shirt... C'mon! Your emperor don't care 'bout you!"

The enemy stood and raised his arms, slow and deliberate, climbing through the layers of sword grass.

"Step back. It's an order, Walt," Raymond yelled.

Oliver lunged forward and grabbed Walt by the collar.

Walter wrestled himself from Oliver's grasp. "I'm handling it."

The Japanese soldier stared at his captor with opaque eyes. Mitt's hackles rose. He'd seen that look before, back home before bad things happened. "C'mon, Walt. Listen to the LT."

Walter came forward and pulled the captive's arms back, tying his hands with a cord. "I told you I got this." He grabbed one of the soldier's crooked elbows and pushed him past Oliver.

The Japanese soldier took a hard step forward with his right leg. With a loud bang, Oliver and Walt disappeared behind a cloud of white phosphorous.

Mitt hit the ground hard, heart thumping.

Raymond came running toward the cloud of debris. Mitt leaped from the ground and followed him. Only Walter could be clearly seen, groaning and holding his head.

Raymond slid to the ground in front of Walter. "What happened?"

Mitt's voice shook. "Must've been a land mine."

An artillery shell landed and exploded on the edge of the ditch, followed by a volley of shots from behind a rise in the distant hilly slopes.

Everyone hit the ground with their rifles in their hands. With the grass only a few inches high, they made easy targets.

"Stay down!" Raymond commanded.

Benjamin called out from behind a large rock. "Over here!"

Raymond signaled to the others to stay down and ran behind the boulder with Mitt.

He took the radio Benjamin handed him. In the distance, Kalberer yelled for more ammo. The LT raised his hand to plug his free ear and reported their location. Mitt leaned closer and listened to the faint response.

"...advanced past your position. No fire support in your sector."

Mitt swore. They were completely on their own?

"We'll take anything you've got," Raymond said.

"My hands are tied. You're the commander. Figure it out."

Raymond's hand gripping the radio turned white. "What do you think I'm—" He shoved the radio into Benjamin's chest. "Don't give up. Squeaky wheel, Benge. Send updates till they get sick of hearing from you."

"You got it, LT."

"What do we do now?" Mitt asked.

"Oliver is gone. You've been promoted. Take your squad and find that fire."

Mitt's heart skipped a painful beat. "Me?"

"*Go*. I'm gonna get Walt."

Raymond ran out from behind the rock. Mitt closed his eyes and inhaled deeply. He twisted away from protection and bear-crawled toward the tree line just beyond the field. A mortar landed close by, knocking him flat. He got back on his hands and knees. Another blast shook the ground, and another. Mitt gritted his teeth. He got back to his hands and knees and inched forward, determined to find the source of that fire. If he was looking for a chance to get back on the LT's good side, saving the platoon was as good a means as any to do it.

TWENTY-SEVEN

A GOOD MOTHER

August 30, 1944

Dear Raymond,

I'm writing you while holding our girl in my arms. It's nice having a little companion during the night now that you're gone, though it means I'm getting little sleep. She has my hair, your nose, and, I'm afraid to say, Jimmie's lungs. Your mother thinks Mary cries so much because she has trapped gas. I massage Mary's tummy through her fits, though it seems to do nothing but make her mad. I've heard that soldiers often come home from war deaf, and maybe you won't mind this handicap when you return.

Enclosed is a snipping of her hair and one of her booties. Can you imagine a foot so small? I know you'll understand it when I say I've never loved anyone in my life like I love her. It's different, having a little one to protect and care for. It's a fearful love, thinking her happiness depends on me, but I'll do my best as long as I'm her mama.

Tonight, I'm thinking of you and our first weeks at Camp Pickett. It was where I learned to love and be loved, and holding on to those memories makes me feel just a bit nearer to you than a thousand miles away.

Yours,
Evie

* * *

August 1944

A cry shattered the stillness of the night.

Evelyn's eyes cracked open.

Moonlight broke through the darkness, tracing the outline of the baby bed in a muted glow.

The cry turned into a plaintive wail. Evelyn's chest tightened. How many more nights like this could she endure? She fumbled for her glasses on the bedside table.

The room sharpened into focus.

Evelyn stumbled toward her daughter in a haze and lifted her from the bassinet. "Mama's here."

For one glorious moment, the crying stopped.

Mary stared with her mouth turned down at the sides.

And then her tiny face scrunched in a grimace again.

"No, Mary. No. Please, don't cry." Maybe she was wet. She fumbled with the buttons at Mary's waist. Evelyn gathered Mary's ankles with one hand and lifted her bum. With a fresh diaper tucked under her and a few pins set in place, it was done.

The effort caused sweat to drip down Evelyn's neck. Her nightgown glued itself to her sticky, heated back.

The screams grew louder, impaling her eardrums and setting her brain on fire.

All she wanted to do was run.

All she needed to do was stay and fix whatever it was that distressed Mary.

Now would be a really good time for you to come home, Raymond.

Evelyn picked Mary up again and held her close to her chest. "Slumber, my darling, thy mother is near," she sang softly. "Guarding thy dreams from all terror and—" her voice caught. Tears slipped down her cheeks. It was the lullaby Mama used to sing to her long ago. "Oh, Mama." Was it wrong to want her here, even with all the hurt between them?

The door cracked open, and Sarah peeked in the room. "Sweetheart, you need help," she said in a quiet, firm voice.

Evelyn shook her head. "You have work in a few hours." Mary's flailing hand caught in Evelyn's hair. Evelyn winced, and, as delicately as she could, she untangled her hair from the little fist.

"For goodness' sake, let someone help you out for once."

Evelyn froze. It was the first time Sarah had talked to her like that.

The two women stared at each other. A stalemate, and Evelyn was in no mood to fight a battle on two fronts.

Mary's cries made it hard to think. Evelyn sank onto the bed and gave up her screaming child to her mother-in-law.

Sarah marched her granddaughter over to the bassinet. "Now, let's see if you need your diaper changed, shall we?"

"Oh, but I already—"

"You'd be surprised how many times I'd changed a diaper only to have to put on another one shortly after."

Evelyn blinked away tears. "I... I don't know what's wrong with her, Sarah."

"Who knows? It's a mystery, sometimes, what goes on in their little heads." Sarah cooed at the irate newborn.

"I've tried everything I can think of, but she just won't stop crying."

Sarah unpinned the diaper and pulled it off Mary. A restrained laugh burbled in Sarah's throat. "Oh."

"What?" Evelyn shot to her feet and peeked over Sarah's shoulder. "Sarah, what's wrong?"

"For starters, she's wearing two diapers."

"What?" Maybe it was the lack of sleep, maybe it was that she could barely hear Sarah over Mary's screams, but it didn't make any sense.

"You put a new one over her dirty one." Sarah made quick work of replacing the old with the new. Mary's cries settled into shuddering hiccups almost at once.

The tightness in Evelyn's chest slackened its grip.

"Evelyn, it's only because you're tired. Why don't you just go back to sleep? I've got this."

"No, that's alright." Evelyn paused. "But thank you." It shouldn't have been so hard to say the words. But still, it smarted that Sarah had been the one to calm Mary.

Sarah squeezed her shoulder. "Fine, but don't be shy if you change your mind." Sarah padded to the door and turned around. "And make sure you rest tomorrow. Chores can wait, including those apples the neighbors gave us. I'll take care of them when I come home."

The applesauce was bubbling, the washed diapers were wrung out and hung on the line. Mary was resting, quiet, draped over Evelyn's shoulder like a sack of flour. With one hand on her daughter's back and the other slowly stirring the fragrant apples, a swell of pride filled her chest. Was there anything more homey than the smell of apples and cinnamon simmering on the stove?

How surprised Sarah would be to find eight shiny cans of golden applesauce cooling on the counter when she came home from work.

A light knock sounded at the front entry.

"Coming!" Evelyn turned down the burner and made her way to the door.

A little girl with freckles and straw-colored braids stood on her porch. A wagon was set behind her with a pile of crushed tin cans. "Mornin'. I'm Barbara. I'm here for your tin."

She wasn't the first child to come by collecting tin. The metal had become a valuable commodity with Japan owning seventy percent of the world's tin supply and the military needing every bit for ammo cans and ration storage. The junkyard paid a pretty penny for whatever the kids scrounged up, and it was nice to think that Evelyn's little contribution might help Raymond in some way.

"I sure do. Just a minute." Evelyn shifted Mary a little higher on her shoulder and went back to the kitchen. She gathered the two cans she'd cleaned and readied for donation, pinching them between her thumb and forefinger.

The girl's face brightened when Evelyn appeared again holding the cans. "Thanks!" She dropped them into her wagon. "You sure do have a nice baby there."

Evelyn smiled. "Why, thank you. I think so too."

"I got a baby brother and another on the way. Mother lets me take care of Timmy while she naps."

"That's awfully nice of you."

The girl lifted her foot behind her to scratch at her other leg. "Is yours a girl or a boy?"

"A girl."

She nodded sagely. "That's good. I was a girl baby, and I never caused any trouble at all. Not like Timmy."

Evelyn smiled. "And how would you know? You were a baby."

"Mother said so. She said it was because she was such a good mother."

Evelyn's smile drooped. A hit on two counts. Either Evelyn wasn't a good mother, or Mary was so bad, mothering wouldn't make a difference. On another day it might not have bothered her, but on the heels of last night, it poked where she was most raw. "Is that so?"

"Does *your* baby cry?"

If Barbara's mother had been such a *good mother*, she would've taught her daughter not to trouble strangers overmuch. "Well, yes, but—"

"Can I hold her?"

Evelyn leaned back and gave a quick glance at the stove. "No, but you can look at her, just for a quick moment. I have something on the stove."

Evelyn kneeled and the young girl came forward.

Barbara stuck her face into Mary's and tapped her back with a gentle hand. "She sure is beautiful."

Evelyn softened a little. "She is, isn't she?"

"Hey! She's suckin' on a button! She could choke." Mouth agape, Barbara looked up at Evelyn with wide eyes.

The tightness returned in Evelyn's chest.

She snaked her hand between Mary and her shirt and pulled the button from between her gums. "I—I didn't know." Mary began to cry yet again.

Barbara studied Evelyn with suspicion in her eyes as if to ask, *How'd they let you be a mother?* "Well, you shouldn't let her do that. It's not safe."

"I kn—" Evelyn clamped her mouth shut. She wouldn't stoop to arguing with a little girl. "Thank you. I'll keep that in mind."

"Be sure you do. You don't want that sweet little baby gettin' hurt."

Evelyn forced a smile. "I have to go. 'Bye now." She shut the door, and safely hidden behind it, she breathed in deeply of her daughter's comforting, sweet scent. "You're alright, aren't you, Mary?"

Another smell hit her nose.

An earthy, acrid scent. The applesauce!

She ran to the kitchen. Geysers of smoke bubbled up through the applesauce. She glanced beneath the pot. She'd turned the burner up, not down before answering the door.

With one hand, she wrapped a tea towel around the handle and carried the pot over to the sink. She turned on the faucet. Fumes filled the kitchen. With the counter's edge cutting into her middle, she strained toward the window with one hand while trying to keep Mary steady with the other.

"Evelyn! What on earth?"

Evelyn winced.

She could only imagine what Sarah was thinking, seeing her and the mess and her crying grandbaby.

"Oh, honey. Why couldn't you have left the apples alone?" Sarah gently led her by the shoulders to a kitchen chair. "Sit."

Evelyn obeyed, too defeated to fight back.

Sarah opened the back and front doors and swung the smoke out of the house with her tea towel. "You want to tell me why you're pushing yourself so hard?"

Evelyn slumped, her body cradling around a wailing Mary. The whole story spilled out of her, of determining the night before that she'd make up for her mistakes, of the button Mary had almost choked on, of wanting to impress Sarah, of Barbara and her perfect mother who raised non-crying babies. "Her mother said that Barbara never cried because she had such a good mother. What does that make me? Mary does little else *but* cry."

"Oh, Evelyn. Don't you know a joke when you hear one? No mother knows exactly what to do, and neither did Barbara's mother." Sarah rubbed Evelyn's back. "Now, go take a nap. You're not thinking straight."

Evelyn didn't have the strength to argue. She handed Mary to Sarah and walked out of the room, turning her back on her crying baby.

Evelyn floated in warm, velvety water. Raymond called to her from the shore. He smiled like he had a secret he couldn't wait to tell her. Hot tears slipped down her temples into the ocean. She would be with him in moments. Lightness danced in her heart, joy skipped through her limbs. Leaving the water's embrace, she pulled herself toward the beach.

Then, it was gone.

Evelyn reluctantly eased open her eyes. She was on her back, lying in darkness.

The room was quiet. Too quiet.

Mary!

Evelyn threw on her robe and rushed down the stairs to the living room.

There Sarah sat in an armchair, her eyes closed, feeding a half-asleep Mary with a bottle.

A wave of horror washed over her. Mary had been hungry, and Evelyn had slept right through it. "Oh, Sarah. I'm so sorry. Why didn't you come and get me?"

Sarah opened her eyes. "Do you feel rested?"

Evelyn stopped short. She did, actually. Even though she'd just woken up, her mind was as clear as a bell. "How long did I sleep for?"

"Oh, ten hours or so."

"Ten!"

"You needed it."

Burning shame made it hard to speak. "But... but I can't just sleep however long I want. I have a responsibility to Mary."

"I know you want to take care of Mary all on your own, but I have to take care of you too."

Evelyn slumped into the chair next to Sarah's. "Why is this so hard for me?"

"One day, Mary is going to be asking you the same question."

That wasn't a very encouraging thing for her mother-in-law to say. "I hope not."

Sarah pulled the bottle from Mary's mouth and set the baby on her shoulder. Mary didn't even stir. "Do you think any new mother doesn't struggle?"

"You make it look so easy."

Sarah rubbed circles in Mary's back just like she had Evelyn's. "I'm not dealing with the exhaustion that comes from trying to do it all on your own." Sarah gave her a pointed look.

Evelyn hung her head. "I feel so alone." Her voice cracked, her throat thick with unshed emotion. "He's missing it, Sarah. He's missing all of it. And it's not the same, telling him about it in letters."

"But you're not alone. You have me." Sarah lifted Evelyn's chin and peered into her eyes. "People think my husband left when the boys were teenagers, but he was gone long before that. The nighttime feedings, the attention young children require... it was all me." She stated it matter-of-factly with no tinge of self-pity. "And I felt a failure. The first years were a blur, Evelyn. Do you know, Jimmie asked me what his first word was, and I can't for the life of me remember? I don't regret a moment of it, but it was hard. So I don't cast any blame on you for struggling, and neither should you."

Evelyn laid her head on the wing of the armchair and studied the two of them. Mary looked so peaceful, so content. Evelyn was overwhelmed sometimes by how much she loved this little creature. And the woman sitting beside her, this dear woman who'd taken her and Mary in and given them a refuge in the midst of a storm—what a stroke of genius it had been for Raymond to send her to live with his mother.

"Will you let me help you a little? Just until Raymond comes home?"

Evelyn squeezed Sarah's hand and braved a smile. "I'll try."

TWENTY-EIGHT

THE FLYING COFFIN

Dear Raymond–

Just like me to follow you like a puppy dog across the ocean. Can't tell you where I am, but all I'll say is that it makes me wish I were back in Hawaii. First thing I did when I got there was get a big glass of cold milk at the Royal Hawaiian. (Yes, milk.) Gee, here I am talking about a cold drink when you haven't had any for months. Remember Mother letting me drink straight from the bottle? She never let you, as I recall. Sometimes it pays to be the baby.

In other news, someone stole my brand-new fountain pen. I suspect it's one of them no-good ground pounders. I get paid in a week, and I guess I'll have to go and buy myself a new one. I'll need to buy some stamps too, as everyone here thinks I'm a regular old United States post office.

Love,
Jimmie

Stinker–

Just received a letter from you dated months ago. It must be hard tracking us with our movements. Wonder where you are in all this mess. Hard to believe the cute little guy who couldn't tell a lug nut from a hose is now in charge of a machine gun. Just don't look down the barrel, okay?

Sorry to hear about your fountain pen. The bad news is soldiers steal from each other all the time. The good news is, if enough of them steal, you'll get your pen back eventually.

Speaking of soldiers, I've got one in my unit you'd love. His name is Mitt. It took some work to get him Army-fied, but there's no one I depend on more over here. I hope you'll get to meet him when we get back.

Are you flying over me as I write? Between you and me, we sure could use the air support.

Don't do anything crazy.

Love,
Raymond

* * *

December 1944
Philippines

Jimmie was about to do something crazy.

Lieutenant Jensen dismissed the crew from the pre-flight inspection to get chow before they went up. Schnepp stayed behind, still deep in conversation with the commander.

Jimmie ran a hand over the plane's fuselage, pretending to inspect the seams. At last, Schnepp put on his hat, signaling an end to his conversation. "Okay, sir. See ya in an hour." The navigator eyed Jimmie. "Sorry you have to stay down tonight."

Jimmie sniffed and brushed imaginary lint off his shoulder. "We'll see about that." Jimmie's back still bore the deep eggplant-colored bruise from slamming into his machine gun the week before. It hadn't faded one bit, and neither had the pain. Thanks to Norm squealing, Jensen had done just what Jimmie feared he would—ground Jimmie until he recovered.

"Whatever you say, bud." Schnepp walked away, whistling.

Jimmie stepped in front of their commander. "Sir?"

Jensen glanced up from his clipboard. "Why aren't you already gone? I've never known you to be late for food."

All he had to do was convince Jensen to send him back up, but the look in the pilot's eyes was enough to dim any hopes of Jimmie getting what he wanted. If fat chance married suspicious, it'd have a kid with Jensen's face. "I want to go up with the crew tonight, sir."

Jensen laughed. Laughed! The tips of Jimmie's ears turned pink. "You're nuts if you think I'm going to let you up there with your back like it is." The lieutenant glanced at his watch and began to walk away.

Jimmie skip-walked to catch up to Jensen's side. "C'mon, sir. Lemme go up. My back's fine. The accident was ages ago."

"Ages? Funny way of marking time. Try five days. Give it another five, and I'll consider it."

"But—"

Jensen held up his finger to interrupt him. "Uh-uh. Not another word."

Jimmie steeled himself for one more try. He couldn't be more grounded than he was. "It's not paining me anymore."

Lieutenant Jensen stopped and crossed his arms. "Oh yeah? Bend over and touch your toes."

Jimmie's heart hammered. "Gimme somethin' hard to do," he said. "Want me to load ammo boxes? How 'bout"—Jimmie forced himself down to his toes and back up again, biting back a groan. A sheen of sweat broke across his forehead—"washing *Gert*'s windows? Really, Lieutenant. I'm golden." For good measure, Jimmie twisted from side to side. Stars dotted his vision.

Jensen narrowed his eyes. "If you're so set on going, get clearance from the doc first."

"But—"

"No buts... go. We're wheels up in an hour."

Fair and square, Jensen got him. No doctor would let him go up like this. "Aye aye, sir."

But as Jensen walked away, Jimmie couldn't bring himself to admit defeat. Not yet. Ever since Raymond's last letter mentioned needing air support, no way would Jimmie stay on the ground.

He swiveled in the direction of the ship's surgeon. It might be a last-ditch effort, but he had to try anyway. Up in *Dirty Gerty,* he could shoot down enemy planes carrying troops on their way to Raymond. He could bomb weapon depots supplying the Japanese army Raymond fought on the ground.

Raymond aside, he *wanted* to fly, even with his back on fire like it was. Going up, there was a guaranteed rush of excitement, whether from a Zero on his tail or the plume of antiaircraft fire from a ship they'd just strafed. He might not come back down unless it was in a ball of fire, but what a way to go! Adventure and risk were a package deal, and Jimmie would pay the going rate no matter how much it cost him. He was finally part of something important, and nothing, not even a back injury, would stop him.

Jimmie found the surgeon's office and knocked on the open door.

"Yes?"

Jimmie walked in on a bespectacled man sitting behind a metal desk, rifling through a mess of papers. "Hey, Doc. I need you to clear me for takeoff. The lieutenant wants to check a box before we go up."

"And what problem am I clearing, exactly?" The doctor dropped a sheaf of papers onto the floor and bent to pick them up with a grunt.

"No problem. Just checking a box, like I said." Jimmie leaned his shoulder against the doorjamb, pretending nonchalance.

"Sleeping well?"

"Like a baby." *A baby who wakes up a lot, that is*. Mother had written about Raymond's new baby, and from what he'd heard, little Mary sure had a set of lungs on her. No one was getting any sleep in the little house on Guerry Street.

"Taking any medication?"

"Nope." Unless aspirin counted, but it might as well be a sugar pill with how little it helped him.

The surgeon's glasses slipped down his nose, and he shoved them back up. "Hmmm." He licked his thumb and flipped through several pages in the stack he'd retrieved from the floor.

"So can I fly?"

"Fine, fine." The doctor waved Jimmie off without looking up from his paperwork.

Jimmie stepped forward and placed his clearance form on top of the stack.

The doctor scratched his signature onto the carbon-backed paper.

Jimmie grabbed one of the corners of the form before the doctor finished writing.

The surgeon slapped his hand on the paper before Jimmie could take it, finally focused on the gunner in his office. "What'd you say you're here for?"

"I got what I needed. Thanks, sir!"

Jimmie yanked the slip off the desk and quickstepped out of the office as if his pants were on fire. Which they were.

Jimmie made his way to *Dirty Gerty* and walked up to Jensen, waving the duplicitous chit.

Jensen narrowed his eyes and snapped the form out of Jimmie's hand. "I don't even want to know what you said to pull this off."

"It took no doings on my part, sir."

"If I had the time, I'd go and have a little chat with the doctor and see how true that is." Jensen sighed. "Fine. Climb aboard. But if I get one hint you're not able to do your part—"

"You won't! And thank you, sir."

Jensen eyed the guy next to him. "Sorry, Junior. No pulling gunner today, but don't get comfy. I have a feeling we'll need you soon enough." Jensen said the last part loud enough that Jimmie couldn't mistake it was meant for him.

Jimmie hurried away before Jensen could change his mind and climbed into the bomb bay carefully so as not to hurt his back.

The crew greeted Jimmie with whistles and hollers as he made his way back to his seat.

Norman leaned over and punched Jimmie on the shoulder. Jimmie's eyes crossed in pain. "Welcome back, you scammer."

"No thanks to you."

"You better pull your weight." Norman shot him a worried glance.

"I wouldn't have had to do this if you'd kept your mouth shut."

Dirty Gerty taxied down the runway, a dirt strip dug out of a bamboo thicket lit by oil fires to guide them on their takeoff. The sun dipped its head below the horizon, pulling down the velvety curtain of night to drape along the sea.

The plane settled into a glide one hundred feet above the water. Jimmie walked back to his post and settled in for the night's ride, hands in position on his Browning. Window hatch open, ocean spray came through the window, pelting his face with cool droplets. It was downright pleasant, with the breeze whistling through the fuselage.

He massaged his aching back with one of his hands. They better shoot something down tonight. The ship's surgeon would allot them a nip of whiskey if they did, and there was no better pain reliever than that.

He gazed at the passing water. How many crewmen hid in the deep of the watery grave below? *Dirty Gerty* better not have to ditch tonight. With Jimmie's back the way it was, he didn't have a chance of surviving if they went down.

Maybe he had been crazy to weasel his way on board.

Hours passed without seeing anything. The haze of the midnight sky gave way to purple. They climbed in altitude and veered toward the Japanese naval port of Cap St. Jacques in French Indo-China. Just below a ceiling of clouds, Jimmie caught sight of something dark heading away from the port. Just a speck, but at that distance, it wasn't a bird.

"*Hey, Jack, you see that?*" Jimmie asked the gunner manning the turret in the nose. "*Bogey. Five o'clock, just below the thunderhead.*"

"*Yeah, I see it. You catch that, sir?*"

"*Put your masks on,*" Jenson said. "*We're going up.*"

"*Aye aye, sir.*"

Jimmie's body leaned toward the stern as the plane veered off its course and climbed in elevation.

The speck separated into two and became well-defined planes. On their sides were the distinctive red meatballs confirming the aircraft as the enemy's. Two Tabbies. They'd run into trouble with those before. Even though they were transport planes, they still had at least one machine gun for protection. Less had taken down a B-24.

Jimmie lowered his goggles and released the safety on his gun. He swiveled it in the planes' direction.

The planes were now within his sights.

"*Take 'em down,*" Jensen said.

Jimmie swung the gun to the left, zeroing in on the left wing, and jackhammered bullets at one of the Tabbies.

It returned fire, a stream of bullets laying down a strip on *Dirty Gerty* from front to back.

The smell of hydraulic fluid filled their cabin.

"Why, you little..." The Tabby got their brakes. Jimmie increased his volleys, following the plane as it dipped under *Dirty Gerty*.

The aircraft caught fire and spiraled to the ocean.

The gunners attacked the other plane, concentrating on its engines. Flames broke out on the Tabby's right wing. Jimmie didn't stop shooting until the fire engulfed the plane's fuselage. For good measure, he kept up the barrage until it teeter-tottered into a nose-dive and exploded.

An electric thrum coursed through his body.

Dirty Gerty began its descent to the ocean. The bombardier opened the bomb hatch and air whistled through the cabin, letting the acrid fumes from the hydraulic fluid escape.

"*Masks off,*" Jensen said.

Jimmie lit a match to test the oxygen levels. Bright blue shifted into orange-tipped gold as oxygen fed the flame. He threw the spent match on the metal floor and rubbed it with his boot. Ripping off his mask, he breathed in air laced with hot metal and fuel.

The hatch doors closed again, and the plane veered back toward home.

"*We've just enough gas to double back.*"

One thousand more miles to go, alone over the silent depths.

Five hundred miles passed without another run-in. Then six, then seven. They were getting closer to home. The bombardier dropped the last of their bombs into the ocean so they could land without fear of explosion.

Towering thunderheads billowed across the horizon, streaks of lightning zipping through the murky depths of the clouds. The gloom that had been a side note before now commandeered center stage. Sheets of rain fell and blurred the line between sea and cloud. There was no other way to fly than through it.

They hit the wall of water, the sound like a million firecrackers exploding.

Jimmie scrambled to pull his gun in and close the metal hatch.

Just as he reached up to the flap, one of the engines sputtered and died.

He looked out onto the wing. Still propellers. A stalled engine. First the storm, now the engine? "C'mon, you bucket of bolts!" Jimmie slammed his hand against the wall of the plane by his side as if that could jolt the propellers into action.

Jensen's voice came through the intercom. "*You know what they say about engines... three outta four still gets us ashore.*"

"*What if it's ashore but in pieces?*" Jacquette asked.

"*Zero zero visibility. We're diverting to Mindoro. They'll have to guide us in by radar,*" Jensen announced.

Mindoro? Jimmie ran a hand over his face. Out of everything they'd experienced during their patrols, going in by radar scared him the most. The strip on McGuire Field ended close to the ocean's edge. It was hard in the daylight, let alone in a storm, to hit the landing just right so you didn't end up plunging into the ocean.

If that wasn't enough, mountains rose up on nearby islands, close enough to Mindoro to be a threat to airplanes by hampering visibility. Overshoot the strip, and you might find yourself planted into the nearest peak. Schnepp was the best navigator there was, but even the best would have trouble getting them home through a storm like this.

"Get in your seats and brace for impact. Brakes are out."

The plane lurched to the side. All he could do was grab onto his gun and hold on for dear life.

Dirty Gerty hit a current. Jimmie's feet lifted for a fraction of a second, and the plane plummeted, jamming his spine into his pelvis.

With another jolt, Jimmie's hands were ripped from his weapon.

He was thrown to the ground on his stomach, knocking the wind from his lungs.

Jimmie's vision faded to black. He came back to awareness as a large metal tank barreled toward his head. He jerked his body to the side just in time for the canister to roll by.

Norman yelled over the rain. "You okay?"

Jimmie answered with a guttural groan. He'd have been a dead man if the canister had met its target, and all because he'd come up with *Dirty Gerty* when he should've stayed down.

The landing gear lowered with a whirr. This was it. They had to be close to the landing strip. Or worse, the mountains, if Schnepp was off. Hopefully, there'd be no bailing from a fiery wreck. It wouldn't be all that bad if they did, though. From what he'd heard, the nurses in the burn tent were real lookers.

He bear-crawled to his seat and buckled in. He grabbed the metal washer on the chain around his neck in one hand and the wall with the other. He squeezed his eyes shut and, for the first time in his life, resorted to praying. *It's me, Robert James Sellers. Jimmie. I know I ain't livin' a clean life and don't deserve to be got out of this fix. I'll give up cards. I won't drink too much, neither. I'll go to services every Sunday, if you help us.* The plane hit another current, jerking him to the side. He whimpered. *And please help Ray with whatever fix he's in too. Sincerely, Jimmie.*

The plane's wheels slammed into solid ground and bumped into a pothole, slamming Jimmie's shoulder into the metal wall of the plane. He doubled over in another shudder of agony.

Jensen steered the plane off the runway to put a stop to its momentum before it hit the ocean. The jungle vegetation screeched against the underside of the aircraft.

Crack! The plane fell downward. Was that the landing gear? One of the wings tilted, scraping the ground and grinding the plane to a halt.

Jensen cut the engines.

Silence filled the fuselage.

For a moment, they sat, stunned.

Jensen ripped off his headgear. "Get out!"

The men unbuckled and stumbled out of the plane. Jimmie fell to the ground in a heap and almost screamed in agony. Shaking himself from his daze, he forced himself to his feet and hobbled to where the others stood under the wing of another plane further down the runway.

Another pilot ran to the plane with a jacket over his head. "Everyone okay? We saw you come down hard."

Without responding, Jensen dashed past him and vomited in the bushes.

The pilot turned to Schnepp. "Jap chatter on the short wave has it those Tabbies you shot down were packed with generals."

Schnepp's face lit. "You hear that, boys? We took down two planes stuffed with Jap brass."

The crew erupted in cheers.

Looking a little less green in the face, Jensen rejoined the group. "What's this I hear about us taking down a plane of generals?" He slapped Jimmie on his back.

Jimmie sucked in a breath and dug his fingernails into his palms to keep from punching Jensen in the face.

"I'd give you boys liberty, but where would you go?" Jensen

guffawed. "How 'bout I twist the doc's arm for the whole bottle of whiskey this time?"

In the midst of the crew's whooping and hollering, Jimmie's grimace slowly morphed into a grin. A whole bottle of whiskey? What a ride! What a night!

The Pacific had churned beneath him. War raged all around him. Death had ridden the tail of his battered and bruised B-24, but he'd come out of it alive.

Maybe going up hadn't been such a crazy idea after all.

TWENTY-NINE

"COME SEVEN, COME ELEVEN. DOUBLE SEVEN HAS LANDED."

—Major General Bruce's invitation to the waiting 7th and 11th Divisions advising them of the 77th's success at Ormoc

December 1944
Leyte, Philippines

Mahony stuck his head in the tent. "Fresh fish!"

"'Bout time." Mitt jumped to his feet and followed Mahony outside the tent.

The Japanese had been funneling tens of thousands of reinforcements through the port at Ormoc since the eastern half of Leyte fell to the Americans. The platoon needed every man it could get before fighting the Japanese there.

Mitt eyed the two men standing with the LT. Another group of newcomers stood behind him. Their uniforms weren't aerated by rips yet; there was no mud caked on their boots and knees. Their faces clean-shaven and their hair freshly trimmed, they might as well have arrived for a night on the town, not a dance with the devil. Mitt glanced down at his bare chest and scraped at some dried mud with his forefinger. A dip in the ocean couldn't hurt. He lowered his nose to his shoulder and sniffed. The sooner the better.

"Mitt? This is Searles and Zampini. Show 'em around."

Mitt put his hands on his hips. Searles and Zampini were too clean behind the ears to be good at fighting, but they'd get there. "Okay. I've been where you are, and it ain't so bad once you get used to the stink. Number one rule: You got the runs? Hold it or wait until you can get to that slit trench over there."

Searles grimaced. "You get a lot of that? The runs, I mean?"

"You'll see. Second, you lucked out by getting 3rd Platoon. The LT's a good guy. He's got our backs, and we've got his, so relax. We'll take care of you too."

Zampini ran his hand up and down his rifle strap. "When do we get to shoot Japs?"

"We're shipping out in a few days to the other side of the island. That's where the real fun starts. Okay, let's find you a spot." He shoved them in the tent and shoved them toward a couple of empty cots.

"Benge, Jas." The privates looked up at Mitt. "Get these two settled, okay?"

"You got it, boss."

"Where you from?" Benjamin asked the two men. "I'm a Jersey boy myself. You had chow yet?"

Mitt left the men behind and made his way to the cot he'd scouted out as the best spot in the tent. But just as he started in that direction, Martinelli made a beeline toward the same cot. Mitt ran, pushing the would-be thief out of the way and launching himself onto the bed just before Martinelli reached it.

Martinelli threw his bag on the neighboring space with a thud. "Just keep your paws off my stuff, and we'll be okay."

"You got nothing I want, anyway."

"You gonna write my sister?" Martinelli asked.

"The teacher? How 'bout you ask Allen? He'd make a good teacher's pet."

"Allen ain't from New York. Besides, you look like that actor she likes... what's his name?" He snapped his fingers quickly. "Tyrone Power. You look like him."

Mitt rolled his eyes. Tyrone Power? "You been drinkin'?"

"You're from the Bronx, she's from the Bronx. She wants to stay close to Ma."

"So now you got me marryin' her? Stop pushin' me." He couldn't imagine settling down with a girl, anyway. He'd have to become somebody worth marrying first.

"I'll stop if you tell me how you got that scar."

"Onion business."

"Onion business?" Martinelli grabbed one of the support poles and pulled himself up. He slapped the wall above his cot, the vibrations scaring a giant spider carrying a white bulbous sack of eggs into the corner.

"Yeah, onion business. It means *none of your business*," Mitt said. "It's how I used to say it when I was a kid. Cute, huh?"

"I'm just saying, you walk around with a face like that, people are gonna ask questions."

Why couldn't they drop it? Every time they asked, he had to live that day all over again. "Shut up, Marti."

Martinelli scraped a sock off his foot and threw it in Mitt's face. Mitt gagged and tossed it back.

"Fine. I'll tell the others you tripped in your heels at dancing lessons."

"Will you quit bugging me if I tell you?"

Martinelli held up his right hand. "Scout's honor."

Mitt stood and backed up to one of the tent poles. Moving up and down, he scratched against it. "Listen up, 'cause I'll only tell this once." It had to be spicy. A little bit crude. Something just believable enough that Martinelli wouldn't know he'd been had until the end. "There I was, standing two feet from the biggest, meanest-looking guy I'd ever seen. This guy says, 'I heard you been sniffin' around my girl.' And I didn't say nothin', 'cause it was true—I'd just been slobberin' over her the night before. 'And I heard you been workin' on my sister too,' he says. I couldn't say nothin' 'bout that neither, because I'd seen her right after I'd seen his girl." Mitt winked. "'What's more,' the guy says, 'I saw you leavin' out the back door when I got home today. No one was home but my mom. What were you doing there with my mama, Mitt?' Well, I says to him, 'I did everything you think I did, and more. And you know what? They liked it.'" Mitt smirked. Martinelli was hooked, alright. Hooked on stupid bunk. Like he'd ever treated a girl like that. The furthest he'd ever gotten with a girl was to stammer out a hello to his best bud's sister like an idiot. Girls were delicate things, and he was too loud, too rough. What if he crushed her hand when he'd just wanted to shake it, or she ran off screaming once she saw the scar on his face?

"Well?" Martinelli's hands motioned for him to continue. "What'd he do?"

"What'd he do? Well, he said, 'I got me another sister. How 'bout you take care of her too?'"

Martinelli let out a growl and tackled Mitt to the floor.

Mitt guffawed. "You shoulda seen the look on your face!" Mitt wiped his eyes and then screwed his face into a menacing glare. He jabbed a rigid finger in Martinelli's chest. "Like I said —onion business."

Two days later, the 77th sailed to the western side of Leyte and, after a fight to secure the beachhead, conquered both Ipil and Ormoc. They swept northward to the Tagbong River, where the crossing had to be secured for Americans to continue the fight northward. This would be their riskiest battle yet if those kinds of things could be ranked. They were coming up on an entrenched enemy holding a river crossing. There was no other way to approach but headlong and across a fast-moving river. In every other battle, Raymond could picture the way out. But with this one the outcome was just as murky as the waters of Tagbong River.

On the day of the planned attack, Raymond approached Benjamin, standing with Jasper in the assembly area. "Wade's attaching you to headquarters. Their radioman was taken out by a sniper this morning. Wish we could keep you with us, but it'll be good to hear a friendly voice on the other end of the line. Jasper, carry the radio for now."

Benjamin took the radio off his back and handed it to Jasper. "I'll direct all the firepower your way, LT."

"Why do you think I offered you up to the captain in the first place?" Raymond smiled. It had been more than that, though. He'd wanted to get Benjamin out of harm's way. If one of his soldiers had a chance to get out of the battle to come, why not the one with kids?

"Thank you, LT." Benjamin handed him the book of leaves he'd been collecting for his boys. "Do you mind? If you find any interesting leaves."

"You sure you don't want to keep it on hand? It'll be safer with you."

He shook his head. "I'll be stuck in that command post tent as you guys go north. Don't want my boys to miss out."

"Okay, then." Raymond took the book. "I'll keep my eyes out for good ones."

"Thanks. Oh, and good luck, Jasper."

"See ya when it's over, Benge." Jasper watched Benjamin walk away.

"You alright?" Raymond asked.

"Just a little relieved Benge got a ticket out of the action."

Raymond nodded. He'd breathe easier with Benjamin

leaving the platoon too. "Okay, let's get this done. Move 'em out."

The three platoons of Company A marched along the Tagbong River, alone except for the cobras hissing deep within the rice paddies. The soldiers ignored the cobras' warning and stepped deeper into the marshy lowlands following the river's winding path to the bridge.

At the designated crossing point farther down from the bridge, Raymond stepped into the water, rifle above his head. The current nudged him downriver. Wading back to the front of the platoon, he lowered himself in the water to his shoulders.

His eyes skittered across the opposite bank for signs of the enemy.

As if the action conjured it, a bullet zinged into the water a foot away from Raymond, followed by a storm of fire.

"Move!" Raymond yelled.

To his left, Harry Pulaski, leading his own platoon, and three of his men were mowed down in the first barrage, face-down in the water within seconds.

"*No!*" Raymond ran toward Harry and grabbed him by the collar. Harry hung back, limp. Raymond dragged him out of the water and pulled him to the bank. Raymond and Harry hadn't spent much time together since they'd been assigned separate platoons, but he was the first of their friend group to die. A bullet whizzed by Raymond's head. He didn't have time to grieve for Harry. He'd save it for when all this was over.

He crouched low, taking inventory of his men. So far, none were injured. Several men from other platoons waited on the banks for medics who couldn't come until the company took the bridge.

The men surged from the river and ran to the fingered ridges jutting out from the hill, covering down behind the walls of raised earth.

A blast pushed the Japanese from the bridge, splintering

wood and rope, and the enemy fell back into the hills where their snipers and machine gun nests continued to fire.

Raymond signaled his men to take cover in the shadow of a shelled tank, which had fallen nose-first into a downward slope.

A hail of bullets rained down on them from a machine gun nest on higher ground.

Jasper crouched down behind the tank next to Raymond. "We're pinned down by a machine gun! Below the high point past the bridge," he yelled into the radio's receiver.

"Gimme that." Raymond ripped the phone out of Jasper's hand. A bullet zipped by and pinged the wheel well inches from his head. Raymond flinched and gripped the radio tighter. "Get us cover, Benge." He'd better, or Evelyn was going to be a widow in the next few seconds.

"*Artillery's on it.*"

"Not from where I'm sitting, they aren't."

An explosion went off on the edge of the hill, raining debris on the men trapped behind the tank.

"*2nd Platoon is en route—hunker down and give it a few.*"

"We need cover now."

Beside them, Martinelli screamed. The private rolled up his trouser leg. Rivulets of blood streamed down his calf.

Martinelli took a knife to his shirt. With shaking hands, he tore off a strip to make a tourniquet for his calf. "Went clean through," he muttered through a knife clenched between his teeth.

"*Who was it? Who got hit?*"

"Just get help!" Raymond thrust the radio into Jasper's belly and twisted his body to train his rifle on the high point where the heaviest concentration of fire came from.

THIRTY

A GOOD MAN IN THE DIRT

Tagbong River, Philippines

Jasper brought the radio up to his ear. "Get these guys off us, Benge... Benge? *Benge!* D'you hear me?"

A thick drawl came through the radio. "*This Lieutenant Sellers?*"

"Who's this? Where's Benjamin?"

"*Put your commander on.*"

The LT was yelling at his men to keep their heads down.

"He's busy."

"*Alrighty. You tell your lieutenant your radioman just ran off a little bit ago. If I had a guess, he's headed in your direction.*"

Jasper slammed a hand into the tank's side. "No!"

The LT whipped his head to face Jasper, streams of sweat marking trails through the dirt on his face.

Jasper craned his neck behind him. His heart took off like a shot. A man ran toward them through the smoke, slightly bent, stumbling through the tank tracks and pockets of earth left behind by shelling—a man just Benjamin's size and bearing. He ran, pistol in hand, through a storm of bullets. He skidded to the ground behind the tank with the platoon.

Jasper gathered Benjamin's shirt in his fist and shook him. Benjamin's shirt was still wet from the river crossing. "What are you doing?"

Panting, Benjamin closed his eyes and caught his breath. "You needed the help."

Jasper shoved him back, releasing his shirt. "When I asked for help, I didn't mean you." Jasper thrust a canteen into Benjamin's chest.

Benjamin took a swig and replaced the cap. He raised himself on one knee as if he was readying to stand.

The LT yanked him back to the ground. "Get down!"

"We gotta get you guys outta here."

"What do you think we've been trying to do?" Jasper asked.

Benjamin squinted an eye and pointed to the top of the hill where most of the fire came from. "That where the nest is?"

"Yes, but—"

Benjamin ripped away from the LT's grasp and ran to the front of the tank.

Jasper clambered to his feet.

"Stay where you are and cover him!" Raymond shouted.

Jasper cursed and trained his rifle on the path Benjamin followed.

The tempo of the enemy's fire increased, concentrated on the charging private.

Benjamin's upper body twisted, his arm grazed by a bullet. He righted himself and surged ahead, eating up the yards with his mud-splattered boots.

Another explosion rocked the tank, knocking the men flat.

Jasper faced Raymond. "We stay, we die. *He* dies." Staying behind the tank would be worse than being exposed to fire in the open.

Raymond nodded. He turned to Martinelli, whose

wounded leg would prevent him from making a run for it. "Fall back to where we were. Searles, stay with him." Raymond scrambled to his feet, motioning his men forward. "Move!"

The platoon scattered into the open. Zampini stumbled back with a shot to the head and fell, instantly dead. Jasper vaulted over Zampini's body and up the path, the rest of the platoon in pursuit of Benjamin.

The enemy's fire swung from Benjamin to the other quarry headed in their direction.

The unit dove to the ground, trying to avoid the shots firing from the nest.

Benjamin crept to the side of the compacted dirt housing the machine gun and the enemy. Distracted by the men coming their way, the Japanese soldiers didn't see Benjamin come up behind them. Benjamin fired two shots in quick succession, and their bodies fell limp over the wall of dirt.

Benjamin sprang back to his feet.

"Come on!" he yelled, motioning to the platoon before taking off once again over the hill in the direction of more enemy fire. Benjamin became a speck on the horizon and disappeared from Jasper's line of sight.

The enemy's fire picked up from every direction.

"We gotta go after him!" Jasper yelled to Raymond.

Raymond signaled for him to stay put.

The firing didn't let up. An eternity of seconds passed.

Then there was a break in the fire.

Jasper didn't wait for permission. He jumped to his feet and surged past the LT, tripping his way down the hill and up the next. His boots slapped through clinging mud up the next rise. Explosions went off behind him and to his side. He didn't look to see where they'd come from or what kind of weapons were used. He just ran, stumbling through the torn-up landscape for what felt like hours. He crested the height of another rise and scanned the horizon for his friend.

And at the bottom of the slope lay Benjamin on his side, grunting in pain.

"*No*!" Jasper tore down the path and skidded to a stop on his knees in front of him. "Hang on, Benge!" Jasper bent down and laid his back on Benjamin's abdomen. He reached over and pulled Benjamin's leg over his shoulder, and rocking forward, he rolled the rest of Benge's body around his shoulders, warm wetness seeping through Jasper's uniform at his back. He pulled one knee up, and with a grunt, he rose and shifted Benge's weight.

Benjamin groaned. "Have to tell... LT... what I saw."

"Save your breath. I'm getting you to the medics."

Jasper turned around, almost colliding with the LT.

"Go! Get him out of here!" The lieutenant then motioned to Allen. "Cover them."

Jasper ran with Benjamin on his back, past the stalled tank and across the bridge, somehow without being hit.

"Medic!" Jasper yelled. He heaved another lungful of air. "Medic!" Within seconds, two men ran up to them with a stretcher held between them.

Jasper rolled the private onto the canvas and grabbed the top of the prostrate man's boot. "Hang on. You hang on for your boys, Benge."

The medics punctured Benjamin's thigh through the cloth of his pants with a dose of morphine. They swung the stretcher off the ground and took off. Jasper followed, keeping his rifle up and ready.

The medics pulled the litter onto a waiting truck and drove down the road behind the river to a hospital tent.

The medics went to work cutting Benjamin's shirt.

He swatted their hands away and tried to sit up. The medics pushed him back down, but he twisted away from their hands.

Benjamin fisted Jasper's shirt and pulled him close. "Get... me... command."

"Save your breath."

"*No.*" The word came out loud and strong. Too full of fire for someone whose light was fading. "I need... I need to let them know..." Benjamin coughed, blood sputtering from his lips.

Black terror twisted Jasper's stomach. This couldn't be happening. Not now that they were friends. Jasper turned to the medics. "You can fix him, can't you? He's going to be okay?"

One of the medics pushed Benjamin's shoulders back to the cot. "Calm him down, will you?"

Jasper leaned close to Benjamin. "Don't worry. I'll get somebody."

Benjamin jerked a nod and relaxed back onto the cot.

Jasper stumbled out of the tent and stepped in front of a moving jeep with hands raised.

"Get out of the way!" The driver swung his arm to point to the side of the road.

"There's a dying soldier with intelligence. I need someone who could use the information."

The man must've seen something in Jasper's face, because he cut the engine and leaped from the vehicle. "Take me to him."

Jasper turned on his heel with the officer following close behind.

When they entered the tent, Benjamin pulled away from the medics working on him.

"I came... from the hill... 'cross the river."

The officer came to stand at Benjamin's side. "Lie back, son. Let the medics work. You're not doing yourself any favors by refusing aid."

Benjamin collapsed to the stretcher. "There's a mountain gun, hiding in... in a tangle of... vines. Their strongpoint..." He stopped and grimaced, doubling over. Panting, he straightened. "They're waiting... just over the third rise." Through halting words, Benjamin used his dying breath—for surely it was that—to speak of the other fortifications he'd seen, the disposition and placement of the Japanese riflemen, and where the men might best attack.

The officer stood, a grim line at his mouth, and squeezed Benjamin's shoulder. "The Army won't forget what you did. I'll make sure of it."

Benjamin dismissed the officer's words with a slight upturn of his hand. "They're up there. Go."

Jasper kneeled next to Benjamin, tears welling in his eyes. "Why'd you do it, Benge?"

"I couldn't... let you all... die like that."

"Your boys, Benge. Tell me what I can do. How can I make it right?"

Benge's breathing picked up. "Tell 'em I love 'em."

"I'll tell them, Benge. I promise I'll tell them."

Benjamin nodded and closed his eyes.

"I'm sorry, Benge. I'm sorry we gave you such a hard time at the start. We were stupid and—"

"Forget it. I did." Benge's face, gray and waxy, eased into stillness.

Jasper shot up. "Medic!"

A medic came over and, after one glance at Benjamin, shook his head. "He's gone."

Jasper looked down once more at Benjamin's face. He tore out of the tent to the road. He flagged down a truck headed to the bridge and climbed in. He tightened his helmet strap and checked over his weapon. A sob escaped through his clenched teeth. He was going to make sure Benjamin's sacrifice made a difference. And then he was going to go home and take care of Benge's boys, even if he hadn't been able to do it in the way it counted most.

. . .

Raymond and his men trudged silently through sticky mud to the bivouac area. It was too much, too far—too much effort for Raymond's already weary limbs. Two rough-hewn slabs of wood sat on four battered oil drums set with the platoon's after-battle reward of deep-fried donuts sprinkled with cinnamon and sugar.

The soldiers filed through and picked up a donut in each hand. Everyone ate mechanically, as if they followed orders. Some soldiers stood, chewing and swallowing, as quiet as the grave. Others made their way to fallen trunks or piles of palm fronds. The rest collapsed on the ground, not caring as mud seeped into their trousers.

Sitting on a fallen tree, Mitt grabbed some donuts from a passing tray. Grimly, he stuffed one in his mouth, chewed, and swallowed. He put the others in his pocket and slumped over, staring into the distance.

A local Filipino boy of only a few years poked his head through the green, holding out his hand toward the private. Mitt eyed the child and held out a donut to him. "Here." The child took a step back. Mitt tossed the donut to him, and the boy caught it and ate it like a rabid animal. Mitt's mouth turned down at the sides, looking as if he would cry. He held out another donut. The boy took a cautious step toward him. The unkempt boy crawled on top of Mitt's lap and grabbed the donut. Mitt ran his hand over the toddler's head and handed him his canteen. Two, three more heads appeared. Mitt emptied his pockets of his fruit bars and gum and handed them over along with the rest of the donuts.

Raymond blinked away tears, so proud of Mitt he could cry. The men had been ordered not to share food with the local population due to supply concerns, but Raymond would turn a blind eye as far as Mitt was concerned. Filipinos hadn't had it easy under Japanese control. Company A came to the Philippines, at least in part, to liberate the Filipinos, and if Raymond was willing to give his life in that cause, it was ridiculous not to give them such a little thing as a leftover donut. He would hope that if Mary were in the same situation, that someone would take pity on her.

Mitt's gaze slid to Raymond's, no doubt checking to see if he'd been caught. Raymond gestured toward the donut table with his chin. Mitt nodded once, catching Raymond's unspoken message. He set the child off his lap and approached the slabs. Charming the cooks out of an entire tray of donuts, he went back to the log and set the tray behind him on the jungle floor. More children rushed to the private's side.

A wave of fatigue swept over Raymond. He lifted his helmet and wiped the sweat beading at his forehead. He was tired. So very tired.

Raymond walked over to Jasper and sank down next to him on a slanted tree trunk a few yards away. "You gonna eat your donut?"

"Don't feel like eating."

"Me neither." The smell of hot grease and cinnamon in the clearing had assaulted him with memories of humid nights walking back to campus munching on College Café's donuts without a care in the world. Harry at his side, laughing so loud he'd wake the neighborhood dogs. A stab of grief cut him to the quick. They'd been so young then. It was too strange, too jarring to be reminded of the creature comforts of home when they had just emerged from hell only hours before.

Jasper made a face and threw his donut into the tangled mess of leaves and vines behind him. Tracks of tears began to run down the private's face.

It was the first time Raymond had seen any of his men cry, although sometimes he'd heard muffled sobs from the trenches at night when he couldn't do anything about it. Raymond knelt on the ground in front of him. "Hey. It's okay."

"No, it ain't." Jasper's tears made splatters on his faded olive trousers. "It was supposed to be me, LT. I was supposed to be the one to die so his boys wouldn't lose their daddy."

Raymond's stomach flipped. Those little boys were asleep in their beds at home, not even knowing their daddy was dead. *Please, God. Not me. Not Mary.* "You can't control these things. You know you can't."

"It just ain't fair." His wracking sobs drew the rest of the platoon's attention, and Raymond angled his body to shield him from curious eyes.

"He made a choice, and we have to respect that."

"*Why?* He wanted to get back to his boys. I *know* he did. So why'd he do it? After how we treated him."

"What would you have done if you'd been him, listening to us getting picked off over the radio? You wouldn't have stayed put, either. You know you wouldn't have, no matter how badly we'd treated you."

"What Benge did..." Jasper shook his head. "I don't know that any of us could've done that."

Raymond nodded slowly. It had been a shock seeing Benjamin charge up the hill to take out the machine gun nest, and afterward, urge the platoon forward with a waving pistol and fire in his eyes. The information from Benjamin passed along over the radio had saved the platoon from walking into a trap.

Raymond couldn't believe Benjamin was gone. Benjamin had known what it was like to have a child waiting at home. A wife that he loved with all his heart, like Raymond had with Evelyn. Benjamin had known the risk in not coming back. He'd understood all that and still did what he did. "We'll find those boys and make sure they know the kind of man their daddy was, alright? Here." Raymond handed Jasper the book of leaves Benjamin had been collecting for his boys.

Jasper raised his head. "What's this?"

"It's something Benge had been making for his boys. I thought maybe you could make sure it gets back to them."

Jasper took the book and laid his hand on the cover.

"We'll live good lives in honor of Benge."

Jasper nodded.

Chaplain Taylor came over and knelt beside Jasper. "I'll take over." He glanced at Raymond. "Come see me once this is all over. I want to see how you're doing too."

Raymond nodded and stood. He leaned down and spoke quietly into Jasper's ear. "Don't forget you became his friend before the end. That counts for something."

Raymond strode to the planks of wood set on the oil barrels and grabbed an empty tray. He raised it high in the air. "No leftover food is permitted to be thrown away. Place it here before we move out."

Raymond signaled Mitt with a nod.

Mitt came up next to him. "On it."

"Oh, and here." Raymond dug in his pockets and held out a nutrition bar.

"What's this for?"

Raymond was sure Mitt hadn't held anything back from the Filipino children. "Just take it."

"I don't need it, LT. You keep it."

"Please."

Mitt took the food and stuffed it in his pants. "Think Marti made it?"

"Wade's checking for us," Raymond said. "But I'm sure Searles got Martinelli to the medics."

Mitt was quiet for a moment. "Yeah, probably."

Raymond picked up his hand-held radio. "Let's move out."

THIRTY-ONE

HOME FIRES BURNING

January 1945
Florence, South Carolina

Evelyn wandered up the aisle, trailing her fingers over a row of cans. What had she come down this aisle to get? Beans? *77th Trounces Japanese at Ormoc. Hell to Come,* this morning's newspaper had read. *Thousands lost in the last push.* Her fingers trembled. Maybe it was corn. Or was it cornmeal? She turned to the opposite side of the aisle and studied the sacks of dried goods.

Is he safe? His last letter arrived three weeks ago, every passing day since then an agony. She grabbed a bag of flour and put it inside her basket. She glanced at it again and sighed. She retrieved the bag and once again held it in her hand, staring at it with unseeing eyes. *Is he alive?*

The burning flame of their short time together flickered and grew faint; still, she held it up against the obsidian, starless night of their time apart, hoping it would be enough to beat back the pressing darkness. She shut her eyes tight and willed the flicker brighter. *Remember.* Her heart grew warm as she blew on the embers. That first year of marriage, a blur of adventure, following the 77th from camp to camp, renting a room in each new place the Army sent him—Virginia, Pennsylvania, Florida. Then California to see him off. Raymond, staying over on weekends or whenever he had a pass. Belly-deep joy as she discovered he was exactly what she'd suspected him to be—achingly, beautifully perfect for her, just as he'd promised. Her life was better with him than without, every moment a wonder to her, a balm to her cautious heart.

With every new set of orders, Evelyn rejoiced. It meant more time—more dinners for two set atop Raymond's old Army trunk with them sitting cross-legged on either side. Evelyn proud of her efforts with his meager pay, Raymond so enamored with his wife she could've served him crunchy beans and he'd have eaten them with a smile. She knew because she had, and he did. It meant rambling moonlit chats as they lay hand-in-hand beside each other on their mattress on the floor, pretending they weren't hurtling toward separation and an uncertain end. The future stretched before them like the endless horizon off the coast of Florida. During their time there, they'd escape to the beach and sit together, toes curling in the seaweed and broken shell-pocked sand, her body curving into his. They'd look out over the incandescent ocean, seeing only sky and sea rolling together into perpetual blue. Such beauty filled the edges of her heart, leaving no room for worries of war or of an end.

At Fort Pierce, she'd begun to hope the war might be over before he ever left their shores. She knew better, deep down, but still, just like when she chose to marry Raymond, she ignored her fears and hoped for the best.

"Evelyn!"

Her head jerked up. A sweaty, agitated Abigail Winters hurried down the aisle in her direction, mouth pulled tight with tension. Evelyn's heart skipped a beat. *Bad news*. She could tell in an instant, like a watchman perched on a tower, on the lookout for the slightest flicker of movement on the horizon. The warmth from her memories of Raymond cooled. Evelyn turned away from Abigail's approach and, with a shaking hand, set the bag back on the shelf. She closed her eyes and tried to steady her nerves. She felt so fragile it wouldn't take much to shatter her into a thousand shards of glass.

"Yoohoo. Evelyn." Abigail flapped her arm back and forth, the excess skin undulating under her arm. "Excuse me," she said, squeezing past a woman eyeing sacks of sugar. She rounded a bin of peanuts and stood right behind Evelyn.

Evelyn took a deep breath and turned around with a smile pasted on her face. "Hello, Abigail."

"Steel yourself. I have the most awful news."

Evelyn broke into a cold sweat. "Did Sarah send you to find me?"

Abigail ignored her question. "A telegram. Delivered just this morning."

The breath left her body. Evelyn's legs wobbled and she clenched her fingers on the closest metal shelf. "I... I have to... excuse me, Abigail." She had to get home to Mary. If she could just hold her in her arms, everything would be okay. She turned away from the woman, knocking over a stack of cans with her basket. The tins rolled under the shelves and through the aisle, but Evelyn stepped over them on her way to the exit.

"Evelyn. *Evelyn!* Come back. What on earth is wrong with you? You didn't pay for any of your things. Oh, for heaven's sake. Stop her!"

The ribbon-thin man at the register could only gape at Evelyn as she marched right past him.

Evelyn reached the door and pulled it open just in time to release the dam of pent-up tears which poured down her pale, thin cheeks. They dripped soundlessly as she rushed along the path back home, following memory more than sight. It couldn't be Raymond, could it? It would be unusual to have someone else find out before the widow. Not only unusual. It just didn't happen. *It's not him. It's not him!* She rushed down the pathway, telegraphing the words again and again to her heart, but hopelessness doused every new spark of belief as soon as she struck the flint.

A faceless enemy hunted her steps at every turn. Every day could be the one in which she received a telegram.

She hated keeping the house tidy in case they'd have to entertain sympathetic callers later in the day. She hated the sound of footsteps on their porch, knocks on the front door, the mail slot creaking open, and the soft sound of an envelope hitting the ground. She knew, she *knew* it would be given into her hand if it were bad, but her heart always seemed two steps ahead of logic. She couldn't bear fearing devastation in every waking moment. It wasn't natural. What human could bear the constant pressure?

Thousands lost in the last push. She hated Raymond for not telling her how bad things really were. His letters were at odds with newsreels and newspapers and nosy neighbors like Abigail Winters. They didn't allow her to believe the kinder truth Raymond fed her, so she hated those things too.

She stopped to dry her eyes. It wouldn't do to arrive home a mess. Mary needed her to be strong. And just as soon as she had that thought, the tears flowed once again. She hated, absolutely hated, that she had to be strong. It was as if revealing any weakness—anything less than utter faith—might prevent Raymond from coming home.

She stubbed her toe on a root jutting up above the path. Her arms shot out in front of her. Her basket flew to the side, and all the contents spilled onto the grass. She stooped to pick up the scattered groceries and turned her eyes to the canopy of bare branches overhead. "I'm not cut out for this. I'm going to break, you hear me?" She shut her mouth before she went any further, but her heart couldn't be so controlled. *Don't you see me?* A new fear curled around her heart. Maybe God didn't. Or even worse, maybe he did see and did nothing.

The thoughts propelled her to her feet. She brushed off her dress and ran a hand over her hair. She pressed on until she stood in front of the little two-bedroom house on Guerry Street.

She ran up the porch steps and swung open the front door, banging it against the wall. "Sarah? Sarah!"

"You're home quicker than expected." Sarah approached with little Mary in her arms. "Here. Someone's been a little fussy." Looking at Evelyn, she did a double take. "Are you alright?"

Mary leaned over and reached out her chubby arms. Evelyn took her with shaking hands. "Abigail. She said there was a telegram."

Sarah shook her head. "That woman is a ninny." She put her hand on Evelyn's back, rubbing soothing circles. "It was Donald Johnson, love," she said in a quiet voice. "Raymond's safe, as far as I know."

Evelyn curled into Sarah's comfort. Pulling Mary to her chest and cradling her baby's head with her hand, she buried her nose in the crook of Mary's neck and breathed deeply. "Poor Mrs. Johnson." She waited for her heart to settle its pounding rhythm.

Sarah sighed and reached out for Evelyn's basket. "I hope the cornmeal doesn't have weevils this time."

Mary reached out and grabbed Evelyn's simple strand of pearls, banging it on her mother's chest. "Ma-ma."

Evelyn and Sarah looked at each other with wide eyes. "Did you hear that?" Evelyn asked. Instantaneous joy bubbled out of Evelyn in a laugh. "Oh, Mary. You sweet girl." She rubbed her thumb over the roll of fat on Mary's wrist.

Mary gurgled back while she gummed the pearls, and the

two women laughed. Sarah carried the basket into the kitchen, and Evelyn relaxed into a chair at the dining table.

Mary's head fell to her mother's shoulder. Evelyn closed her eyes at such trust and faith—in her. A shudder ran through her. *Oh, Mary. If only you knew how little I can do.*

She was so tired of feeling helpless.

Mary grew still, her dimpled arms lax at her sides and her sweaty cheek on Evelyn's neck. Evelyn put her hand on her daughter's back and felt the slow and even rise of Mary's breathing.

Everything about her daughter was soft and fragile while the rest of the world could be so cold and cruel. She was an undeserved kindness, as if God had seen all this coming and tailored the cure.

Mary exhaled a shuddering sigh, and without opening her eyes, she swung her foot back and forth, soothing herself back to sleep. Evelyn ran her finger over Mary's toes and felt the second toe peeping taller than the first. They were Raymond's toes. She had his eyes too. His gentle, loving eyes. Eyes that longed to see his daughter, separated as he was from her by a distance as great as a wide ocean.

What must he feel, realizing his greatest heart's desire but not able to enjoy it? A child. A family of his own. It must be like watching people from behind the barred window of a prison, bustling on their way to this mundane thing or that, unaware of the gift they had in their freedom to do what they wanted.

She surged to her feet, holding Mary in her arms.

How dare she? How dare she complain when Raymond would give his right arm to sit in his mother's house and hold his sleeping baby girl on his chest, just like Evelyn was doing right now?

Alone? No, she wasn't alone. Not like Raymond was.

No matter what, Evelyn would never be alone. Her greatest fear had already become impossible—because of Mary.

And if Evelyn gave up like Mama had, Mary would be the one to answer for it.

Raymond's words came back to her from the day he'd fixed the roof on her mother's house: *Where's the Evie who put Frankie in his place? She seemed like the kind of girl who wouldn't back down from a fight.*

Where *was* that Evie?

Evelyn strode toward the stairs and climbed them to her and Mary's room.

She couldn't change the situation, but she wouldn't let it change her. She'd set aside her fears and hoped for the best before, and she could do it again. She could show Mary how to love without fear.

It was time to forge a new path for the Noble family.

She placed a firm kiss on Mary's head. "I'm going to write a letter to your grandmother," she whispered into the silky locks. Then, she was going to find something to put her hands to. Something that would put her back into the fight, for both her and Mary's sakes.

She'd been too much of a mouse, but now she was going to be a lion.

Dear Mama,

I was never brave enough to ask why you sent me away when Daddy left. I thought you'd abandoned me, just like he did.

When you asked me to keep away from Raymond, that was a little easier to understand. You didn't want me to feel the same pain you did when Daddy left.

Would you have chosen differently had you known I would still suffer, no matter if I stayed with you when Daddy left or went away, or if I married Raymond or not? You were right—I'm miserable with Raymond gone, but it was worse when I'd ended it with him. So, you see, we can't choose a way forward thinking it promises us less pain. What matters is choosing what's right, and I choose to hang onto hope, for my sake and Mary's.

I've found that I'm becoming a better person for the hurt, and I hope it brings a measure of comfort that it has made me a little more understanding of what you went through.

I'm sorry I didn't call you sooner when I was pregnant with Mary. We'd welcome you for a visit anytime.

Your loving daughter,
Evelyn (and Mary)

THIRTY-TWO

THE ENEMY'S BOOK

January 1945
Northern Philippines

Two weeks after the battle at Tagbong River, the platoon fell upon a quiet Japanese encampment. Raymond sent a squad forward. Once the *all-clear* was given, the platoon crept into the camp. Raymond lowered his hand to a firepit. A small wave of warmth emanated from the rain-darkened wood. If the upended bowls and scattered rice told the rest of the story, the Japanese soldiers had left in a hurry.

He approached the tent behind the firepit. Leaning his head close to the canvas, he listened. A wave of dizziness pulsed through him. He closed his eyes and gripped the tent pole. The vertigo passed as soon as it came. Strange. He listened again, and hearing nothing, moved the flap aside with the tip of his rifle.

The accommodations were uncommonly luxurious for the poorly outfitted Japanese. A wide plank of black, lacquered wood sat on ammo boxes, comprising a desk. On it were neat stacks of paper arranged according to size and a small silver frame with a photograph of a black-haired woman holding a little boy in her lap. A bamboo mat was rolled out beneath the desk, and squeezed in beside the desk was a neatly made cot. On the ground beside it lay a tattered and worn text, tossed to the ground in what must have been haste to escape the Americans.

Raymond tilted his head to read the spine. "*The Death of Ivan Ilych,*" he said aloud. Some Japanese soldiers had been educated in America. Maybe the book belonged to one of them. He picked up the book and hit it with a *thwack* against his thigh to remove the dirt on its surface. He opened it to a dog-eared page and read. A man named Ivan faced imminent death, the pain that had started in his stomach months before spreading, gnawing his life away, bit by bit. But Ivan didn't want to die. Dying was for other men to do.

That Caius—man in the abstract—was mortal, was perfectly correct, but he was not Caius, not an abstract man, but a creature quite, quite separate from all others. He flipped the page. *What did Caius know of the smell of that striped leather ball Vanya had been so fond of? Had Caius kissed his mother's hand like that? Had he rioted like that at school when the pastry was bad?* Raymond felt for the edges of the cot and sank down, the book still held in one hand. *Caius really was mortal, and it was right for him to die; but for me, little Vanya, Ivan Ilych, with all my thoughts and emotions, it's altogether a different matter. It cannot be that I ought to die. That would be too terrible.*

The words blurred. He lowered the book to his lap.

He, like Ivan, was mortal. He, who loved his family with such thrumming power that the joy of it sang through every cell of his body. He, who had a daughter to meet and a wife who needed him alive as proof that not all men left in one way or another. He, his brother's protector and friend, his mother's help.

Too many things left undone.

Too great a cost to bear for others in his leaving.

And a heart so alive with the purpose of these things that it seemed to him impervious to anything less than the hand of God.

He couldn't die. He just *couldn't*. He wasn't finished yet, was he? With his marriage to Evelyn, he'd been given a chance to pick up the pen and rewrite the story his father had authored. She'd trusted him. He'd convinced her to give him a chance even though this was on the horizon. It couldn't just end over here like this, could it?

It could. It had, for Benjamin. Why not himself? *Benjamin... Peach... Oliver... Walter*—he stopped, every name like a knife.

All tragedies. All wrong.

He broke out into a cold sweat.

All this bad. He couldn't find good in any of it. Would he ever?

What had happened with Walter and the land mine had been a lapse in judgment on the private's part—a mistake, but it led to the death of good men.

It could have been him. It could have been any of them. They were all just one bad decision away from the end. One wrong move, and that would be it.

But Benjamin? Benjamin hadn't done anything wrong. His death had been the saving of them, except his kids would have to suffer for it. Raymond had offered Benjamin up to Captain Wade as their radio operator—to give him a greater chance of going home to his boys, and then at least one of them would have a shot at making it back alive.

But none of Raymond's maneuvering had mattered. His decision had set off a chain of events that left Benjamin dead at the end of it.

Tolstoy understood that Death had no mercy, no understanding, no compassion. It couldn't be reasoned with or manipulated. No matter how many reasons Raymond had for staying, he had no power over the end, like Benjamin.

He flung the book away from him as if stung.

In the words of Ivan, it was too terrible indeed.

The replacement rate for lieutenants held at one hundred and fifty percent. Raymond was a marked man living on borrowed time, unless by some miracle he survived. The Japanese had better odds, and they didn't have a chance of winning. Just like Caius, just like Ivan, Raymond had a train barreling toward him, and bound to the tracks, he'd been pretending he couldn't hear the whistle.

What good could come of all this wreckage?

With shaking fingers, he searched his shirt pocket for the treasure he'd carried for months. He pulled out the snipping of Mary's hair and cradled it in his hand. All he knew of his daughter came from Evie's letters and the palm-sized picture tucked in his New Testament. This honey-colored curl might be the closest he came to holding her.

He couldn't leave her. He couldn't abandon her like his father had abandoned him. He'd promised her. Well, he'd promised the stars, the same stars hanging over her, thousands of miles away. He'd promised himself, too, long before he'd known all that would stand in his way.

In a reflex born of years of practice, he bowed his head. *Make a way. Oh, God. Please make a way. Let me go home. Let me go home to my girls.* He swallowed convulsively, knowing he was praying for the same things Benjamin didn't get.

He shot to his feet. Another wave of dizziness ran through him. Grabbing onto the tent pole, he steadied himself until it passed. Within two steps, he was at the canvas opening. He whipped one of the flaps to the side and propelled himself out of the tent.

"Move out!" he yelled to his men as he stepped through their midst.

They looked at him, startled.

"I said, move out."

Kalberer took one look at Raymond's face and repeated the order. "You heard 'im. Let's go."

The men eyed each other and fell in line.

Raymond trudged behind the scouts, his feet moving as if they were wading through a pool of molasses. He pressed on, putting as much distance as he could between himself and that tent.

Beside him, Kalberer rambled on about his plans for after the war, sweat pouring down his face. His men, likewise, appeared resigned to the heat and the swarming mosquitos.

So hot. So cold.

His nerves jangled, turning his skin cool and then burning hot with prickly fire.

Legs trembling, he stumbled to the side of the road and leaned on a severed tree trunk.

Kalberer edged into Raymond's line of vision.

"I don't feel so good, K-Bar."

"You don't look so good, neither." Kalberer's voice trickled to Raymond's ears warbly and muted.

A dark curtain fell across his vision. Raymond fell to the ground.

Mitt ran over and skidded to a stop on his knees in front of him. "Parson!" Mitt gave Raymond's face a few gentle slaps. "Wake up, LT. Don't you do this."

Raymond lifted one of his numb hands, grasping only air when he'd wanted to grip Mitt's shirt.

Hands patted him, turning him over, checking for wounds. His men hoisted him off the dirt. The tingling numbness in his hands and feet worked its way up his limbs. He tried to lift his hand to his pocket to retrieve his daughter's curl, but his leaden arm betrayed him. The burning, stinging wave worked its way to his lips.

Someone grabbed his face. Raymond opened his eyes. Mitt's mouth moved, shouting something to someone out of Raymond's line of vision.

The ringing in his ears became a clanging roar. Raymond closed his eyes. His head fell back. Black gave way to searing white, and his last thoughts were of the honey-colored curl in his pocket tied with a thin ribbon of pink.

THIRTY-THREE

THE LAND OF THE LIVING

He would achieve distinction as an agent for a portable, vest pocket atomizer which deals death to any approaching mosquito or fly.

—Raymond's senior yearbook prediction

January 1945
Leyte, Philippines

"Help me with this bedding, will you?"

"Fine, Gayle."

The women's faint voices drifted to Raymond as if he were stuffed inside a glass bottle.

He cracked his eyes open and then quickly shut them against the brightness. The buzzing in his ears increased to a whine. "Mmph."

"Oh, so you're awake now. Welcome back to the land of the living."

He opened his eyes. The woman hovering above him had nut-brown hair in a pert bob. Twice his age and all business, going by the efficient, crisp movements she used to roll him over and place the sheet below him. She rolled him over to the other side, her midsection squeaking with the movement. "Where... am I?" his voice croaked.

"You're in a field hospital. Malaria."

Malaria? So that's why he felt chewed up and spit out. What had he been doing before this? Where were his men now? He grabbed the woman's arm. Black swirled behind his eyes. "News. Need... news."

She glowered and snapped the top sheet in a billow, letting it settle over him. "You've been out of it for days. Give yourself time before worrying about anybody else."

She chopped her hand under the mattress, tucking the sheet underneath.

Her middle creaked again. What was that sound? She grabbed a folded green wool blanket from another nurse's arms and smoothed it over him. Another squeak. A girdle? He wrinkled his nose. He didn't want to think about anyone's underclothes. Well, no one's except for Evelyn's. Married life had certainly been educational. "C'mon, Squeaks. Paper and a pen's all I'm asking."

"Not until your delirium's gone."

"Aww, you're no fun."

She put her hand behind his back, lifting him up, and the other nurse thumped the pillow behind him. She settled him back on the pillow and straightened. There was that creaking again. Who would want to wear a girdle in this heat? He'd never have guessed all the contraptions women used to pull themselves together into one pleasing whole. Not that Squeaks could ever be called pleasing.

"Yes, yes. I'm no fun and when you get back, you're going to make an atomizer that'll get rid of mosquitos for good." She rolled her eyes at the other nurse.

An atomizer? Had he been so out of it he'd brought up his

senior class's prediction? They'd all known how much he hated mosquitos.

The other nurse patted his shoulder, her eyes shining with not a little humor. "I think it's a fine idea."

Scowling, Raymond relaxed back on his pillow. "I'm tellin' you, the Japs weaponized those bloodsuckers. I just know it."

"Of course they did. That's why you have to rest so you can get back out there." Squeaks gave him a swift tap on his shoulder.

It felt like a bear hug coming from the efficient woman. "Say, you're not half bad, Squeaks."

"Glad to hear it. Now rest."

Sleep sounded like a fine idea. His eyelids felt like they were weighed down with bricks. Urgency jolted through him just as he began to drift off. "Wait."

"That's enough for today. *Rest.*"

"Jus' hol' on..."

Her shoes thudded away from him. He didn't have the strength to call her back.

He awoke some time later to a tent hushed and shadowed in the night's stagnant air. Lying there, he cataloged the sensations in his body. His head, still fuzzy, his eyes, still whirling. He lifted the back of his hand to his forehead, the way his mom used to when he was a kid to check his temperature. Still feverish, as best as he could tell. He dragged himself to a sitting position, careful not to pull his IV line. His cot wobbled, the uneven feet trading turns standing on the floor.

"Keep quiet, will you?"

Raymond peered through the dark in the direction of the noise. All he could see was a white turban floating in the air with the red glow of a lighted cigarette hovering below it. "Sorry."

"I had to listen to your yapper all week. You went a little cuckoo, you know that?"

Cuckoo? He walked himself through the haze of his hospitalization to find anything that could qualify as nutty. A nurse with bobbed hair popped into his mind. *Squeaks*, he'd called her. And he'd told the nurses all about his mosquito atomizer. It sounded stupid coming from a grown man. He closed his eyes with the shame of it. "What're you in for?"

"What are you? The Spanish Inquisition?"

"Just making conversation."

The silence stretched between them. A nurse opened a flap, revealing the earliest tinges of morning light. The man's outline took shape. One of the man's eyes was a puffy and yellow-tinged purple. The floating turban became a head swaddled in snowy gauze marked by spots of dried, rusty red. The man's thick black hair, shoved up by the wrappings and standing on end, made him look as if he'd just flown a kite during a lightning storm.

The man took another drag of his cigarette. "Shell went off to my front. Fell and split my head open like a coconut on a rock."

"Tough luck."

"I'll be out soon. You?"

Had Squeaks said anything about when he'd break out of this jail? Raymond scratched at the gauze wrapped around the IV line going into his arm. "Don't really know."

The man grunted, and they fell into silence.

A wave of heat rolled over him, and he pushed off the covers with his feet. Exhausted from the effort, he lowered himself to his back. Wherever he went, it wouldn't be home. Malaria didn't take men out of the war for good. Not that he knew of, anyway. He'd seen enough men with shot-up limbs and chemical burns get patched up and thrown back into action to know this wasn't a ticket out of fighting.

But whatever happened, he'd be away from his platoon long

enough that another lieutenant would replace him. Probably some newbie who'd never heard a shot fired outside of training.

He couldn't let that happen. He had to recover, and fast.

A shiver coursed through his body. He reached with trembling fingers for the blanket and brought it up to his neck. He swallowed, his throat catching on itself. It was only then he noticed how thirsty he was. He flailed his arm, searching the stand between their cots for a glass of water, and knocked over a metal pan. It clattered to the floor.

The man beside him cursed. "There he goes again," he muttered.

Raymond flung his arm back to the cot, and it landed like a sack of flour. A yell billowed in his lungs, but he didn't have the strength to release it. Weak. So weak. There'd be no going back to his men. Not anytime soon.

He closed his eyes and steadied his breathing. Had he left his men in the middle of a battle? No, they had Mitt. And Kalberer. They would've taken care of things. But there was something else. Something awful, hovering on the edges of his mind.

"Would you like a book, Lieutenant?"

Raymond opened his eyes and lifted them to the nurse who hadn't mocked his atomizer. She held a stack of books in her arms. "Water."

She poured a glass and handed it to him. He gulped it down greedily. Breathing heavily from the effort, he fell back to his pillow.

"Take it easy, soldier. How about reading? You're awake now with nothing to do."

He moved to sit up, and she put a hand behind his back to guide him. "What do you got?"

"We don't have much. How about *The Robe*? I hear it's awfully exciting. About a soldier, just like yourself. Well, sort of. You see, he's a Roman, and..."

She babbled away, but his mind was too tired to follow. He took the book and thumbed through it. "Thanks, ma'am."

"Enjoy."

Raymond opened the book to the first page. The letters doubled. He squinted. The letters wobbled and then flew apart again. Raymond rubbed his eyes and tried again. Now the words were blurry. Forget it. He shut the book and tossed it to the foot of his bed.

He froze. The action unlocked a memory. The book in the Japanese camp. Benjamin. Evelyn and Mary. The train barreling down the tracks. All of it. Death, hunting him. Stalking him.

Even here in this hospital tent.

THIRTY-FOUR

A TIN OF LICORICE

March 1945
Leyte, Philippines

Sitting on his cot, Jimmie thrust a foot into his boot and yanked the shoestrings. He picked up his other boot, turned it over, and shook it. Nothing came out. He positioned it over his eye. There, in the heel, were the tips of three glinty legs backing into the shadows.

He yelped and flung the shoe against a support pole holding up the canvas roof. The boot fell to the ground with a thud, and a spider the size of a fist skittered outside the tent. Jimmie grabbed the shoe and shoved it on his foot, pulling the strings so hard, his hands got rope burn.

Leyte was no better than the last place they stayed.

Just like in Tinian, monkeys pilfered shiny objects from unguarded bedsides; slimy, rotted coconuts littered the path to and from the beach; and just this morning, he'd had powdered eggs again—slimy, just like the rotten coconuts on the path. He'd give his two front teeth for steak and eggs. Real eggs cooked in bacon grease and a charbroiled chunk of meat so thick it would take him an hour to chew it.

"Mail call!"

Jimmie hustled out the tent and joined the men crowding around Jensen. It had been weeks and weeks since the squadron had received their mail since relocating to the Philippines, and even longer since Jimmie had heard from Raymond. He was dying for one of his brother's upbeat letters.

"We're a little behind. A batch was rerouted from Tinian. The rest should start trickling in soon. Schnepp?" Jenson handed him a package. "Sellers?"

Jensen put a stack of letters into Jimmie's outstretched hand.

Jimmie stepped back and rifled through the stack—two from mother, one from Dad, another from Aunt Lil, and two from Evelyn. Nothing from Raymond.

He looked at the postmarks. Late December. He'd received a letter from Raymond after that, so these letters wouldn't be of any help.

A sickening feeling settled in to his middle.

He tossed the letters onto his cot unopened and heading out of the camp toward the Red Cross.

It wouldn't be unheard of to go so long without hearing from someone out here, but almost two months? He'd already checked, and Raymond's company wasn't here in Leyte. Rumor was, they'd been sent on to Ie Shima, one of the islands hugging Okinawa. Maybe that's all it was—a unit on the move and logistics were having trouble keeping up.

After a long trek, he arrived, sweaty and short of breath and strode to the table where two women wearing Red Cross uniforms sat. The first was a matronly stick of a woman with a blank face and bangs jutting out from under her cap. The other was a curvy woman with dimples and hair the color of gold.

He leaned with his hands flat on the table, breathing heavy.

Blondie raised an eyebrow. She dragged her pencil across the table, pushing one of his hands until it fell off the edge. Jimmie straightened and removed his other hand before the nurse could push that one off too. "I'm here about my brother. Lieutenant Arthur Raymond Sellers, Jr. He's with the 77th. I haven't heard from him in a while, and I'm getting worried."

"Get in line over there." Blondie inclined her head toward the soldiers waiting outside the tent. "You can wait your turn just like the others."

Jimmie pressed his lips together. "Look, lady. I haven't seen him in two years."

She sighed loudly. "What's your name?"

"Petty Officer Robert James Sellers."

"We'll call you when it's your turn."

What a battleax. He stuffed his hands in his pockets and joined the line. After an hour of waiting, he sat down against a coconut tree and closed his eyes.

"Excuse me."

His eyes flew open. The skinny older lady with bangs was bent at the waist, peering at him.

He jumped to his feet. "Yes?"

She turned her head toward the tent and lowered her voice. "I'm not supposed to do this, but here." She held out a folded slip of paper.

He grabbed her by the upper arms and laid a smacking kiss on her cheek. "Thanks a million."

She stumbled back from him and wiped at her cheek. "I hope you find him. He's in a hospital right here in Leyte."

In the twilight, Jimmie slipped through the hospital's canvas flaps with the "No Admittance Without Pass" sign tacked to them. He huddled behind a supply cabinet and scoped the room. It was divided by curtained sections, some open and revealing patients in their beds under mosquito nets. A nurse marched past. He retreated farther into the shadows. A cart topped with sandwiches rolled in front of him and paused in place. The nurse pushing it had stopped to chat with a passing doctor.

Jimmie rolled his eyes. How was he going to get to Raymond without arousing suspicion?

A man shouted obscenities, sending several nurses scurrying in the patient's direction. Miracle of miracles, the lady lifted her hands off the cart and bustled off to help the other nurses.

Jimmie grabbed the wagon, threw his shoulders back, and lifted his chin. If anyone tried to stop him, he'd give them the set-down of their lives and send them in search of the doctor. It might buy him enough time to find Raymond.

He nudged the cart down the hallway carefully. *Thunk.* The wheels fell into a crack between boards. Again, it happened, between every crack, a thunk. Jimmie gritted his teeth. Traitorous cart. There was nothing for it but to keep pushing on.

The first partitioned room he passed, he stuck his hand between the curtains and opened them an inch. A man—not Raymond—was hurling into a bucket. Yuck. He dropped the curtains back into place and checked the next bed and the next. Only one bed remained. Raymond had to be in there, unless that Red Cross girl had played a prank on him.

He left the cart and slipped into the enclosed space. The curtain fluttered closed, sealing him in the small space.

Shrouded in a cocoon of mosquito netting, a man lay flat with a shirt covering his eyes. Jimmie's heart thumped harder. Raymond always did that to block the light from his eyes when he was sleeping.

"Ray?" Jimmie whispered.

The man didn't move. Jimmie stepped closer. His heart

pounded so fast, his head began to swirl. "Ray." He spoke louder this time, his voice hoarse from restraint. He moved the net aside.

The man removed the cloth from his eyes. It was his brother, alright, but barely recognizable, with his cheeks pulled tight over his cheekbones under a three-day beard and dark hollows under his eyes.

Jimmie fell to his knees at the bedside. "Ray, it's Jimmie."

"Ji—Jimmie?" Raymond lifted his head weakly off the pillow.

"It's me. I'm here, and I'm gonna take care of you."

Tears welled in his brother's eyes. "Just a cold. I'll be—" A coughing fit seized him. He hacked, doubled over to his side. His eyes squeezed in pain.

Jimmie lifted him up. He could feel his brother's bones through his shirt. Raymond clung to Jimmie, wheezing, his skin burning under Jimmie's touch. Jimmie's heart hammered hard. Just how bad off was he?

Raymond laid back on his pillow, weakened by the attack. "How'd you know... I was here? I—" Another hacking cough interrupted him.

"Weaseled it out of a Red Cross lady."

Raymond's mouth cracked in a ghostly smile. "Sounds... like you."

"Where's your doc? I want to talk with him."

Raymond's eyes drifted closed. "Shell went off. Busy. Lots of patients. " His speech slurred a little.

Determination flooded Jimmie's chest. "Well, you're not alone anymore."

Raymond nodded weakly.

He wasn't even going to fight him on this? Jimmie placed another pillow behind Raymond.

"Are you thirsty? Hungry? I've got sandwiches."

Raymond shook his head.

"Don't make me stuff it down your throat. You need fattening up. Think your doc will let me stick around and be your nurse?"

"Don't think... the stockings would fit."

Jimmie rolled his eyes. "Did the doc say malaria affects the brain?"

Raymond's only response was a crinkly-eyed smile.

Tears pricked Jimmie's eyes. He hadn't known just how lonesome he'd been until he'd seen his big brother lying in his hospital bed. It'd been like pitching with the wrong arm without Ray around. "You're going to get through this, alright? I'll make sure of it."

He slipped between the curtains and marched up to a doctor writing in a chart at the end of the hallway. "Hey, doc. Got a minute?"

The man glanced up and did a double take. "Who let you in? Show me your pass."

Jimmie ignored him. "Your patient, Lieutenant Sellers. Just how bad off is he? I'm Jimmie, his brother."

The doctor looked him up and down.

"You can ask him yourself," Jimmie said.

The doctor took his stack of folders and handed them to a nurse. "Malaria. One of the worst cases I've seen. And now pneumonia from all that time on his back. He's too weak to evacuate. We're doing what we can, but we just had an influx of patients from a shell going off in a command post. If I had more staff, I would devote someone to your brother entirely."

"What if I was that person?"

"If your commander gives you leave, I don't care what you do as long as you keep out of our way." He paused. "Your brother's very sick. You should prepare yourself for the worst."

. . .

It hadn't been hard to gain Captain Jensen's permission to stay with Raymond. Jimmie's commander had a brother of his own in the war and sympathized with Raymond's plight. "I can't promise you all the time you want," he'd told Jimmie. "As soon as the squadron wants us to join them on Mindoro, you come with us, understand? And you'll still go on your missions as scheduled. But I'll see if I can find you a replacement gunner for a mission or two."

Jimmie agreed and headed straight to the field hospital as soon as Jensen dismissed him.

When Jimmie wasn't sleeping or flying, he was at his brother's bedside. He cajoled Raymond into drinking water, fanned him with a banana leaf while he was in the throes of a fever fit, and scrounged food that would tempt him to eat. He kept Raymond upright as much as he could, just as a nurse taught him, and forced his brother to his feet several times each day. The first time, Raymond had collapsed back onto the bed, gripped by dizziness and weakness. But by the end of the first week, Jimmie had Raymond taking steps on his own. Another week, and Raymond was going on short walks around their hospital tent with Jimmie at his side.

In the middle of the third week, Jimmie entered the hospital carrying a plate of pineapple upside-down cake behind his back. To his surprise, he found Raymond sitting in a chair by his bedside, the hollows in his cheeks a little less pronounced. The tight place in Jimmie's chest loosened a little. Maybe Raymond was well and truly out of the danger zone.

"Lookee what I got." Jimmie brandished the plate from behind his back.

Raymond groaned. "Give it here." He pinched the entire piece between his fingers and took a big bite. "How'd you get your hands on this?" he asked around a mouthful of cake.

"A cook owed me a favor."

Raymond laughed. "Listen to you. First the comic books, then the cake. Oh, and the extra pillow. Were those favors too?"

"I prefer to call it a reallocation of assets." He held his hands in front of him and studied his nails. "I'm a scrounger. I find people what they need for a little something in return."

"The less I know, the better."

Jimmie heaved a contented sigh. "You're looking heaps better than when I first found you."

"Well, I'm feeling heaps better." Raymond shoved the rest of the cake in his mouth.

"You know, I take it as a matter of pride you don't look like a skeleton anymore."

"You should. It was all your babying. Or maybe it was just having you around. I'll never forget waking up and seeing you standing at my bedside. Thought I'd died and you were leading me to the pearly gates."

"Does Evie know how bad off you were?"

Raymond shook his head. "She knows I have malaria but not about all this. And we're going to keep it that way, alright?"

"You sure that's a good idea?"

"Trust me. She's better off if I don't give her something else to worry about."

"She'll be spitting mad when she finds out you lied to her."

"It's not lying. It's loving her the best that I can right now."

Jimmie shrugged. Far be it from him to know how to handle a wife. "I have Dotty coming by later to give you a shave."

"I can do it myself."

"Have you *seen* Dotty?" He whistled. "Why you'd turn down a shave from that girl is beyond me."

Raymond's cheeks reddened. "The only girl's looks I care about are Evelyn's."

"You're saying you haven't noticed all the pretty girls in this place?"

"I'm not blind. I just don't care. But now I know why you're so bent on visiting me every day."

"Make no mistake, I'm here for you, brother dear, but the view... the view!" He fell back in his chair with a hand crushed to his chest.

"You ain't gonna be getting any girl's attention looking like that. How long's it been since you had a haircut? And your clothes." Raymond whistled. "I know regulation, and that ain't it."

"Do you know how long the line is to get your hair cut? This place is nearer a circus with all you Army boys on deck."

Raymond laughed. "My men sent me my foot locker. I guess they didn't want to lug it around anymore." He brandished a letter from his bedside. "Remember this?"

Jimmie eyed Raymond and took it.

July 12, 1936

Dear Ray,

I wish Aunt Lil could get another boy to fix her house and send you home to us. Summer ain't fun without you. All my pennies are gone on ice cream. It's so hot I ain't wearing pants right now. I'd swim in the river all day, but Mother says lazy boys tempt the devil. Don't it work the other way around?

You'd be real proud for I can play "Goober Peas" on the piano. Mother wants me to learn a church song next. She says old time religion will get the devil off my back. I'm only eleven years old. What the devil wants with a boy who can't do what he likes is what I want to know.

I dug a swimming hole in the back yard. The old gal kept my supper till I filled it up with dirt again. Hope it don't stunt my growth. I want to be at least as tall as you. (Mother said to write two pages. That's why I'm writing big.)

Your only brother,
Jimmie

Jimmie wrinkled his nose. "I'll never forget the scolding you gave me for calling her an old gal."

"The devil was on your back, remember?"

"Still is, by all accounts." Jimmie folded the letter and tapped it thoughtfully on his thigh. Raymond had kept the letter all these years, even so far as to take it with him across the ocean. Nothing, not even separation by Clemson and then by a war, had been able to break their bond. He handed the letter back to Raymond. "You still sent me more pennies for ice cream."

"You always had a sweet tooth. Speaking of..." Raymond reached for a large tin on his nightstand and set it in his lap. He rubbed his hands together and cracked open the lid. A familiar smell teased Jimmie's nostrils. "The boys sent this with my things."

Jimmie peered inside the container. Licorice. Sweet, pungent chunks of candy. Snaps, with their crunchy candy coating, chewy cigarettes, whips and wheels. Jimmie didn't wait for permission. He grabbed a twisted rope and sank his teeth into it. He groaned and closed his eyes in ecstasy. Around a mouthful of candy, Jimmie asked, "Do I want to know how they got all this black gold?"

Raymond shrugged before shoving a piece into his own mouth. "Wade found it in an abandoned camp awhile back."

Jimmie stopped chewing. "I didn't know Japs liked licorice."

Raymond wouldn't meet his eyes. "Don't think they do."

That could mean only one thing. It had once belonged to an American soldier. Jimmie spat his piece on the ground. Didn't it bother Raymond they were eating a dead man's licorice? Discomfort settled in his middle. The brother he knew would've been sick at all this.

Raymond shook the tin. "Eat up. Call it justice for that poor soul who lost his licorice to the Japs."

In the jungle, away from the watchful eyes of Sunday school teachers and mothers, the logic made sense. Jimmie tossed a piece of licorice into his mouth. "Can't let it go to waste, anyhow." He chewed for a moment. "Don't it bother you, though? Even a little?"

Raymond shrugged. "'Course. But if I got upset every time someone died out here, I wouldn't be able to go on."

Jimmie hadn't seen much death as a gunner. When he had, it'd been from the sky, not up close like Raymond had. He hadn't ever considered what it was like for Raymond on the ground, seeing people die—killing them, even. He shuddered. He couldn't imagine Raymond killing anybody. He was the nicest guy in the whole world who was good even to those who didn't deserve it. But here his brother was, having committed violence so bad as to kill somebody, maybe with his bare hands. How was it even possible? "How can you do it? How can you shoot somebody dead?"

Raymond was still for a moment. "I... I don't think about it much. I try to remind myself that it's keeping other people alive, and that I'm doing a good thing for our loved ones back home," he said quietly.

Raymond choosing to think of the good instead of the bad was the most Raymond-like thing he could've said. Jimmie's middle relaxed. Raymond hadn't changed, not in essentials. "Well, I'll see you tomorrow." He stood to go.

Raymond looked up at him, a worried glint in his eyes. "You know I'm going back out there, don't you? I have to. My men need me."

Raymond only needed to look in the mirror to know that

wasn't happening. His brother looked only a little better than death eating a cracker. "They'll just have to adjust to fighting without you because you're done."

"You don't know that."

"You'll get better, but it won't be in time to join them in Okinawa. Trust me."

Raymond's mouth turned down like he was sucking a lemon. "I think I liked it better when I was the one in charge."

Jimmie bowed, arm extended. "Get used to it, brother. Because this new Jimmie's here to stay."

One month later, Raymond was unbuttoning his shirt and studying the doctor's face.

The physician placed the cool metal of his stethoscope on Raymond's chest. "Sounds clear. Lungs still burning?"

"A little."

"Still wake up at night coughing?"

"No. That stopped a few days ago."

"Sleeping well, are you?" He crouched down and pulled Raymond's foot forward, checking his nailbeds.

"More or less." Raymond continued buttoning up his shirt.

"Hmm." He pinched one of Raymond's wrists between two fingers and stared at his watch. After a minute, he nodded. "I see no further need to keep you here."

Raymond's fingers froze in the middle of slipping a button through a hole. "I'm going back to my unit?"

"You won't be up for fighting anytime soon. You've lost too much weight. I'd put you on the first ship home, but General Bruce requested I send him every man who's had experience on the ground and has recovered enough to be propped behind a desk. You're going to the division's headquarters here in Leyte. Any luck, that's how you'll ride out the rest of the war."

"I don't understand." Not going home, but not going back to

the fight. Not seeing Evelyn and Mary yet, but not seeing how his men fared, either. The words jumbled in his head, duking it out for top billing. "My battalion's on its way to Okinawa. What if I went along for logistics or support?"

"The journey and the living conditions would be too taxing for you. I prescribe a nice bed, good food, and limited working hours. Don't forget you were one of the sickest we've seen, Lieutenant Sellers. I didn't know that we'd ever get to this point of discussing your release."

Jimmie slipped inside the curtain. "Hey, doc." He skirted the chair where the physician hovered over Raymond and plopped down on the bed. "Everything okay?"

"I'm discharging your brother."

Jimmie propped himself up on his elbows and stared at Raymond. "You're going home?"

"Not home. I'll be at headquarters for the rest of the war, apparently."

Jimmie turned his head and stared at the doctor. "You're not pulling our legs?"

The doctor gave Jimmie an indulgent smile. "You did a fine job taking care of him. Safe to say he might not have made it without you."

Jimmie pumped his fist in the air. "At least one of us is getting out of this dump."

"I... I can't believe it." Was it really over? No more fighting, no more worrying he might never make it home? The doctor said he might ride out the rest of the war behind a desk. With Japan on its last legs and him being released to light duty, there was a very real chance he'd be home by Christmas. Sooner, even. He could finally meet Mary. His heart beat faster. He hadn't let himself imagine it too often. She'd be scared of him at first. He'd be a stranger, for all she knew. But he'd take her on walks, read to her, be silly with her—whatever it took to help her be comfortable with him.

"I'll tell the head nurse to prepare you for release." The physician disappeared behind the curtain, leaving the brothers alone.

Jimmie sat up straight and screwed his face together. "I thought you'd be more excited."

"I am."

"Don't lie."

Raymond sighed and dropped his head onto the chair's back. "If I were going straight home, that'd be one thing. But I'm still going to be here. Sitting behind a desk. How can I do that when my men are out there taking the hits we promised we'd take together?"

"Don't you think they'd be happy for you? You've just been given a ticket out of this place. Take it and be grateful."

"I guess it's just hard to believe all this... the war... is almost over." Raymond got up and tossed his duffel bag on his bed next to Jimmie.

"Well, it's a good thing you're moving on. Got word last night I'm needed in Mindoro with the rest of the squadron. I leave tonight."

"Tonight?"

Jimmie looked at his watch. "I'd better start heading over there right now, in fact. We're needed for missions to Okinawa."

Raymond's stomach dropped. Okinawa would be the worst fight yet, as desperate as the Japanese were to keep the Allies off their mainland. "Now, Jimmie. They've gotten better at shooting planes from the sky. You—"

A nurse bustled into Raymond's room, pulling the curtain aside. "Time for discharge."

Jimmie sprang to his feet. "Give us another minute, will you?"

"Sorry. Doctor's orders."

Jimmie faced Raymond with a shade of panic in his eyes.

"You sure you'll be okay without me? You've only just gotten back to normal."

"I'm just dandy. Lookee here..." Raymond broke out into a jitterbug and ended with a flourish, hands fluttering.

Jimmie glanced at Dotty and lowered his voice. "I told you to never do that in public."

Raymond laughed. "See? Still your same old brother. Can't dance worth a lick."

"You just get yourself home to that wife and baby of yours, and I'll forgive the embarrassment."

"Deal."

"Will you still work for Dad when you get back?"

It seemed a lifetime ago when the scariest thing Raymond faced was standing up to Dad. But there was one thing he'd learned since then: Jimmie didn't need protecting any more. "You know, I don't think I will."

Jimmie tilted his head and squinted one eye as if he didn't believe it. "Really?"

"Really. I was thinking of giving teaching a try. Mechanics, carpentry, metalworking..."

"Well, isn't that something." A smile spread across Jimmie's face. "I can't think of anything better suited to you. Those boys'll be the luckiest fellows alive with you as their teacher."

Raymond pulled Jimmie to him for a hug. "If we don't—"

"Nope."

"But if I..."

"You'll be fine."

Raymond leaned back and studied his brother's face. Jimmie's image started to blur. "Don't be a hero. Just come home, okay?"

"Oh now, don't you get all misty-eyed on me."

"Easy for you to say. I'm out of danger, and you're off to Okinawa. It's dangerous out there."

"Do you think *any* of it's been safe?"

"I can't shake the feeling that something bad's about to happen."

"The war's ending soon. You're coming home. We both are. I've never been much without you, and I don't aim to try."

Dotty cleared her throat.

Raymond gave him one last fierce squeeze. "Goodbye, Jimmie. See you on the other side. And don't do anything stupid, alright? We're this close to being done with this whole thing."

THIRTY-FIVE

VICTORY GARDEN

March 1945
Florence, South Carolina

The last section of the two-day test was over. The booklets picked up, the pencils collected. Evelyn stretched her cramped hand.

It had been two weeks since she found out Mr. Franks, principal of the Florence school, needed a math teacher for a few hours a week. Two weeks since Evelyn had written Mr. Cabot, asking him to get her into the next teachers' exam. If Evelyn could hand Mr. Franks the results from this test, he might overlook the fact that she didn't have a degree yet.

Evelyn slipped out the door and down the hallway to the nearest restroom. Once shut into a stall, she released the happy tears dammed in her eyes.

"I did it," she whispered to herself. She bit her bottom lip. "I did it!" She put her hand flat on the door and closed her eyes. "I did it, Raymond. I took the test. I wasn't afraid. Well, I was a little afraid, but anybody would be."

Someone rapped their knuckles on her stall door. Evelyn straightened her jacket, ran a hand over her hair, and lifted the latch.

Sarah peeked inside, her brows drawn together. Poor Sarah had traveled to Columbia to help care for Mary when Evelyn took the test and looked as anxious as she might be if she'd taken the exam herself. "Well?"

Evelyn pushed out of the stall and took Mary, who was leaning toward her with outstretched arms. "We'll have to wait and see. But I think it went well."

"Of course it did. I'm so proud of you, sweet girl." She wrapped an arm around Evelyn's waist.

Evelyn rested her head on Sarah's. "I couldn't have done it without you. How about supper? I'm starved."

"I'll take you anywhere you want to go. My treat."

"How does pie for dinner sound?" Since Raymond left, the two women skipped dinner in favor of pie more times than could be healthy, but who would be cruel enough to say that their enjoyment wasn't worth an extra inch or two around their waists?

A few weeks later the results came in, and they only confirmed what Evelyn had felt in her heart, that she'd score well enough to impress Mr. Franks. And impress him she did, enough for him to put her to work two days a week for a few hours teaching high schoolers math.

Had she really been so afraid only two years before that she couldn't bring herself to take the test? Yet, here she was, exam complete and job offer in hand. When worry crept in about the job to come, she'd pull out Raymond's letter responding to her news, and his ebullient praise and pride would remind her of what she'd overcome. If she could conquer that test, she could certainly deal with a bunch of students.

She arrived at the school for her first day and hesitated

outside the door of her classroom. Her hand went to her gurgling midsection. Of all days to lose a little nerve. She peeked inside.

Some students were caught up in furtive conversations. There were bits about troop movements and rumors of the war ending in Europe. Others compared letters, trying to piece together the details their fathers had thought better unwritten. Their parents would be proud of such savvy offspring, but at what cost? Children shouldn't be thinking about troop movements and combing through announcements of those killed in action, hoping not to find their family listed there.

A boy holding a newspaper read aloud from the war correspondent, Ernie Pyle. Students gathered around him, hanging on every plain-spoken, brutal detail.

"...heard a noise in the brush on the hillside below. He called a couple of times, got no answer, then fired an exploratory shot down into the darkness. In a moment there was a loud explosion from below. A solitary Jap hiding down there had put a hand grenade to his chest. Why he did that, instead of tossing it up over the bluff and getting himself a half-dozen Americans, is beyond any American's comprehension."

The students were quiet for a moment. Evelyn could guess what they were thinking because she was thinking the same. Were the Americans Pyle wrote about, the ones almost dead if not for the suicidal choice of a Japanese soldier, men they knew? Their fathers? Raymond?

Evelyn surged into her classroom and clapped her hands above her head. "Please put that away. It's time for class."

The kids stuffed the letters into their pockets and straightened in their seats, facing forward with their hands clasped together on their desktops.

The boy holding the newspaper didn't move to obey. "I was just paying my respects."

"Paying your respects?"

"Didn't you hear the news? Mr. Pyle has been shot dead. He was with the 77th in Okinawa. That's my brother's unit."

Her stomach twisted. Mr. Pyle gave a voice to all the troops fighting overseas, though Evelyn had never been able to bring herself to read his columns. If he'd been with the 77th in Okinawa, then it wouldn't be too far-fetched to imagine Raymond in Pyle's tableau. "N-no, I hadn't heard that. But I'm sure Mr. Pyle wouldn't want you delaying class on his account."

Shaking his head, the boy folded the newspaper twice. "I can't believe this is one of the last of his columns we'll ever read."

Eighteen glum faces stared at her, students who had likely already faced loss, who might face more still. They waited for her to say something, trusted her to know the words that would help them understand. But she'd been prepared to teach math, not this. "You're right to mourn his death. But the best way you can honor him and help all the soldiers out there fighting for your freedom is to apply yourself to your studies and be kind to everyone so there won't be any more wars."

In the front row, a girl with braids raised her hand. "But how can us workin' hard in school help our daddies?"

Evelyn's gaze traveled over the class. "Why, aren't they fighting for this very thing? For you to be free to go to school and make good lives for yourselves?"

A freckle-faced boy at the back piped up. "I thought it was to help people."

"Well, yes. There's that too."

"I don't see what good workin' hard at school can do when our fathers are out there in the mud and the gunk fightin' the enemy," he said.

What was Mr. Franks thinking, going off one test as proof of her ability to teach? Evelyn's smile turned so brittle it might break. "Alright, we won't settle this in one day. Let's open our books and get to work. I don't think I introduced myself." She grabbed a piece of chalk in her shaking hand and turned to the board. "I'm Mrs. Sellers."

"And I'm David Parker," the boy with the newspaper said. "Is your husband over there?"

She paused writing her name. "He is."

"Then I guess you feel about the same as we do."

She set down the chalk and turned around. "We all have to make sacrifices to get the job done, David. It may seem little, but keeping things going back here so our loved ones have something happy to come home to is important. How do you think your fathers would feel if they came home to their children failing their classes?"

The students had the sense to look abashed.

"Now open your books to the chart on page one hundred, please." She didn't take pride in chastising them into obedience, but she had a job to do.

Through the rest of the class, they answered her questions and scribbled problems on command, but an air of distraction still hovered over them, with doodles being drawn and glances at the clock. Evelyn would bet her first paycheck the doodles comprised battlefield scenes and weapons. It wasn't their fault. They needed something to take their minds off the war, and even Evelyn, with half an hour's experience of teaching under her belt, knew schoolwork wasn't going to get the job done.

On her second day of teaching, Evelyn put Mary down for a nap and traveled the easy distance to the school, juggling her books, a sack lunch, a box with an old paper globe she would cut in two, and a bag of jellybeans. The jellybeans weren't strictly necessary to teach measuring the area of spherical objects, but perhaps a bribe could warm them up to it.

David and his classmates were gathered by the entrance.

Evelyn lowered her head and followed the pathway toward the back of the school. She wasn't ready to face them again just yet, especially in such a disadvantageous position, with her chin holding the globe in place and her arms juggling the rest.

Rounding the building's corner, she stopped short. The bricks had disappeared under vines and leaves the size of umbrellas, annexing territory on the walkway. "What in the world?"

She took a bounding step over one of the leaves and wobbled on a zucchini. One arm shot to the side and caught a cornstalk, heavy with cobs and hanging silk, while the other arm barely held onto her things. What was a neglected vegetable garden doing in a schoolyard?

"Mrs. Sellers?"

Mr. Franks stood behind her. "No one comes this way." He held out his hands, and she transferred the globe and her books into his arms.

"Is this the school's garden?"

"It was. Or still is, rather. It was Mrs. Stillwell's idea to put a Victory Garden back there for students to tend to. Help them feel like they're part of the effort and all that. But her husband came home from Europe, and she left it to us. I haven't found anyone to—"

"I'll do it." It was as clear as day what she needed to do. She'd thought her students needed to keep their minds off the war, but maybe what they needed was to feel more a part of the effort.

He blinked. "You will?"

She gave her head a vigorous nod.

"Well, I won't lie and say I wasn't ready to mow it all down."

"Oh no, don't do that. Do you have tools and seeds and such?"

"We have the tools, but are you sure you need the seeds?"

His gaze traveled to the overgrown jungle of bolted spinach and tomatoes rotting on the vine.

"Well, maybe not seeds just yet." She had enough of a battle ahead subduing the plants' uprising. If all went to plan, she and her restless student recruits would tend to the war in their own backyard.

THIRTY-SIX

77TH HEADQUARTERS

April 1945
Leyte, Philippines

"Something for you."

Raymond glanced up from the report he was working on. He'd adjusted well enough to life at headquarters, but somehow a part of him always expected his brother to show up unannounced like he had at the hospital. A soldier—not Jimmie—held out an envelope riddled with Mitt's familiar chicken scratch. Raymond's heart skipped a beat, just like it did every time he received a letter from one of the men in his platoon. They never said much as to the particulars, but Raymond was able to piece together enough to get a pulse on the platoon's situation. "Thanks." He grabbed the letter and ripped it open.

Parson—

How's the food? I hear you get steak on Fridays. What I wouldn't do for a slab of meat.

Things are okay. The replacements can't tell a Jap from a rat in the leaves. Our new LT just got himself killed. Liked his salutes and sirs, just like all these new 90-day wonders who come straight from training. K-Bar and me tried, but he wouldn't listen. Hope the next one has better sense.

Everybody asks when you're coming back. Between you and me, I'd stay where the steak is. But since I'm me, I'll just say, get better soon.

—Milton Solomon

Raymond fell back against the chair, letter still in hand. A lieutenant who insisted on salutes with Japs around did it at the risk of his own life. The general nixed formalities on the battlefield for a reason. Mitt's mention of replacement troops didn't bode well, either. If they were needed, his platoon was hemorrhaging men. Badly.

That new lieutenant had been a fool.

Not a fool—probably just as scared as you were when all this mess began.

A shadow covered his desk.

Frankie, the same annoying tag-along from Clemson who'd lashed out at Evelyn for reading at the diner, sat on the edge of the desk. Raymond swallowed his irritation. It had been a shock when he'd run into his old acquaintance at headquarters. One would think Frankie would've learned to keep his mouth shut in their time apart, but he was as stuck in his ways as mud-logged tank tracks.

Raymond stood and nudged Frankie. "Do you mind? I've got to find Colonel O'Brien."

Frankie fiddled with his lighter.

Flick. Flick. Hiss.

Clink. He flipped the lid closed.

Again, he opened it. *Flick, flick, hiss.* "What for?"

"I have work to do. Don't you?"

Frankie smirked. "Gave it to the new guy."

Raymond ground his teeth together. Frankie still had the same punchable face he'd always had. If the fellow wasn't careful, Raymond would go ahead and give him what he'd deserved ever since he bullied Evelyn. He bumped Frankie's legs again. "Move it."

Frankie didn't budge but instead lifted himself off the desk a little and straightened his leg so he could tuck his lighter into his pants. "Looks like you're working hard enough for the both of us. Be careful, or they'll see your potential and send you back out." He looked Raymond up and down. "You know, you could always ride out the rest of the war here. Go home to that little bookworm you married. Picture it: home-cooked meals and a bouncy bed. Wake up when you feel like it. Be there to see your kid grow up."

Yearning stabbed through Raymond like a knife. He grabbed the stack of reports. "See you tomorrow, Frankie."

The disagreeable lieutenant jumped off the desk and planted himself in Raymond's way.

Raymond went around him without a word.

Frankie walked backward, facing him. "Don't tell me you never thought about it. C'mon. We've got ourselves the best seats in the house." He spread his arms wide. "If you play this right, you go home wearing a rack of medals without the bullet in your head."

"I'm not stuck at headquarters because I want to be."

"You know you can game the system. I did. Wait it out,

idiot. This isn't going to last forever. Right now, there's ten-to-one odds it'll all wrap up by Mother's Day."

Ha. Joke's on him. No one would be able to sit things out if the Allies had to take the fight all the way to Japan. Frankie was a fool if he thought he could stay back in the rear indefinitely. "We've all got to do our part, Frankie. The men out there can't do their job if the people behind the scenes don't do theirs. What's an army without their bullets and beans? But to cheat your way out of the action? Your friends are out there."

"So are yours."

Raymond ignored the sickening feeling that gripped his stomach at Frankie's words. "You know just as well as I do they have a steady stream of replacements coming over from the States every day shipped express by the squids. Scared-out-of-their-mind newbies who have no idea what they're getting into. Do you know how long it takes to get your bearings out there?"

"No, but I bet you're gonna tell me."

Raymond came to an abrupt halt, and Frankie collided into him. "Some scared kid from who-knows-where is doing your job for you. Maybe taking a hit as we speak because you took the easy way out. You can't scam the system without somebody paying."

"Like your men are paying while you're here taking it easy?" Frankie looked Raymond up and down. "Seems you're more like me than you think."

Raymond grabbed him by the collar and pushed him against the wall. "I'm not you."

Frankie lifted his hands. "No need to get so worked up." He wrested his shirt away from Raymond's grasp and laughed. "I was just trying to help."

If this was Frankie's help, Raymond would stick with the problem. "I don't need your help."

Frankie straightened his shirt. "You're lucky I'm in a good mood today."

"Look, I'm sorry, but I'm telling you, you're gonna regret this someday."

"No, *you're* the one who's going to regret this." Frankie shouldered past him. He turned and pointed at Raymond. "I tried to warn you." He sauntered away, yelling as he went. "You're the dummy. You hear me? Not me."

As soon as Frankie disappeared, Raymond turned a corner and collapsed against the wall. In the shadows, he shut his eyes tight and leaned his head back.

Was Frankie right? Were Raymond's men paying the price because he was here while they were out there with an untried lieutenant?

His men's faces flashed through his mind, now at the mercy of whatever new lieutenant the brass assigned to them. Raymond's guess was that he'd be just as green as the rest of them. Why send someone else when Raymond was sitting at headquarters, almost as good as new? He would have to convince General Bruce of that.

His heart thumped. Was he actually considering going back to the fight? Would they even let him? He might not have the stamina to sling mud and bullets as he had before. The quinine had left him with ringing ears day and night, and he still had bouts of dizziness, probably from the weight loss. Going into battle with handicaps didn't seem ideal. Going into Okinawa in any way, shape, or form didn't seem ideal, but he might be ready enough. More ready than any of these newbie lieutenants, anyway.

Evelyn wouldn't like it. Although she didn't know how sick he'd gotten, she was aware he'd been sent to headquarters for light duty due to a bout with malaria. She might have begun to hope that he was at the end of his fighting days and would be home as soon as the surrenders of both Germany and Japan were secured.

Jimmie wouldn't like it, either, with all the work he'd put into doctoring Raymond back to health.

But did Raymond have a choice?

Raymond had been through hell and back with his men. For all that he'd done to gain their trust, it had taken time and experience to turn them into a powerful fighting whole. The new commander would have to hit the ground running from the start. There'd be no time to figure out what he was doing, and with what Raymond had heard predicted about the battle for Okinawa, it was time the new lieutenant wouldn't have.

How could Raymond stay at headquarters, knowing what his men were facing?

How could he risk his life and fight, with all that Evelyn had endured already?

It was an impossible choice, and he didn't have much time to decide. His men had just wrapped up fighting on Ie Shima and were on their way to Okinawa.

THIRTY-SEVEN

THE PARSON AND THE CHAPLAIN

"Raymond?" John Taylor, the 306th's battalion chaplain, halted.

Raymond lifted his head. "John? What are you doing here? Why aren't you in Okinawa?"

"I'm on my way there as we speak." He eyed Raymond from head to toe. "I was hoping to run into you. You're better then?"

"I'm good enough."

"I'm glad to see you alive and kicking. The men miss you. We all do."

Raymond pushed himself off the wall. "When was the last time you saw them?"

"Last week."

"How'd they look?"

Taylor's glance shifted away from Raymond. "Oh, well enough. Morale is high."

Raymond narrowed his eyes. "You're a terrible liar, John."

"Good thing I'm a chaplain, then. That's one of the job requirements."

Raymond couldn't bring himself to return John's smile. "What happened?"

"You know how it is. One day up, another down. Before long, there'll be another up."

"So it's bad, then."

"It does you no good to know."

"But I have the right—"

"I know how much your men mean to you. If I had to guess, you're thinking right now about how to get those men home. Leave it alone, for your sake. Especially since there's nothing you can do about it."

"There might be."

"Oh?"

"You got time to talk?"

"For you? Always. Come with me."

Raymond followed Taylor down the hallway.

"How do you like it at headquarters, Raymond? It must be a change, working directly under General Bruce."

"I've been getting along okay."

Taylor led Raymond to an empty office and locked the door behind them. "Just so we're not disturbed." Taylor lowered himself into one of the chairs.

"So, what got you laid up, anyway?"

"Malaria and pneumonia." Raymond hesitated a moment before adding, "And dehydration."

"After all your harping on your men to take their salt tablets and keep their canteens filled?"

"I know, I know. I'm feeling stronger, but it comes and goes."

Taylor sobered. "What is it really?"

Raymond blew out a puff of air. Where to begin? He stared at the roof. "You ever read Tolstoy?"

"Tolstoy? *Tolstoy's* got you twisted up?"

"Not Tolstoy. *Reality*. Tolstoy gave me a big, fat dose of reality, John."

"Okay." Taylor sat back and brought his interlocked fingers to the back of his head. "Let's talk reality, then."

"I know we're at war. I knew on some level I could die." Raymond shook his head. "I just never believed it might actually happen. Not until Benjamin."

"But why are you worried about getting killed? You have no need for that, being here at headquarters."

Raymond hesitated. "What if I said I was getting sent back to my men?" A hypothetical wasn't a lie. Technically.

Taylor winced. "Ahh. So your worries aren't hypotheticals, are they?"

"They weren't hypotheticals for Benjamin. He had every reason to live, but he was killed anyway. He had children, John. What do I do about *my* family?" Raymond raked his hands through his hair. "All I've ever wanted was to be a father. A good one. I wanted to come home, every night, and never give my daughter a moment's worry that I won't. Same goes for my wife."

"Alright, let's say the worst happens. You're already worried it might. What happens then?"

"Evelyn... alone. Again. Just like she feared. Do you know she didn't even want to be with me because of this very thing? It didn't stop me, John. I didn't listen to her. Not like I should have." Raymond grimaced and fell back into silence once again. "What about my mother? And my brother? It was always me and him, putting up with our dad together. What'll he do if I'm not there to look out for him? I've been doing it his whole life." The memory of Jimmie's confidence and maturity in the hospital came unbidden to his mind. "Well, he used to need me." He pinched the bridge of his nose and sighed. "If I die, I'm afraid they won't be okay. But do you want to know the worst of it? I *want* to stay and fight. I feel guilty, John." There it was, laid bare before another person to judge. What kind of man wanted to risk his life when his family waited on him back home?

Taylor set his hands on his knees. "I don't know exactly what Tolstoy wrote to put you in this frame of mind, but let's set him and all that gloomy reality aside for the moment. Let's talk a different reality, no less true. You're an ocean away from your family, Raymond. There's nothing you can do to change that fact or what might happen if you don't come home." He searched Raymond's eyes. "There's some freedom in that. Do you think God can take care of your family without your help?"

Raymond's mouth tipped in a rueful smile. "I know the answer's yes. If I believe in a God powerful enough to make the world and everything in it, I have to believe at least that."

"Exactly so. Whether you live or die, Evelyn and little Mary are safe because good men like you are over here keeping evil at bay. Don't you see? You're protecting them still, even from a distance. You might do more in this than you ever would by their side." Taylor paused. "Who's to say what may be done through your answer to this call? There's a reason you're here, Raymond. We're caught up in something bigger than ourselves. All we can do is go with the current and trust that our sacrifices won't be without an answering good."

"What good was there in Benjamin's death?"

Taylor studied the scratched wooden floor. "You must think that because I'm a chaplain I should know the answer to that question."

What else were chaplains for? "I suppose so."

"I have no more an answer for that than I did before I entered this war. I must trust in a wisdom higher than mine. *Greater love hath no man than this, that a man lay down his life for his friends*. And it's true. No greater love. Love means blood spilt on the ground over here. That's what Benjamin showed you."

Raymond's throat tightened. "If only I could've helped him..."

"No one could've helped Benjamin. He knew the risks when he left the command post."

"But—"

"It was his time, Raymond. You told me a long time ago you had to do everything right so your men would survive."

"I remember." He'd thought he could ensure that they all came home if he followed every procedure to the letter. But no matter how badly he wanted to keep them safe, bad things still happened.

"It was an impossible burden for you to take on then, same as it is now. Let it go. You can't control things any more than I can."

Whether he could fix any of this remained to be seen, but the facts were these: Evelyn and Mary weren't in any immediate danger. His men were. There was no going around it—he had to go back. "You're right in one regard. All I can do is what has been put in front of me. And from where I'm sitting, that's going back to my men and giving them my all." He stood, and Taylor did too.

Taylor's eyes were troubled. "I've always wondered, why you young boys? Why not old men like me who have everything to gain by going down in a blaze of glory before I have to drink my meat through a straw?" He shook his head. "You come to me anytime you need your old friend, the chaplain. I don't think Tolstoy cares about you as much as I do. All you boys are like sons to me."

Taylor's face radiated with acceptance and love, while Raymond's heart throbbed with a sudden grief. How different everything might've been if he'd had a father like Taylor. "John, thank you. You've always been good to me." Raymond picked up his hat and readied to go.

Taylor put his hand on Raymond's arm. "Wait."

Raymond turned and looked at him. "Yes?"

"Although I won't deny you'll pass on some day—you are

human, after all—you don't know the how or the when. Only God does. Don't count yourself a goner just yet."

Raymond forced a smile. "You mean, just because I've got a load of Japs with Arisakas pointing at my back?"

"You might have a thousand trains coming at you, but there's only one that gets you." He grabbed Raymond's shoulder like a vise. "It's not over, you hear me? You stay alive. You fight to get back to your family. Tolstoy doesn't have the last word. You fight like you're coming home, you hear me?"

Raymond looked Taylor dead in the eyes, grabbing hold of the chaplain's strength for what lay ahead. "As long as there's breath in me. I ain't giving up without a fight."

Raymond left the small office, his stomach in knots. He hadn't exactly lied to Taylor. He never outright said he was being sent back, but if the chaplain knew there was more of a choice involved, he might've dissuaded Raymond from doing what had to be done. There was only one thing left for him to do. If all went according to plan, Evelyn and Jimmie wouldn't find out until he got back. Even better if they didn't find out at all.

He retrieved some files off his desk and made his way to General Bruce's office.

An aide sat at a desk outside the general's door.

"I'm here with the reports General Bruce asked for."

"Go right in, Lieutenant Sellers." The aide jerked a thumb behind him. "He's been antsy for them."

Raymond nodded and rapped on the general's door.

"Enter."

Raymond came in and snapped a salute. "Here are the reports you asked for, sir."

General Bruce leaned over the map, the heels of his hands gripping the edge of the table. "At ease." The telephone rang. Bruce held up a finger and picked up the receiver. "Bruce." He pointed to his desk, and Raymond laid the reports on top of a stack of other reports, stepped away, and held his hands behind his back.

The general shook his head at whatever the other person on the line was saying. "You've made that quite clear, but—I wasn't finished." Bruce said the last in a clipped tone, his face positively purple. "They're headed for slaughter, and you're telling me to wait? Yeah, I understand, alright. I understand you care more about optics than the survival of my men." Bruce slammed the receiver into its cradle. He ripped off his spectacles and threw them to the desk. He exhaled slowly and focused on Raymond. "These are the reports Major Peterson wrote up?"

"Yes, sir."

"Thank you, Lieutenant."

"You're welcome, sir."

"If there's nothing else..." Bruce pointed his glasses at the door behind Raymond.

Raymond lifted his chin. "Yes, sir, there is."

"Go on."

"Sir, I respectfully request to be sent back to my unit."

Bruce sat in his chair. He rolled his pen back and forth across his desk with his forefinger, studying the lieutenant. "You do, do you?"

"I'm ready, sir. I haven't had a fever for days."

He eyed Raymond from head to toe. "Days, huh? I'd bet one of my stars it's not more than two."

Raymond kept steady under the general's perusal. The general couldn't scare him. He'd faced worse on the battlefield.

"Do you know who I was just on the phone with?"

"No, sir."

"Washington. Bastards know what we're facing in Okinawa and still won't give us what we need. Do *you* understand what we're up against?"

"I believe I have some idea. I've read the reports, and I've been in the meetings, sir. Still—"

"Thousands like you climb through the meat grinder all because I ask them to. Maybe I decide to keep one of you back." He picked up the pen and pulled out his memo pad. "You know what I like about you, Sellers? You're not a butt-kisser. I hate butt-kissers. You may not be flashy, but you're solid. Shame to see it go to waste." Bruce scribbled a note and handed it to Raymond. "We need someone to fill Garrity's spot in Logistics."

Raymond looked down at the paper and glanced back at the general. This wasn't part of the plan. "For how long?"

"We need men who've been on the ground to help G3 make informed decisions. My hope is that you'll be with him for the duration."

"For the duration," Raymond repeated slowly. Another ticket out of the fighting, just like with the doctor sending him to headquarters. Was God trying to tell him something? "Who'll lead my unit?"

"Lt. Frankie White hasn't seen any action yet."

A white-hot flame combusted in his chest. "All due respect, sir, but no one leads my men but me." He handed the slip back to Bruce. "They stand a better chance with someone who's actually led men into battle before."

Bruce raised his eyebrows. "You do understand you're talking to the commanding officer of the 77th Division, don't you?"

"My men need me. I can't ignore that. It's what you've taught us from the beginning—not to leave our brothers behind."

"You're sly to use my words against me." The tiniest of smiles lifted the corner of his mouth. "Let's not let emotion override common sense. Someone has to stay and push paper. Why not you?"

"I could never look myself in the mirror again if I took the easy way out. I can't sit back while my men are in danger."

Bruce tilted his head and studied Raymond. "I heard you have a little girl back home, Lieutenant."

Raymond's throat tightened. "She's one of the reasons I'm doing this. I want to be the kind of father she can be proud of."

The general sighed and swept his pen across the memo pad once again. "Alright, then. Have it your way. Hope I didn't just sign your death warrant."

Raymond took the slip and skimmed the words. It was done. He expelled a breath, squelching one last flicker of doubt. He couldn't dwell anymore on the ifs or the whens. His men needed him, so that's where he'd go. "Thank you, sir. I really do appreciate you letting me go."

"Thank *you*, Lieutenant. You've served us well during your time in our headquarters. Good luck over there."

"I hear luck's a fickle lady, sir."

"Well, then, Godspeed. Any objections to that?"

"I'll take whatever I can get."

THIRTY-EIGHT

BRUCE'S BATHLESS BASTARDS

The Fighting 77th
We're Bruce's Bathless Bastards,
rugged men are we;
Heroes of the Pacific
The Statue of Liberty.

We slaughtered the Japs at Ormoc
And butchered them at Guam.
We got that way from eating Spam,
Calisthenics and Pommpom.

We're the rugged boys of the Infantry—
Fighting Sons of B's
Backed by those fighting fools
The boys of the artillery.

We'll fight for Uncle Bruce
And cover him with fame—
We're the boys of the 77th
We earned ourselves a name.

When MacArthur left the Philippines
He said he'd be back or rot;
But he ran into a stalemate
And things didn't go so hot.

He called the 77th
And hell began to crack
We hit them on December 7th—
Pearl Harbor Day, in fact.

Now we're waiting for the bugle call
To line us up for Reveille
And tell us we're going back
To our homes across the sea.

We'll march down Fifth Avenue—
The people will cheer and call
"They're Bruce's Bathless Bastards,
The heroes of them all!"

—Written by an unknown 77th Division soldier

* * *

May 1945
Okinawa

Raymond and the other latecomers to the island stood in silence watching the shoreline bob in cadence with the waves rocking the boat. There were no more islands to hop. Okinawa was all that stood between America and the Japanese mainland—the last sputter of fireworks before the grand finale. Not only would they be in the cur's backyard—they'd soon be riding the back of the mangy beast itself.

"Alright. That's far enough." The sailor cut the engine.

Raymond climbed out and stepped into the surf.

Free. The word pounded in every step he took toward the island. Free from the prison of his sick bed in the hospital tent. Free from the protected confines of the 77th's headquarters in the Philippines.

Funny how returning to war felt like freedom.

His chest expanded. He drank in the familiar scent of metal and gasoline from machines moving supplies. It was good to breathe something other than carbon and typewriter ribbons in canvas-walled and plank-floored tents.

He trekked over the water-logged sand toward a man with a clipboard directing the tide of new arrivals. The soldier pointed down the road leading away from the beach. Raymond shouldered his pack and turned in that direction.

Just when Raymond reached the narrow road, a jeep rolled to a stop in front of him.

"Look who finally decided to show up," Jasper said, arm draped over the side of the door.

Raymond grinned and threw his gear in the back of the jeep. "Hello, boys. Miss me?"

Mitt whistled. "What'd they serve you in the rear? Water and air? Maybe you should reclass as a spy—the Nips wouldn't hear your feet hit the ground behind them with as much weight as you're carrying."

Raymond climbed in the back next to Kalberer.

He nodded at Raymond. "Sir."

Mitt twisted around from the front passenger seat. "We've been ready for you to come back since the day you left. It's good to have you back, Parson."

"The new LT we got last week can't wait to give your men back to you, bless him," Jasper said.

"And we can't wait till he does," Mitt added.

Raymond laughed and leaned forward, giving Mitt's shoulder a friendly jostle.

"You sure you're up for this?" Jasper's eyes creased with worry.

"What are we looking at, exactly?" Raymond asked.

Jasper remained quiet. Kalberer and Mitt eyed each other.

"You three want to tell me what I'm getting myself into?"

Mitt spoke up. "All I know is we're replacing the 96th. George Pakorney's company was thrown back from the ridge three times and came down with only fourteen men out of eighty-ni—"

"Alright. We get the picture." Kalberer gave Mitt a slight shake of his head. "Nobody thinks Okinawa's going to be a picnic. Let him adjust a little before you throw him into the frying pan."

Raymond had already heard whispers about the 96th and the battle raging on the Maeda Escarpment, the last line of defense protecting Shuri Castle and the headquarters for the Japanese army. What he'd heard had been enough to chill him to his bones. "It's alright. I'll find out soon enough."

"Sure you can't push out your TDY a little longer?" Mitt asked.

"And leave you guys on your own? Never."

An explosion punctuated the "Amen" of Chaplain Taylor's benediction. Raymond flinched, having already forgotten how shellings shook a man to his bones. Taylor grabbed a bottle filled with amber-colored liquid from the corporal beside him. He held it up before the men as if he were Moses holding up the bronze snake that would make his people well. "A little fortification, for those who want it," he said.

The corporal pushed back the men who crowded the chaplain. "Get in line, get in line. No pushing, no shoving, or no booze." The men who wanted it lined up and held out their canteen cups for a shot. Each man gulped it in one swallow and left the line to join the staging area where vehicles would convey them to the front lines.

Trucks drove by, bearing men returning from the escarpment. The men swaying in the truck bed were gray paper shells, just shadows of who they must've been before going up on the ridge.

Raymond pushed down his niggling guilt. With any luck, Evelyn and Jimmie would find out about this when he came home, if at all. He thought on the letters he'd left behind in his foot locker. If he didn't come home, they would find out why through those letters. He wouldn't chance them finding out from somebody else that he'd chosen to stay.

A truck with an empty bed pulled up and stopped in front of Raymond and his men.

"Third Platoon?"

"That's us."

"We'll take fifteen. Climb aboard."

One by one, the men stepped into the truck. Raymond grabbed the side of the truck and pulled himself into the bed.

The truck lurched forward and joined the convoy trekking up to the escarpment. He looked over his men, quiet as the truck bounced over the war-torn road. There hadn't been enough time to get to know his replacements. Tricky thing, going into battle with those you hadn't trained yet.

"Where's home?" he asked the white-faced private on his right, the freckles scattered across the bridge of his nose reminding Raymond a little of Jimmie's.

The boy swallowed. "Missour-ah." The truck went over a large dip in the road, and the boy's loose helmet wobbled on his head.

"Peters, right?"

The boy gave a jerky nod.

Raymond undid the chin strap and lifted the boy's helmet. An orange shock of sweat-slicked hair greeted him. "Well, Peters, what are your plans for when you get home?" Raymond tightened the straps, eyeing the private's head to guess its size.

"Pa wants me to help out on the farm."

Raymond plopped the helmet back on Peters. "And is that what you want?" He shifted the helmet to the left and the right, gauging the fit.

Peters set his mouth in a stubborn line. "I want to go to college."

"Well, now. That's a fine thing. Have you told your pa?"

Peters looked down. "No."

"I'd say you're doing the work of a man out here, Peters, and a man can make up his own mind about what he wants to do." Raymond connected the boy's chin strap and leaned back to survey his handiwork. "Who's to say you can't help out in the summers?"

"You don't know my pa. He don't give up once he's got an idea in his head."

"Oh, I know a thing or two about stubborn fathers. To tell you the truth"—Raymond leaned closer as if he were sharing a secret—"I'm about to have the same talk with my own dad when I get back." Raymond winked.

Peters stuck a finger under his chin strap and pulled. "Is this thing supposed to be this tight?"

"Yep." Raymond tapped the top of the helmet. "You don't want it slipping off. Your hair would draw Jap fire quicker than lightning."

The boy sat back with a scowl, scratching under his helmet, reminding Raymond of Jimmie again, this time wearing a starched shirt and tie at Dad's.

Raymond turned his attention to the others, cataloging how many were left from Fort Jackson. Martinelli had survived and was back with the platoon, and there were still Mitt, Mahony,

Allen, Jasper, and Kalberer. So few. He swallowed bile. *Please don't let us end up like George Pakorney's unit.*

As soon as he said his *Amen*, a shell hit the front of their convoy. Raymond's truck veered into a field. "To the caves!" Raymond yelled, grabbing Peters by the scruff of his shirt and hauling him out of the truck. Everyone ran to the tombs carved into stony cliffs to their right. Just as the last man ran into the field, the truck exploded, hit by another shell.

They scattered among the caves. Climbing over stone markers, they entered the muted light of the rock-hewn tombs filled with ceramic jars full of ancestral bones. Searles squeezed into the tomb with Raymond, Peters, and Mitt and bumped into one of the jars, knocking it forward into the others like a bowling ball into some pins. The last one fell to the ground and cracked on impact, spilling bones onto the ground.

"Oops," Searles said.

"Yeah, oops." Mitt leaned down and grabbed the cracked jar. He lowered his hand as if to scoop the bones inside but shrank back just before touching them. "Can't do it." He righted the jar and wiped his hand on his pants. "Sorry, Grandma. Or whoever you are." He settled down on his haunches beside Raymond, crouching by the tomb's entrance.

Wade's voice came over the radio. "Stay put. We're dialing in now."

"Roger." Raymond sat back and leaned against the stone wall at the side of the tomb, the chill of the stone seeping through his shirt. To have been ready for battle and then forced to wait—to have time to think over all the things he'd made his peace with—it wasn't a reprieve. It was going to be agony, here in the quiet, trying not to second-guess what he'd done.

He closed his eyes. He could still see Evelyn as she was when they'd said goodbye, one hand cradling her rounded middle, the other lifted in farewell. He'd stood at the ship's railing and watched her until land faded into infinite blue. He'd been so confident then. So sure their parting was for only a time.

It was hard not to think this moment a second chance to tell her how he felt. Without wasting another moment, he pulled out his map and scribbled a note on its back as fast as he could.

"Parson?" Mitt whispered after some time had passed.

Another explosion went off in the field across from them, the sound reverberating in the earthy coolness of the tomb. "Yeah?"

Mitt cracked his knuckles, one by one. "I wanna come clean about something."

"Did you finally write Marti's sister?"

Mitt rolled his eyes. "Like I've had time for that."

"No, don't tell me. You and Miss Angelina are getting married as soon as you get back, and you want me to do the honors." Raymond grinned. "I told you, Mitt. I ain't that kind of parson."

"Just listen, will you? It's about something I told you. Back at Fort Jackson."

Raymond sobered at the look on Mitt's face. He folded the letter and put it back into his pocket. "What's that?"

"You remember when you asked me where I'd learned to handle a gun, and I told you it was because my old man was a cop?"

"Yeah?"

"He *used* to be a cop. Before the drink got to him. My pops attacked my ma, and I stepped in. My face took the knife he tried to put in her. Mean old drunk. Don't know what happened to make him turn to the drink like he did." Mitt peered out of the opening of the tomb. "Ma took out her needle and cried the whole time she put me back together. Guess that's why my scar's so crooked. Couldn't sew straight through all her tears."

Raymond's mouth tightened. "I'd give your old man a piece of my mind if I could."

"He kicked me out to the streets that day." Mitt looked down. "I lived a rough life back then, Parson. I never hurt a soul, but I took stuff that wasn't mine so I could survive and ran with guys who were no good for me. Yeah, I knew my way around a gun, but I swear I'd never used it on anybody till this war."

"I believe you. You have a good heart, Mitt."

The private scoffed.

"No, you do. You were the only one to be nice to Benjamin from the start."

Mitt was quiet for a moment. "Thanks for taking a chance on me, is all I'm saying. I didn't want you to know I was a lowlife before I got into the Army, but you gave me a real shot. I just wanted to say thanks."

Raymond squeezed his shoulder. "You deserved every bit of that shot."

"I turned out pretty good, huh? For a mangled-up Yid from the City?"

"Good thing you stuck it out. You've saved our backsides more than a time or two."

"I know." Mitt smirked. "So, you gonna tell me how you got the name Parson or what? Fair's fair."

"I'm no parson, Mitt. I just helped an old lady, that's all."

"Nuh-uh. You don't get off so easy as that. C'mon. Spill."

"It was nothing like what you did. You were real brave to go up against your dad like that."

Mitt gave a pointed look around the cave. "What else we got to do but share our deepest secrets?"

"You can be a real pest, you know that?"

"So? What's the story?"

Raymond sighed. "Fine. My friends and I were parked at the picture house and an old teacher of ours ran over one of our bikes. They were spitting mad and were going to go after her to pay for it." He paused, twisting his mouth to the side. He'd never actually shared the story before.

"And?"

"I told them to leave her alone. I'd build a cart and haul kids up a hill for a penny a ride, and they could coast down on their own. After a whole lot of rides, I could pay for the bike myself, and the lady would be none the wiser."

"And the parson part?"

Raymond looked up at the carved rock ceiling and shook his head. "When my friend asked me why I'd done it when the lady deserved to pay, I told him that I'd rather be wrong in one direction than the other. He called me *Parson,* and the name stuck. Happy now?"

Mitt laughed a little. "Aww. Little Raymond, getting a head start on his sainthood."

"Yeah, a real Holy Rabbi, just like you called me at the start." He thought about the letter in his trouser pocket. "Can you do something for me?"

"Anything."

"If I go down—"

"Don't talk like that."

"*If I go down,* grab this letter from my pocket and a couple others in my footlocker. Will you take them to Evelyn? Make sure her and my daughter are okay?" He'd known Mitt had a soft heart underneath all his gruff once Raymond saw him caring for the little Filipino boy back at the donut slabs. Evelyn and Mary would be safe with him.

Mitt gave a tight nod.

"While you're at it, check in on my brother. There's a letter for him too."

"How old is he?"

"Twenty."

"Twenty?" Mitt scoffed. "Hate to break it to you, but he can take care of himself."

"Maybe so. I just want to know he has a friend. Someone who'll be there for him if he needs it."

"Sure, LT. I can do that."

Raymond allowed himself a moment to imagine the two of them together. If they got along, and Raymond was pretty sure they would, Jimmie might even invite Mitt to St. Simons just for the fun of seeing Dad and Virginia deal with a scar-faced bruiser with hands the size of skillets arriving on her doorstep. Now *that* would be a fireworks show worth sticking around for.

Wade's voice crackled through the radio. "All clear. Move out."

Raymond turned to Mitt and exhaled a breath. "Well, this is it."

"Uh, Parson?"

"Yeah?"

"Say a prayer for us? Before we walk out?" Mitt fiddled with his gun strap, avoiding Raymond's eyes.

Raymond nodded and bowed his head. "Lord, jam their guns and bend their sights. Give us victory, so we can all go home. Amen." He looked up at Mitt. "Will that do?"

"It'll do," Mitt said.

Raymond held his gun at the ready. "Alright, let's go. Searles, you might want to watch your step as you leave. You know, because of the bones."

"Yeah, yeah."

Raymond laughed and pulled his rifle off his shoulder and held it at the ready. "Okay, let's get this over with."

THIRTY-NINE

ON THE SHURI LINE

Too soon, they pooled at the base of the Maeda Escarpment.

The still air carried shouts, screams, explosions, and the crank of machinery from the battle happening above them. Raymond shifted his rifle to his back. Placing a boot on the incline and gripping a ledge above his head, he strained upward. He moved as if he were an automaton, each step lifting him closer and closer to the sounds of hell above. The man above him was struck by a bullet and toppled backward. Raymond turned his head, watching the man's descent to the hard ground. The landscape whirled. He faced forward and closed his eyes. Resting his forehead on the wall of rock, he breathed slowly, waiting for the spinning to stop.

He hurled himself into motion again. Arriving at the top, he pulled himself over the ledge and spilled onto the flat surface. He scrambled to the cover of a boulder to his right. Allen dropped to the ground beside him and set up the BAR on its tripod. Martinelli, bearing ammo, dropped beside Allen. One by one, the rest of his unit got into position.

Raymond peeked around the rock. Other platoons from Company A were already grappling with the enemy, and at the forward edge of the slope, more Japanese soldiers poured over the side, coming straight toward them.

A blast obscured the sight of the rushing enemy. The flying rock and dirt settled, and the enemy materialized again, still charging toward them.

Beside him lay Searles, stunned by the blast. Raymond grabbed him under his shoulders. "Grab his legs."

Mitt rushed to them and took hold of Searles' legs. Together, Raymond and Mitt scrambled to the shell hole. Raymond dropped to his belly alongside his soldiers and fired. The enemy who made it past the line of fire swarmed onto the platoon's position like hornets on overripe peaches.

Raymond fired his pistol at an enemy soldier, knocking him to the ground. The downed man raised himself to his forearms and crawled toward Raymond, dragging a leg behind him. Raymond fired again, only allowing himself the briefest of glances to confirm the man was dead.

Jasper yelled, "Behind you!"

Raymond whipped around just in time to dip from a raised knife. He rolled away, tangling his legs in the man's, knocking him to the ground. The enemy scrambled on top of him and raised his knife again. Raymond shot his hands upward and blocked the blow. The man's arm flailed for freedom. He slipped from Raymond's hold. The knife slashed downward, and Raymond raised his forearm to deflect it. The knife scraped against Raymond's metal helmet.

The man grinned at him, baring a row of perfect, ivory teeth. He lifted the knife yet again. Raymond discharged a shot from his pistol into the man's chest.

Raymond heaved, adrenaline coursing through his veins. Hand-to-hand combat, already. Not a good sign.

Returning fire for fire, fist for fist for hours on end, darkness descended, mingling with smoke and fire. As quick as they came, the Japanese retreated to the protection of their caves and tunnels.

But it wasn't over yet. Not by a long shot.

A voice crackled through Raymond's radio. "Sellers? You there?"

"Reporting."

"Take command of Company A. No other officers surviving."

Raymond's heart beat like an executioner's drum. How could he be the only officer left out of seven commanding the company? He closed his eyes and slid the receiver to his forehead. How would he lead an entire company in the bloodiest struggle he'd ever seen?

The reedy voice came through again. "Do you copy?"

Raymond yanked the receiver back to his ear. "Roger that."

"Also, need headcount of NCOs."

Raymond's eyes swept the smoky ground to catalog the remaining sergeants. "Kalberer and Solomon are still with me, best I can tell."

"Medics are coming up for an evac from B's lower ground. Make it quick. Japs are regrouping as we speak."

"We need water and ammo. Reinforcements. We're getting pretty thin up here."

"We're down by fifty percent. I'm sending what's left of Companies B and C to you."

Raymond's chest tightened. So few, when untold numbers of the enemy still lurked beneath their feet in their maze of tunnels.

"Hold that ridge, Sellers."

Raymond turned to K-Bar. "Have the men gather ammo and prepare for a counterattack. Dig in as far away from the forward slope as you can. Double time."

"Yes, sir."

"Allen? Keep your BAR at the ready. It won't be long till they're back."

The men spread out, collecting magazines of ammo from the dead. Raymond signaled to Mitt. "Get evacs ready. You're in charge."

Several yards away, there was a slight wobble of green.

Raymond squinted. Under a fallen tree hugging the border of Company A's and Company B's sectors, a soldier in a tell-tale American uniform cowered beneath a roof of tangled roots.

Who was that? Raymond ran in a crouch and ducked under the roots.

The man lay with his arms wrapped around his knees, head bowed.

"Everyone's getting shuffled to Company A. Get up and start digging in." Raymond grabbed the man's arm and pulled.

The man jerked back from Raymond and lifted his face.

Raymond's heart stopped. *Frankie?* Seeing a familiar face in a sea of death knocked the breath right out of him.

Frankie whimpered.

"Shhh. It's okay. C'mon, I've got you." Raymond pulled one of Frankie's arms from his deadlock around his knees. Frankie uncurled from his hunched position. Dark crimson blood seeped through a hole in Frankie's lower abdomen.

Raymond pushed him back and pressed the wound with both hands. He had to get back, but he couldn't leave Frankie like this. "Medic!" he yelled. The window for evacuation would be closing soon. "It's okay. You've got help now." Raymond twisted his head and yelled again, "Under the tree!"

Frankie's gray face was a mask. "Guess what?"

"What's that, Frankie?"

"I found out how long it takes to get your bearings out here."

Their last conversation came back in a rush. "Shh. You'll be okay."

"I asked to come out here. Because of what you said. I put my name on the list. Typed it up myself."

It would be like Frankie to lie just to get a dig in. Raymond pressed the wound with the heels of his hands. "You did, did you?"

Frankie grabbed Raymond's forearm with a bloodied hand. "I knew you were right when you said I needed to go."

Their eyes met. The look in Frankie's eyes removed any doubt as to whether he was serious or not.

Frankie panted in pain. "At least I made the right choice while I had the chance. For once, I'm proud of myself."

"Your grandkids are going to get tired of hearing about it too."

A laugh grated out of Frankie. "You sure got me pegged."

A medic stumbled under the roots. Two litter bearers crouched beside the tree, waiting. "Okay, boys. What have we got?"

Raymond lifted his hands slightly to show the wound to the medic.

The man nodded. "Alright. Step aside."

Raymond looked over his shoulder at his men building their defensive positions on the ridge. He'd been gone too long. He squeezed Frankie's shoulder. "I have to get back. You're in good hands now."

Frankie clasped Raymond's shirt. "You come visit me when this is all over. Except I'm the one rescuing you in this story, got it?"

"Don't worry. I'll make you look good." Raymond took a step back. Once they'd been fresh-faced, naive boys eating donuts and squabbling over a golden-haired waitress, and now they were here, in the middle of all this darkness. "Goodbye, Frankie."

The litter bearers put Frankie on the stretcher and lifted him in one big jostling swoop. Frankie squeezed his eyes shut and lifted feeble fingers to wave goodbye. Raymond ducked under the hanging roots and ran in a crouch to Kalberer, huddled in a foxhole.

"You okay?" Kalberer asked.

Raymond lowered himself to the ground beside him. "Okay? Not exactly the word I'd use for it. How many we got left?"

"Of the three companies together?" Kalberer took a swig from his canteen. "About two hundred, give or take."

Two hundred. Two hundred against maybe thousands waiting below. God have mercy.

"What are the odds of us getting out of this alive, you think?" Kalberer asked.

"Enough that we shouldn't give up now."

They took opposite sides of the crater and watched the distance for ripples of movement. The rest of his men dotted the landscape, lying low in pockets carved by explosions. Only a temporary reprieve before the storm to come.

An hour passed, then two.

His hand gripping his rifle cramped. He let go and wiped his sweaty palm on his trousers.

A movement in the distance caught his eye.

Mahony had raised his rifle in the foxhole at the front of their line, signaling the enemy was in sight.

Beyond him, dark specks were getting into position.

The counterattack had begun.

FORTY

THE QUIET ISLES

For the next two days, the company seesawed over the ridge with the Japanese. Keeping the ground they'd gained was like trying to hold onto a fistful of sand without letting any slip through their fingers.

In a rare moment of respite while the Japanese regrouped, Raymond and a few of his men gathered in a low-lying area.

Raymond chewed his nutrition bar mindlessly. "Everybody taking your salt tablets?"

"I've been making sure of it," Mitt said.

"Good." Raymond closed his eyes and let his head fall back to a tree limb. In the stillness, a roaring buzz swarmed in his head. His limbs were heavy, twitching, trembling with exhaustion. But he was alive. Alive and, with his men, holding onto Rocky Ridge, even if it was by the skin of their teeth.

The divide between night and day had eluded them as they fought through a sleep-deprived, adrenaline-fueled daze. Even through the stupor, they'd held their ground. They'd lost too many lives over this ridge to give it up now. *Just one more day,* Raymond had told them, and the next day, *It won't be long now.*

Now on the seventh day, he was starting to believe it. The battle had to come to its breaking point soon.

His mind swirled, dragging his eyelids down, down. If he could sleep, just for a little while. A minute or two, and he might be clearheaded enough to get through the next hour.

"LT, Command Post's on the line for you."

Raymond jerked awake and grabbed the receiver from Mitt.

"What's your status, Sellers?"

"Twenty or so waiting for evacs. Still need water, ammo."

"As soon as it cools down, we'll send it up. Hang tight. By the way, Germany surrendered. War's over. In Europe."

Raymond blinked.

"Hello? D'you hear me? I said, *Germany surrendered.*"

Raymond gritted his teeth. "I heard you."

"Thought you'd want to pass it along to your men. For the morale boost and all."

"I'm not telling them that." It made no difference for them if the war was over in Europe. Raymond shoved the receiver at Mitt.

Mitt took it, his eyebrows raised in question.

"Germany surrendered."

Mitt looked like he'd just taken a whiff of rotten cheese. "Well, good for them."

"My feelings exactly."

"Maybe they'll send those guys in Europe to us now."

"You know how long it takes to get from there to here? Won't be soon enough for us."

Muffled booms sounded, one after another.

The ground shook beneath them.

Raymond yelled at Kalberer. "Fall back!"

The men scrambled away.

The Japanese were setting off charges in their tunnels, attempting to collapse the ground underneath the company.

The land in front of them exploded in a geyser of rock, leaving a large crevice open to the tunnels below.

Small clouds of dust dotted the landscape, billowing out of hidden cave openings.

Eyeing the pillars of debris, an idea sparked in Raymond's mind. "Hit those caves with satchel charges," he commanded, hooking three charges over his own shoulder.

The men scattered to do his bidding.

There was a cave directly in front of him, on an elevation by the line of the ridge, but Mahony and Peters were already crawling toward it.

Something near Mahony and Peters caught his eye—an undulation on the rocky soil. Two Japanese soldiers climbed toward the men, bayonets glinting in the sun. No guns—a sign that they'd run out of ammunition, perhaps. It wouldn't make much of a difference if the enemy didn't have their guns, though. The Japanese were just as good with their bayonets as they were with anything else.

Raymond dumped the charges and ran, pistol in hand.

One of the Japanese soldiers leaped at Mahony and gripped Mahony's head with one hand, holding a knife at his throat with his other.

Raymond slid to a stop in front of them.

The enemy's arm jerked in surprise. The cut angled up from the side of Mahony's neck to under his chin. Mahony fell back at an unnatural slant. Peters fumbled with his rifle and jumped back. Raymond grabbed Peters by the collar and pulled him back just as the other soldier thrust his blade toward Peters' midsection. The knife sliced the bottom half of his leg instead.

Raymond pulled Peters down the incline. The other soldier lunged forward, grabbing Peters' boot, and held on. Raymond turned his pistol on the enemy, shooting him in the arm. The man howled and let go.

At the bottom of the crevice, Raymond ran, half-carrying

Peters. Just ahead was a crater where Mitt and some of his men huddled.

"Behind you!" Mitt yelled.

A Japanese soldier ran at Raymond with his blade raised.

The enemy jerked backward, a bullet slugging him in the chest.

Raymond swung around, chest heaving.

Mitt had his rifle pointed at the fallen Jap. "Get in here, Parson."

Raymond shoved Peters in Mitt's arms. "I'm going back for Mahony."

Mitt cursed. "Cover him."

Raymond climbed the crag once again. Behind him, his men fired from abandoned foxholes and behind rocks, covering his back.

Raymond reached Mahony's hiding place. The private looked as bad as Raymond had expected, but alive. "Can you run?"

Mahony shook his head back and forth, blood trickling from the side of his neck.

Raymond allowed himself the barest of glances outside of their hiding place. His heart stopped for a painful beat. A horde of Japanese soldiers were climbing over the edge of the ridge. Another counterattack was underway, and the ones who'd made it over the side were running straight toward Raymond's dug-in company below.

Raymond shoved his pistol into Mahony's hand. "Stay here. I'll be right back."

Victory was close. He could taste it. Tenth Army would have a clear path to Shuri Castle, the heart of the Japanese defense, if they finished this now.

Mahony grabbed the bottom of Raymond's trousers with his free hand. "Don't do it, LT."

Raymond whipped his leg from Mahony's hold and took up Peters' and Mahoney's discarded satchel charges.

Crawling over jagged rock and spent shells, he scrambled to the highest point of the outcropping. He pulled the ignitor and hurled a charge into the midst of the enemy. Just as soon as it left his hand, he pulled the ignitor on the other charge and threw it. He dropped to the ground and covered his head. *Boom*. The ground shook. *BOOM*. A second explosion cracked the air like a clap of thunder. Raymond heaved, dragging dirt into his lungs. Nerves on fire, he sprang to his feet and peered below.

Debris tumbled down the sloping, rocky ground, knocking men down on its descent. A multitude of the enemy lay dead. Even more were struggling to their feet, stunned.

Raymond scrambled back from the edge.

"Run!" he yelled to his company on the other side of the rise. They could regroup in the shell craters where their heavier weapons waited and finish the battle from there.

He ran on shaking legs to Mahony and dragged him to his feet, placing one of the man's arms around his neck.

"Leave me," Mahony rasped.

"Not a chance."

The tide had turned.

Through seven days of horror, they'd held on, no matter how many times the Japanese had tried to throw them back.

There might be a few dozen of the enemy to deal with, but Company A had won the ridge.

Raymond ran toward his men, Mahony in his arms.

Mitt sprinted to them. "Give him to me."

Raymond released his burden into Mitt's arms. He couldn't have borne the physical burden much longer.

Another explosion rocked the ridge.

Raymond hit the ground with a grunt.

An artillery shell landed again, this time to his right.

Breathing heavily, he hugged the ground as soil rained down on him.

Mitt yelled, but it was drowned out by a shell falling ten yards away.

Raymond's hearing blunted into a dull whine.

Kalberer ran to them and was yelling too, signaling them toward the cover of a fortified shell crater. Mitt handed Mahony to Kalberer and pulled Raymond to his feet.

A wave of dizziness swept over Raymond.

Mitt took off running. He turned around and yelled, waving Raymond forward.

Raymond stumbled into a run, forcing his aching legs forward. There was no one else to save except himself, so he ran with every ounce of strength he had left in his body. He ran toward a chance at home and a life with a golden-haired waitress who waited for his return. Toward his chance at being a father in more than name only, because Mary waited for him too.

Mitt dove into the crater and turned around with an outstretched arm.

Raymond strained forward.

Just as their fingers touched, a crack of blinding, searing heat slammed him back.

The chaos shuttered behind a flash of light, ice-cold shock replacing the fire of battle.

In a pulse, he plummeted into a greater light.

A moment—not even that. A tearing, a rendering, from this world to the next.

He knew at once, but he was not afraid.

FORTY-ONE
BEST-LAID PLANS

May 1945
Florence, South Carolina

Evelyn raced up the stairs two at a time. "Be down in a bit," she called down to Sarah. She cracked her bedroom door and peeked in on Mary. Her baby was lying on her side in her crib, one rosy cheek squashed against the sheet and a soft snore coming from her parted lips. Evelyn smiled and quietly shut the door.

She tiptoed down the hallway to the rocking chair in the window nook and sat. It was the place she fed Mary, overlooking the quiet goings-on of sleepy Florence under the cover of moonlight. But today, in the bright sunshine of early May, she didn't care one bit about Florence. With trembling fingers, she reached inside the pocket of her sweater and pulled out the thick envelope with red and blue stripes lining the top. The letter had been lost for months, making Raymond's news old, but old news was still news.

Dear Sweet,

How are my girls? I think of you every moment. I can't wait until I'm home with you. Sometimes I look up at the starry sky at night (when I can... sometimes the jungle's so thick I can't see the sky through the leaves) and remember they're the same ones hanging over you. It makes me feel like we're together somehow. I'm no poet, but the closest thing I've ever had to a poem in my head is when I'm looking up at those stars and thinking of you.

We lost a good man yesterday. He got us out of a tight spot, but it came at the cost of his life. If his wife wasn't in New Jersey and you weren't in South Carolina, I'd ask you to look in on her. When I get home, I want us to go up and visit her and her boys. I want to make sure they understand what a good man their father was. I've written her and told her so, but I feel uneasy about leaving it at that.

Life's too short, Ev. Tell me your dreams in the next letter, and I'll tell you mine. We'll do them together. I love you. You're more to me than any earthly comfort. You and that darling baby girl of ours.

All my love, Raymond

Evelyn sat back in the rocking chair and closed her eyes, pressing the sheets of paper to her heart. Hope threaded through her. If they were making plans, surely Raymond would be coming home soon. She read the letter twice more and tucked it into her sweater pocket. The scent of butter and caramelized sugar wafted up the stairs. She clomped down the steps and entered the kitchen. There stood her mother-in-law at the counter, damp tendrils escaping from her pinned-back hair.

Evelyn grabbed an apron and tied it around her waist. "Can I help?"

Sarah smiled. "'Course you can. I'm making a batch of candy for the boys." She handed Evelyn the roll of wax paper, and together they wrapped caramel candies and chit-chatted about their day.

"How's the garden coming along?" Sarah asked.

Evelyn couldn't speak for the grin spreading across her face. "We harvested so many green beans and tomatoes that we had enough for every student to bring some home to their families *and* for the older folks without gardens. I can't tell you how good it's been. For everyone."

Sarah peeked up at her. "And you too."

"I'm making a difference, instead of just sitting back and waiting for something to happen."

"How's that Parker boy doing with his math?"

Evelyn heaved a dramatic sigh. "Alas, I still haven't been able to convince him of its importance."

Sarah grabbed three candies and dropped them in Evelyn's apron pocket. "Well, maybe you can use these as an incentive."

"They might just do the trick." Evelyn folded the wax paper over a candy and twisted the ends. "The school wants me to fill in for Mrs. Harper when she retires. Maybe even take her place. It would only be a few hours a week teaching pre-calculus and statistics, but it means I could follow my students when they went up a grade."

Sarah glanced at Evelyn. "Oh. Well, I can't imagine it being long before Raymond comes home, and then they'll be in a lurch looking for someone else."

"I guess that's true. But it's a good opportunity anyhow."

"Well, think on it."

Evelyn did think about it, all through wrapping and packaging the candy. She could continue teaching and stay with the students she'd begun to think of as her own. She and Raymond could buy a little home, and she'd put red gingham curtains above the kitchen window. They'd have a small garden for her, a garage for him, and a tire swing for Mary and any other children who came along. Mama had come up for a visit once already, and there was every hope there'd be more in the future.

She ran upstairs, and seeing Mary still fast asleep, she sat at her little writing desk and poured out all her hopes in a letter she'd send along with the sweets.

Someone knocked at the door downstairs.

She quickly jotted her name, stuffed the letter in an envelope, and hurried to the stairs.

Raymond's mother sat on the bottom step, one hand splayed to the wall. Her back shook as if… as if…

No. *No!* Evelyn's cry came out as a strangled moan. Her legs collapsed, and she sat down hard.

Sarah turned to face Evelyn.

There were tears streaming down her face.

And a telegram clutched in her fist.

FORTY-TWO

WHERE THE FAULT LIES

Dear Evelyn,

I received the radiogram yesterday telling me about Raymond.

Wish it could have been me instead of him, and I mean that, Evie.

He was the best brother I could ever hope for, and I knew he would be the same as a husband when he married you. Raymond talked a lot when he was with me about what he thought of you. He had so much to like with an excellent wife and a cute little baby.

I am so glad he had you. You were always so thoughtful and made his life a joyful one. I wish he could have seen little Mary, for she meant so much to him. Does she really look like him? It's nice that a part of him is still here with us.

Write me, even if it's just to tell me it's raining outside. I promise to look after Mary as best I know how. I'll always be there for the both of you.

Love always,
Jimmie

* * *

Leyte, Philippines
September 1945

The projector whirred, illuminating curls of smoke rising from flame-tipped cigarettes. Flickers of shadow and light flittered across everyone's faces. An elbow jabbed Jimmie in the ribs, but he sat, unmoving. There was a guffaw from the soldier beside him on the rough-hewn bench, a roar of laughter from the soldiers around him. Abbott and Costello's "Lost in a Harem" was playing.

It didn't matter what movie they played. The same nightmare ran through a loop in his mind, ever since he'd found out about Raymond's death: Just home from the war, Jimmie would walk through the door. His mother, crying, would hug him. He'd hug her back, then go to his room and sleep on a real bed. Wake up. Eat biscuits with ham. Grits and butter. Then what? It hurt too much to think what his days would be like without the person he loved more than anybody. He wouldn't see Raymond, sitting on the porch drinking from a bottle, working on some car part or another. Their kitchen table, with only two chairs. One toothbrush missing from the cup. It had been like that for a little while once Raymond left for training, but now, he'd never get those things back.

How did Raymond ever end up in Okinawa? It didn't make sense. The doctor had said he wouldn't clear him to fight. He'd like to put his hands around the moron who'd messed this one up. His mistake cost Raymond his life.

"Hey!" the soldier beside Jimmie protested.

"Move over. There's plenty of room for the three of us," a deep voice replied.

Jimmie looked up. A swarthy-skinned man with wavy dark hair shoved Jimmie's bench mate aside and plunked down beside Jimmie.

Jimmie ignored him and turned back to the movie.

"You Jimmie? Parson's little brother?"

Jimmie sucked in his breath. He faced the newcomer. "How'd you know that?"

"Wasn't hard. You look just like the picture he'd pin by his cot."

Jimmie's heart beat wildly. "You fought with him?"

"Yeah. Name's Mitt. Mitt Solomon. He tell you about me?"

Mitt... Mitt... the crack shot from the Bronx? "You shoot a bullseye on your first shot?"

Mitt chucked. "Yeah, that's me."

Jimmie held out his hand. Mitt took it, his large, calloused hand engulfing Jimmie's.

"Why'd you track me down?"

"Raymond asked me to."

"*Shh.*" The other man on the bench scowled at them.

Mitt smirked. "C'mon, Jim. Let's let this little fella watch his movie." The guy beside them made an obscene gesture, but Mitt just laughed. "Where do we go for some quiet?"

"Follow me," Jimmie said. Leading Mitt down a path to the beach, Jimmie's mind raced. Was the radiogram wrong? Was that what Mitt was here to tell him? Was Raymond really alive and stuck in some hospital somewhere? He'd heard of it happening before. Some poor jerk reported as dead turning up months later a little worse for wear but as alive as anybody.

They stopped at the water's edge. "Well?" Jimmie asked, hands on his hips. "What happened? Why are you here?"

"Just wanted to check in on you. See how you were doing."

A wave of sorrow hit him so hard it might as well have been a sucker punch. He'd been stupid to think he was going to get good news. With every letter, radiogram, and impromptu summons into his commander's presence, he expected to find out that Raymond was still alive. Who'd have guessed that hope would become his greatest enemy out here?

It took a moment before Jimmie could speak again. "I'm fine, considering. Heading home soon. Just waiting on a transport ship."

Mitt studied him with his mouth turned down at the sides and his eyes sad as if he could see right through Jimmie's act.

He looked all too much like Raymond had whenever he was concerned about Jimmie's state. Jimmie plopped down on the sand and stared at the long trail of moonlight rippling in the gentle laps of water. "How 'bout you?"

Mitt lowered himself to Jimmie's side. "I'm free as a bird after all this."

"Family?"

"The visiting kind. Ma's the only one I care to see, and she moved in with her sister in Jersey after I left."

"After you visit her, then what?" Jimmie asked.

"I've saved up a bit. Looking for a new start. Maybe some kind of business. You?"

All he knew how to do was handle a gun and acquire goods through technically unauthorized means. The only jobs he was aware of that would require those skills wouldn't do him any favors in Dad's eyes. "Was thinking of a new start myself. Saved a little, but not enough." Jimmie could feel Mitt's eyes on him once again.

"We could go in together. Bet we got enough together for a decent something."

Jimmie set his jaw to the side. Mitt wasn't the only person who could see through people's acts. The last thing Jimmie needed was someone thinking he could take Raymond's place. "You don't even know me."

"The LT did, and that's enough for me. He didn't love nobody as much as you, 'cept his wife and baby. And he's the smartest guy I know." Mitt winced. "Knew," he corrected.

"Yeah, he was." Jimmie picked up a stick by his feet and dragged it through the wet sand.

"Besides him deciding to go and fight. Can't say it was all that smart, though it saved our bacon."

Jimmie's heart stopped. He forced his voice into a deadly calm. "Go and fight?"

"You know, before Okinawa. When he asked to come back to the platoon."

Jimmie couldn't breathe. His mind whirled, trying to make sense of Mitt's words. "Stay... before..." Jimmie shot up. "*Before Okinawa*?" White dots sparked his vision.

Mitt scrambled to his feet. "I assumed you knew."

"Why would I know that? That Ray *chose* to get himself killed? To leave his baby behind?" *To leave* me?

"C'mon. He didn't want to get killed any more than the next guy."

Jimmie's chest rose hard and fast. "You're telling me he took a chance like that? On *purpose*?" Jimmie narrowed his eyes. "I don't buy it."

Mitt stared at Jimmie for a moment and then rubbed the back of his head. "You know, now that I think about it, it was the colonel's idea."

Liar. Jimmie sagged down to the fallen tree. It was true. Jimmie didn't know how, but Ray chose to go to Okinawa when he had the chance to stay back.

Mitt sat beside him and sighed. "If you knew what we were facing out there, you'd understand."

"This is my fault. He wouldn't have done it if he wasn't fighting ready. And guess why he was like that? Who forced him out of bed and made him walk and beefed him up with extra chow? Me."

"What would you have done instead? Leave him to die?" Mitt scoffed. "Nah. You'd never do that. Besides, nothing could have kept your brother back from doing what he thought was right."

Jimmie shook his head. "Except being too sick to stand, which is how he was when I found him."

"If you want to talk blame, what about me writing him letters telling him how bad off we were? You don't think I regret that?" Mitt tossed a broken shell into the sea. "I was an idiot not to see what he'd do after reading them." He pulled a letter out of his pocket. "Which reminds me."

Jimmie shrank back and stared at the wrinkled and stained envelope Mitt held out to him.

"Where'd you get that?"

"He told me to give it to you."

Jimmie snatched it out of Mitt's hand. With shaking fingers, he broke the seal and pulled out the single sheet of paper.

Dear Jimmie,

I know you were counting on me to come home, but I couldn't step away from the fight. A man does what needs doing, even when it's tough, remember? Well, a man wouldn't leave his friends to die. I don't know how else to say it. I have to stay until it's done and pray to God I get through this. If I don't come home, know I love you. More than life itself. If you understand that, maybe you can understand why I had to stay.

It was always you and me together, and I'm sorry you'll have to go it alone. I did my best to be a good brother to you. I hope you'll look back on our happy times and be glad for them. If you don't know it already, I'm proud of you. Everything you've accomplished out here is more than ten men could hope to do in their lifetimes. I always knew you had it in you. I've always been the one protecting you, but you don't need protecting anymore, do you? It's one of the reasons I decided to return to my men. I wouldn't have left you if I didn't think you'd be okay on your own.

Keep an eye on my girls. Marry a nice girl and be happy. Don't hold a grudge against Dad, and don't forget to go to church. I'll be waiting on you.

Love,
Raymond

P.S. You're the best friend I ever had.

Jimmie's hand dropped to the sand still clutching the letter. Unrestrained tears rolled down his face. "He was—"

"I know."

The roaring in Jimmie's ears slowly dissipated, leaving only the sound of the gentle laps of water.

The letter was a revelation.

All his life, Raymond had been there. He'd seen Jimmie for who he was and loved him anyway. He'd believed in him. He'd believed in him so much he'd staked his life on it.

He'd been the one to teach Jimmie how to throw a fishing line, shine his shoes, change a tire. Face a bully, ride a bicycle, drive a car. Raymond had shouldered the role of father all for the love of a little boy with wheat-blond hair who monkeyed everything his big brother did.

All this time, Jimmie had been chasing his dad's acceptance, when Raymond's—the only one's who really mattered—had been there all along.

Freedom, that's what Raymond had given him. Freedom to be who he was. Who cared what Dad thought? Jimmie didn't, not any longer. He was going to go home and stand on his own two feet, just like Raymond thought he could. "About us pulling our money together. What ideas do you have?"

FORTY-THREE

THE MOUSE AND THE LION

October 1945
Florence, South Carolina

October in Florence was the first hint of relief after months of sweltering heat. The barest of oranges and reds traced veins in deep green deciduous leaves, an omen of their eventual demise. Unlike the prophecy of fall told in dying leaves, there'd been no hint, no warning of Raymond's death. One second she was planning a reunion, the next, his memorial. The rendering had been worse than even she could imagine. But she'd survived, and now it was October, Raymond buried out of reach in a dirt plot in Okinawa with a small wooden marker. He would be moved, eventually. There was talk of a national cemetery at Pearl Harbor. She'd never see it, more than likely. With no grave to visit, it was the end, truly. One moment, she was married, and the next, not. But still his. Evelyn Sellers, her last name a chain, reminding her over and over at every mention of the one who'd given it to her.

If it was the end, why couldn't she let him go? Questions still haunted her over what had happened in Raymond's final days. The letters sent by Chaplain Taylor and the commanders in Raymond's unit had been full of platitudes. They praised him as a soldier, a friend, a beloved leader and hero, but his death was described in such flowery terms that she began to think their letters were more art than truth. She couldn't blame them. What commander wanted to tell a widow her husband's life had been wasted?

It made her think the truth was something they didn't want her to know, and in the vacuum of facts, nightmares assailed her. Her mind cooked up scenarios that, were she less fragile, she could have dismissed out of hand as ridiculous. She'd heard the whispers and seen the newspaper headlines about Okinawa. Enough to know that her thoughts weren't ridiculous. They were probable.

But there was one scenario that plagued her the most.

The atomic bombing of Hiroshima and Nagasaki secured the surrender of Japan, scuttling the plans for America's assault on the Japanese mainland. With the invasion off the table, had the battle for Okinawa been unnecessary? Had she and Mary given him up for nothing?

She looked in the little mirror by the front door and twisted her pearl necklace until the clasp was at the back of her neck. Men from Raymond's unit planned to visit today.

They could tell her what everyone else was too scared to tell her. But would they?

She held her finger out to little Mary, and her daughter grabbed hold of it with her chubby hand. A few months past one year old, Mary still needed her mother's hand to steady her. Evelyn led her outside where they sat on the porch swing of Sarah's house. Seeing the neighborhood dog approach, Mary slid off Evelyn's lap, the layers of organza scrunching up behind her head. Evelyn straightened Mary's dress and patted her bottom before the little girl toddled off to the dog.

A car slid to a stop in front of their house. Evelyn's heart jumped. She stood and ran a hand over her skirt. One of the car doors opened and out came a wide-shouldered man with a swoop of black hair. Behind him stood another man, taller and more leanly muscled, with golden hair and steel-blue eyes.

They took off their hats. The muscular man with dark hair stepped forward, his hand outstretched. "Hello, Mrs. Sellers."

Her tension settled a little at the warmth in Mitt's eyes. Her gaze traveled to the scar running down the side of his face. A little of her nervousness returned. Had he gotten it over there? Evelyn clasped his hand in hers. "You must be Mr. Solomon. I've grown familiar with you due to my husband's letters."

"Mitt is fine. The LT didn't mention anything about my swimming in those letters, did he?"

Her mouth tilted. "Why, no, he didn't. But he did mention your love of donuts. I made sure to have some on hand today." She motioned them toward the door. "You must be Mr. Hall?"

"Yes, ma'am. Call me Jasper. Thanks for letting us come and visit." He shook her hand.

Evelyn caught her daughter up in her arms. The two men studied the squirming honey-haired girl.

Mitt held out his hand to Mary, and the toddler stilled. "Hello there, little lady. My name's Mitt." He kept his hand in place, frozen between them.

Mary stuck her finger in her mouth and stared back at the older man. She laid her head on Evelyn's shoulder and swung her foot back and forth. The next moment, Mary took her finger out of her mouth and laid her palm on Mitt's larger one for the barest of moments. Mitt's face softened like melted butter.

Unbidden, tears came to Evelyn's eyes. She turned away and opened the door. "Come on in. Donuts are warm."

Jasper took Evelyn's place holding the door, and they followed her to the dining table.

"She's got his eyes," Jasper blurted out as soon as he sat down.

Evelyn nodded quietly and placed a donut on each of their plates before sitting down in her own chair. "Are you both well?"

"Yes, ma'am. Just fine," Jasper said.

Mitt took a dainty bite of the donut and placed it back on the plate. "Nothin' to complain about."

"Jimmie'll be coming back in a few months, I hear," Jasper said.

Evelyn brightened a little at the mention of her brother-in-law. "Yes, he's coming back to South Carolina for school when the Navy's done with him. It'll be good to see more of him."

Mitt nodded. "I met up with him in Mindoro a few months back."

"You did?"

"Jimmie and I have some ideas cooked up for what to do once Uncle Sam's done with us. Nothing official, but I'll be sticking around South Carolina for a little while, at least."

Evelyn smiled. "I'm glad to hear it." And she was. Mitt would be good for Jimmie, going by what Raymond had told her of him in his letters. Mitt could look after Jimmie and make sure he didn't get into too much trouble, taking over where Raymond had left off. Her husband had probably guessed that and orchestrated it ahead of time.

"And you, Mrs. Sellers?" His eyes were still on Mary, but the gentleness in Mitt's voice was a balm for her bleeding heart. "What are your plans?"

Her stomach sank. It was another question that had been plaguing her. "I... I don't know. Raymond made provisions for me to finish school, so I might do that, in time."

"He did say you were the brains of the outfit, meaning the both of you," Mitt said.

"Yes, that does sound like something he'd say." The ache in her chest throbbed. "What about you, Mr. Hall? What will you do now that you're home?"

"*Jasper*," he reminded her with a smile. "I plan on visiting another widow in our unit. George Benjamin's wife. He's the one who got himself a Medal of Honor for what happened in the Philippines. I want to stay on a bit and make sure her and her two boys get on okay." Jasper snapped his fingers. "Oh, I almost forgot. Mitt?"

Mitt held out a thick envelope. "These are full of letters from the boys. They wanted to record their memories of the LT for Mary so she would know how much he meant to them. Your husband was the best man we ever knew, Mrs. Sellers."

She took the letters and set them in her lap. It surprised her little that Raymond's earnest concern for his men had drawn this level of devotion. "That's very thoughtful."

Jasper stood and pulled something wrapped in tissue paper out of his pocket. "There are a couple more things." He pulled back the tissue and held the bundle out to her. "Raymond had them on him when he... well, you know."

She looked down at his hand. Cradled in his palm was Mary's curl set on top of a small knitted sock. Mary's baby bootie. The air left her lungs. She didn't know he'd carried it on him as he went into battle. She took them and stared at them in her own upturned hand. The booty was frayed. Flattened. No longer the lily white it had been when she'd sent it. She saw the miles it had trudged with Raymond, the hardships, the battles. It had seen and understood more than she ever would.

Mitt held out a letter to her. "And one more thing. He gave me this to give to you."

Heart galloping, Evelyn took the letter. She'd already worked so hard to separate her life from his. To transition him to memory instead of the stationary arm of her compass. Her beginning but no longer her end. She'd put his letters away. His pillow. His clothes. At one glimpse of her name written in his hand on the envelope, he came crashing back in all his smiling, masculine reality. She tucked the letter in her sweater pocket, right next to her aching heart. She'd have to save it for later when she was alone. She swallowed the lump in her throat and looked up at the men. "Please. You were with him on the ridge. At the end. I want to hear it from you."

Both men exchanged looks.

"You sure you really want to know?"

"I need to understand."

Mitt cleared his throat and studied the table. He tapped his forefinger on his leg. The clock ticked by the seconds on the wall behind him.

She'd wait as long as it took for Mitt to speak. She pasted a bland but interested look on her face as if his answers didn't matter.

At long last, he spoke. "I won't go into how bad it all really was. I don't think I could explain it, anyway. We knew we were facing something scary before we got up there. Other units hadn't been able to hold the ridge so far. The few survivors we saw coming down, they looked..." He paused. "They looked like they'd seen the Devil himself."

A shudder ran through Evelyn.

"In the first few hours up there, six of our seven officers went down, meaning Raymond was the only one left to get the company through the rest."

How scared he must have been, knowing all those lives depended on him. She blinked back tears. "How many men were left?"

"Oh, I'd say about two hundred." He swiveled to Jasper. "Wouldn't you say?"

Jasper nodded. "After that first day, yeah."

"The Japs, well, they mighta had a thousand or so. Can't say for sure because they kept coming from below. It wasn't a fair fight from the start."

A knot formed in Evelyn's stomach.

"The battle went into the next morning, and the next. We

were stuck up there for days, going hand-to-hand with those bas—"

Jasper coughed.

"—the other guys. They were blowin' up the ground beneath us from their tunnels. They just wouldn't quit. Now I know why those men looked like they did coming down from the ridge." His face turned ashen.

Evelyn slid her hand on the table toward Mitt, her fingertips almost reaching his. "It's alright. Please." She placed her hand back in her lap, grasping it in her other.

Mitt exchanged glances with Jasper. "Well, they kept comin' over the other side and from underneath. We'd get one guy down, and two more would take his place. Headquarters couldn't send reinforcements, the fighting being too hot, so we were on our own. On the seventh day, we were down to forty, maybe fifty of us, but we'd knocked down the enemy a good amount too." He stopped, as if he needed to gather strength for what he was about to say. "We were takin' cover in a hole when they came chargin' at us. We thought for sure it was the end. We were sitting ducks, all of us." Mitt twisted his hat in his hands. "Parson risked himself to throw two charges into them, blowing most of them to kingdom come. He gave us time to get out. It whittled down their numbers enough so we could finish it. It was over after that, but too late..." His voice caught.

"A shell got him, Mrs. Sellers. He wouldn't have known what hit him," Jasper added gently.

Evelyn winced, her nails having made crescent moons in the palm of one hand.

"The worst part about it was..." Mitt's voice thickened. He tore his tormented gaze away as if he couldn't bear to look her in the eyes. "The worst part was that we were off that ridge one day later, eating donuts."

She sucked in a breath. *Oh, Lord.* She couldn't bear it. It was much worse than she'd imagined. *Why?* One day. One day and he would have been safe. How could she go on, knowing that?

He took a moment and then spoke again. "I want you to know... I wouldn't have made it. None of us would have if it hadn't been for him. He kept us alive up there when we didn't have any hope of winning."

Eyes burning with unshed tears, she forced her hand to loosen its grip on the other. "I'm glad for that." Her voice trembled. "Truly." Mary climbed up into her lap as if knowing her mother needed her close. Evelyn tucked her daughter into her chest and held her tight.

"We just had to hold on to that ground, Mrs. Sellers. And we did, for seven days. Headquarters said they'd use that ridge as a pivot to get through the defenses of Shuri, and that's what happened because of what he did." He placed his hand flat on the table and leaned forward. "Without him, we wouldn't have been able to hold that ridge, and without the ridge, there'd be no getting through to Shuri. No Shuri, no winnin' Okinawa. Who knows how many other battles it would've taken if we hadn't won Rocky Ridge? He saved a lot of lives, Mrs. Sellers. A whole lot of lives."

It was an answer. His life given in return for others. His sacrifice hadn't been a waste, no matter what had ended the war. But the cost. Oh, the cost. The tears she'd held at bay poured down her cheeks. The men stared at her, helpless. "I'm sorry to embarrass you."

Mitt held out a handkerchief to her. "Aww, you just let it out. He was a brother to me, Mrs. Sellers. I'd've followed him through the gates of hell. Not that it's anything to your loss but maybe it would help you to know we thought the world of 'im."

Silence filled the room. Mary fussed and slid off Evelyn's lap. She toddled over to Mitt. He took the floppy bunny he'd found under his chair and waggled it at her. She pulled herself up on his leg and reached for the bunny.

"Hello, puddin' pie. I'm Daddy's friend. Mitt."

"Da-ee."

Mitt's head reared back as if he'd been struck. "No, Mitt. *Mitt*." His gaze crept to Evelyn's.

Evelyn winced. So much pain. Would there ever not be moments that tore at her wounds?

"Mip." Mary grasped the bunny and fell on her bottom between his legs. She stayed there, gumming the stuffed rabbit at his feet. Mitt looked up at Evelyn, flustered. She couldn't help but smile. He must not have been around many babies before.

Evelyn released a shuddering breath. "Thank you, Mitt. Thank you, Jasper. You're welcome anytime. I think it'd be good for Mary to hear about her father from his friends when she's older."

Jasper nodded.

Mitt looked up from Mary. "I'd like to come and help. I noticed a few shingles were off, and the house could do with some paint."

"I'd have to ask Sarah, but I'm sure she'd be happy to have your help."

"You just holler, and I'll be here in a jiffy."

She looked at the two men, opposites in looks and manner but united in their love for her husband. And now, in their care for his widow and daughter. It was the closest she'd felt to Raymond since he'd left for the Pacific. They'd seen him, laughed with him, maybe cried with him too. They knew what he looked like after months of hardship in war. They knew, more than she, the parts he'd hidden from her in his letters. It could have made her jealous, but it didn't. He hadn't been alone at the end, and it helped to know it. "Thank you. Thank you for everything."

"Tate-too," Mary said from in between Mitt's legs.

Everyone laughed. A half-hearted laugh, but it was a start.

May 5, 1945

Dear Sweet—

We're about to move out, so this letter won't be nice and newsy like you like. Mitt Solomon will pass it along in case the worst should happen. He's a good man and will tell you what you want to know. I figured as smart as you are, you probably guessed I haven't told you everything that's happened over here. I didn't have the heart to make you worry, with all you're carrying on your own.

I've lived a good life, Ev, and I don't have any regrets except one. I knew the risk you took in marrying me, and I still wanted to make you mine. Forgive me. All I could see was you.

Speaking of regrets, you may hear some things about me choosing to go back to my men. I want you to know there was no real choice. I couldn't choose my own happiness if it came with risking their lives. If I did what I wanted, I would be AWOL and on my way home to you. I'm here with them and in this awful time for a purpose. I may never know this side of heaven what that might be, but knowing there's a reason helps a little.

Tell our little girl I loved her. Tell her I felt every inch her father even though I never once got to hold her. It tears me up to think that I'll never get to see her grow up. I wish I could've seen her, just once.

I only hope that what I did over here keeps you and little Mary happy and secure for the rest of your lives. If it did, I would do it again, even knowing what it came to. I pray that you'll have a good life, and that God will take care of you. I couldn't go on out here if I thought He wouldn't.

We're in the last push, and I expect I'll know soon what my fate will be. This isn't the end, no matter what happens. Life will go on, and so will you. Live a good life, take care of our girl, and be happy.

I love you more than life itself.

Raymond

Evelyn sat in the rocking chair by the window, staring unseeingly into the waning light. Jasper and Mitt's visit three days ago had left a trail in its wake. Her cheeks were tight from tears she hadn't had the heart to wipe, her muscles aching from her sobbing. She'd fallen apart after they'd left, the bit of lightheartedness at the end of their visit doused in reality.

She had her answers now, but it came at a cost. Her nightmares now had the tinge of truth to them, and she couldn't push them away. It was like her first days as a widow all over again.

The letter from Raymond had been like getting him back for one glorious moment, but once she finished reading, he was dead once more. The words he wrote were the last she'd ever hear from him.

Mary squirmed in her arms, and Evelyn looked down, startled. Sarah must've given Mary to her, although she couldn't remember when. She let her head fall back on the chair.

He'll break your heart, Evie, Mama had said. And he had. Oh, how he'd broken her heart.

What had Mama done with all this pain? She thought back to their life after Dad had gone. Their home, dreary and comfortless. Her mother, mute and unreadable. Those new grooves in Mama's forehead became permanent installations. It was why Evelyn had said no to Raymond once she knew he was going away. She could see the end before it even began because she'd seen it in her mama's face.

The stairs creaked. "Evelyn?"

Sarah approached with cautious steps and knelt by Evelyn's side.

Evelyn glanced at her mother-in-law through the shadows.

Sarah's red-rimmed eyes peered up at her. "Are you alright?"

Evelyn could only shake her head, unable to speak.

"I've been thinking..."

"Yes?"

"I thought you might be worried about what to do next, and I want you to know you can stay as long as you need to." Sarah reached up and placed her hand on Mary's back, rubbing her thumb back and forth. "Longer, even. But only if you want to."

Evelyn swallowed, panic rising in her chest. Couldn't she just stay here with Sarah forever? "I..." Tears welled in Evelyn's eyes again.

"There's no rush on deciding anything." Sarah stood and reached for Mary. "Why don't I take her so you can have some more time to yourself?"

Evelyn hugged Mary closer. "I want her with me, Sarah."

"Alright, then." Sarah's arms dropped to her sides. "I'll be downstairs if you need me. No matter how late." She walked to the stairs, stealing backward glances at Evelyn holding Mary in the darkness.

Evelyn could stay. Forever, even. Sarah wouldn't force her to go. She'd never have to leave the house, and Sarah could help her with Mary. Evelyn could lie in bed, pull the covers over her eyes, and leave the world to itself.

But even as she considered the idea, her heart rebelled against it.

That wasn't who she was anymore, not since that day with Abigail. "Wait."

Sarah turned around, hand still on the railing. "Yes?"

"I'll stay. For a little while, at least. Until I figure out what to do next. And thank you. For being there for me and Mary through everything." She might be sad for a long while yet, but she was going to finish what Raymond started when he pulled her out of that alcove all those years ago.

With love shining from her eyes, Sarah nodded. "I wouldn't have it any other way."

FORTY-FOUR

A SCARRED SAINT AND A LITTLE SINNER

April 1946
Florence, South Carolina

Mitt followed the flow of people into the church and almost turned right back around and left. Fancy geezers in fancy clothes waved and called out to each other, ignoring the big bruiser in his new shoes and suit. Which was fine by him. He wasn't here for them, anyway.

This was his first time in this church even though he'd been in Florence for months building his new life. The seeds of what he and Jimmie discussed back in Leyte were finally sprouting. They'd pooled their money and bought land to develop on the outskirts of town, and while Jimmie was away at college learning about the business side of things courtesy of the GI Bill, Mitt worked alongside a crew to clear the land and did odd jobs to pay for his bed and board. On Sundays, his only free day, he joined Sarah, Evelyn, and Mary for dinner. It kept him busy enough. And being too busy to think was exactly how he wanted it.

A man in a tailored linen suit headed straight toward him,

his hand held out and his mouth spread in a toothy grin. "Hello there. Welco—"

Mitt pushed past him into an arched doorway and found himself smack dab in the middle of a palace—what he imagined a palace looked like, anyway, with its gold-leafed columns, plush red carpet, and soft music flowing through the wall of pipes at the front of the church. It couldn't be more different than the dark synagogue back home. The inside of the Jewish assembly had been simple, except for a brass chandelier that hovered above the *aron,* the carved cabinet where the Torah scrolls were kept. A manager from Rockwood candy attended the Congregation Kneseth Israel and gave chocolate candy to the kids every Friday night. It was the only reason he didn't complain too much when his mother dragged him to the Faile Street synagogue for Shabbat.

A man bumped into him. "Pardon me." He sidestepped Mitt and entered the sanctuary, removing the hat from his head.

Mitt scanned the crowd of people.

All the other guys had bare heads too.

He snatched his hat away and smoothed his hair. That tailor must've seen him coming from a mile away, talking him into buying a hat he didn't even need.

He edged the wall running the length of the sanctuary and peered down the length of each bench. Four pews down, he found them.

Sunlight streamed through a stained-glass window, painting Raymond's wife and daughter in reds and oranges. Mary sat in her mother's lap, happily gumming a string of Bakelite beads. Evelyn leaned against the pew's tall arm, her eyes closed and an arm draped around Mary.

"Mrs. Sellers?"

Evelyn jolted upright and wiped at the corner of her mouth as if she expected drool. "Why, Mitt. What are you doing here?"

"I thought I'd take you up on your invitation." Going by the look on her face, she was just as surprised as he was that he came. "Mind if I join you?"

She smiled up at him. "Of course not. And I thought I told you to call me Evelyn." She scooted down and patted the empty space beside her.

Mitt tried it on for size in his head. *Evelyn.* He shook his head a little. Nope. She wasn't the kind of lady he was used to being on a first name basis with. He'd probably never be on that basis with her, new suit or not. Mitt dropped into the seat and waggled his fingers at Mary. "Hello, little lady."

The organ blasted the first notes of its prelude. Both the congregation and the choir surged to their feet. Evelyn shifted Mary to her hip and wrapped an arm around her so she could hold her hymnal open with both hands.

Mary grabbed for the book. Evelyn swung it away from her, but it wasn't fast enough. Mary caught a page in her fist and pulled it toward her, ripping it a little. Eyes still on the choir, Evelyn encircled Mary's wrist and gently untangled the page from her grasp.

Mitt leaned close to Evelyn. "Want me to take her?"

"No." She shifted Mary higher on her hip. "I can do it."

Mitt shrugged and flipped through the pages, but by the time he found the right hymn, the organ played its last note. He rolled his eyes and shut the book.

"You may be seated," the guy in the robes at the front said.

Everyone sat. A beat too late, Mitt joined them.

The man talked about committees and church picnics, and then a lady went to the front and made a weepy plea for helpers in the children's Sunday school. Evelyn propped her elbow on the seatback and rested her temple on her fist. The undersides of her eyes were darkened with shadows. If Mitt had to guess, that little rug monkey of hers must've kept her up all night.

"You alright?"

"I'm fine."

Is that what they were calling it these days? Poor woman needed a nap. Or a nanny.

Mary grabbed bits of Evelyn's clothing and hair and pulled herself to her feet. Evelyn didn't stir, seemingly unfazed by a wiggly human using her for a playground.

The lady yapping about plans for the children's program sat down at last.

The pastor took her place, laying down a tidy stack of notes.

Four verses into the reading, Mary let out a bright, off-pitch shriek.

It bounced off the walls and into the massive dome above them.

A look of utter joy filled her face. She shrieked again, and in her excitement, flung her beads into the row in front of them, hitting a little boy in the head, who began to bawl.

A few people turned their heads toward them. Their mouths looked like they'd just finished sucking lemons. Mitt glared right back at them.

Evelyn grappled Mary back onto her lap and dug another toy out of her purse. "Be quiet, Mary. Please."

Mary fussed and shimmied her way down Evelyn's lap, plopping on the floor. She went to her hands and knees and crawled toward the pew's exit. Evelyn bent over and dragged her backward by the hips. When Mary took off again, Evelyn picked her up and set her down hard in her lap.

Mitt screwed his mouth tight. It wouldn't help matters any to laugh. *Poor kid.* He didn't like sitting still any more than she did. He unclasped his watch and dangled it in front of Mary.

Her eyes lit up, and she stopped squirming. She tugged the watch out of Mitt's hand and stuffed one of the straps in her mouth. The soggy sound of Mary's chewing filled the empty spaces of the pastor's sermon.

With her eyes closed and mouth slightly open, Evelyn's

head had fallen and rested on her neighbor's shoulder. The old lady leaned her head forward and peeked at him with an amused smile.

Mary gagged and pulled the wet, spongy leather out of her mouth.

Mitt chuckled. "Hungry, huh?" He pinched it between two fingers and wrapped it in his handkerchief.

The sides of Mary's mouth turned down, and her chin began to quiver.

"Now, don't you even think of—"

Mary let out the very beginning of what promised to be an ear-piercing wail.

Mitt clapped a hand over her mouth and glanced at Evelyn. She didn't stir, but the pastor stopped in the middle of a sentence and eyed them both. Mitt could recognize a chew-out when it was coming. "I ain't gonna go down like this," he muttered. He swooped Mary up in his arms. "What do you say we break out of this joint?"

The organ bellowed its final song.

Evelyn startled awake. Her hands went to her empty lap. *Mary.* She twisted behind her. There was nobody but an older gentleman. She bent and searched under the pew in front of her. Empty. A wave of heat and ice trickled down her spine. Mary was gone.

The woman next to her leaned close. "He took her outside."

Evelyn didn't wait for the *Alleluias* and the *Go forths* to be said. She hurried down the aisle and flung open one of the front doors, crashing it against the brick facade. The grounds were empty. A car drove past the church, drawing her attention to the road and the grassy park beyond.

There stood Mitt, leaning against an oak tree, and Mary, lying on his jacket spread on the clipped lawn.

She ran across the street as fast as her pumps would allow.

He raised a finger to his lips when she approached.

She ignored him and dropped to the ground beside Mary, who was sleeping peacefully in the oak's shade. At least he hadn't been so mindless as to lay her in the sun. Head bent, she blinked away tears and brushed her hand over Mary's curls.

He pushed off the tree. "I'll be right back." Soon enough, he returned from his car with a quilt and spread it on the ground beside her. "You might as well take a break while she rests."

She surged to her feet. "What were you thinking?"

"What was I thinking?" He cocked his head and studied her. "I was thinking you might want a break."

"I woke up, and she was gone."

"And I was about to get bawled out by your preacher."

Evelyn stopped short. "You were?"

"Let's just say Mary wasn't happy when I took my watch away from her."

She closed her eyes, knowing exactly what Mitt had felt in that moment without him having to describe it. How could she blame him when she herself had been half-tempted to run out of the church with Mary and never look back?

Mitt stuffed his hands in his pockets. "Don't worry about it. These things happen."

She didn't have to ask what he meant. He'd had a front-row seat to her troubles. "It's embarrassing."

"Who cares what those people think? I don't. Besides, you weren't the one making a racket that would call down Moses."

"I lost my temper with her."

"Lady, if that's losing your temper, I'd like to see you on the days you really let it fly."

"No, you wouldn't." Mitt couldn't understand. She was a war widow with a gold star hanging in her window. A living symbol of the sacrifices paid for America's victory and the closest thing to a saint America had. A mother to a hero's only surviving child. Raymond had grown up in that church, and every one of its attendees expected her to do right by his little girl.

"You were tired."

"And that excuses it?"

"You're not a saint."

She laughed without humor. "Definitely not." A surge of anger swept through her and not for the first time. She'd always stuffed it down, ashamed to feel it for a moment. How could she be mad at Raymond? He'd sacrificed his life for the greater good. There were men who now lived because of what he did. But what if the greater good should've been her and Mary?

She wouldn't have struggled today in church if Raymond had been there to provide a lending hand. She wouldn't have to be a saint if Raymond was taking care of them, just as he'd promised.

She wheeled her gaze back to his. "How could he have left us, Mitt?"

He drew back a little. "He didn't want to."

"But he did it anyway."

"You and Mary, you meant the world to him. He would've never hurt you on purpose."

She didn't miss the defensiveness in his voice. "I know, but sometimes...sometimes I'm just so *mad* at him."

"You shouldn't be angry with him." He'd turned pale, almost as white as the scar that ran down the side of his face. "You should be angry with me."

"Mitt, why would I—"

"I was so close. You can't know how close I was. If I would've just reached out a little further, that's all it woulda took." His haunted eyes begged for understanding. "You wouldn't be going through this alone if I'd just tried harder."

"Oh, Mitt." She sometimes forgot she wasn't the only one affected by Raymond's death. "If you could've done it, you would have. I shouldn't be blaming anyone for today. We all have our troubles, and we all just do the best we can."

"You care more than any mother I've seen. Everyone in that church sees it too." He looked at her steadily as if he willed her to believe it.

Evelyn hugged her arms around her middle. "What if Mary doesn't turn out well? What will people think if Raymond's daughter gets sent to prison?"

"Prison?" The tightness in his face faded away. "*Prison?*" He cackled.

Evelyn shot him a dirty look. "You don't know." But despite herself, a laugh bubbled up from her belly. She tightened her mouth, but there was no use. A giggle escaped, then two, and soon, she was laughing just as hard as Mitt.

After fits and starts, they settled down. Spent, Evelyn leaned back on the tree, arms crossed lightly on her stomach. How good it was to laugh again!

Mitt lowered himself to the blanket and laid on his side, propping himself with an elbow. "It's heatin' up out here. Seems early for April." He loosened his tie.

His action drew her attention to his neck. Even relaxed, his muscles could have been cut from stone. There was something dangerous in the bridled strength of his well-built body. It seemed at odds with the way he'd taken the blame so readily for her pain.

She joined him on the blanket and curled her legs to her chest. He was right. She wasn't a saint. And she did care. She cared so much about Mary that sometimes she couldn't sleep at night for watching her breathe. Maybe in trying to become a lion, she'd gone too far in the other direction.

"Why did you come to church today, Mitt?" she asked softly.

"You wanna know the truth?"

"Of course."

"Because I hated the idea of you being there alone."

The admission stole Evelyn's breath away.

Mary stirred. She went to her stomach and lifted her bum in the air. Pushing up on her hands, she plopped onto her sitter. The pigtail Evelyn took so much care in crafting lay askew, leaving sweaty strings of hair plastered to one side of her face.

Evelyn held out her arms. Mary crawled toward her and plunked herself in Evelyn's lap. "Do you know my only regret for today, Mitt?"

"What's that?"

"I didn't plug my ears with wool today. It would've helped with Mary's screaming."

"We stuffed bullet casings in our ears." He shrugged. "But wool'll get the job done."

FORTY-FIVE

A PORCH AND A TIRE SWING

May 1947

"Halloo? Evelyn?"

She peeked through the curtains hanging at her open kitchen window. She grinned and wiped her hands on her apron. "Uncle Mitt's here."

Clapping, Mary ran to the door and reached for the handle. "Uncle Mip!"

Evelyn chuckled. "Yes, Mip is here." She swung open the front door.

He greeted them, arms open wide. "Hello, dolls."

Evelyn grinned. "Hello, Mitt."

He squatted to catch Mary, who ran into his arms. He lifted her and jiggled her in the air. The three-year-old screeched with laughter. He smiled at Evelyn and set Mary down.

"I have banana bread, fresh from the oven," Evelyn said.

He clapped his hands and rubbed them together. "Hot dog!" He took his hat and tossed it on the entryway table.

Mary grasped Mitt's pinky finger and dragged him forward.

"Alright, sugar. I'm coming."

"Watch out. She's a little cranky today. She barely got any sleep at all last night with the heat."

He sat down at the dinette and leaned against the wall with his hands interlaced behind his head and his legs stretched out. He exhaled a hearty sigh. "Smells good in here."

Mary made a beeline to the counter and strained with her hands toward a decorated double layer round cake under a glass dome.

"No, Mary." Evelyn shoved the cake away from Mary's reach. "It's for Uncle Jimmie's birthday."

Mary plopped down and threw herself backward, crying.

Evelyn crouched close to her daughter. "Now stop that. You can have some later at the party."

Mary's wails grew louder.

"You can have banana bread. It'll be just as good, I promise." She tried to pick Mary up, but the girl twisted away and swatted Evelyn.

Tears filled Evelyn's eyes. She didn't have to look at Mitt to know he watched them closely.

His chair scraped against the floor. He took Mary gently from Evelyn's arms. "Now, you can't hit your mother, alright?"

Mary stared up at him, quiet now except for her shuddering breaths. She nodded and placed her head on Mitt's chest. "I sorry, Mama."

"Good girl." He set her down and marched to the counter, pulled out his switchblade, and stabbed the cake, right in the middle. He swung it down and sawed a sliver. "Here you go, baby," he said, handing Mary the piece. Mary sat on the floor and happily munched on her spoils.

"Mitt!" Evelyn stared at him, mouth gaping wide.

"If this is the hill you wanna die on, be my guest. You got any extra icing?"

"You're spoiling her."

"You said it yourself. She's tired. And so are you. Cut yourself a little slack."

As if her arm had a mind of its own, she pointed to the bowl on the counter with the leftover icing. He grabbed the frosting and pulled the cake closer. Pushing the sides of the round cake together, he filled the gap with icing, dabbing it to make decorative peaks to match the rest of the cake.

She crossed her arms and studied him. "You've done this before, I take it?"

Wiping his hands with a tea towel, he waggled his eyebrows at her. "I never could wait for cake. I got good at hiding it. Here." He wiped his blade with a tea towel and folded the knife. "You know, you really oughta let go of the little things."

She collapsed into one of the chairs at the table and slumped over. Leaning on an elbow, she covered her eyes with one hand. "I don't know what I'm doing."

"Who does?"

She dropped her hand to the table and glared at him in jest. "You, apparently."

"You'll figure it out. You're already a better mother than anyone I know. Just relax, and it'll all work out, alright?"

She'd spent the whole of last year trying to relax. When she'd decided to stand on her own two feet, she'd known she couldn't fret over the future any longer. Worrying only made her want to crawl back under her covers. "I wish I could be more like you."

"I think you're just right." He winked.

Heat rushed to her cheeks. "Want your banana bread?"

"Sure."

He pulled Mary onto his lap and played zoo with the shakers and utensils in the dining room. Evelyn bustled to the cabinet and gathered the plates. She peeked back at them, her heart squeezing. He'd been just what they'd needed, these past two years. He was so different than any other man she knew.

Raymond had been earnest and good—so set on doing what was right. Mitt took every day as it came.

"Jimmie here?" Mitt called back to the kitchen.

"Oh, he's all wrapped up in that new girl he met at the college bookstore. Betty."

"Tell him I came by, would you? I've got papers for him to sign. For the business."

"Sure, Mitt." She carried plates in one hand and a dish of banana bread in the other and set them on the table.

"Have you met her? Betty?" She placed a slice on his plate and sat down.

He nodded. "Nice girl. She's a little thing. Spunky, like him." He lowered his gaze and ran his thumb over a wrinkle in the tablecloth, smoothing it out. "He's lucky to have her."

The quietness in his voice made her lower her fork back to her plate, bite uneaten. She tilted her head. "Do *you* have a girl, Mitt?"

A flush inched its way from his neck to his temples, making his scar even whiter. "No."

She twisted her mouth to the side. *No?* Just no? No joke or rambling silliness? Either his blush was lying, or he was. She sat back in her seat and studied him. Did he have feelings for Jimmie's girl? She shouldn't be surprised at him wanting to get on with his life after the war. Of course that would include a wife. Still, the idea made her feel like she wore a too-tight girdle—squeezed in all the wrong places.

His reticence reminded her of when he first came around to mow their grass and repair their leaky faucets. He'd been respectful. Too respectful. *Mrs. Sellers*, this. *Mrs. Sellers*, that. Treating her as if she were a fragile thing who'd fall to pieces with one sudden move or one wrong word. He'd always come with his hair tamed and pomaded, just like he did when he came to church with them. It was only in the last few months he'd allowed his jet-black waves to be wild and free. Wild and free, like him.

Mary reached over with a crumby hand and brought Mitt's hand up to her face. She leaned against his hand and munched her bread, her honey curls crushed against his palm. She squeezed one of his fingers. "My Mip."

He looked down at the little girl and grinned. "Yeah, your Mip." He patted her on the head. "You're the only gal for me, Miss Mary."

The toddler stroked his head and left a trail of crumbs in his hair. Something warmed inside Evelyn, watching the two of them together. Mitt was a force, an untamed wind who had blown into their home and chased out all that gloom of those terrible early days. His muscled bulk and scarred face had intimidated her at first, but that was before she'd seen his gentleness with Mary. Great strength, tender heart—that was their Mitt.

He popped a bite of the bread into his mouth. "Any more thoughts about what you'll do after you graduate?"

"I'm thinking about moving on and getting a place of our own. There's a school in Clemson that wants me on fulltime. With Jimmie here now, I feel better about leaving Sarah."

He studied her, quiet for a moment. "That's a big change."

"There's nothing left for me here. Nothing besides Jimmie and Sarah."

His eyebrows knit together, as if he couldn't quite formulate the words he wanted to say.

She reached out to pat his hand. "It's not like I'm leaving for good. Why, I'll probably be here every weekend."

He slipped his hand out from under hers. "Suppose that's true." He stood, avoiding her eyes.

She got up from her chair and followed him to the door. "You're leaving already?"

He glanced down at her, his face smooth. "Seeing as Jimmie's not here, I guess I better get a move on."

He looked so serious. Evelyn couldn't help but giggle at those crumbs Mary had left behind in his hair. Bringing a hand up to his head, she brushed her fingers over the dark strands. His hand shot up to her wrist, holding it in place. He stared at her, somber.

"What're you doin', Evie?"

Her heart flipped at his mumbled words.

"I... I'm just... you have..." Her words fled at the look in his eyes.

"I have what?" Gone was the gentleness he'd used with Mary. It had been replaced with an intensity that made Evelyn's knees tremble.

"N-nothing."

His grip loosened on her wrist. He trailed his hand over her forearm until it nestled in the crook of her folded arm.

"Nothing? You sure?" From the dark depths of his eyes rose a question she wasn't sure she should be answering.

To her surprise, tears pooled at her eyelids.

His face blanched. "I'm sorry, Evelyn. I'm really sorry." He stepped back.

She reached her hand out. "No, wait."

"I don't know what I was thinkin'." He shook his head as if to clear it. He took another step back. He grabbed his hat on the entryway table. "Just tell Jimmie I came by, okay?" He squatted at Mary's level. "Bye, squirt." He tweaked her nose, and just like that, he was gone.

Evelyn stirred in her bed, sheets twisted around her legs. It had been a week since Mitt had left, and he hadn't visited once. Her mind replayed the scene of him holding her wrist in his hand, over and over. Her skin still tingled where he'd touched it.

She huffed and sat up, breathing hard. It wouldn't do to keep on like this. She threw back the covers and stepped quietly past Mary's crib to her door. She stalked down the stairs and turned the corner to the kitchen. There, wreathed in a halo of light, sat Sarah, drinking a glass of milk.

"Couldn't sleep?" Sarah asked.

"No."

"Come sit."

Evelyn slumped down in a chair, her head propped by her hands.

"What's wrong, Evie?"

She groaned. "I don't know."

Sarah eyed her. "I see." She nudged a plate of cookies toward her. "Thinking about Mitt?"

Evelyn's eyes skittered up to Sarah's. Her mother-in-law was too perceptive, by half. "I don't think he's happy with me..." Her voice trailed off at the look in Sarah's eyes.

"What I can't figure out is why you haven't told him you love him yet."

Evelyn's head reared back. "What?" Love? *Mitt*? She'd just lost Raymond, and Mitt was only a friend. A handsome devil of a friend, sure, but it'd never been like that between them.

Sarah reached out and patted Evelyn's hand. "You know I love having you and Mary here, but I've been preparing my heart for you two to leave me. I've known it was coming ever since that boy started coming around."

"But Sarah—"

She cupped Evelyn's jaw and peered into her eyes. "But nothing. You don't want to miss your chance at a new start. I never got one, but I'd like to think I would've taken it if it had come to me."

Unbidden, images of a life with Mitt infiltrated her thoughts. Not just visits like they'd had, but all the moments of a day spent together. Enough came to mind to make Evelyn's cheeks burn. "W-what about Raymond?"

"Who gave Mitt the letter to bring to you?"

Evelyn's mouth fell open to object, but she closed it. Had that been what Raymond had done? Brought Mitt to her and Mary? It would have been the most natural thing in the world for Raymond to be as selfless as to think of her happiness if he were to leave them. He would've known Mitt would take care of them. *Oh, Raymond. Why did you have to be so good?*

Evelyn got up and kneeled on the floor by Sarah's feet. She placed her head in Sarah's lap and wept. Wept for the life she'd wanted but didn't get. For the man she missed oh-so-much but couldn't have. She was finally saying goodbye.

Sarah stroked her hair.

Evelyn lifted her head and faced her mother-in-law. "But I don't know if he likes me back," she wailed.

A laugh burst past Sarah's lips before she could stop it. She laughed until tears poured down her cheeks. "Where have you been over the past year, Evie? Have you seen the way that man looks at you?"

The memory of Mitt's eyes flashed across her mind, intense and... well, there was no other word for it but... yearning.

Sarah's mirth-filled eyes coaxed a sheepish smile from Evelyn.

"Now, dry your eyes. You don't want them puffy when you talk to Mitt tomorrow."

Evelyn raised her head from Sarah's lap. "But what if he doesn't want to listen?"

"Not another word. March on up those stairs and get some sleep. You have a big day ahead of you."

Evelyn got up from the floor but hesitated.

Sarah gave a playful slap on Evelyn's bottom. "Scoot."

. . .

Evelyn slowed the car to a stop in front of the grassy lot and peered out of the car window. There Mitt stood in the garish morning light, nailing boards into the side of the unfinished house. Her heart skipped at the sight of him, at his windblown hair and burnished skin, his hammer slamming into the boards as if they deserved a beating.

She got out of the car and smoothed her dress with a shaky hand. She stepped carefully through the field. "Mitt!"

His hammering drowned out her greeting. She trudged forward, her heels penetrating the soft sod. "Drat these heels." Her lips a thin line, she took off her shoes and tested the ground with one foot. Dew dampened her stockings, blades of grass stabbing through the silk to her skin. She glanced at Mitt and pressed forward.

The path emptied into a lot of bare soil with the house standing in the middle. She was close enough to see the sweat glistening on his forehead. He was the only man she knew who looked better wearing a white tee shirt than a dress shirt and tie. "Mitt?"

He whipped around, hammer raised. His eyes trailed over her, head to foot. He lowered his hammer. "Where are your shoes?"

She held up the pair, hooked in her fingers.

His eyes glittered fire and ice. "Why are you here, Evelyn?"

"We miss you, Mitt."

He turned his back to her and walked away.

If he thought that would deter her, he was about to find out how determined she could be. She trailed behind him.

He put his hammer in his tool bag and stooped to pick up the bag of nails from the concrete path leading to the porch. "I've been busy."

He turned around and slammed into her. He backed up, keeping his eyes to the ground. "Excuse me." He swerved around her, but she stopped him with a touch on his forearm. He looked down at her hand.

"What's troubling you, Mitt?"

"Nothin'."

"Why won't you look at me?"

"Evie, I..." Her heart tumbled at him calling her that. "Just give me a little bit of time. I'll come back around. I just need time."

"For what?"

"Until I can come around you without makin' you cry." He gently took her hand off his arm and took a step back. He walked away from her toward his car.

She followed close behind. "I cried because I was scared."

He stopped and turned around, anguish written across his face. "Of me."

"No, of myself."

His eyes narrowed. "Keep talkin'."

"I was scared of what I was feeling."

He shook his head. "Look, Evie. I get it. You're lonely. Ray was the best man I ever knew. He took a chance on me when I didn't deserve it. If it weren't for him, I wouldn't be here. With you. It's messin' with my head, Evie."

"But if you'd just come back, it might feel normal again." The wind blew her tresses across her forehead.

"I can't. Bein' around you and Mary, it makes me feel things... *want* things I have no right to ask for. Look at me." He held his arms open at his sides. "Do I look like the kinda guy who goes around with a girl like you?" There was a vulnerability in the hazel depths of his eyes she'd never seen before.

She took a small step forward. "You're a good man, Mitt. You're kind and patient and gentle with Mary. You're thoughtful, and you're teaching me how to enjoy life a little more. And besides, if you're saying a nice man like you doesn't go with a girl like me, well, that isn't very nice of you." She poked him in his side.

His mouth tilted and then fell. "I'm not him, Evie. I'm loud and rough and joke too much. He was the Parson. I'm tryin', Evie, but I still got a little bit of a devil in me."

She took a deep breath. "I don't want you to be him. I love *you*." Her heart beat as fast as a hummingbird's wings. She wouldn't have been this bold years ago. But Raymond had drawn it out of her, bit by bit, unwittingly making her ready for a man like Mitt. And oh, was she ready.

His troubled eyes searched hers.

"I mean it, Mitt. He's gone. I'll never not be sad about that. But I think I knew from the start he wouldn't be mine forever."

He turned his face away from her, jaw clenching.

Evelyn ached to touch him. She took a step toward him. "You make me feel stronger." She brought her fingers to his neck, brushing upward to his jaw. His Adam's apple bobbed. She ran her fingers over his scar. "And free." She lifted herself on her toes and put her lips to the flexed muscle in his jaw. "And loved. Almost as much as I love you."

He groaned. "C'mere." He pulled her to him and buried his face in her hair, inhaling deeply. "I can't think straight when you're doin' that." He pushed her away so he could peer into her eyes. "You sure?"

She nodded, her throat too tight for words. She curled herself in his warmth and tucked her hands between them. Eyes closed, she drank of his nearness.

He grabbed one of her hands and moved in the direction of the porch, pulling her behind him. At her protest, he turned around, eyebrow quirked. He looked down at her feet. "Whoops. Sorry." He swooped her up into his arms.

She yelped, arms flailing for his neck. "What are you doing?"

"Forgot about your shoes."

He carried her to the porch and set her down gently. "I built this house with you and Mary in mind, even though I didn't have a hope of you two livin' here." He shrugged sheepishly. "Over there"—he pointed to an oak tree, its branches ribboning across the sky—"a swing. For her. And here"—he stretched out his arms the breadth of the porch—"another swing. For us. Where we can keep an eye on her while we smooch." He winked.

A thrill bloomed in her chest. "And who says we're smooching?"

He pulled her to him just like he had after she'd kissed his jaw. "Me."

She grinned into his face, but he wasn't smiling back.

"Do you think you could be happy here? With me? I'll be the man you deserve, Evie. I'll give you everything you want—"

She put her fingers on his lips. "I just want *you*."

With his thumb, he brushed aside a wisp of hair the wind had blown across her forehead. "I'm going to kiss you silly, Evie. Just thought I should warn ya."

And so he did.

FORTY-SIX

MARY

April 1961
Florence, South Carolina

I was almost to the end of the letters now—some touching, others comical, and a few, excruciatingly sad. Letters between brothers. Letters between fathers and sons. Letters between my mother and father. And finally, a letter with "*For Mary, when she's eighteen and ready*" scrawled across the envelope.

I sat with it for a full minute, trying to decide whether to read it. Something in me told me there'd be no going back once I did.

My family had taken care that I knew him, but this was altogether different. Maybe I didn't want to be disloyal to Dad, my Mip. Or maybe I was scared of loving a man I'd never get to meet.

I broke the envelope's seal, and once I caught sight of my name in his strong, tight script, my decision was as good as made.

My dear little Mary,

It's your Papa here. I wanted you to have something in my own hand to remind you how much I love you on days you start to forget. You might hear how I chose to stay and not understand how I could love you so much and leave you behind. It was the hardest decision I've ever had to make. The thought of coming home to you and your mother has been the only thing that has gotten me through at times. But I knew in my heart that I would be abandoning my men when they needed me most and maybe at the cost of their lives.

I can guess what you might be thinking, that you needed me too, but I'm certain you're not suffering for a lack of love being surrounded by the same people who loved me.

Now, if you'll indulge your daddy, I aim to fit all the fatherly advice I would've given to you over my lifetime onto this page.

1. *Love God and your family, for either won't steer you wrong.*
2. *Go easy on your mother. She's taken on a heavy load. Trust she's doing the best she can.*
3. *Keep an eye out for the quiet ones. Maybe they just need a friend.*
4. *Have Uncle Jimmie teach you his mean right hook before you set out on your own. (Knowing him, he probably already has.) You never know when it might come in handy.*
5. *Sometimes the way someone looks on the outside doesn't match what's on the inside. It goes both ways with this piece of advice. Be wise enough that you don't get taken in by a charmer and charitable enough that you don't miss a good heart hiding underneath the gruff.*

6. *If you're ever unsure which way to go with something or someone difficult, it's better to be wrong in being too gracious than not gracious enough. But that doesn't mean being weak. Stand your ground when it's important, and let it go when it's not.*

That's about it. I figure your mother has taught you the rest. Love you, honeypie. Be good.

Love,
Papa

I couldn't breathe. I couldn't even see the words through my tears. If I were honest, it wasn't just Uncle Jimmie's toast that had drawn me to the desk. It had been building for a while, this feeling that what was a hole was actually a gaping chasm. And now the space stretched wider than it ever had before, maybe so far that I'd never cross it.

Someone cleared his throat.

I closed the book with a snap and jumped back. "Uncle Jimmie!" I brushed the tears from my cheeks. I'd forgotten he'd decided to stay the night.

He stood there, quiet and grave. Too quiet. Too grave. Was he still upset over what had happened at supper? He leaned down to kiss me on the top of my head, and I automatically tipped my head to his movement. He lowered himself into a chair across mine. "Couldn't sleep?"

"I—I wanted to know more. About *him*. About what you said at supper."

He rubbed a hand over his mouth. "You know I've only ever wanted your life to be good and happy, don't you?"

I nodded.

"Tonight, I got to thinking that you don't really know who

your father was and that maybe part of that was our fault. We didn't want to hurt you, honey. We told you just enough so you wouldn't go digging for more. Not until you were old enough to understand."

I couldn't pretend I didn't know what they hadn't wanted me to find, not after reading the letters. The discovery had hurt just as much as they'd expected it to. "You sounded angry at him."

"No, not angry. I just wish he could've been a little more selfish. Though he wouldn't have been Raymond if he had." He pulled out a chain from his shirt and dangled a flat metal circle in front of me. "Remember when you used to play with this?"

The washer. The one my father had given to him when they were younger. The one Uncle Jimmie wore during the war. I'd read about it in the letters.

He slipped the chain off his neck and dropped it in my hand.

The circle was dinged and rubbed thin in places and warm in the palm of my hand.

"I'll never forget when he handed it to me. I'd needed a father badly at the time, and Ray was the one who showed up. I was supposed to put the washer back in the engine, but I couldn't bring myself to do it. To me, it was a promise that he'd always be there for me, just like he was that day. It took me some time to sort that out after he died."

"But you still wear it."

"Because he's still here for me, though in a different way. For one thing, he's kept me out of heaps of trouble just by the things he taught me. When I choose to listen." He winked.

I handed it back to him.

He slipped the chain over his head and tucked the washer inside his shirt. "Did you find what you were looking for in those letters?"

"I found out he chose to stay behind and help his men." I couldn't keep the bitter note from my voice.

"He would've come back to us if he could've."

"I know." And I did. At the time he'd made his decision, I wasn't at risk. His soldiers were.

"No, I don't think you do." He peered into my eyes. "When most of us boys were cooking up trouble, he was thinking about what it would be like to have a family of his own."

"But why?"

"Because he had a lot of love to give, for one thing. And because your grandfather was the meanest ol' stinker there ever was. Raymond wanted a do-over."

The only thing I'd remembered of Granddad was sitting in his home on a plastic-covered sofa while the grownups talked, the backs of my legs slippery with sweat and stuck to the covering. He'd shushed me when I'd asked to go to the bathroom, and it was a good thing for him the couch was covered by plastic. I never went back after that, and he'd died just a few years later. It was fine by me that I had little to do with the man who left my Grandma Sarah. "Whatever happened between you and Granddad after the war?"

"He sent for me right before he died, you know." He leaned closer, as if he were sharing a secret. "He told me he regretted leaving your Grandma Sarah... that he wished he'd had the chance to make it right with Ray before he left. He was saying sorry, in his own way."

"And did you forgive him?"

"No." He grinned wryly. "I guess I was enjoying myself too much at the justice of it all to think of that."

"Uncle Jimmie! You should. Forgive him, I mean."

He studied me, a strange light in his eyes. "You know, you remind me of Ray sometimes."

My heart jumped in an unexpected thrill. "I do?"

"He could be stubborn. He'd get on me about doing this or

not doing that, and of course, he was always right. Like you. He'd asked me in his last letter not to hold a grudge against Dad."

"So, will you? Forgive him, I mean?"

He laughed. "Well, I guess I can let it go, for Ray's sake."

"For *your* sake."

His eyes twinkled. "Alright, for my sake."

I sobered. "Why didn't Dad ever tell me that he fought with him?"

"I don't think Mitt likes to talk about what happened over there. None of us do." He shifted his head away from my gaze, but not before I caught a shimmer in his eyes. "It was a real bad time for those men. A real bad time. But Mitt has you and your mother now, and he loves you both." He looked at me again. The storm in his eyes had cleared, leaving only traces of red in its wake. "Ray made Mitt promise to look in on us. He knew, somehow, that Mitt would be just what we needed. Ray wanted us to be okay. He was always protecting others like that, so I shouldn't be surprised that he's still doing it, even after he's gone."

I sat back against my chair, overcome. Because of my father, I had Mitt, who loved me like his own flesh and blood. What would I have done without Dad? He'd taught me how to ride a bike and how to put enough snap in my voice if a boy ever got too handsy. He came to every one of my piano recitals and school plays and played with me in the ocean surf when we visited Nana Solomon in New Jersey. Uncle Jimmie would've given me a cookie behind Mom's back, but Dad? He would've bought out the bakery if I'd asked him to. His boisterous laugh was so loud it would reach me wherever I was in the house, usually in the warm cocoon of the reading nook he'd made in the house he built for us. My mother's answering laugh was all I needed to know that she'd found her happiness too.

I traced my fingers over the gilded edging of the portfolio.

All the joy, all the love in my life, I could trace back to my father. Papa.

I had been drawn to the letters in the desk, thinking them the last tangible evidence of a man long gone. But that wasn't true. He was still here, stitched into the fabric of our family.

Maybe in his dying I'd learned more about him than his living ever could.

"I do know a little of what it's like, finding out secrets where Raymond is concerned," he said.

"You do?"

"Your mother told me that Ray only went to Clemson to keep Dad from messing with me. Gave up his plans, just for me. Who knows what would've happened if he hadn't become a cadet? He would've still joined up, somehow, but maybe he'd still be here if he hadn't."

"Oh, Uncle Jimmie."

"I've made my peace with it. Mostly, I just feel loved by the greatest brother there ever was."

"If only I could've met him, just once. I'd have so many questions for him."

He patted my knee. "We should've talked about all this a long time ago. You can ask me anything you like. Go on. What do you want to know?"

Anything. *Everything*. "What was he like? Before the war."

A spark of mischief lit his eyes. "Did I ever tell you about the time we threw those cupids into the pond behind Granddad's house?"

A LETTER FROM THE AUTHOR

Dear Reader,

Thank you for reading *What the Silent Say*.

If you would like to join other readers in keeping in touch, sign up to my email newsletter here:

www.stormpublishing.co/emerson-ford

If you enjoyed it and could spare a few moments to leave a review, that would be hugely appreciated. Even a short review can make all the difference in encouraging a reader to discover my books for the first time. Thank you so much!

In my office hangs these lines from the 10th century poem, "The Wanderer": "Where has the horse gone? Where has the warrior gone? How that time has passed away, dark under the cover of night, as if it had never been."

It's just how things are—great men and women, forgotten, their stories footnotes in the great annals of history. People move on. Civilizations rise and fall. We eat, sleep, work, and die, giving little thought to those who came before.

I was a teenager when I found Raymond's letters in my father's desk. They were all we had left of my Papa Jim's beloved brother, besides a few pictures and the mystery of what exactly happened when he was fighting overseas. As I held the fragile onion sheets with fading blue ink, I couldn't help but wonder—what if they'd been lost in a move? Burned in a fire? Passed on to indifferent heirs? Would he have disappeared along with these letters?

It didn't seem just, his twenty-five years amounting to letters buried in a dark, dusty drawer as if he'd never been. I wanted to change it somehow, to bring him back to life so no one could forget him. Something about his story seemed significant, and I couldn't have guessed at the time how true that really was.

So I started writing. Then I promptly wrote myself into corners with as little information as I had to go on.

I dug deeper and found the stories of the men he fought with. All that was left of Private George Benjamin, for example, was his picture and the riveting account of his heroism that earned him the Medal of Honor. After what he did, that was all there was? I then wanted to resurrect him too.

I also thought about Raymond's wife and all she experienced. I myself was a military wife and had added a daughter to our family while my husband was gone. Even though he'd deployed in the era of email and faced only a fraction of the danger Raymond had, it helped me to at least envisage a little of what she went through. It became important to me to tell her story—the story of those who stayed behind. Sometimes courage looks like dying on a battlefield, and sometimes it looks like pressing forward when you have no control of the outcome, like she did.

And on that day when we discovered what Raymond and his unit did, I decided I would do whatever I could to get their story into the light of day.

It was of utmost importance that their experiences were portrayed as accurately as I could. I relied heavily on archival documents, first-hand accounts, and interviews. I only took liberty where research yielded scarcity, and any fictionalized aspects or inaccuracies were well-meant and in service to the story.

So what was fictional and what was not?

I'm sorry to report that Mitt is only an interpretation of Evelyn's second husband. While Raymond's widow did marry a man who fought beside him, there wasn't enough information about him to build a story on. What I do know is that Bill, like Mitt, was kind and generous, and he raised Raymond's daughter as his own. By all reports, he was a loving father and husband who took on Raymond's role with grace. The couple continued to include Raymond's family in their lives, and Jimmie and Sarah were especially thankful that their connection to Raymond through his daughter wasn't severed.

In addition to Mitt, I took infrequent liberties with biographical details, including names, of a few real-life characters in an effort to protect their privacy and in order to reconstruct their pasts. As one example, while I did uncover that Benjamin was an accountant and had a wife and two sons, the details of his home life beyond that are of my own imaginings. Lastly, for the purpose of a cohesive storyline, I put the Blue Raiders in Tinian a few months earlier than their actual arrival and switched the order of the 77th's training at Camp Pickett and Camp Hyder.

What I've come to believe is that there are untold thousands just like Raymond, Jimmie, and Benjamin who deserve to have their stories told, but the aftermath of war is messy, and acts of bravery, faith, and perseverance, no matter how inspiring, are lost in the rebuilding. As Marc Antony says in Shakespeare's *Julius Ceasar*, "The evil that men do lives after them; the good is often interred with their bones." I hope I breathed a little life into the history of these men and their families, who waited at home and suffered through the unknown. Learning about their endurance and courage has changed me forever.

Until next time,

Emerson

www.emersonfordwrites.com

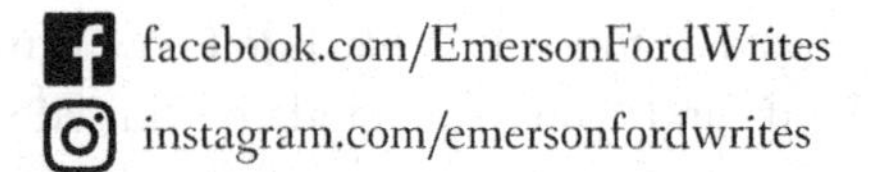

ACKNOWLEDGMENTS

Thank you to:

My dad, who carried this story in his heart long before I found the letters in the desk. You said yes without hesitation when I asked you to meet me at the National Archives so we could search for answers about your dad and uncle. You spent countless hours with me on the phone as we tried to piece together the puzzle of what happened, and you were there when, stunned, we realized what Raymond and his unit achieved in Okinawa. It has been one of the most meaningful experiences of my life. Who knew all your permissiveness with my reading at the dinner table would lead to our adventure? I think you must have, a little. My mother, likewise, cheered me on and helped without complaint when life came calling. I couldn't have done it without you both.

My Papa Jim, who thought writing big would get him out of writing two pages. You were always Jimmie in your heart, even while raising a family, running your business, and going to college at age fifty-five (because you wanted to). Raymond would have been so proud of you.

My husband, Keith, who encouraged me to pursue writing and gave up time and energy to help me do just that. You propped me up, slept through my laptop lighting our room late into the night, and tag-teamed dinner. Your countless sacrifices make this book yours as much as it is mine.

My children, Wyatt, Hudson, Emmalyn, and Arianna. I

wanted you to see me work hard at something I loved and to know that you can do it too. You'll always be the best story I'll ever write.

My editor at Storm Books, Claire Bord, for taking me on as an author. Your sharp instincts, kind spirit, and enthusiastic support are beyond what any author could hope for. I consider myself to have the best editor in publishing and am grateful for our partnership in every way.

My writing group and friends, some of the most insightful, fun, and gifted women I know: Emily Leininger, Gina Sheridan, Katie Staker, Rebekah Stocking, and Stevie Young. I can say with certainty that I wouldn't have finished this book without you. Each of you have left an unmistakable fingerprint on this story, and I'm forever thankful we found each other. Here's to many more years of Emily's savvy, Gina's instruction, Katie's plot wizardry, Stevie's eye for beauty, and Bekah's drive.

April Barcalow, whose friendship and fortification on this journey is immeasurable. You answered the lit beacon too many times to count. As long as I'm writing, it'll be alongside you.

Jennifer Major, who made the journey easier with her wisdom, honesty, and wit; Ashley Worrell, both a kindred spirit and a trusted sister; John Walker, who welcomed me into the writing community and guided me along the way.

Marissa Graff, who gave me what I needed to bring the story in my heart to the page.

Denise Harmer and Carrie Walker, editors extraordinaire.

My creative writing students, who inspire me each and every class, and my English Literature students, who walk with me through the beauties of Beowulf, Shakespeare, Dickens, and Lewis.

To D.V. Caitlyn, who encouraged me to stay true to my voice; Arthur Fogartie, whose generosity and wit won't ever be forgotten; Rachel Garber, who helped me see my book through new eyes; Jessica Fortenberry, who has eagle eyes for the little things; Elizabeth Reed, M.M. Finck, and Idria Barone Knecht, for their whip-smart suggestions; Jeff Staker, for lending me his experience; Cheryl Fitzgerald, Joyce Long, and Linda Samaritoni, for their welcome and kindness.

And lastly, the knowledgeable staff at the National Archives; Jim Sciaretta, who shares the heart and the mission to preserve the 77th's stories; Alan C. Carey, for his advice and insight; Bill Beigel, for digging up morning reports and personnel files; Rodney Foytik and Lori Wheeler at the U.S. Army War College Library; Nathan Cross at the Veterans History Project; and, with enormous gratitude, the relatives of the men and women in this book, who trusted me with their stories.

Soli Deo gloria.